Diane Chamberlain

SECRETS AT THE BEACH HOUSE

(Previously published as
PRIVATE RELATIONS)

PAN BOOKS

First published 1989 as *Private Relations* by Berkley Books

Reissued by HarperCollins in 1996

This edition published 2018 by Pan Books
an imprint of Pan Macmillan
20 New Wharf Road, London N1 9RR
Associated companies throughout the world
www.panmacmillan.com

ISBN 978-1-5098-6416-4

1 3 5 7 9 8 6 4 2

A CIP catalogue record for this book is available from the British Library.

Typeset in Scala by Palimpsest Book Production Ltd, Falkirk, Stirlingshire
Printed and bound by CPI Group (UK) Ltd, Croydon, CRO 4YY

Dear Reader,

Private Relations was my first novel. I was working as a hospital social worker as I wrote the story, and back then I approached my writing as a hobby. Gradually, that hobby became an obsession and after a few years, I had a complete manuscript – way too long and quite a mess! My agent and a few editors all had the same suggestions: focus on the romance between Kit and Cole, remove extraneous characters and sub-plots, and tighten, tighten, tighten. I took their advice and *Private Relations* sold to the first editor who saw the revised edition. It went on to win the RITA award for Best Single Title Contemporary Romance of 1989 – an incredible thrill for a newbie writer.

I've made some very minor changes to the novel, mostly related to structure. I haven't updated the story, though in a few instances I've changed a character's behaviour or speech to be more in keeping with my present day thoughts and feelings. I've also added an epilogue to satisfy my longing to know what happened to these people I cared so much about. For the most part, though, I've left the story and its characters alone. I hope you'll enjoy this tale of love and friendship, and I look forward to your thoughts.

Diane Chamberlain, 2014

SECRETS AT
THE BEACH HOUSE

1.

She only ran at night when she needed to escape. The Atlantic churned next to her, bottomless and black, and she played a game with it, matching four of her breaths to each crackling roll of its waves. It was her first after-dark run in Mantoloking, her first since she'd left Seattle where nearly every night she'd slammed the door on Bill and pounded the streets lined with identical houses until her head was free of him.

The Chapel House came back into view, silvery in the moonlight and beckoning, as always. It was the first time she'd seen it from this angle at night. It rose out of the sand and the beach heather, a huge gray whale of a house, two stories high and rock solid. No storm could touch it. No wonder she felt so safe inside. The bay window of her bedroom reflected the moonlight in its wavy glass, and she knew that her whole room would be bathed in a pale yellow glow by now.

She slowed her pace and climbed the hill to the house, spraying powdery sand behind her. The lights were still on in the living room, but maybe the others would be through talking about Cole by now. She was tired of listening to it, the glorification of him, the plans for his homecoming. She'd heard it all week at the hospital where nurses she'd respected were suddenly giggly with anticipation. And now she had to listen to it in the house as well. Odd how a man she'd never met was beginning to seem like her nemesis.

They were just as she had left them, Janni cross-legged on the floor in front of the fireplace, Jay stretched out on the blue camelback sofa, and Maris flung sideways across an overstuffed chair, the tiny gold sphere in her right nostril catching the glow from the fire.

"Kit!" Janni jumped up. "We were getting worried about you. It's not such a great idea for you to run on the beach at night." She was six inches shorter than Kit, but she put an arm around her shoulders and led her toward the fire. "Sit with me," she said.

It was too hot to sit by the fire, but Kit let herself be pulled onto the pale Persian carpet without protest. When Janni gave an order you were expected to obey. Not that she minded. She knew in the darkest part of her heart that it was Janni's attention she would miss most when Cole returned.

She imagined Janni would want a fire every evening all summer long, just as she had during the spring. That was all right. Kit loved the big slate fireplace, and the blaze gave a cozy feeling to the enormous living room and its eclectic clutter of furniture.

She remembered Janni's response when she asked if she could move into the house for a while. "Only if you bring something for my living room," Janni had said. Janni'd hardly needed any more furniture for the living room, but it was not aesthetics she'd had on her mind. Kit understood as soon as she set her wing chairs in the corner of the room and stood back to see them blend in with Maris's sleek white couch, Jay's camelback sofa, Cole's antique French tables, and the patchwork of furniture Janni had inherited along with the house. The room was a melting pot. It tied them all together, made it hard to think about leaving.

"How about a little after-run refreshment, Kit?" Jay held a bottle of Chardonnay in the air. Of the three of them he presented the most hedonistic image, lying on the camelback sofa, a wine glass in one hand, the bottle in the other. His rumpled plaid shirt was only half buttoned and completely free of his jeans, the sleeves rolled up to his elbows. He looked as if his speech would be thickened by alcohol, but she was certain that he'd actually had very little to drink. At any moment the hospital might call about one of his patients, and he'd be instantly alert. In her six months in the Chapel House she'd seen it happen a dozen times. He would tuck in his shirt, make an attempt at smoothing his wild black hair with his hands, give Janni a quick kiss, and walk out the door without the slightest complaint over the hour or the intrusion on his privacy.

"Just a sip, Jay," she said. "I need to do a little work tonight."

"You work too hard, sweets," Janni said, licking the rim of her wineglass.

Kit stared at the flames, thinking that Janni had no idea what it was like to change careers at thirty-one, the effort it took. Janni Pitney had been the social worker on the

Adolescent Unit at Blair Medical Center for the past eight years. Nothing was new to her. Nothing surprised her. But for Kit, every day held some fresh terror.

They'd met two years ago at a conference in Seattle where Janni had presented a workshop on teen pregnancy. Kit had been fascinated by this diminutive woman dressed in a silk blouse and jeans—probably the only pair of jeans at the conference—strutting around in front of a group of overdressed, overly serious high school counselors. Janni was animated and confident, maybe just a tad too cocky. She looked like a teenager herself, although she was nearly thirty. Her fine, glossy dark hair swung when she moved; her long bangs touched the top of her glasses.

Kit made a point of meeting her after the workshop, and for the next three days they were inseparable. She hadn't felt that kind of emotional bond with a woman since college. She talked Janni into staying at her house instead of the hotel. Bill was rarely around, anyway. "He's at a meeting," she told Janni the first night. The second night she told her the truth: she didn't know where he was, and to be honest she didn't care. She said it without anger because she felt none. She was at the point in her marriage where she felt trapped and numb. She'd grown dependent on a man who no longer meant anything to her.

She moved to Mantoloking when she and Bill split up. It was the perfect choice for a fresh start—as far from Seattle as she could get. Janni persuaded her to apply for the Public Relations opening at Blair. Kit was interested but not optimistic. Why would they hire a high school counselor to do PR? But they did, and she always wondered if Janni—or maybe Jay—had had something to do with it. That worried her. She'd spent the last six months trying to prove she was worthy of the job.

She loved the work. It was a relief taking care of an institution instead of the people inside it for a change, and her confidence was growing. But today the old insecurities had surfaced again.

"I got a new assignment this morning," she said, her eyes on her housemates. "I have total responsibility for the PR on the Fetal Surgery Program." Just saying it out loud made her jittery. She didn't know why the director had handed this to her. It felt like a test to see if she'd sink or swim under pressure, but why would they take that risk with something so important? Her coworkers, all of whom had been there longer than she had, seemed as confused as she was by her selection. A little miffed as well. They'd been talking for months about the Fetal Surgery Program and the PR challenge it presented. Competition for funding the program was stiff. Five medical centers on the east coast were battling for the funds already. So why had this honor been bestowed on the only person in the department who wanted nothing to do with it?

"That's fantastic, Kit." Janni grinned at her. "That's one of the biggest things Blair's ever gone after."

Jay sat up. "Cole's got four years of his life tied up in planning that program. I'm impressed they'd give it to you." His tone was complimentary, but the words felt like a warning.

"I don't *want* to be responsible for four years of someone's life," Kit said. "I want to say, no, sorry, I can't do it, but I'm still playing the game . . . you know, pretending I'm competent, and I'm afraid that if I turn it down they'll know I'm a fraud."

The three of them smiled at her. Even Maris's usual melancholy expression had lifted.

"You're good, Kit," said Janni. "If you're pulling the wool over anyone's eyes, it's only your own."

"You're going to love working with Cole," said Maris.

Kit wasn't so sure. She'd heard Cole could be demanding and temperamental. He'd spent the last nine months researching fetal surgery techniques in Paris, and he'd come back ready to put the program in gear. He'd have high expectations of the person assigned to the PR.

"I guess it's about time I got to meet this guy," she said, trying to sound convincing. "I've heard enough about him. The women at Blair are constantly pumping me for information on him."

Jay laughed. "The Chapel House has fueled the hospital grapevine for many years."

His accent made her smile. Unmistakably Brooklyn. How could anyone well-educated sound like that? She'd been shocked when she first met him. He sounded like a high school dropout, and looked like the kind of guy most people would cross the street to avoid—big and brawny with a mop of unruly dark hair. She tried to imagine how his surgery patients felt the first time they met him, when they pictured this thug taking a knife to them in the operating room.

But close up he had the face of a man at ease with himself, calm and unflappable. His placid style was the perfect foil for Janni's theatrics. They'd been balancing each other for a decade.

"The nurses used to ask me if I actually lived with both Jay DeSantis and Cole Perelle," Janni said now. "And I'd tell them, 'yes, and with another woman, Maris Lavender, too.' You could see the wheels turning as they tried to imagine what decadent things went on inside these four walls."

The four of them laughed, sharing a kinship Kit was pleased to be part of. How would she fit in when Cole returned? She was the newcomer. Cole's inferior substitute. After all, he'd been with the others for years. His room was directly across the wide upstairs hall from hers, and even though he'd been away, Janni still had the housekeeper dust his antique French furniture and keep the shimmer on the hardwood floors.

Maris had been in the Chapel House just a year and a half longer than Kit, but she had a connection to it that couldn't be taken from her. She was an architect and Janni and Jay had hired her a few years earlier to help with remodeling. Her touch was everywhere, her innovations always dramatic, like the huge half-circle windows in the living room and the intricate tile design of tropical fish that circled the kitchen on the backsplash above the counters.

Sometime near the end of the remodeling, Maris's husband was killed. Kit wondered what project she'd been working on when she learned of his death. Was there some patch of hardwood floor, perhaps, that she couldn't look at now without remembering what she'd lost? She'd moved into the house just a few days after his death. A smart move, Kit thought. This was the place to be when you needed to piece your life back together.

It had taken Kit a while to realize that the gloom in Maris's face was not the result of Kit's moving in and that Maris was, in fact, pleased to have her there. She helped Kit settle into her room, planned dinner menus with her, took her out to lunch. Kit liked being with her. The company was low-key and comfortable. And she liked Maris's dark, exotic looks—her warm spice-colored skin, the eyes a pale brown, nearly gold, with sharp black rings around the irises.

By contrast, Kit was fair. "Alabaster skin and angel hair," Bill had said once, when he was still interested enough to notice. There was something ethereal about her hair with its soft, unruly curls. She never wore it longer than chin length—any longer and she'd have to spend most of the day sorting out the tangles. It framed her face with a blend of colors—dark honey, a little gold, a touch of red. A hairdresser once told her she was lucky her skin was so pale—any color in her face would have competed too much with her hair, he said. Her gray eyes were competition enough.

"I can't believe Cole's moving in with Estelle," Maris said now.

"He's not going to live here?" Kit tried to hide the relief in her voice.

"You weren't here when I read his letter." Janni fondled the thin blue envelope on the carpet in front of her. "He and Estelle are moving in together. I think she's tired of sharing him with the rest of us." There was no sympathy for Estelle in her voice.

"He's moving into Estelle's condominium." Maris wrinkled her nose as though the elegant Point Pleasant condominium were the equivalent of a gym locker.

"He's coming back a few weeks before she does—she's still working on the translating—and going straight to the condo," Janni said. "He says he doesn't want to take a chance coming here first. He's afraid he wouldn't be able to leave."

Kit understood. There was something about this house that drew you in, soothed you, then drugged you a little so you lacked the motivation to leave. She'd meant her stay in the house to be a mere stopover, a month, no more. But the evenings with her housemates were hard to give up. It was new to her, coming home to people who cared what had happened to her during the day, who squeezed her hand when she walked in the house with a frown.

She leaned away from the fireplace to look up at the picture above the mantel. It was a photograph of the house, huge, blown up many times from a snapshot that Cole had taken. The view was from the street side, on a day when the air was gray and threatening. The house blended into the sky, everything the color of pewter. Even the small patch of lawn in the center of the circular driveway had taken on a vaporous gray hue. You could tell it was Christmas time, though. Each of the thirty windows glowed with the faint silver light of an electric candle. It was a beautiful picture, misty and surreal. Obviously this house meant something to Cole. She wondered how he could leave.

Janni opened his letter and reread it to herself. "I can't stand this part where he asks if he can use our beach this summer," she said. "*Our* beach! It's his beach, too, it always will be. We have to let him know that."

"It's not the end of the world, Jan," Jay said softly.

"How can you take his moving out so calmly? After ten years?" Janni asked him.

"Eleven for me," said Jay. He and Cole had been together since medical school. "I've always expected this to happen. He and Estelle can hardly settle down together living in two different places."

Maris sniffed. "I thought it was a superb arrangement."

"Superb for us maybe, but Estelle never got much of his time," Jay said.

Janni had rested her head against his knees. Now she pulled it away as if punishing him for the thought. "How can you be so sympathetic toward her?" she asked.

"She's not that bad."

"Oh, Jay, she's a bitch!" said Janni.

"You're sounding pretty bitchy yourself." He cushioned his words by stroking her cheek with the back of his fingers.

"If Cole's so terrific, why would he want someone who's not?" Kit asked.

Maris swiveled in her chair to face Kit, curling her long cinnamon-colored legs beneath her. "Cole has one monumental flaw," she said. "He's a sucker for beauty. When you meet Estelle you'll understand."

She already knew Estelle was beautiful. The women who worked at Blair had described every inch of her in elaborate detail. In voices edged with contempt—or was it envy?—they talked about how Estelle could transform a stiffly tailored suit into something soft and seductive merely by putting her body into it. And you could always see lace beneath her blouses. Nothing lurid, they were quick to admit, but still it couldn't help but provoke the imagination, could it? Some of them said they remembered seeing her picture in magazines years ago when she modeled lingerie for Caprice and Company.

No one mentioned that Estelle could translate medical terminology into six languages and that she was indirectly responsible for Blair's international status—the status those same women saw reflected in their paychecks. No one mentioned it at Blair, and no one was mentioning it now, here at the house.

Kit's bedroom was one of ten in the Chapel House. The rooms were all off the meandering upstairs hallway, half of them facing the ocean, the other half the bay. Jay and Janni's room was the only exception. It stretched the entire north side of the house with a view of both ocean and bay. One of the two upstairs fireplaces was also in their room. The other, with its Victorian mantel, was in the den.

All the rooms were large, and Kit had plenty of space for the walnut bedroom furniture she'd brought with her from Seattle. It looked beautiful against the soft buttery walls, and the carved molding around the ceiling looked as though it had been stained to match. She loved this room. It was warm and peaceful and usually settled her the moment she stepped inside.

But tonight she was finding it hard to sleep. Her windows were open and she lay on her back, naked under the sheet, listening to the rhythmic roar and whisper of the ocean. The moon left a lacy pattern on her ceiling, and she watched it change shape as she mulled over the warning Jay had given her before she came up to bed. He'd told her about the beach on summer nights, how the city crowds would converge on the neighboring towns and she could never know who might be lurking over the next sand dune. Although, he added with a smile, he was certain she could outrun just about anyone.

It still surprised her to be thought of as an athlete. She'd told them the truth, but they shook their heads in disbelief, only able to picture her slender and healthy. For most of her life she'd been anything but.

Bill had badgered her daily to run with him, and she had balked every time. It had become a joke between them. "Join me for a run?" he'd ask, standing at the front door in his shorts and T-shirt, a white sweatband in stark contrast to his dark curls.

"Oh gee, honey, I don't know," she'd answer as though she were actually considering it. "I think I'll pass today." He'd leave, both of them smiling at the ritual.

When her two closest friends, teachers at the high school, began jogging after work, she felt left out. It was no different from all those times when she was a kid, watching her classmates play softball while she sat on the bench on doctor's orders, morosely swinging the only legs on the playground that never wore Band-Aids. Her teachers had united together to demand that note from her pediatrician. None of them wanted the responsibility for her asthma. After all, this kid could have attacks sitting calmly in class.

Who knew what would happen if she joined the others on the playground?

She couldn't trust her own body. The day she took her tennis shoes to the track to run with her friends she was terrified. She felt her heart pounding against her ribs just lacing up the shoes.

Her friends slowed their pace for her, and she walked and jogged, walked and jogged six times around the track, a mile and a half. Afterward, when she looked in the mirror of the teachers' lounge, her cheeks were a lively pink. High quality color, not like the powder blush she angled across them each morning in a painstaking attempt to emphasize nonexistent hollows. The next day her legs ached with the sweetest pain in the world.

She couldn't stop. Bill was amused. "Did you take your little jog today?" he'd ask. When she finally accepted his invitation to join him, his face fell. "Oh, well, honey, I mean, I really do this for the exercise, and if I have to slow down for you it'd blow my routine."

Within a few months he didn't need to slow down for her, and that's when the marriage started to crumble. Or perhaps, as she admitted to herself later, it had been falling apart bit by bit for many years.

2.

From the air, the buildings of Newark looked like a charcoal drawing, and the sky between the city and the circling jet was dense with chemicals and ash. Yet there was no place Cole would rather be than suspended above that smoky city, spiraling toward the airport where his parents would be waiting for him and where the past nine months would be no more than a memory.

Those last few weeks in Paris, Estelle had acted as though his departure was a betrayal. Her eyes walled him in with suspicion. He'd been relieved when Elliot wired him to return to Blair ahead of schedule. He didn't want to spend another month with Estelle while she finished her translating and his feeling of suffocation grew in the French summer heat.

The dark-haired flight attendant broke into his thoughts to hand him a warm, powder-scented hand towel.

"You're almost home," she said, lingering by his seat.

For what he hoped was the last time he gave her a restrained smile and returned his gaze to the city below. Once during this trip he had thought she was going to proposition him. She sat in the empty seat next to him and told him that she didn't usually say things like this to a passenger, but "I can't seem to stop myself from telling you that I really find you attractive."

He felt her body next to him, all hopeful energy.

"Thanks," he said. "But I'm already in a permanent relationship."

"I . . . um . . . I wasn't looking for permanence."

He smiled patiently. "Sorry, but I am. And now I really need to get some reading done." He rustled the papers in his lap, and with the color rising in her cheeks, the attendant excused herself. She gave up easily, he thought. More easily than most.

He wasn't sure what the attraction was. He didn't see himself as exceptionally good-looking. He liked the straight line of his nose well enough but his eyes were an alarming turquoise color that he himself described as unearthly, and his smile was more than a little lopsided.

He watched the flight attendant make her stop-and-smile way down the aisle. She was pretty all right but he hadn't touched a woman other than Estelle in six years, and he wasn't about to start now.

The jet, so graceful in the air, lumbered awkwardly to the terminal. Cole squinted through the window to make out his parents standing behind the tinted glass of the waiting area. He was surprised to see Corinne standing next to them, looking like a scared rabbit. At first he thought he was mistaken, and he stared hard until his eyes burned and he began to feel that gnawing blend of love and hate his sister always evoked in him. Wendy and Becky were with her, and he waved to them from the little window even though he was quite certain they couldn't see him. They looked taller, stringier.

His father kissed his cheek when he reached the waiting area inside the terminal. The same gesture Cole had pulled away from as a teenager gave him a lump in his throat these days. Lately, when he looked in the mirror, it was his father's face he saw reflected there. There was no gray in his dark brown hair yet, but the lines were deepening in the same places. He had the same subtle cleft in his chin, the same deep hollows in his cheeks that his mother generously referred to as dimples. He hoped he would never take on his father's gaunt defeated look.

His mother looked, as always, as if she'd been taking very good care of herself. Her hair, which had once been Cole's color, was now silver. Her skin was smooth and unlined despite the perpetual tan. She embraced him and nodded toward Corinne.

"Look who's here," she said proudly. "In an airport."

"The twins wanted to welcome you home so I forced myself to come too, but I'm absolutely dying to get out of this place." Corinne laughed nervously as Cole knelt down to hug the girls. They were as towheaded as he had been as a child.

He took his sister's hand. Her palm was damp and her fingers trembled in his own. He kissed her pale cheek.

"Would you like to wait outside while I get my luggage?" he asked her, surprised at his own gentleness.

Relief softened her features as she nodded and turned to find the exit.

*

The ride from Newark to Watchung was cramped and noisy with everyone competing for his attention. The girls sang preschool songs for him, trying to outdo each other in volume. They clung to him in the backseat of the sedan, smelling sweetly of baby shampoo. Wendy sat on his lap, toying with the buttons on his shirt.

Cole furrowed his brow at his nieces. Their father had walked out on them a year ago, saying he'd had it with Corinne and her phobias. Since then the girls attached themselves too easily to other men.

"You don't need to worry about those two," Estelle told him. "They're survivors." But Cole saw only two little girls made of glass that could shatter in the slightest breeze.

He took Wendy's hand away from his shirt and squeezed it, wishing he could turn back time and shield them from everything worldly.

Corinne left with the girls shortly before dinner, as the fireflies were beginning to light the yard with their maize-colored glow. He and Estelle would have to come over when Estelle got back, Corinne said as she hugged him good-bye. He nodded, knowing Estelle would ask him to invent a reason to turn down the invitation.

His parents exchanged looks of surprise across the dinner table when he told them he'd be moving out of the Chapel House.

"What does that mean, Cole?" Phillip asked, setting his fork down. "Will you and Estelle be getting married?" The beautiful smoothness of his father's French-Canadian accent struck him as if he were hearing it for the first time. Phillip

Perelle had grown up in Montreal. He'd met Virginia Cole there when she was on spring break from Smith, and they were married six months later. They saw to it that their children spoke French as easily as they did English. Still Cole's French had never met Estelle's standards. She'd lived the first ten years of her life in Paris, as well as a few years during high school and college. His French couldn't compare.

Cole returned his father's quizzical look. "I'm not sure what it means." He pushed his plate away, annoyed at the knot in his stomach. He wanted to marry Estelle. He had for several years, but the conflict over where to live always got in the way. That was a small obstacle, though, compared to Estelle's fear of marriage itself. It wasn't the commitment that frightened her—he knew there was no one else in her life. It was putting her faith in an institution she saw as doomed. Her mother had been divorced three times, her father twice. She was afraid that the moment they married Cole would begin to grow tired of her. But he was patient. He figured that in time he could convince her otherwise.

Virginia was eyeing him closely from across the table. "I've always thought Janni's grandfather had something of the sorcerer in him to build a house with such a pull on the people inside," she said. "It must be difficult to get out from under that spell, not to mention leaving Jay and Janni after all these years."

What is very difficult, he thought, *is having a psychologist for a mother.*

"It won't be easy." He tried to avoid his mother's perceptive gaze. He'd always suspected her of eavesdropping on his thoughts—how else could she know what he was thinking and feeling with such accuracy? His childhood friends could get away with lying about why their homework wasn't done or where they'd been the night before. When he tried it, his mother invariably knew the truth, as if she'd left a little part of herself attached to him at his birth to serve as an informer.

Now she leaned across the table toward him, trying to grip his blue-green eyes with her own. "This is Estelle's idea, isn't it?" she asked.

Phillip looked at his wife. "What if it is?" he said. "She's a smart girl. It's about time, if you ask me."

"It's a mutual decision, Mom," he said, keeping his voice even. He wished he could say that the last nine months had drawn them closer together, but his mother would know in an instant he was lying.

They had made few friends in Paris. Had it been the long work hours or had Estelle reeled him in each time he stepped away from her? He didn't know. They worked together in the daytime and slept together at night. They spoke only French with each other. They tried to master the current patois, making and incorporating the same mistakes in usage until the language they spoke was very much their own and their symbiosis was complete.

She clung to him with a bewildering fierceness. Her possessiveness grew as if she could be certain her heart would beat only in his presence. She began asking him to account for the few hours he spent apart from her, then she'd tearfully apologize for doubting him.

He blamed Paris, not Estelle, and he was certain she

would be her old self again when they were back in New Jersey. She convinced him that her Point Pleasant condominium was big enough for both of them and that the time was right to move in together, away from the Chapel House. She was hard to refuse. At times he felt weakened by some Circean quality in her that made him give in to her with no thought to the consequences.

He couldn't very well describe that power to his mother when he didn't understand it himself.

He arrived in Point Pleasant on Sunday night and opened up the condominium. He expected a musty, stale smell to greet him, but it was Estelle's scent—that unique blend of soap and roses and earth—that enveloped him, as if she'd just walked past him into the hallway. Amazing that the sterile white and chrome condominium would hold her scent for all these months. Right now, as he stood in her living room, she was sleeping three thousand miles away from him. He could picture her, the splash of mahogany-colored hair across the pillow, one arm reaching out for him in her sleep. A sudden longing ran through him to the tips of his fingers.

He set his luggage down by the front door, balancing a bag of hamburgers on top of his suitcase, and walked across the living room to the balcony that overlooked the inlet. He wanted to see the water before he did anything else. The inlet was never calm, and this evening was no exception. Its waves inflated and died over and over again with no true rhythm. A few fishermen were scattered on the flat rocks of the jetty, colored pink by the setting sun.

He opened the refrigerator. It gaped discouragingly at him with its white and silver emptiness, like the room behind him. He filled a glass with tap water and carried it to the kitchen table. He ate two of the hamburgers, chewing and swallowing without tasting. The third he threw in the garbage.

He wouldn't call the Chapel House until at least nine, when it would be too late for him to drive there. He couldn't take the chance of being asked to stay the night or feeling the walls of the house close around him like a lullaby. His dreams in Paris had been full of the house. Even when the dream itself made no sense, the setting held it together. He dreamt often of his bedroom or of the kitchen with one of Janni's fires burning in the fireplace. How would he survive in this condo?

The waves of the inlet disappeared in the dusk, and the lights clicked on one by one in the handful of boats foolish enough to attempt the inlet at night. The fishermen packed up their gear, calling to each other in muffled words he couldn't decipher, but which he imagined signified resignation and defeat.

Nine o'clock came and went without a call to the house. Still too early. Mantoloking's only ten minutes away, he thought. He pictured driving down the barrier island, the ocean on his left, the bay on his right, the thick salty air filling his car. He could drive to the house, visit for an hour, and drive back. He had a sudden mental image of an alcoholic at a party claiming he could take just one drink, and he laughed out loud at the comparison.

At nine-thirty he made the call. The voice that answered was unfamiliar.

"Maris?" he asked, wondering if he'd tangled the digits of the number in his memory.

"No, this is Kit Sheridan."

He felt a sharp twinge of loss; the Chapel House was not the same house he had left. There was a stranger living there, answering the phone as if she belonged.

"Is Jay there?" he said. "This is Cole."

"Oh, *Cole*," said Kit. "I'll get Janni." The stranger was gone so quickly she left ice on the line.

"Cole! Are you in Point Pleasant? Can you come over tonight?" Janni's voice was quick and eager and brought a smile to his lips.

"It's too late, Jance," he said, as if the hour of his call had been dictated by some force outside himself.

"God, we've missed you. You should have come here for the night. Aren't you going to be lonely there all by yourself?"

"No, it's fine," he lied.

She told him that Jay was out of town until Tuesday, but she'd meet him for lunch the next day. It felt strange, having to make arrangements to see her. He was used to simply knocking on her bedroom door when he wanted to talk.

Estelle's big bed looked inviting, but the bedroom was too full of her. He remembered so many mornings lying beneath the sheets of that bed, watching her brush her thick, wavy hair at the dressing table. She'd wear slips of lace and satin, and she'd use the names of fruit to describe their colors.

"This one's apricot," she would say, or "this one's raspberry with a hint of watermelon." She used mango when she could think of no fruit the color of her slip, because she said mangoes turned a different color nearly every day as they ripened.

He loved watching her. Sometimes when she would catch his smile or his look of contentment, she'd say, "Isn't this better than spending the night in the Chapel House?" And he would have to agree because he liked to see her so relaxed, so comfortable in her own home. The lure of the house was, it seemed, selective.

She'd certainly been relaxed this past weekend, his last in Paris. They'd driven through the Loire Valley in the leased Renault. He hadn't wanted to go, but it would be his last look at the chateaux country for a while. He'd expected Estelle to spend the time questioning him again about his plans for the next three weeks, when he'd be in New Jersey without her. But the interrogation never came, and as the enchantment of the valley surrounded him, he began to unwind.

They'd spent the morning exploring Chenonceau, his favorite of the chateaux. It wasn't the architecture or the manicured gardens that captivated him. It was the water. The Cher River flowed under and around the castle—he could see water from every window.

Afterward, they shared a lunch of salmon in sorrel sauce and cold asparagus.

"I wish you could stay just two weeks longer," she said,

sipping her wine, her deep blue eyes watching him. "The chateaux concerts would begin then."

It was as close as she came to the dangerous topic, and she let him ignore the comment without reprimand.

After lunch they sought out a road that Estelle remembered from a dozen years earlier, when she had been a student in Paris. She sat forward in the car, brow furrowed, map in her hand.

"Turn here," she said.

He turned onto a narrow road, forested on one side, a rolling vineyard on the other.

"Now here." She pointed to a barely noticeable opening in the woods. He turned onto the road, and she sat back. "This is it." She smiled. They were in a leafy green tunnel, shut off from the rest of the world.

They drove for a while in silence. He felt pleasantly disoriented by mile after mile of overhanging greenery. They rounded a bend in the road and, suddenly, laid out in front of them was a sea of vermilion poppies. Acres upon acres of them, the breeze blowing across them like a wave on the ocean.

Cole stopped the car in the middle of the road. "Look at that," he said.

"They're still here," said Estelle. "*Les coquelicots*. Aren't they beautiful! Let's get out."

Her spontaneity surprised him. She'd often stop the car in the middle of the city when a boutique caught her eye or she needed a closer look at a painting in a gallery window, but rarely had he known her to ask for a closer look at nature.

He pulled the car onto the barely existent shoulder of the road and got out. He followed Estelle into the field at a distance. He wanted to watch her. She was wearing the dress she liked to travel in—yards of pale green fabric that wrapped around her in so many turns he could never figure out how to unwrap it without her help. Her hair was shades darker than the poppies but in perfect harmony with them. She turned around and waved.

He hadn't known this childlike part of Estelle still existed. He caught up to her and took her hand, feeling dizzy from the flow and sway of the flowers.

They walked toward a cluster of trees that would shelter them from the road, and she didn't complain when he sat in the midst of the poppies and drew her down next to him.

"Let's make love," she said, as if she hadn't known that was his plan.

"Your dress will get dirty." He laid her back into the poppies. "And your hair."

"I don't care," she said, in that dusky voice that scared him sometimes. He never knew what was hidden beneath it, sometimes tears, sometimes anger. Whatever it was this time, he knew there would be a desperate edge to this lovemaking. She was breaking all her own rules. She wanted this to be the memory of her he took back with him to the States.

He slept now under a single sheet on the couch in the living room so he could hear the water slapping against the rocks of the jetty. The cooling breeze that streamed steadily through the window smelled of salt and seaweed and he slept more deeply than he had in months.

It took him only five minutes to drive to Blair the next morning. Quite an improvement over the fifteen it used to take from the Chapel House. He told himself that living in the condo might not be so bad after all, especially when he got those middle-of-the-night emergency calls.

The hospital looked good to him. The building was a striking arrangement of concrete and black-tinted glass that jutted out over the water of the Manasquan River. It was a good-looking building at any time, but particularly at night when it lit up the water with its lights.

Blair was gaining national attention for its transplant programs and eye surgeries. The addition of a fetal surgery program would put it on the map in obstetrics as well. That's why Blair had been willing to pay him—and pay him well—for spending nine months in France, studying the latest techniques in fetal surgery. They'd even spared Estelle from the Research Department to go with him to help with the translation. The critical thing now was to get funding. He couldn't tolerate the thought of all his effort in these past few years going to waste.

The carpet of the Maternity Unit was new, and the walls now had murals painted on them. Trees and grass and rainbows. He had the feeling he was in a dream, walking through some alien hospital on springy green carpet. He couldn't remember the color of the previous carpet, or if this hall had been carpeted at all.

Elliot Lehman, the director of the Maternity Unit, was

waiting for him in the reception area of the offices they shared. He shook Cole's hand, a wide smile on his bronzed face, and handed him a piece of coffee cake and a pint carton of milk. "We have a lot to talk about," he said. "Let's go in my office."

Cole settled into one of the maroon-colored chairs in front of Elliot's desk. He loved the leathery smell of this office, an office that was just a bit bigger, a bit more comfortable than his own. He sipped at his milk, thinking that Elliot looked grayer. His eyebrows were nearly white. And there was something strange about his smile, something held back.

"The work you sent me looked excellent," Elliot said.

"I feel completely confident with the open-uterus technique." Cole sat forward, wishing he could read Elliot's face. "Do you know what that means? Spina bifida . . . bone transplants . . . the fetus will be literally at our fingertips."

"At *your* fingertips."

Cole frowned. What was that supposed to mean? There'd never been any rivalry between them, on this or any other topic. "Well," he said, "even if I'm heading the team I still think you should be a part—"

Elliot held up a hand to stop him. "I'm not going to be here," he said.

"What do you mean you're not going to be here?"

Elliot leaned his forearms on his desk. He seemed to be enjoying Cole's confusion. "I've been offered the position of director of Perinatal Research at Stewart. And I've accepted."

Cole's mind raced with uncertainty. No Chapel House. No Elliot. His life was precariously out of balance. "Well, congratulations," he said halfheartedly. "That's quite an offer. But it's hard to imagine Blair without you. The prestige of this unit is owing to you more than to anyone."

"Thanks," said Elliot. He was grinning. "That was only part of what I need to tell you." He leaned across the massive desk, his meaty hands spread flat on the leather top, his fingers pointing in Cole's direction.

Cole shifted uncomfortably in his seat. He couldn't handle another piece of news like that.

"You've been selected to be my replacement. We'd like you to be the new director of Maternal and Fetal Medicine here at Blair."

He stared at Elliot in disbelief. He had imagined that, years from now, when Elliot retired, he might take over. Or perhaps in four or five years he would take on the directorship of a smaller medical center. But he had never imagined that at the age of thirty-four he would be handed an opportunity like this.

A smile broke free from his face. "I don't know what to say."

"You have a few days to decide." Elliot sat back in his chair. "You're the right person for this, Cole. I hope you plan to accept."

If he had been deaf and blind, he still would have known he was following Janni in the cafeteria line. She was as frenetic as always. At times she made little jumping movements while she waited, shiny dark hair bouncing, and she walked backward so she could talk to him without pausing.

She was wearing a denim jumper over a blouse with a tiny Mickey Mouse print running through it. Something new, he thought. He'd never seen this particular outfit on her, but it was typical of her clothes. He wondered what other adult woman would buy a Mickey Mouse blouse.

He watched her affectionately as she loaded her tray with nearly every raw and cooked vegetable on the counter. She frowned when he put a cheeseburger next to the milk on his tray.

"The latest study I read found a definite relationship between eating meat and having pungent perspiration," she said.

"And vegetarians sweat Chanel Number Five, I suppose?"

"Something like that."

He had decided not to tell her about Elliot's offer. He needed time to think, and he wanted to be the one to tell Jay. How could he tell his best friend that he'd taken a quantum leap ahead of him? It would be a decade before Jay could receive such an offer, the hierarchy in general surgery was so intricate.

The cafeteria was buzzing as usual, and he felt a little nostalgic. He'd actually missed this place, mediocre food and all. They found a table in the corner, out of the mainstream of people anxious to welcome him back.

"So how's the new Chapel House resident working out?" he asked, remembering the voice that had chilled him on the phone the night before. He tried to picture the stranger in the house. He saw a faceless woman eating with the others at the old oak table in the kitchen, laughing with them in an intimate way.

"She's great. Jay and Maris liked her right away, but I knew they would. She'd planned to stay at the house for a month or so while she was looking for a place to buy. She found a great house on a lagoon in Point Pleasant, but when it came time for her to move into it . . . well, I bet you can guess what happened."

"She couldn't leave the Chapel House."

"Right."

"Did she rent out the Point Pleasant house?"

"Yup."

He laughed. He had acted out the same scenario years earlier.

"Wait 'til you see the changes she's made in the *Communicator*. You won't recognize it. She's a runner, too. But she eats meat, can you believe it? You'd think she'd care what she puts in her body. Plus she's doing the PR on your Fetal Surgery Program."

"What?" He put down the cheeseburger. "I don't even know her. How can they expect her to get the funding when she doesn't know the first thing about me or the program?" He knew as he spoke that it wasn't the PR that made him uncomfortable. This woman was moving into his territory much too quickly.

"Don't worry. She's good. And you'll know her tomorrow. She has an appointment with you in the morning."

He shook his head. "I'm seeing patients in the morning."

"She's coming to see you *as* a patient. She's had a raging

infection for weeks, but I talked her into waiting until you got back."

"Janni, you savage. She's probably got PID by now."

Janni didn't flinch. She took off her glasses and leaned toward him, her silky dark bangs grazing her eyelashes. "I want her to go to *you*."

He shook his head, smiling at her. "You haven't changed a bit," he said with some relief. "You always have your own plans for your friends, don't you?"

"Uh-huh." She sounded as though he had complimented her on an outstanding personality trait. "And my plan right now is to talk you into staying at the Chapel House."

"Jance, don't do that to me, please. It's going to be hard enough as it is. I gave Estelle my solemn promise that this is it. I'm going to start boxing things up when I come over for dinner tomorrow night."

"Well, that should make for an uplifting evening." She put her glasses back on.

He asked about Maris. She was dating finally, Janni said, no longer moping around the Chapel House gym. He and Jay had installed a barre in the gym for Maris's thirty-second birthday, and it and Tchaikovsky had become her escape.

"I hope I can still use the gym," he said.

"That's out of the question. You want to use the torture chamber, you have to be a resident."

He stiffened. "Janni, I'm serious. I don't want to be badgered about moving back in." He let his eyes burn into hers to make his point.

She looked down at her plate, and he noticed her eyes

glistening behind her glasses. She looked like a little girl who'd just been scolded.

"I'm sorry," he said. "But I don't want to feel as if I have to choose between Estelle and my friends."

Janni nodded. "I know. It's just the hysterectomy."

"What do you mean, the hysterectomy?" He always felt guilty when she brought that up, as if he were responsible for the fibroid tumors just because he was the one to discover them. "That was two whole years ago."

"Yeah, well, most of the time it doesn't bother me, but every once in a while I think to myself, Janni, you'll never, ever have a family of your own. And then I think, well, I've got Cole and Maris. They're like a family. But now you're leaving . . ." She shrugged, a wounded look on her face. "I couldn't believe it when you wrote you'd be moving out." She poked at the corn and spinach on her plate with her fork, the little Mickey Mouse figures smiling insipidly at him from her sleeves.

"Did you think I'd be living with you and Jay forever?" he asked.

"I guess I did."

"Well, I'll be around so much you won't realize I've gone."

Janni nodded, her expression as hollow as the sound of his words.

3.

Kit was surprised by the man who reached out from behind his desk to shake her hand. For a fleeting instant she thought she was in the wrong office. The doctor in the blue plaid shirt who motioned her into a chair looked nothing like her mental image of Cole. He had no trappings of a physician. No white coat, no stethoscope circling his neck. Because Cole and Jay were best friends, she had expected him to look like Jay—wild dark hair, a gently handsome face that was slow to register joy or sorrow. But Cole wore his dark brown hair short, and his expressions were quick and sharp. His pale eyes looked right through her, and his smile was so immediate that for a moment she was caught off guard. Maybe it had been a mistake to let Janni talk her into seeing him as a physician. He would have all the power in this first meeting.

"So you're Kit Sheridan," he said. "I'm glad to finally meet you." He walked around his desk and sat in the chair across from her.

Nice touch, she thought. With one move he had equalized them, and she wondered if he allowed all his patients that degree of control.

She folded her hands in the lap of her beige skirt. "I've heard a lot about you," she said.

"I can imagine." He smiled, a little crookedly. "I have to say that I'm envious of you, living in the house. What room are you in?"

"Right across the hall from yours."

"Oh, that's a great room." He wore a pained expression as though he couldn't bear to remember it. "I used to sit on the window seat in there to read or catch up on paperwork."

She felt guilty, as if she'd stolen something from him. "The whole house is remarkable," she said.

He nodded. "Magical. I'm looking forward to having dinner there tonight, but it's going to be hard, being there without belonging there anymore."

"I think you belong there more than I do."

"I don't know about that. When Janni wrote that you'd moved in, I thought, 'well, I'll just have to get used to the idea that somebody's taken my place. I've been usurped.'"

She looked at him suspiciously. Would he really let himself be that transparent or was he playing some kind of game with her? He seemed genuine enough.

"I've been resenting you a bit, too," she said, deciding to trust him. "I was afraid that when you came back they'd forget I existed."

He grinned. "It's a toss-up as to which of us is more neurotic."

"We'll have to get over that if we're going to work together to get the Fetal Surgery Program funded."

"Ah yes. I've heard that my professional future's in your

hands." He looked more comfortable now. He was slightly slouched in the leather chair, his hands folded across his belt buckle. She noticed he was wearing jeans.

"Well, let's just say I'll share the responsibility with you," she said, pleased by the strength in her voice. "Will you have a chance to work on the proposal for the Devlin Foundation in the next few weeks?"

"It's nearly done. Just needs the finishing touches."

He was going to push for this thing. A twinge of anxiety tried to latch on to her, but she ignored it. "I'll time the first press release with the submission of the proposal," she said. "That should generate public support that can make a big difference in Devlin's decision."

He sat up a little straighter, his hands moving to the arms of his chair. "But what about public *criticism*? I've heard there's been some flak from religious groups already."

He was as anxious as she was about the whole thing. When she spoke her voice was reassuring. "All the competing medical centers are facing that obstacle," she said. "We'll work closely with the media to get them in our corner." For the first time she noticed he was very good-looking. "We'll get you on TV. On the news and maybe the local wake-up show."

His eyes were very wide now. "Wow," he said.

She smiled and only then realized that her face had been a solemn mask. "It'll be easy. You'll see."

He made notes on her chart as she spoke, slowing her when she tried to rush. She pictured the other women in the waiting room, tapping their feet impatiently and glancing at their watches. She told him about the infection. She'd had them before, but this one wouldn't let go. Stress, he suggested. She nodded. She couldn't remember a more stress-filled year.

"Are you using birth control?" he asked.

"I've used an IUD since I was first married." She told him the brand and he nodded his approval. "I plan to get my tubes tied the next time I need it replaced."

"You don't want children." It was a statement, not a question.

She shook her head. "There are too many other things I want to do," she said, and then bit her lip, imagining he was thinking she was a hard, selfish bitch.

"Why put off the tubal ligation then?"

"Well," she said slowly, not really sure how to answer. "I don't have any problems with the IUD. And frankly, sex is the last thing on my mind."

He raised his eyebrows.

"I haven't been interested since my divorce. Not at all. Work and running keep me totally occupied."

"Have you tried any of those provocative novels Janni leaves around?"

She nodded with a grin. "No impact whatsoever." It did worry her a little, that she never felt the longing anymore. "I haven't even masturbated in months," she said impulsively, startling herself with the words.

Cole looked unruffled. He laughed, a quiet laugh, barely more than a smile. "Did you ever stop to think what throwing yourself into your work is costing you?"

She wanted to defend herself, but his voice was so soft, so tentative that she felt closer to tears than anger. "It's a matter of deciding what's most important to me right now. And that's work and running."

He nodded. "Okay," he said. "Okay."

She undressed in the examining room and sat on the table, covering herself with a mass of crinkly paper sheeting. He walked in followed by a young nurse. He was frowning over her chart. "You wrote that your last period was in March. Is that a mistake?"

She tensed, wondering how he would handle this. Her periods had been unpredictable since she started running. She worried that some doctor would tell her to stop running, that being fat and asthmatic was preferable to skipping periods.

But Cole didn't seem alarmed. He asked her what tests she'd had, told her to keep track of her cycle, and dropped the subject. She let out her breath in relief.

He listened to her heart for a very long time. She could feel the unfamiliar warmth of his face close to her own and see the laugh lines at the corners of his eyes. He finally looked up.

"You're either very healthy or near death," he said. "Fifty-four."

"I must be a little nervous." She smiled.

He motioned her to lie down. "How much are you running?" He pressed gentle circles around her breasts.

"About sixty miles a week right now, but I want to start building it up so I can run in the Somerville Marathon in October. I'm hoping to qualify for Boston."

"Sixty sounds overwhelming already. Do you run on the beach?"

"In the mornings. Then I usually run home from work."

The nurse groaned.

"That's got to be five miles," Cole said.

"Only four. And all flat. I need some hills."

"When was your last Pap?"

"About a year ago." She held her breath as he slipped a speculum inside her.

"What about the bridges?"

"What?"

"As hills. They're not like Boston but they're better than nothing."

She'd never thought of the bridges. "I could take Bridge Avenue home from work and run over the canal. I could go back and forth over it a few times. That would be a workout."

"If you don't mind that passersby will think you're nuts. Your cervix looks beautiful, by the way." He said it all in the same breath, and it made her laugh.

"Thanks, I guess. No one's ever told me that before." It was hard not to like him.

She nibbled the edge of her garlic bread. She had barely touched the spaghetti on her plate, but her second glass of wine was almost empty. The quivering in the pit of her stomach wouldn't let her eat.

Maris sat queen-like at the head of the long cherry table in the formal dining room. She'd replaced the gold sphere in her nostril with a diamond chip sometime during the day. She wore one of her usual outfits, a long white skirt over a scoop-neck black leotard. She had the lithe look of a dancer, which she was by avocation if not by profession.

Kit sat next to Janni, caught between Janni's steady chatter and the life returning to her own body. Jay and Cole sat across the table from them, looking entirely different from one another. Jay's face calmed her like the wine, but she imagined that Cole could see into her, that somehow he knew that her blood was pumping faster and harder than it had been an hour earlier.

She had been the one to answer the door. Cole stood on the step holding a bottle of wine in one hand, a bunch of flowers upside down at his side in the other.

Those eyes. How had she missed their color during her appointment that morning? She stared at him as though she'd never seen him before, and he grinned back, long subtle dimples on either side of his lips.

"May I come in?"

"Of course." She regained her composure. "Janni and Jay are in the kitchen."

He walked past her with a nod, and she followed, dazed and jelly-kneed.

In the huge kitchen, Jay and Cole embraced while Janni leaned against the empty fieldstone fireplace, watching them with a smile. Kit walked uneasily into the pantry to hunt for some unneeded ingredient. When she returned to the kitchen, empty-handed, they were laughing at how Jay's sauce-spattered apron had transferred a tomato stain onto Cole's jeans.

Janni wet a kitchen towel and rubbed at the denim

covering Cole's right thigh, and Kit felt the pit of her stomach roll over.

Now, at the dining room table, her appetite was completely gone. Her head felt as if it were floating, and her teeth, when she touched them with her tongue, seemed strangely soft. She had to fight with herself to pay attention to the conversation. It was lively, the air in the room light and electric, as though the house itself had been waiting for Cole's return to spring to life.

They were reminiscing, using her as an audience. Something about Jay and Cole's first apartment near Columbia. Torturing roaches with water pistols. Eating cocaine? Had she heard that correctly? Maintaining a string of women and going to classes red-eyed from lack of sleep. She wrinkled her nose or smiled or laughed in what she hoped were the right places.

". . . but when Jay first brought Janni to the apartment, I knew it was serious," Cole said. He was talking to Kit, his eyes resting on her as though she were the eighth natural wonder of the world. "I thought to myself, oh God, a social worker. A vegetarian social worker."

Jay laughed. "It *was* an adjustment," he said.

She tried to picture Jay and Janni getting to know each other, a tentativeness in their relating that was hard to imagine.

"Well, Cole," said Janni. "I thought you were a nice guy, great to look at, very sociable, but shallow."

"Shallow?" He looked insulted.

"Every woman you brought home was gorgeous. Every

one of them looked like they'd stepped off the cover of *Vogue*."

"It was purely coincidental." Cole gave Janni that completely attentive look. His charm was uncanny. "I was attracted to brains that just happened to belong to good-looking women."

Kit tried to imagine what she looked like at that moment. No makeup, flyaway honey-colored hair, pale skin that was incapable of taking color from the sun. A runner's tight body under her white short-sleeved shirt and khaki shorts. She sighed and took another swallow of wine.

"Do you remember the night the three of us moved in here?" Janni was talking to Cole and Jay. "The storm?" She turned to Kit with a shudder. "The lights went out. The wind was howling in the rooms upstairs, and the ocean was up to the beach heather. The three of us huddled in the library, straining our eyes to watch the water getting closer and closer in the dark. We thought it was a bad omen, as if moving in here had been a mistake."

"Best mistake I ever made," Cole said. "Wasn't it five years ago this month?"

"You're right!" Janni jumped out of her seat. "We should break out the champagne and celebrate."

"Except for the fact that one of you is no longer living here," said Maris.

Janni shot her a warning look. She had told them not to talk about his moving out.

"Sorry." Maris bit her lip.

Cole cupped his hand around hers where it rested on

the table. "And it must be about two years for you, Mar," he said.

"Two years next month," Maris said without a smile, but she turned her hand to latch her fingers with his.

Janni left the room and Kit stared at the two hands twined together on the embroidered tablecloth, one wide and square, the other dark and slender. The room was suddenly very quiet, and she was relieved when Janni returned with the champagne.

"We've been waiting all night to hear your news," Janni said as she poured. They had asked him earlier in the evening but he'd put them off. "After dinner," he'd said. "I don't want to talk about it yet."

He still looked reluctant, unsure of himself for the first time all evening. He sat back from the table. "Elliot's taking a position at Stewart," he said, "and I've been asked to replace him." The room was so quiet that the waves seemed to be breaking just outside the back door. "I haven't decided yet," he added.

"Good lord." Maris frowned. "You're just a kid."

Kit watched Jay's face. It was hard to read. He had told her once about the competitiveness between them. "We didn't want to outdo each other as much as we didn't want to be outdone by each other," he had said. What was he thinking now? When he finally spoke, everyone else was quiet.

"You'd be a fool if you turned it down," he said.

Cole looked relieved. "I won't then."

*

They moved to the living room after dinner. Cole sat on the floor, leaning against Janni's chair, and she stroked his hair lightly with the tips of her fingers. It was odd to see her touching a man other than Jay in that familiar way.

Jay stretched out on the blue sofa, and Maris and Kit sat on the floor in front of the fireplace. Kit watched the men, looking for a sign of friction between them. But they were laughing, talking about the *Sweetwater*—the motorboat they docked on the bay, a couple of blocks from the house. If there was tension in their faces, it was well hidden.

They talked for hours, finishing the champagne and switching to coffee, one by one. By that time Kit was lying on her back on the rug, wondering if Cole had any idea of the effect he was having on her. She liked what she could see of his body, the broad chest and shoulders, the flat line of his stomach under his jersey, even after a meal of pasta. She liked the way he carried himself—self-confidently but without a trace of arrogance. She watched him from the floor, staring at the patch of curly hair in the unbuttoned neck of his jersey. It was a few shades darker than the hair on his head, and she imagined running her lips over it. It was becoming an obsessive thought. She could almost feel it brushing against her mouth.

It was late. She'd had too much to drink.

Maris was the first to go to bed. She knelt in front of Cole, her hands on his knees, and kissed him lightly on the lips. "It's wonderful to have you home," she said.

"I'll come up and tuck you in."

Kit frowned at the ceiling as Maris and Cole headed up the stairs to Maris's room. She sat up, a little dizzy.

"Are Maris and Cole . . ." she said. "Are they . . ."

Jay and Janni watched her struggle for words.

"Lovers?" Janni offered with a grin. "No way. Cole's a one-woman man." She stood up and stretched, held out a hand to Jay. "Bed?"

Jay nodded. "Tell Cole good night for us, Kit," he said.

She thought of going up herself, but she wanted to see Cole one more time. She needed another look at those eyes, needed to feel that shock wave roll over her again. She wanted to take that feeling with her to bed.

She pulled the wide French doors of the living room shut and began collecting glasses and cups from the tables. Maybe he wouldn't come downstairs after all. She wasn't convinced that he and Maris were just chatting in Maris's bedroom.

But within minutes he was back in the living room. He smiled at her but said nothing as he walked around the room, stroking a tabletop, looking out the window at the black water of the Atlantic, stopping to stare at the photograph of the house over the mantel.

She carried the last of the cups into the kitchen, and after a few minutes he joined her there.

"I want to sit out on the beach for a while," he said. "Come with me?"

The beach was high and level close to the house and covered with beach heather that changed colors with the seasons. Beyond the heather, the sand began its gradual decline to the sea.

Tonight the beach was the color of moon glow, the heather a deep sea green. Four big white wooden chairs faced the water. Kit started to sit in one, but Cole stopped her. He grouped the chairs together, tipping the backrests of the two in front onto the seats of the two in back. He'd obviously done this many times before.

"It's for stargazing," he said, pointing to the sky.

Kit looked up. The stars were crisp little diamonds in a black sky.

"You have to be careful getting in," he said, holding her arm as she slid into the seat. She felt the warmth of his fingers on her skin.

He slid into his own seat next to her. "Janni's grandfather built these chairs," he said.

"I didn't know that."

"If you look underneath, you can just make out the name 'John Chapel' where he carved it into the seat. But they've been painted so many times that his signature's nearly disappeared."

She'd noticed that about these chairs, that the paint was so thick she could dent it with her fingernail. She thought of how Janni struggled to preserve John Chapel's mark on the house, keeping all his old furniture, never seeming to care that it didn't fit in with the new, and for the first time she felt some of Janni's sense of loss.

It was warm enough tonight to be out here in her shorts and shirt. This was new for her, these summer nights in New Jersey. She liked the salty air, the occasional breeze that slipped past her shoulders. She liked being barefoot in the dark with the thunder of the ocean so close she could feel it in her bones.

She could identify only the Big Dipper. She defended

herself, telling him that astronomy had been incompatible with Seattle's low ceiling. Cole outlined the constellations for her with an outstretched arm, describing the genesis of each. His favorite, he told her, was Scorpios.

"Orion was very egotistical and claimed he could kill all the poisonous reptiles on earth, so Diana sent the Scorpion to kill him. That's why you never see Orion and Scorpios in the same sky."

"Undone by a woman," Kit sad. "Brains against brawn. Is that why you like it?"

She could see the glint of his teeth in the moonlight and knew he was smiling. "You're reading way too much into it, Kit. I like the curved line of the stars. That's all."

Suddenly, two stars fell, long silver trails streaming into the sea.

Cole sighed. "Where else can you sit in your backyard and have a show like this?" he asked.

Kit remembered Janni's warning how he'd get angry if anyone mentioned his moving out, how she never liked to be around when Cole got angry. But Kit felt safe. She thought she could ask him anything at all. "Do you want to move back into the house, Cole?"

"What I want doesn't matter right now." He told her that he and Estelle were tired of splitting their time between her condominium and the Chapel House. He wanted Estelle to move in with him, but she wanted privacy. "I can't fault her for that," he said. "So I'll move into her condo." He shrugged as if it were a solution to which he had no objection.

"Tell me about Estelle," she said. When he had spoken

about her at dinner, she sounded loving and vibrant. Did he know how other people—how his own friends—talked about her?

Cole leaned his head back and studied the constellations again. "Estelle means star, you know."

Kit said nothing. He was moving away from her, out of reach.

"She's exceptionally beautiful. She's smarter than I am. Much smarter." He lowered his head and looked at her. "We have a lot in common. But she hates the Jersey Shore." He tightened his lips as if confronting a hard reality. "She belongs in the city, in Manhattan. She was even offered a job at the UN a few years ago. She's here because of me, because I love it here, and I could never live in the heat and pace of New York. She's sacrificed a lot for me, so it's my turn now."

"I can sympathize with her," Kit said. "Mantoloking is not exactly cosmopolitan." She knew that she wanted to be friends with Estelle, not just because she sounded like an extraordinary woman but because it was as close to Cole as she could hope to get.

Cole smiled at her. "I want to apologize for what I said to you in the office today, about you taking my place here. I think you fit in perfectly."

She watched the lights of a boat slip across the dark horizon. "I feel so lucky," she said. "I was afraid I'd never fit in anyplace again. I felt lost when I moved here."

"How long had you been married?"

"Eight years."

"What happened?"

She thought about how to answer that. Nothing had happened. That was the problem. They'd fallen into a monotonous routine. They never fought, rarely made love. It was her fault as much as it was Bill's. She should have done something, tried to bring the spark back. But it hadn't seemed worth the effort.

"I think our relationship bored itself to death," she said.

"Is that when you lost interest in sex?"

"I guess so, but I think my interest has suddenly returned." She immediately wished she could take back the words. Her ears burned with embarrassment.

"What do you mean?" he asked. "You mean . . . me?"

She felt his eyes on her. "I should have thought that through before I said it," she said.

"Maybe you're a little drunk."

"Maybe."

For a few seconds he said nothing.

"Listen, Kit, I'm flattered, but I think you understand how I feel about Estelle."

"Oh, I know," she said quickly. "Even if you weren't involved with someone I wouldn't pursue it because I really don't want a relationship with anyone right now. Nothing serious anyway." She was telling him the truth—she wouldn't allow herself to be suffocated in a lifeless relationship again. "I'm just glad to know I'm still capable of feeling attracted to somebody."

"I'm sure the feeling's transferable," he said. "Tonight Cole Perelle, tomorrow the entire male population at Blair."

"That's an exhausting thought," she said, marveling at how safe it felt to talk to him.

She woke in the middle of the night on the verge of an orgasm. She was so close that she came just by rolling onto her stomach and pressing into the mattress. She tried to piece together the dream that had brought her to that pitch, but it was evasive, and she fell back to sleep with the hope of recapturing it.

4.

Cole moved back into the Chapel House that Saturday. He made his decision the night he came to dinner. On the beach, under the stars, he felt himself surrender. He didn't ever want to feel like a guest in the house again.

How he'd hated waking alone in the condominium. He woke chilled every morning even though it was June. He raced through showering and dressing to get to work, to get out of those empty white rooms as quickly as he could. His inability to stay away from the house embarrassed him; his weakness must be so evident to the others. But they welcomed him without taunting, as though his return had been entirely expected.

He was relieved to be back in his room, surrounded by the homey rich smell of his own furniture. He had collected a lot of it over the years. It spilled out of his room into the den next door and down into the living room. His was not one of the larger bedrooms, and it had no ocean view. Yet he had chosen it himself because of the balcony and the view of the bay, two blocks to the west. The colors of the sunset warmed his room every evening and made size and a view of the ocean unimportant.

The hardest part of moving back in had been the phone call to Estelle. He heard the trembling in her voice over the crackling line. The silences when he knew she was swallowing hard, trying not to cry. He could see her eyes, the darkest blue imaginable, filling with tears she despised. She loathed any loss of control.

"You're being selfish," she said.

"I'm not denying that."

Silence.

"Is it the condo?" she asked. "We could find a place of our own."

"We could never find one on the ocean that we could afford."

That made her snappish. "Why don't you just admit it, Cole? It's not the ocean. The problem is that you can't break away from your precious friends."

"Maybe you're right." What was the point of arguing when he had no defense? He told her he was sorry. He was wrong, unspeakably selfish. But there were no tears, no words of reasoning that could make him change his mind.

"What if we took the whole south wing of the house?" he asked.

"How many times have we been through this?"

At least once a month for the last five years, he thought. "I guess we'll have to keep things the way they've been," he said.

"That's what you've wanted to say all along, isn't it?"

He knew, of course, that she was right.

*

In the mornings he felt the presence of other people in the house even before he opened his eyes. Before any of the floorboards in the long hallway creaked or the aroma of coffee floated up the stairs, he knew they were there. If he wanted to, he could knock on Jay and Janni's door, sit on the edge of their bed, and tell them his plans for the day while they smiled and yawned, still dusty with sleep. He half expected Maris to come into his room like she used to, to tell him one of her nightmares. Fiery dreams, full of smoke and flames. Did she still have them? He doubted it. She didn't seem to need his comforting as much as before.

By the time he'd been back in the house for two weeks he'd worked out a morning routine. He'd rise before the sun and pull on a T-shirt and shorts and go out to the beach where he knew Kit would be running. She ran four miles south of the house and four miles back. He'd run about a mile and wait for her to come back to that point, and then they'd walk the final mile back to the house together.

She liked to walk along the chain of shells left behind by the night tides. She said it was her reward for the run. She'd pick out perfect conches when she could find them or fragments of orange periwinkles, admire them, and then toss them far into the surf. She had quite an arm. Occasionally she spotted colored glass smoothed by the sea, and she grew as excited as a child plucking the piece out of the shells and dropping it into the pocket of her shorts.

Sometimes he'd cup her elbow in his hand as they walked. He could tell that she liked to be touched by the way her flesh seemed to melt under his fingers. But he was careful. He could never tell her that he felt drawn in by her smoky eyes or that when he watched her in the Chapel House gym, her face tense with effort, he wanted to run his hand over the shimmery fabric of her tank top. It would be unfair to tell her any of it. She might begin to expect things from him that he couldn't deliver.

He liked the way she dressed, everything in layers. She'd wear a tank top under a soft, boxy shirt with lots of pockets, then drape a sweater over her shoulders. It made him want to touch her, just to see where the clothes ended and her body began.

She was enigmatic. She had interviewed him for an article for the hospital newsletter. She sat in his office in a white linen suit, her legs crossed at the knee and a pad and pen in her lap, asking him questions with a directness that stunned him. She was pure business, and she was very, very good at it. She wanted to combine the article on his research with the announcement of his promotion, but Elliot had said no, it wasn't time yet. So she went to see Elliot, in that same suit with that sane candor.

"Very persuasive woman," Elliot had told Cole after he'd given her the go-ahead. "She made sense."

And then there was that fragility that came out of nowhere. On the beach in the morning, her skin was so pale that it looked translucent; her gray eyes were wide and rimmed by feathery amber lashes. She had the most enticing lips he'd ever seen—full and velvety. She ignored the dampness that wove itself into her hair. Estelle would never walk on the beach in the morning for that very reason. When Estelle came home, these early morning outings would come to an end. That made them assume greater importance; he didn't want to miss a single one.

One morning, when it was barely light enough to see the row of shells on the sand, she told him there was a man in the respiratory department who seemed interested in her.

"Oh yeah?" he said, hoping he sounded nonchalant. He was startled by jealousy, unreasonable and unnerving.

"His name's Sandy Cates. I think he's kind of nice-looking. Tall and skinny with dark hair and big eyes and sunken cheeks." She sucked in her cheeks in a way that made him laugh.

"So what do you plan to do about it?"

"I don't know. I get nervous when I talk to him. It's been a while."

"Pretend you're talking to me," he offered.

Kit laughed. "I could never tell him the things I tell you."

"Sure you can. Just say, 'Gee, Sandy, I haven't even masturbated in a year.'"

"But that would be a lie." She was still laughing.

He skirted a clump of mussels and seaweed. "Why don't you ask him out to dinner?"

She shuddered. "I don't know if I can. I'll have to think about it." She sat down on the damp sand as though she were going to think about it right then. "I want to watch the sunrise," she said.

The water and sky, the sand and the shells, were all the color of ripe peaches. A gull dipped into the wave rolling toward them and soared into the sky, carrying breakfast in its beak.

He sat down too, but not so close that he'd be tempted to put an arm around her. It worried him that he wanted to lift the damp tendrils of amber-colored hair off her neck and set his lips on the skin below. He missed Estelle, he told himself. That was all.

5.

He tried to see the house of his childhood through Kit's eyes as they traveled up the long driveway in his old white Mustang. Was it obvious to her that his family had money, that he had never wanted for anything? He no longer felt guilty about that. The first time he'd visited Jay's family—seven people in a steamy frame house that smelled of tomato sauce in every corner of every room—he had wanted to apologize for his past. But no longer. Background was unimportant. They had all been equalized by time.

"This is beautiful, Cole." Kit was taking in the vast green lawn, the towering oak trees, and the little pond that he and Corinne used to skate across in two long strides when it froze over in the winter.

The house itself was set far back from the street, stark white against the lush green of the grass and shrubs. He thought, as he always did, that it looked like a museum with its two-storied, pillared portico. He hoped Kit wasn't put off by it.

He'd had a hard time convincing her to come. "My parents know my friends as well as they know me," he'd told her. "They want to meet you."

On the patio, his parents settled them into lounge chairs with glasses of iced Perrier. Both his parents were dressed in white as if they'd just played a few sets of tennis, but that was a ridiculous thought.

His father had made the potato salad and wrapped chicken breasts in foil to put on the grill. He'd even made the salad dressing from the fresh herbs in his garden. Since his retirement from the airline, he did most of the cooking. It was a good arrangement; Virginia had never been comfortable in the kitchen.

Kit complimented Phillip on the dressing and juiciness of the chicken and the dill in the potato salad. Phillip beamed like a shy little boy trapped in a body that was growing very old. He was ten years older than Virginia, nearly seventy now, and Cole was struck again by how white and sparse his hair was. His father seemed more withdrawn than ever, a fading shadow in Virginia's presence.

"Corinne was going to come, but at the last minute she called to say she wasn't feeling well," said Virginia, pushing the potato salad in Cole's direction. They were sitting at the glass-topped patio table, eating off black stoneware plates.

He guessed that Corinne had backed out after learning that a stranger would be present.

"She's planning on starting therapy again," his mother said.

"I'll believe that when I see it." Cole passed the potato salad on to Kit. He thought his father had overdone it on the dill.

Virginia turned to Kit. "I don't know how I raised two children so different from one another. Corinne's just as intelligent as Cole, I really believe that, but she's always been held back by her fears. As a psychologist, it's been frustrating for me not to have been able to help my own daughter."

Kit nodded in sympathy.

"I just hope she can pull out of it with this new therapist."

"She doesn't want to pull herself out of it," said Cole.

"Of course she does. Look how she came to the airport to meet you. And she's gone grocery shopping by herself several times lately."

He was relieved when his mother changed the subject.

"How's Maris?" she asked.

"She seems better," he said. "I don't think she has the nightmares anymore."

"She's had just one since I moved in," said Kit. "She woke up screaming. I thought she was being murdered."

"She never worked any of those losses through," Virginia said, shaking her head.

Cole remembered the old Maris, the Maris they'd hired to remodel the house. He'd admired her, the way she'd seemed to have overcome the tragedies in her life. Her mother had died when she was fourteen; her brothers were killed in a fire a few years later. And she'd had miscarriage after miscarriage. Still, she'd been full of sparkling energy when she started on the house, busting out walls for bay windows, overseeing the work on the long back porch. He remembered her sitting day after day at the kitchen table, painting the tiles for the backsplash above the counters. She'd been pregnant again, optimistic because this time she'd made it to her sixth month. But then Chuck was killed, hit head-on on the Parkway, and Maris lost her baby the same night. She didn't want to go back to the house she and Chuck had been working on. And there was so much room in the Chapel House.

"She always looks so tough," said Kit.

"It's a facade," said Virginia. "Some day it'll catch up with her."

"How do you know her so well?" Kit asked.

Cole laughed. "You can't spend an evening with my mother without her learning all your secrets."

"Now, Cole, that's not true." Virginia looked at him sternly. "You'll make Kit nervous about being here."

But it *was* true. By the time dessert was finished, Virginia knew about Kit's marriage and divorce, her career change, her longing for independence, as well as her increasing desire for a relationship with a man with no strings attached. Virginia had a knack for getting information from people, and Kit poured it out.

"Why don't you come up here on Saturday mornings so you have some hills to run on?" There was a light in his mother's eyes that Cole hadn't seen for a while. "We can have lunch afterward."

"I'd *love* to." Kit smiled, a look of delight on her face.

Cole and his father were quiet, not wanting to tread on the electricity between the two women. Yet Cole couldn't help but be annoyed with his mother. Why hadn't she ever taken to Estelle that way? He wished he could introduce

Estelle to her again and have them start over. As if that would make any difference.

"When does Estelle get back?" Virginia asked as they walked across the thick lawn to his car. It was the first time his parents had mentioned Estelle all evening.

"The end of next week."

Phillip put his arm around Virginia. "Give her our love," he said, as though he were speaking for them both.

Kit sat in one of the wicker chairs on the balcony of his room the following evening. She had on a pair of blue shorts and a white T-shirt, with one of her soft shirts—this one dark blue—unbuttoned over it. The circular driveway of the Chapel House was beneath them, along with the tiny circle of lawn they took turns cutting in the warm months. It was the only grass on the Chapel House property, and it was easy to forget it was there.

Barnegat Bay stretched across the horizon, above the rooftops of Mantoloking. An enormous red sun was falling toward the water, staining everything on Cole's balcony a metallic pink.

Kit's bare feet were propped up on the white railing, and on her knees she held a picture of Estelle, framed in silver. Cole felt jittery, as if she were holding something priceless too casually on her knees. Something she might at any minute abuse.

The black-and-white picture was his favorite. It was actually an advertisement cut out of a magazine from the days when Estelle had had to "sell her body," as she called it, to make ends meet. She stood against a background of black and gray foliage in lacy panties and a bra that seemed too diaphanous to hold her breasts. Her huge eyes looked past the camera, focusing on something that caused her to part her lips expectantly.

Kit ran her fingers lightly over the glass, over Estelle's body. He wished he could read her thoughts.

She finally spoke.

"If you're a man, and Estelle's a woman, I must be a third sex," she said, a wry smile on her lips.

She tended to do this—put herself down. He thought of telling her how attractive he found her, how hard it was to sit next to her without touching her, but thought better of it. "No one would mistake you for anything other than a woman, Kit."

"You must miss her."

He hesitated, squinting out at the bay. He could just make out the pier they rented and the tail end of the *Sweetwater*. He loved that boat. It was nothing special and had barely enough power to pull a skier, but he and Jay were taking it to work these days. He could think of no better way to begin the day than with that cool glide across the bay, up through the canal to the river, where the hospital clung to the water's edge.

He hadn't told Kit about the problems with Estelle. He hadn't wanted to damage the chance of a friendship between them. But right now he wanted to tell her more.

"She's angry about my moving back in here," he said, frowning at the dusky sky. "And things were rocky between us when I left France. She's changed during the past few years. It's been gradual, but it came to a head in Paris. She was so possessive of me. She criticized anyone I wanted to spend time with."

Kit turned in her chair to face him. "But she was in a strange country and probably felt very dependent on you."

He smiled. She was defending Estelle, the way one woman would shield another from the callous reasoning of a male. But she was wrong; it was more complex than she could imagine. How odd it felt, though, to have someone take Estelle's side. That was usually his task.

"She speaks French better than I do, and she loves it there, so I really doubt that's the problem."

He decided to say no more. He wanted Kit to like Estelle. Estelle had never had a friend, never a confidante. Women pulled away from her. He'd seen them stare at her, absorb her from head to toe. He'd seen the spiteful look come into their eyes before she'd even said a word.

With Kit it would be different. He'd watched her with Janni and Maris. In the hospital he'd seen her laughing with other women, touching their arms lightly with affection. He'd seen her with his own mother, not an easy woman to elicit warmth from. Kit had some kind of magnetic attraction that drew women to her. He hoped Estelle would allow herself to be touched by it.

6.

Every time she pressed on the clutch or the brake, pain shot through her legs. Bona fide pain. It had been a long time since she'd pushed herself so far. Nothing could feel as good as the fire in her legs.

When Virginia Perelle had seen her hobble in the back door after her run, she'd steered her in the direction of the master bathroom. "Forget the shower," she'd said. "You need a long soak."

Kit had settled into the sunken tub, navy blue to match the print of the wallpaper, and shut her eyes. She had nearly fallen asleep when Virginia called her down to lunch. They ate chicken salad on china plates while Virginia asked her about her divorce and how she liked living in the Chapel House and all sorts of questions that might have been considered prying if they hadn't been so compassionately delivered.

After lunch with Virginia she'd felt so invincible that she drove to Blair, tracked down Sandy Cates in the respiratory office, and asked him out to dinner for Friday night. She walked in and blurted out the invitation before she had a chance to change her mind. He looked surprised, his round eyes even rounder, and smiled widely.

"I thought you were married or living with someone," he said.

"No, I'm completely unattached. So, what do you think?" She wasn't sounding like herself at all. Too quick and bold. And she felt out of place here at Blair in her drawstring pants and T-shirt, sunglasses dangling from her breast pocket.

"Sure, why not?" he answered, his eyes running over her body, scaring her a little.

The purest pleasure of the day would be telling Cole about it. She pulled into the Chapel House driveway, parking next to the already full three-car garage, and ticked off on her fingers the things she'd tell him about: Lunch with his mother. How good her legs felt. The case of nerves she was getting over the thought of a potentially intimate relationship with a man other than Bill.

Why was it she could say anything at all to Cole, that she emerged unscathed from every disclosure? She told herself that she no longer wanted him sexually, even though his steady gaze still made her shudder and he appeared regularly in her dreams. But sex with him now would feel almost incestuous.

The door to his room was closed. She could see the pink light of the sunset shining in the crack between the door and the floor. She pictured the view from his balcony, the sun dropping over the rooftops and sinking into the bay.

She knocked quietly on his door, then walked in without waiting for his answer. She knew in an instant that she'd made a mistake. Cole and Estelle sat in his four-poster bed, propped up by pillows and covered only by a sheet.

"Oh, God, I'm sorry!" She clapped her hand to her mouth and turned to leave.

"Wait a second, not so fast!" Cole laughed. "Say hello to Estelle. Estelle, this is Kit Sheridan. She's the one I told you about who's doing the PR for the program."

Kit reached her hand across Cole, looking apologetically at Estelle. "I've been looking forward to meeting you," she said. "Though not like this."

It seemed as though minutes passed before Estelle drew her hand out from under the sheet and reached up, barely touching her fingers to Kit's.

"Hello," she said, her voice flat. She turned her eyes away from Kit to look out the window.

Maybe she'd walked in on a fight. "I've got to go," she said to Cole, her eyes begging him for release. She reached for the doorknob.

"What did you want to tell me?" he asked.

"Just that it was great to run in Watchung, and that your mom is terrific."

Estelle looked at her at the mention of Virginia, and Kit avoided her eyes. *Let her wonder what I'm doing with her lover's mother,* she thought uncharitably. But she decided to keep the rest of her news for later, when Cole was alone.

"I've got to go now." She forced herself to look at Estelle and suddenly felt sorry for her. There was sadness in those big, dark blue eyes. It was unmistakable. "I'm glad you're here, Estelle," she said. "Cole's really been missing you."

*

Cole had told her that when Estelle walked down the street all eyes turned to follow her. Kit guessed that he was more than a little biased. But when Estelle walked into the kitchen an hour after their awkward meeting in Cole's room, she knew he hadn't exaggerated. It would have been impossible not to stare.

Her cream-colored satin robe hugged her body, her nipples dimpling the fabric that stretched over full round breasts. Her face was perfect in its symmetry—square jawline under high cheekbones, enormous eyes, straight nose. Her heavy auburn hair hung in soft waves to her shoulders.

Janni was slicing bread. She looked up. "Hi, Estelle," she said, as if she had last seen her minutes earlier rather than ten months ago.

Kit thought Estelle looked a little lost, a regal presence in a common kitchen, though this kitchen could hardly be described as common, with its beamed ceiling and huge fireplace. It didn't fit Estelle, though. Estelle would need something sleekly modern and uncluttered with sentiment. No wonder she couldn't tolerate the thought of living in this house.

Kit walked across the room to where Estelle was standing. "I'm very sorry that I walked in on you and Cole," she said.

Estelle didn't look at her. Her gaze wandered around the room until it settled on the wide sliding glass doors at the rear of the kitchen and the beach heather outside. "It's all right," she said.

"Really, it was thoughtless of me and I . . ."

"I said it's all right. You don't need to make a big deal out of it." She was looking at her squarely now, the look of a woman who could devour people whole, and Kit felt a sudden lump in her throat.

Jay walked into the kitchen just in time to rescue her. He moved between them and put his arms around Estelle. His hands slid over the satin of her robe as he kissed her cheek. "Welcome home," he said.

She nearly smiled at him, her hands on his shoulders. "Thanks," she said.

Kit watched Janni turn away from them, back to the counter and the bread.

"Move in," Jay said. "Nothing would make Cole happier."

She shook her head, her hair shimmering in the kitchen light. It was redder than Kit had imagined. Estelle pulled away from Jay and took a couple of plums out of the fruit bowl before heading toward the door.

"There's no *privacy* here, Jay." She looked directly at Kit when she said the word and turned to leave the room.

Cole and Estelle didn't come out of Cole's room all evening, not even for dinner, and Janni froze the leftovers, muttering under her breath. The others were quiet at the dining room table, and Kit guessed that they felt it, too, the impenetrable wall that had suddenly been erected between them and Cole.

7.

In the dim light of the Szechuan restaurant, Sandy looked more delicate than she remembered. He was reed-thin in his loose brown shirt and baggy pants. Deep shadows filled the hollows of his cheeks, and his brown eyes reminded her of a fawn's. But his cockiness belied any delicacy.

"I could tell you were a runner the second I laid eyes on you." He picked up a shrimp expertly with his chopsticks.

"You could?"

He nodded. "You have that hard-as-a-rock look to you."

She wondered how he could tell. She thought her body was well camouflaged under the conservatively tailored clothes she wore to work, as well as under the flowered skirt and yellow cardigan she had on tonight.

"It's nice," he continued. "I like a long, lean, tight body on a woman." He dragged each word out and finished with a long pull on his tea.

She didn't know why her heart was racing. There was something unbearably intense about him that attracted and frightened her at the same time. "You're rather thin yourself," she said. "Do you run?"

He laughed. "If you knew me a little better, you'd know

what an idiotic question that is. No, I'm just a natural ecto-morph. But I know a lot about running. I know that you should be in training by now if you plan to do Somerville in October."

"I *am* in training." She described her running schedule to him, and he nodded his approval. "I thought I'd try running on the dunes at Island Beach once a week, too," she said.

"That's a great idea. It's very pretty out there, practically my favorite place in the world. You can see horseshoe crabs screwing on the beach if you're lucky."

"Well, I'll keep my eyes open."

"Seriously, you can. My point being that Island Beach is so unspoiled the horseshoe crabs feel secure enough to do it right on the beach."

She smiled. "Oh."

"And the shells are abundant. They haven't been raked over by the masses."

That did sound appealing. "I look for shells every morning on the beach," she said.

"You must have quite a collection."

She shook her head. "I throw them back."

He set his chopsticks on the table and leaned back in his chair. "Let me get this straight," he said. "Every day the ocean presents you with its treasures and you throw them back?"

She wasn't sure if she should feel defensive or guilty. "I didn't realize it was a major offense," she said.

"Next time we go out I want you to bring me a couple of shells that you find, okay? You need a lesson in sea lore."

He poured himself another cup of tea. "Shall we go back to my place after dessert?" he asked.

She was caught off guard. What did that mean? If she said yes, what was she agreeing to? He was looking at her with those innocent doe-eyes and she laughed. "It's been so long since I've been out with someone, Sandy . . . I'm not certain what you mean when you ask me to your place."

"Oh." He looked incredulous. "How old did you say you are?"

"Thirty . . ."

"I'm teasing you." He covered her hand with his. "You sound about fifteen right now. Are you saying you don't want to make love tonight?"

"Yes, definitely, that's what I'm saying. I don't even know you."

He narrowed his eyes at her. "Don't give me that self-righteous stuff. *You* came on to *me*, didn't you?"

"Yes, but . . ."

"So I figured that when we were done with dinner, we could go to my apartment, smoke some weed, and"—he shrugged— "enjoy each other. I thought that was what you were after."

Oh God. She would never ask another man out. She took a deep breath. "I can't jump into bed with you, just like that."

"Why not? I've been tested. I'm clean, and I'm careful who I sleep with. I figure you're a pretty safe bet."

"I still can't. I'm worried about . . . disease, yes, but also

I've had one lover for eight years, and I need some time to get used to the idea of having another."

He grinned at her. "Okay, we can take our time," he said. "But you should know right upfront that I don't want marriage or anything like that."

"That's the last thing I want!"

"Good," he said. "I don't want to see one woman exclusively. I wouldn't want either of us to start thinking we own each other."

When she was certain he had finished laying his ground rules, she reached across the table to shake his hand, surprising him. "It's a deal," she said. "Why don't we go back to the Chapel House? My friends are there. Maybe we could play a game."

"A game!" He laughed. "Golly. I wouldn't want to miss out on that."

8.

The house was different with Estelle there, and she was there much of the time. It seemed to Kit that she took up more than her share of space. Every room she entered shrank in size.

That Cole loved her was enormously clear. He couldn't take his eyes off her, and he touched her every chance he got, stroking her arm in the upstairs hallway, kissing her in the kitchen. They went out nearly every night, to the band shell or driving great distances to find movies they hadn't seen, and when they returned they cut themselves off from the others by conversing in French.

Estelle was two people in one body. When Cole was around she seemed content, and while Kit would never have called her friendly, she was at least approachable.

When he wasn't around, she was sour and moody, and Kit dreaded every encounter with her. Those first few days she tried every possible conversation starter, but she could rarely catch Estelle's eye, much less engage her in any exchange.

It was even worse to be in a room with Cole and Estelle together. Kit felt small—at five-seven a new feeling for her—and insignificant. She imagined that she looked like Estelle's prepubescent daughter.

She couldn't remember the last time she'd felt so intimidated by someone. This was what a woman could be: brilliant and beautiful. With every miserable encounter she scrutinized her feelings of jealousy and resentment, certain that they were to blame.

She missed Cole. She wanted time with him, time to talk the way they had before. There was so little of him left for her with Estelle there. In the mornings she walked the last mile on the beach alone, trying to keep her mind out of Cole's bedroom where he and Estelle would be waking up together.

She was still working with him on the Fetal Surgery Program. An hour here, an hour there, but it was work and little more. She lived for those moments when he would squeeze her shoulder or rest his hand on her back as she left his office. Her need for his attention, for his touch, frightened her. Dependence on anyone was the last thing she wanted, and dependence on Cole struck her as disastrous. Yet it was a feeling she had little control over.

She had no fear at all of needing *Sandy* too much. There was little about him that she could imagine wanting for very long, although she did find herself enjoying his company. She had to attend so carefully to propriety during her workday that it was refreshing to be with someone loose and unorthodox in the evening. Since that first night, he had never pressured her, never mentioned sex. When they finally did make love, on the night of their fourth date, she was more than ready.

The house had been breathless that night. The heat of the day continued into the darkness, and her sheets were damp before they'd begun. Sandy was a generous lover, patient and appreciative. She needed that. She worried that she'd forgotten how to make love, that she was out of practice. But that was not actually the case—she'd been making love to Cole for over a month now, if only in her mind.

She was still awake long after Sandy fell asleep, and sometime after midnight she heard the screams. She wasn't certain at first if they'd come from the beach or the house, but then she remembered she'd heard those screams once before.

She looked over at Sandy. His eyes were shut, his breathing regular. She lay still until she heard heavy footsteps in the hall. Then she got up and pulled on her robe. By the time she reached Maris's door Cole was there, sitting on her double bed and holding her close to him. Her screams had turned into a choking moaning sound, and she was clawing at Cole's back, her nails leaving tiny red welts on his skin.

Estelle was just inside the door, leaning against the wall with her arms folded against her green negligee. She looked coolly detached. Except for tiny droplets on the bridge of her nose she gave no sign of being hot.

Kit stood frozen in the doorway, not certain if she should join Cole at Maris's bedside or not. Seeing Maris so out of control was a shock.

"Was it the fire again, Mar?" Cole asked quietly as she began to pull away from him. Her cotton nightgown stuck to her skin in damp patches across her breasts.

She nodded.

Estelle said something in French, but Cole didn't respond.

"I'm okay." Maris looked up. Her skin glistened in the moonlight, and she was rubbing a long pink discoloration on the inside of her left arm. "It's so hot. When it's hot like this, I . . ."

"Why don't you sleep on the porch tonight?" Cole suggested.

She shook her head. "No, I'm okay. I'm sorry I woke all of you." She looked at the three of them and then down at her bed, still rubbing the scar on her arm.

Estelle spoke again, and this time Cole turned quickly to face her. He snapped at her, also in French, and Estelle laughed in a way that gave Kit gooseflesh.

Cole stood up and turned back to Maris. "You want me to get the fan?"

Maris shook her head.

He leaned over and kissed her forehead. "Good night, then," he said.

At the door he took Kit's arm. "Can you stay with her a while?" His hair was damp against his forehead; his body gave off heat.

She nodded and Cole walked down the hall to his room, Estelle following close behind.

Maris lay back against the damp pillow. Her eyes were wide open, staring at the ceiling. "You don't have to stay, Kit. You've got Sandy with you. Cole thinks I can't handle it, but I'm okay."

"I'd like to stay. And Sandy's sound asleep." The heat

was even worse in this room, and Kit sat on the very edge of the bed, trying not to crowd Maris.

"I hate this," Maris said. "I feel like such a fool when it happens. The dreams take me over. It's as if I'm there, going through it all again, and I start screaming before I realize that it's only a dream."

"Do you want to talk about it?" Kit asked hesitantly. She wasn't certain that she wanted to hear.

Maris looked at her. "I *can't* talk about it. Cole knows the most because he used to try to make me talk. He thought it would help. But I can't stand to remember the whole thing. I've never understood why I was the one to survive. Why I was left with nothing more than this little reminder." She held up the arm with the scar. "It's been sixteen years. That's a long time to be haunted by something."

Kit nodded.

"When I first moved in here I woke them up nearly every night. Estelle accused me of faking the nightmares to get Cole into my bedroom." She chuckled and Kit envied her sense of superiority over Estelle. "He always gets here first since his room's just down the hall and he sleeps light as a feather." Her voice was getting sluggish.

"I don't think Estelle's my biggest fan," said Kit. She wanted Maris's opinion on the subject of Estelle, but Maris didn't seem to hear her.

"Thanks for staying, Kit," she said. "I'm exhausted."

Maris shut her eyes, but Kit remained on the edge of the bed. Her head felt heavy from the heat. She looked around the moonlit room. The walls were covered with African art—drawings and masks that would be enough to give anyone nightmares. One of Maris's drafting tables was in front of the window facing the ocean. The other faced the house next door. Maris had told her she used the ocean view for creating, the house next door for detail.

Kit looked down at her again. She was sleeping now, her breathing slow and regular. The stud she usually wore was missing. There was just a tiny black dot on her nostril where it belonged. Her face looked as if it had been sculpted in fragile, spice-colored porcelain. Maybe the power behind Maris's strong facade was in the tiny gold orb.

She leaned forward and kissed Maris's forehead in the same spot Cole's lips had touched and walked back to her own room.

A few days later, she was halfway through her seventh mile under a sky the color of creamsicles when she spotted Cole. A blue T-shirt, white shorts. He was stretching up to the sky, and he was alone, waiting for her. It had been a long time since he'd joined her on the beach. Estelle must have spent the night at her condominium.

She slowed her pace as he walked toward her, and without a word he put his arm around her shoulders. She slipped hers around his waist. It was as simple as if they'd done it a hundred mornings before. They walked in silence for a few minutes, more slowly than Kit ever would have alone.

Cole stopped suddenly. "Isn't that a piece of smoothed glass?" He was pointing with his foot at a blue disc buried among the shells.

"I don't want to let go of you to pick it up," she said.

He tightened his hand on her shoulder, and they walked on, leaving the glass behind.

"Monday's the big day," he said.

She knew he was talking about turning the proposal in to the Devlin Foundation. The press release was all set to go, too. She'd worked and reworked it so many times that she could recite it by heart.

"I played up the ethics committee in the final draft," she said. "It's the one area that all the centers are handling differently so we can make our way look best."

"I never thought the ethics committee would be an asset."

"It is, but you're actually the biggest asset we've got," she said. "You're attractive and charismatic and—"

He made a face. "I'd prefer this whole thing to fly on the merits of the program rather than my looks or personality."

"That's the perfect attitude." She laughed. "So humble. They'll love you."

He let out a long sigh but when he spoke again his voice was playful. "So tell me," he said, "how are things with Sandy?"

She was walking in the tire tracks of a Jeep. "Well, he's one hundred and eighty degrees from Bill and that's what I like best."

"He's damn good at charades, I'll say that much for him."

They'd played charades with the others after their date at the Szechuan restaurant, and Sandy had turned out to be something of a ham.

"He knows everything there is to know about the beach," she said.

"Uh-huh. And how is he in bed?"

She smiled. Coming from Cole, the question didn't surprise her. She thought back to the night she'd spent with Sandy and tried to think of an appropriate adjective. "Attentive," she said.

"Attentive? That doesn't sound like fireworks."

"It was nice."

"Sitting on the porch in a rocking chair is nice, too."

"*Cole*." She laughed. "It felt . . . friendly. You know, kind, gentle, satisfying sex." And safe. She knew part of the reason she enjoyed Sandy was that he would ask nothing more of her. No commitment.

"Sounds kind of staid. Wasn't he at all inventive?"

"What do you want, every graphic detail?"

"Yeah." He looked sheepish.

She shook her head. "You are very, very nosy."

"I want to be certain you were well taken care of."

He frowned when she told him Sandy would still be seeing other women.

"It's what I want, Cole. Someone I can enjoy for the moment who won't end up suffocating me like Bill did. I don't want a man to be all that important to me."

The Chapel House came into view above the twisted line of the storm fence, and she wished they had farther to walk.

"How are things with Estelle?" she asked.

"Good." His eyes lit up. "I'm glad she's back." He went on to tell her more—their plans for the next few weeks, a couple of conversations they'd had, how good it was to wake up with her next to him.

She wished she hadn't asked. Imagining the two of them together was painful enough; hearing the reality of it only made it worse.

"She doesn't like me," she said.

"I know she gives people that impression, but that's just her way. She's been grumpy since she got back because I'm still living in the house and she had her heart set on us living together." He stopped and turned to face her. "Don't give up on her, Kit. Please? She doesn't know how to react to a woman treating her as a friend. She's never had it, not even as a kid. Please keep trying."

She thought of her last encounter with Estelle. They'd been in the Chapel House library, one of Kit's favorite rooms in the house. One wall was made up of windows that overlooked the beach and the water; the other three walls were covered with bookshelves, the wood dark and smooth. She liked the insulated feeling of being surrounded by books, floor to ceiling.

She was reading in one of the black leather chairs, her feet on the ottoman; Estelle was hunting for a book in one of the bookshelves, the one filled with Cole's medical collection. She seemed to be in a good mood. It gave Kit courage.

"Would you like to meet for lunch tomorrow, Estelle?" she'd asked.

Estelle turned around. "Why?" She sounded as though she couldn't imagine a more inane suggestion.

Kit's throat went dry. "I know I got off on the wrong foot

with you," she said. 'I'd wanted us to be friends. Maybe we could start fresh."

Estelle folded her arms and leaned against the books, her eyes never leaving Kit's. "I have no interest whatever in becoming your friend, Kit, so don't break your neck trying to invent ways of making that happen."

Kit was more hurt than angry. "Why do you dislike me so much?"

"I don't dislike you. I simply have no interest in you. You're not interesting to me in any way. So give up, okay?"

She turned to go but stopped at the door to face Kit again. "How the hell did you get into the Chapel House anyway? You don't belong here. You sashayed into this house as though you owned it. Janni's a bleeding heart— she takes in all the strays. But Jay's not. Do you really think he wants you here? Have you ever stopped to think about it, Kit?"

She never told Cole how Estelle belittled her. It was the one thing she kept from him. She was afraid her complaining would sound too much like envy.

"Some of the effort needs to come from her, too," she said to him now.

"I know." He reached down and scattered the shells with his fingers to pick up a smooth gray periwinkle. He handed it to her, and they turned toward the house.

"It's like a magnet," he said, putting his arm around her again.

"What is?"

"The house. I don't know how I ever thought I could leave."

"I know what you mean. When I'm running away from the house it takes twice the effort as when I'm running toward it."

"Honest?" He grinned at her.

"Honest."

He laughed and pulled her closer to him. "I really love you," he said.

She was quiet, afraid he'd regret speaking impulsively. She glanced at him. He was smiling to himself, and they walked across the beach heather in silence.

9.

"Thanks for agreeing to spend the weekend here," Estelle said, laying her legs across his thighs.

They were sitting on the balcony of her condominium in their bathing suits, passing a bowl of boiled shrimp between them. The afternoon sun was hot and boats crammed the inlet below.

He didn't dislike these condominiums so much now that he didn't have to live in one. They were very modern, full of angles, and painted the gray of weathered wood, different from the warm silver-hued gray of the Chapel House. They were located where the ocean met the inlet, and it was that feeling of being surrounded by water that made the condo tolerable for him. In all other ways it was too small, too sterile, too new and unseasoned.

Estelle's face was calm and beginning to turn pink under her straw hat. He didn't dare tell her that he was on call for the Emergency Room this weekend. He was hoping any obstetric crises could wait until Monday.

"It's good to have you all to myself for a change," he said, wrapping his hand around her ankle. He could handle the condo for one weekend.

She passed him the bowl of shrimp, and he took a handful.

"The Chapel House feels cramped these days, don't you think?" Estelle peered at him from under the brim of her hat.

"Cramped?" He laughed. "Hardly."

She looked down at her hands. "Aren't you tired of it yet, Cole?"

"No." He tensed, hoping they weren't headed for another fight.

"No, I guess you wouldn't be. You thrive on being around people who need you."

He shrugged. "Is that so terrible?"

"You know," she said, "I think part of our problem is that you don't realize that *I* need you. You treat me as if I'm incapable of feeling hurt or scared. You comfort everyone else, but you've never comforted me. Never."

He frowned. That couldn't be true. He searched his mind for examples. The time she'd found the dead woman in the stairwell at Blair? Hadn't he comforted her then? No, not really. She hadn't seemed that upset. Years ago, after the abortion? She'd gotten through that far more easily than he had. It was true that he never thought of her as needing him in that way.

"I think it's your strength that's always attracted me to you," he said.

"But I do have needs." Her voice was one he'd never heard before.

"What do you mean?"

She pulled her legs from his lap and leaned toward him.

"I need you so much that sometimes it scares me. When I was alone in Paris I felt, I don't know, *desperate*. I'm afraid of losing you." Her eyes were so wide that he could see the reflection of a sailboat in them.

"What do you mean, you felt desperate?" The word alarmed him.

"I've always been afraid that one day I'll wake up and you'll be out of my life. Also"—she hesitated, looked at him almost shyly—"lately, sometimes, I feel . . . well, out of control. It's frightening."

"I've never given you reason to worry about losing me."

"I know, I know. But, are you listening to me, Cole? I feel . . ." She hunted for a word. Her hands were fists at the sides of her head. "I feel trapped by my own head."

"Estelle." He leaned forward to take her hand. "Why haven't you ever told me this before? How can I help unless I know?"

She leaned back suddenly, pulling her hand out of his. "It's really nothing. I don't know why I brought it up. Forget it." Her eyes had cooled.

"Forget it? You just told me you feel desperate and frightened and trapped and now you want me to forget it?"

"Yes."

She'd let him inside her for a fleeting instant, and he hadn't recognized her at all.

"I'm worried about you."

She laughed and crossed her legs. Her look was almost mocking.

If it had been anyone else, anyone at all, he would have

pursued it. He would have questioned her until he'd uncovered the truth. But this was Estelle, and he knew better than to try. Once she closed a subject there could be no reaching her.

10.

Janni asked him to wake Kit for dinner, and he climbed the stairs, thinking about how good the week had been and how much of it he owed to Kit. The first wave of local reaction to the proposed Fetal Surgery Program had been overwhelmingly positive, and she was keeping the topic alive in the papers and on the news.

Estelle had spent the week in New York and he'd been able to walk with Kit on a few mornings. He envied her the sense of ownership she had over the beach. It was obvious that her endurance was up. She was running farther, yet she was still full of energy by the time he joined her for the mile back to the house.

And she was seeing Sandy nearly every other night. But maybe it was catching up to her if she needed a nap in the middle of the day.

He knocked on her door. There was no response. He opened the door slowly and started to call her name but stopped himself when he saw her.

She was lying on her stomach, her face turned away from him. She was covered only by a sheet that clung to her from her heels to the middle of her back. Her shoulders were bare. He forgot about dinner. The only thought he had was of running his hand slowly up her leg.

What would it be like to make love to her? It wasn't the first time he'd thought about it, but it was the first time he could see the possibility taking shape in front of him. He could move into the room, shut the door behind him, turn the key in the lock just in case anyone . . . Then what? He'd wake her slowly by kissing those incredible lips, touching her all over. She'd be too aroused to want to stop him when she finally realized what was happening.

Damn, what was he thinking?

He stepped into the room without closing the door and walked past the open closet with its double row of running shoes. He sat on the edge of her bed.

"Time to get up for dinner, Kit," he said quietly.

She started, and he held the edge of the sheet so she wouldn't lose it when she rolled over. She smiled sleepily at him. She looked pretty. She wore no makeup, but her eyes always had that smoky look to them. Right now they were watching him from above the creamy pale skin of her cheeks. There was little comparison between her face and Estelle's, which sparkled with color from the first moment of the day. Yet the feeling welling up inside his chest as he looked at her was familiar.

"You're going to have to start getting some sleep at night," he said. "Tell Sandy he'll have to see more of his other women."

"Not a chance." She grinned.

He smoothed the hair away from her damp cheek and let his finger trace her lower lip. It was as soft to his touch as he'd imagined. She didn't move. Didn't even look surprised. What would she do if he kissed her?

"I was watching you sleep from the doorway," he said, the words coming out before he could stop them. "I was thinking about . . . what it would be like . . . I wanted to make love to you."

She shut her eyes. Fine blue veins in the lids. "I wish you hadn't told me that," she said. She looked up at him. "That's something we can never do."

"Have you wanted to?" He'd often wondered if whatever she'd felt for him that first night under the stars was still alive.

"Of course," she said. "But it would be fatal to our friendship, and it wouldn't do your relationship with Estelle any good."

It excited him to hear that she'd thought about it. His own brain was burning up. "We'd just have to keep it in the proper perspective," he said.

Proper perspective? What the hell was he talking about?

Her eyes were unsmiling. She sat up against the dark wood of her headboard, holding the sheet tightly in front of her. "No, Cole, never. I couldn't compare to Estelle. I don't come the instant I'm entered."

He winced. He never should have told her that. He'd started confiding in her lately. He knew now that he'd taken it way too far.

"I can't whisper sweet nothings in French in your ear," she continued. "Remember that the next time you think you want to make love to me."

"Those things aren't important." He was confused. He

ran his hand through his hair. He couldn't remember the last time he'd tried to talk a woman into sex. He could feel blotchy color creeping up his neck, and he wished he could erase the last five minutes from his life.

He stood up. "I'm sorry," he said. "You're right, of course. Not that you don't compare to Estelle, but that it would be a mistake. I'm sorry. Kit, I wasn't thinking."

She nodded slowly, and he turned and left the room.

Sunday morning was clear and golden, and Janni decided they should eat brunch on the beach. Cole was relieved when Kit agreed to join them. Since Friday night she'd held herself apart from him, skipping meals and staying out late, he was certain, just to avoid him. Even now her attention was riveted on the ocean.

She looked very young, he thought, sitting cross-legged on the beach blanket, faded jeans hugging her thighs. He tried to catch her eye, but she wouldn't look in his direction. She was concentrating on her scrambled eggs, pushing them from one side of her plate to the other with her fork. He could kick himself for his lack of restraint. When would he ever learn to think before he spoke? Certainly she was right; if talking about it forced this kind of distance between them, what would happen if they ever did make love? What would be the point, anyway? He was with Estelle. And even if he weren't, Kit had made it clear time and time again that she didn't want a permanent relationship with a man. It would be hard for him to think of her on any other terms.

She was the first to head for the house after brunch, but he called her back.

"Can we talk, please?" he asked.

She looked at him, then at the house, then back at him again. "Okay," she said finally, and she turned away from him to sit down on the sand once more.

11.

She woke with rumbling bowels. She walked around her bedroom between bouts in the bathroom, cursing her nerves and fighting tears at the growing certainty that she'd be unable to run that morning.

It was seven o'clock. How would she be ready to face the Jersey Shore Women's Association at nine? And it was so hot. She stopped in front of the full-length mirror on her closet door. The long, well-defined muscles of her thighs comforted her. Her face was so pale, though. She hated to see it first thing in the morning. And her *hair*. It was impossibly frizzed from the ocean air. She ran her fingers through the stubborn curls.

What the hell did Cole want with her anyway?

She felt toyed with. Oh, it wasn't intentional. He didn't mean to tease her. Estelle had been out of town, and maybe at that moment he sincerely thought he wanted her. But for what? To satisfy some immediate craving, when for her the longing would go on and on.

That he regretted asking her was certain. On the beach after Sunday's brunch, he'd made it very clear. They'd sat at the water's edge, on opposite sides of a patch of shells and seaweed, while he begged her to forget it and she promised him she would. But the memory of his face the night he'd asked her, the hunger she'd seen in his eyes, would stay with her for a long time.

When they had finished talking, when they understood each other as well as they could, she impulsively began complaining about Estelle as if she were trying to undo the fragile peace treaty they'd created between them.

"She treats me badly behind your back," she said.

He looked unimpressed.

"She says cruel things to me."

"Like what?"

She hesitated. What could she say without humiliating herself? Estelle insulted her body, her hair, the way she talked. She told her that Cole made jokes about the sounds coming from her bedroom when she was with Sandy. She couldn't tell him she knew about that.

"She once told me that I was only capable of getting a man who would see me on a part-time basis." She felt as if she were ten years old, tattling on a schoolmate.

"But that's all you want," he said.

"That's not the point, Cole. The point is that she said it, and it was insulting."

"Estelle's not famous for her diplomacy, but I thought your skin was a little thicker than that."

"She says other things. Nastier things. Too embarrassing to repeat."

"What do you want me to do about it?"

She really wasn't sure. "I just want you to know what she's like."

His face went cold. "I think I know her a little better than you do, thank you." He stood up and walked toward the house.

"Cole!" She stood up herself and he turned around. "Please don't be angry with me." Her throat was tight.

"I'm not angry. I'm just sick of people telling me what's wrong with Estelle. I thought it would be different with you."

He turned, and this time she let him go.

She didn't have time now to stew about Cole, though. She got into the shower and turned on a cool spray of water. Her legs still ached from the day before, when she'd run like some kind of animal over the clean white dunes at Island Beach. Sandy had perched himself on the top of a dune, brazenly smoking a joint while he waited for her. She'd felt a little crazed, running in bare feet through the sand and sea grass with the sunbathers as an audience.

When she'd finished, she leaned against Sandy while he told her everything imaginable about beach grass and the shifting sand. He knew the name of every bird, and he pointed out the osprey nests scattered among the tops of the trees. She listened, too exhilarated to talk herself.

That night in bed she cried with the sharp pains in her calves and thighs, and Sandy rubbed them with oil, making long expert strokes with his thumbs. Then he smoothed the oil over the rest of her, telling her in a voice laced with honey that he would take the pain away. And for a while, he did.

*

There were many more of them than she'd anticipated. They eyed her as they took their seats in the crowded meeting room at the Y, jangling their bracelets and patting beauty parlor hair. Kit kept a frozen smile on her face as she nursed her coffee at the podium. There had to be a hundred women here. At nine in the morning. This was a hot topic.

They'd given her a microphone, and her voice sounded stilted to her ears when she began to speak, but soon the words were flowing easily. She turned her notecards upside down. She knew this so well. The history of fetal surgery. The specifics of how the center at Blair would function. Cole's reputation. She even mentioned Estelle, how with her help they had access to international developments in the field.

Then she showed the slides Cole had given her. Tasteful shots of children who could have been helped by surgery before they were born. Oohs and aahs went up from her audience. Most of the babies looked healthy, but she described the abnormalities hidden inside that could cripple or kill them. One picture showed a baby with a swollen, fluid-filled head and the women gasped. She was glad that she'd vetoed the slides of the babies who were born dead.

"But this is what it's all about." Cole had looked distressed.

"I know, but you'll have these women throwing up their Danishes," she'd answered.

When she finished with the last slide, the lights went up and she invited questions. At first they were easy, full of examples of children they knew who suffered from conditions that might have responded to surgery in utero.

But then it got harder.

A tall, graying woman in the middle of the room stood up. "I think there comes a point when the continued development of technology is dangerous." She paused, a self-serving smile on her lips, and the room was silent. "Dangerous in a moral sense. What gives us the right to tamper with something that is God's will?"

"You had surgery for your gallstones last winter, Hallie!"

Kit was grateful to that brave soul in the rear of the room, whoever she was.

"That was different," Hallie continued. "I'm an adult. These are unborn children who God in His divine wisdom has planned for in His own way."

Kit was glad now that she had the microphone. When she spoke, her voice easily overrode Hallie's. "It's certainly true that there are differing schools of thought on the topic of fetal surgery," she said. "But it's a fact that the technology exists to help these children live fuller lives and in some cases, to live period. The parents whose children have been helped by these advances are certainly very grateful for them."

A woman near Hallie stood up. "What about those babies who are spared death through surgery only to be left so severely crippled that they become a drain on the family? I think all of us would agree that sometimes it's better to die than to live a fraction of a life and burden those around us."

Did she have to sound so eloquent?

"You raise an important issue," Kit said. "It's very difficult to decide who should be treated and who shouldn't, and many variables need to be considered. At Blair we will have an ethics committee made up of a minister"—she looked at Hallie—"a neonatologist—that is, a medical doctor specializing in newborn infants—and several professionals and parents from the community. Every case that is to be considered for treatment will be discussed by this committee in order to make the best decision possible with the healthiest outcome for the child and his or her family. Yes?"

"I read about twins where one was saved at the expense of the other."

"I think you're referring to the recent case in which one twin was diagnosed as having a fatal condition. The parents wanted to abort that fetus but spare the second fetus, which was healthy. The fetal surgeons were able to withdraw blood from the sick fetus while it was in the uterus, and the mother continued her pregnancy and delivered the healthy second twin."

There were some gasps in the audience as she related the story, and she wondered if there might have been a better way to tell it.

"Those doctors didn't perform any miracle there," said Hallie. "They performed murder."

Several heads bobbed up and down in agreement and Kit's palms went damp.

"I can see why you might think that," she said carefully. "However, the surgery was the parents' choice and their legal right. Different parents make different choices, and what is right for me might not be right for you"—she nodded at Hallie—"or for you." She nodded at a woman in the front row. "Through fetal surgery we're increasing the available choices for those parents and their children."

She wasn't certain if her last few sentences had made any sense. She just wanted to get out of there.

She set the air conditioner of her car so that it blew right in her face and took long slow breaths of the cool air. This was supposed to have been an easy group. She had to stay in better control of her audience. She'd done okay at first, until the case of those twins sprang out of nowhere. She'd panicked. She couldn't afford to freeze up like that. Maybe she was the wrong person for this job.

12.

Cole snapped off the ultrasound and turned to the woman lying on the examining table. Her dark eyes were questioning and he wondered if she could tell that his insides were tied in knots.

He lowered the hospital gown over her belly, too swollen for twenty weeks. How much did she already know?

"You understand that Dr. Benfield wanted me to check your baby's development with the ultrasound, right?"

She nodded.

"Did he tell you what I'd be looking for?"

She shook her head.

Don't feel too bad, he thought. *He didn't have the courtesy to warn me either.* He took a deep breath. "There's a problem with your baby," he said. "I can switch on the machine and show you, or we could just talk about it first. Whichever you think would be easiest for you."

She looked frightened. "I don't want to see," she said. Thick tears already lay unshed across her eyes.

"Here, sit up." He helped her into a sitting position, and the tears spilled over her cheeks. "Your baby is hydrocephalic," he said. "Do you know what that means?"

She started to shiver. "Something about its head?"

He nodded. "That's right. Your baby's head is filling with spinal fluid and is quite a bit larger than it should be by now." He waited for her reaction, not wanting to give her all the facts before she was ready to hear them. He took a blanket from the shelf above the table and draped it over her shoulders, freeing her long dark hair from under it with his hand.

"Will it be okay?"

"His or her head will continue to fill with fluid, and I'm afraid the prognosis isn't very good." He waited. She looked dazed. He handed her a tissue, and she held it in her lap while her tears fell on the blanket. He wished she'd ask him another question. He hated plowing ahead.

"Do you understand what I'm saying, Mrs. Carselli?"

"It'll be retarded?"

He nodded. He explained the situation to her. Her baby would probably not live. If it did, the retardation would be severe.

She pulled the tissue apart with quivering fingers as he spoke. He wished she'd wanted the ultrasound screen left on so that he could focus on something other than the torment in her face.

"Abortion is one option," he said softly.

Her eyes flashed angrily. "I would never have an abortion!" She sounded as though that was something he should have known.

"Okay," he said, "but I feel obligated to let you know what your options are, and that's one of them. There may be one other possibility. Hydrocephalus can sometimes be treated by fetal surgery—surgery on your baby while he or she's still inside you. It's not commonly done, and you must understand that it's still considered experimental."

She looked excited. "I want to do it. I don't care if it's experimental or not. When can you do it? How does it work?"

"Listen to me," he said, smiling at her enthusiasm. "First of all, not all fetuses with hydrocephalus are treatable. That needs to be determined first. And soon. Unfortunately I can't do it because only certain medical centers are allowed to perform fetal surgery at this time. The closest is in Boston. I can call them right now and see if we can—"

She shook her head, tears flying off her face. "That won't work! I can't travel."

"Sure you can. It's only a few hours and—"

"No! I don't mean I can't because I'm pregnant. I mean I can't. I could hardly force myself to come here. I go to Dr. Benfield because his office is just a block from my house. And sometimes I can't even make myself get there."

He suddenly felt very tired. "You're agoraphobic," he said.

She nodded.

She'd come to the wrong place for sympathy. Corinne and her fears had worn him out long ago. "When you first walked into this room you told me how important this baby is to you," he said, hoping he sounded more patient than he felt. "What's a few days' discomfort now when you compare it to the chance of having a healthy baby?"

She was weeping openly. "You just don't understand."

No. He guessed he didn't.

*

Her husband came to see him later that week. John Carselli looked about thirty. A gray, hot-looking three-piece suit hung loosely on his slight frame. His hand was clammy in Cole's grasp.

"I'm very sorry about your baby's condition," Cole said, gesturing toward one of the leather chairs.

Carselli swept away the sentiment with a wave of his hand. "I saw an article about you in the paper yesterday," he said. "It said you can do this . . . fetal surgery. That you're the best in this area. I . . . my wife and I want you to do it."

Cole shook his head. "Believe me, I wish I could. We're trying to get a grant to start a fetal surgery program here, but right now I don't have the authorization or the equipment I would need to perform the surgery."

"But you have the expertise! You could get the equipment. My baby's going to die when you could save him."

He felt misunderstood. "My hands are tied," he said. "They limit the number of medical centers in the country that can perform fetal surgery so that all the cases will go to those few centers and a high skill-level can be achieved. If everyone did it, the cases would be too spread out for anyone to develop a—"

"Do you think I care about all that crap?"

No, probably not, Cole thought. "Right now the closest center is in Boston. I'm certain that I can get her seen by someone good there."

"She can't go to Boston!"

Cole stood up. "Look, Mr. Carselli There's nothing I can do. You and your wife can stay here and deliver a hydrocephalic baby who may or may not live, or go to Boston and get the best treatment available. It's that simple."

"No, it's not." He stood up as well. "You haven't lived with Peggy for seven years. Seven childless years. She can't do it. But you—you have the skill to help and you're withholding it from us."

By the first week of September he had forgotten about the Carsellis and their baby. He was orienting Kevin Mastrian, his new associate, and the hospital absorbed much of his time.

He would have forgotten about them completely if it hadn't been for the call from Orrin Chavek. He was about to leave his office for the night when the phone rang. He thought twice about answering, then picked it up.

"Dr. Perelle?" The voice was unfamiliar.

"Yes?"

"This is Orrin Chavek. The attorney for Blair."

Cole hesitated, hoping that by some miracle this was a social call.

"I'm afraid that the hospital's received a complaint from one of your patients naming you as a codefendant," Orrin continued.

"I'm being sued?"

"Yes."

He sat down behind his desk. "Damn."

'It could be serious, I'm not sure. It's an interesting case they have. According to their complaint, you have the necessary skill to perform surgery on their unborn baby, and the wife is unable—"

"Unable to go to Boston where she could get the treatment she needs. The Carsellis."

"Right. You remember her?"

"Yes. Damn. What happens now?"

"Well, you and I had better meet."

"Will this be in the papers?" He saw the funding for his program going down the drain.

"I wouldn't be surprised," Orrin said. "How about ten tomorrow morning?"

It would throw his schedule off, but this was too important. "All right," he said.

"The chief-of-staff should be there," Orrin added. "And the person doing the PR for the Fetal Surgery Program. She'll need to see what the program is up against."

Cole had to pass the central reception desk to get to the Fairchild Room the following morning. He could never walk past that desk without remembering the day he'd met Estelle. She'd been standing there talking with someone, he didn't remember who. Her back was to him. He knew who she was from the lines of her body beneath her wool skirt and green blouse and by the way the red in her hair caught the light from every direction. She had to be the woman everyone was talking about.

When she turned around, he didn't bother to avert his gaze. She was still talking, but now her eyes were on him and there was something like recognition in them, as though she'd been looking for him for a very long time.

They'd slept together that same night. He hadn't meant to move that quickly; he'd wanted it to be special this time.

But there was a current that passed between them at dinner, a kiss in his car that made his thinking fuzzy. After they made love, they told each other about their childhoods, every word in French. He discovered they'd been born on the same day, just hours apart—he took that as a sign—their fates were inextricably linked. Somehow, talking about his beginnings in the language he'd used as a child tapped the tenderest part of him, and Estelle listened to him as though every word had special meaning for her.

When he was being honest with himself, he knew that they'd stopped listening to each other a long time ago.

Kit was alone in the Fairchild Room. She gave him a weak smile. "You look as if you'd rather be anywhere else," she said.

He sat next to her. "You're very perceptive."

The air-conditioning was set too cold in this room, and the stark white walls, long conference table, and hard chairs did nothing to warm it up. He found himself shivering under his suit jacket.

Stu Davies and Orrin Chavek came in together. Davies held out his hand to Cole. "You're in the right, Perelle," he said in the rumbling voice that grew gruffer every year. Cole wondered if some malignancy was eating away at the chief-of-staff's vocal chords.

Orrin was younger than Cole had expected. Early thirties, he guessed, with jet-black hair that was silky and straight and gray eyes that matched Kit's except for his thick black lashes.

Orrin read the complaint. Cole ached when he pictured

Peggy and John Carselli sitting with their lawyer, struggling to put the words on paper that might save their baby.

He shook his head sadly. "They should be able to have the help they need."

Davies looked annoyed. "They can have it. In Boston."

He thought he'd better say no more.

"You understand that they're not after money." Orrin looked at Cole. "What they want is an injunction ordering you to perform the surgery."

"How can a court order me to perform surgery?" Cole asked.

"Under usual circumstances, they can't. But there have been a few cases recently involving the rights of the fetus that have turned the entire legal process upside down."

"It's impossible for him to perform that surgery," said Davies. "We're not set up for anything like that yet."

"That's the kind of information I need to be able to put together an answer to this complaint."

Davies turned to Kit. "This absolutely must stay out of the press, young lady."

Kit's expression held the proper blend of apology and pain. "Unfortunately it's not within our control, Dr. Davies. Their lawyer can make certain it gets splashed throughout the media if he's clever enough. What we need to do is prepare a rebuttal—a defense that doesn't sound defensive—in case it comes to that."

Cole knew that she'd been calling people and reading articles most of the night to learn the angles of this suit. He was glad she was there.

"You're right." Orrin smiled at Kit. He'd had his eye on

her since he walked in the door. "But for now, let's look at how we can answer this complaint. They didn't specify the exact skills Dr. Perelle possesses that would be necessary to perform surgery on a hydrocephalic fetus, so we can respond in just as general terms that you don't have them."

"But I *do* have them," said Cole. "Wouldn't it be more ethical to say that they haven't been specific enough to answer?"

Kit kicked him under the table and he looked at her.

"It just seems as though we're trying to find new ways of twisting words to our own advantage when the health of this fetus is at stake. What should be happening is that someone should be counseling them on how they can actually get some help instead of letting them beat a dead horse."

Orrin leaned back in his chair with a sigh and a smile. "Dr. Perelle, they're not asking for guidance. They're asking for the court to order you to perform surgery you are not authorized to perform. And that is what we need to address. The problem as they define it. And we have exactly thirty days to get our answer to them."

"Thirty days? That'll make her"—he figured quickly in his head—"nearly twenty-six weeks. That doesn't leave much time for them to play with. The surgery can't wait much longer than that."

"That definitely works to our advantage, doesn't it?" said Orrin.

Cole leaned on the table. "I can't go along with this," he said.

"Cole, you discussed the options with them." Kit spoke

quietly, and he guessed she was trying to keep him calm in front of Davies. "It's their choice to proceed with this. They know the risk they're taking. It's out of your hands."

Davies coughed. "You'd better worry about your own skin, Perelle. This is no time for the bleeding heart routine."

Kit slipped a sheet of paper in front of him. Across the top she'd written, *You're absolutely right, but incredibly naive.*

He leaned back with a sigh. "Okay," he said, 'let's get on with it."

"Bonnie?" He tested the name on the young girl in the bed, and she nodded. Either she was very polite or he'd hit the right one.

He should have checked the chart. The names of these women were beginning to congeal in his head. Six deliveries in the past twenty-four hours. The annual September baby boom, and he was practically doing it alone. Kevin would be good in time, but he wasn't ready to carry his share of the load yet.

"Remember I told you if your pressure didn't come down I'd have to do a c-section?"

She nodded again. Her eyes were tiny black stones in her bloated face.

"Well, it hasn't responded to treatment at all. I wanted to let you know that I'll be doing your c-section in about a half-hour and—"

"No!" she wailed. "It's too soon! My baby will die!"

"Shh." He took her hand. He was struck by how pulpy it felt in his own. "Your baby has a much better chance if we deliver him or her now." *And so do you*, he thought. He stood up. "I'll see you in a few minutes, okay?"

She was sniffling, watching him with those button eyes. She needed something more.

He sat down again. "Are you afraid of the c-section?"

She shook her head. "No. I know what it'll be like. You told me a hundred times, even though I never thought it would really happen. It's just . . . my baby is too little."

"A special pediatrician will be right there. I'm going to call her as soon as I leave your room. Your baby has a good chance, Bonnie."

The second labor room was in a shambles. He had to duck when he walked in because Marion—was that her name?—threw her water glass at him.

"This Demerol ain't doin' shit!" she screamed.

He'd never seen her before today. Heroin addicts were notorious for avoiding doctors during their pregnancies. In a few hours she'd deliver a baby who would shake like a derelict with DTs, sucking the skin off its fingers and spitting up every feeding.

"I need a fucking epidural!"

He examined her and shook his head. "It's too soon. It'll slow you down."

She glared at him across the bed. "What's your name?" she snapped. "Cole?"

"Dr. Perelle."

"Well, *Dr. Perelle*, I've had babies before. I know what I need!" She cried out with a contraction, her bravado gone. She grabbed the sheet with clenched fists, and the veins on her arms stood out, stippled with track marks. She ended the contraction with a sob. "You just want to watch me suffer, don't you?"

"No, I don't. Not at all." He moved toward the door. "I'll see what I can do about switching you to something a little stronger."

He walked to his office after delivering Bonnie's three-pound baby boy. She'd done very well, with no complications, but still he was running late. He was supposed to meet Estelle in the Research Department in five minutes to take her to lunch. He'd promised her Pierre's, and maybe an hour or so in the hotel next door to the restaurant. Now he didn't even have time for McDonald's. He'd better tell her in person rather than use the phone. Let her see how harried he looked.

He stopped at the reception desk in the Research Department.

"Could you buzz Estelle's office," he asked the clerk.

She grinned at him. "Oh, I think Estelle may be in the process of getting unemployed, Dr. Perelle."

"What?"

The young woman laughed, tossed her head. "She's in with Miss Hampton." She nodded toward the director's office. "Can I give her a message?"

The women in the circular reception area were staring at him, he was certain of it. Not the way women usually looked at him, either. This group was smirking.

"What's going on?" he asked. He knew this receptionist. One of those women who gave all women a bad name.

"I think it's confidential," she said. "But you could probably find out if you go down to the Emergency Room."

He didn't have time for this. He turned on his heel and
walked to the elevator.

He walked casually into the ER, carrying a chart he
could pretend to be working on while he tried to figure out
what was going on. He didn't have to wait long. Rick, one
of the Emergency Room nurses, nudged him from behind.

"Your girlfriend's a real animal, isn't she?" He grinned.

He didn't know whether to return the grin or not. He
wished he knew the rules for the game he was playing.
"How is it going down here?" he asked.

"I guess they're sending Vicki home. She's in there."
Rick nodded toward one of the treatment rooms.

Vicki? Who the hell was Vicki? "How is she? Vicki?" he
asked.

Rick grinned again. "I didn't think it was possible to lift
a chunk of flesh out of somebody's arm with a pencil. But
there was lead in the wound so I guess it's the truth. You
didn't see Vicki's arm?"

He shook his head, his stomach churning.

The door to the treatment room opened, and a woman
he recognized as one of the secretaries for the Research
Department walked out, her forearm bandaged, her face
red. She stopped when she saw him.

"You should lock her up," was all she said.

He took the stairs instead of waiting for the elevator.
He felt the eyes of the clerks on him as he walked toward Estelle's door. Heads poked out of the other offices.

Everyone knew what was going on except him. But he was beginning to figure it out.

"Dr. Perelle?"

He turned around. Agnes Hampton walked toward him. Dressed in black, as usual. He couldn't remember ever seeing her in any other color. She had the sharp nose of a witch, and her long salt and pepper hair was pulled back in a bun. She looked as though she spent her nights with a statistics book.

She locked her bony hand around his arm and pulled him aside. "I hope you can get her some help. It should be quite obvious after this that she needs it. Her temper is simply out of hand."

"I'm not her parent, Miss Hampton."

She ignored the remark. "You know, I'm sure that the Research Department would be at a loss without her. Perhaps it was an accident, so I'm giving her a second chance. But there'll be no third chance, I can tell you that." She let go of his arm. "Frankly," she continued, "administration would have my head if I fired her. But something is radically wrong with her thinking."

"I'll speak with her," he said, wanting to get away from Agnes. She smelled like flowers at a funeral.

Estelle was waiting for him just inside the door of her office.

"Take me home, please?"

He shut the door before he spoke. "What the hell is going on?"

"They're making a big deal out of nothing." She sat down at her desk. She was wearing the beige silk dress he'd bought her in Paris and thick gold chains around her throat and wrists.

"You stabbed the secretary with a pencil?" It sounded so bizarre that he laughed.

"Vicki's been telling me you had an affair while I was in France."

"That's not true," he said quickly.

"I didn't believe her at first, but she kept rubbing it in. She said it was some nurse on the eighth floor. She said that's why you wanted to stay at the Chapel House, so you'd have some freedom to see this other woman."

"That's bullshit." He felt abused by rumors, touched in private places by strangers he had no control over. Yet he couldn't help but wonder who this nurse was he'd been linked to.

"Deep down I know it's bullshit," she said, touching his arm. The gold chains whispered against each other at her wrist. "But when I hear it over and over again, I go berserk."

"Tell me the truth, did you stab Vicki?"

"It all happened so quickly. I wanted to hurt her, and my words didn't feel like enough. But I didn't actually *stab* her. Her arm and my pencil were just at the same point in space and time."

He looked at her quietly for a long time before he spoke. "Agnes Hampton's an old prune, I'll grant you that, but she suggested you see someone and I think it would be a good idea."

She looked insulted. "Why?"

"Well, today's fiasco aside, a few weeks ago you told me

you were feeling desperate. I'm still not certain what you meant, but—"

"Cole, I was in a peculiar mood that day. It was nothing."

"Doesn't it bother you that you can't get along with other women?"

"I don't need women." She smiled at him. "All I need is you." She leaned across the corner of her desk to kiss him, and he felt the weight of her breast on his arm. How long had it been since they'd made love in one of their offices? Two years? Three?

He stood up. "I have to get back to the unit."

"What about Pierre's?"

He shook his head. "Not today. I'm swamped."

"You haven't slept in two days."

"Don't remind me."

"And now you had to get dragged into this. I'm sorry, darling." She stood up and touched his cheek. Her fingers were cool and dry.

It was March, early spring, and Paris still had a chill to it. Their breath turned to smoke as they walked across the piazza in front of the Pompidou after the Matisse exhibit. He had to admit his feelings about that building had changed, although he still found the architecture ugly. He turned to look back at it. Hideous, with its garish colors and exposed pipes. It reminded him of a baby he'd delivered once, with her bowels outside her abdomen.

But inside it was paradise. He'd jumped at the chance to rent a tiny restored house close to the Pompidou, despite the cobblestone street that was taking a toll on the Renault. He and Estelle spent most of their free time inside that museum, taking advantage of all it had to offer.

Estelle had no problem at all with the building. She loved it, inside and out. But on this evening in March she had something else on her mind.

"It's extraordinary, Cole. Wait till you see it." She put her arm through his as they walked down one narrow street and into another. The dark river smell mingled with the aroma of baking bread, and they passed people walking home from work, baguettes clutched under their arms.

She'd found a gallery the night before, while he was still at the hospital. And in it, she'd found the perfect painting for the living room of her condo. She'd kept him awake much of the night talking about it. Yet from her description, he couldn't get an image of it in his mind.

"It's pale," she'd said, eyes aglow. "It's incredibly pale."

Now she steered him toward a doorway, then up a flight of crooked stairs, the walls close to their shoulders on both sides.

"How did you ever find this place?" he asked.

"Fate," she said.

The stairs sprang open into a large room, its wall covered with paintings, all of which Cole could have described as "pale".

"Can you guess which one?" Estelle asked.

"Uh . . ." He laughed, looking from one nearly identical painting to the next. "No."

"*Cole.*" She pointed to a huge white square on the far wall. "*That* one. Won't it look perfect above my lilac settee?"

He smiled. "I guess." He walked over to the painting. Once close enough he could see ice-blue brushstrokes in the lower third.

Estelle stood back to look at it, framing it with her hands. "A lake," she said. "Newly frozen. Dusted with snow. Do you see it, darling?"

"I thought you liked the Matisse," he said. "I thought you liked the colors."

"I love Matisse. But I need something pale for the condo."

A young woman appeared from a side door. She spoke to them in French. "*Bonjour*, Mademoiselle Lauren, you've come to take another look at the painting?"

"I've brought my friend to see it."

Cole reached out his hand. "*Bonjour, Madame. Je m'appelle Cole Perelle.*"

"Oh, English, please. I want to practice." She shook his hand. "My name is Nicole Eduard."

"You don't sound as though you need any practice," he said. She had blond hair, shorter than his own, and a smile far warmer than the paintings in her gallery.

"I'd like to buy it," said Estelle. She reached into her purse for her checkbook.

"How much is it?" he asked Nicole.

"Twelve thousand francs."

He wondered if she'd made a mistake in translation. "*Douze mille francs?*" he asked.

Estelle gave him a warning look. "Twelve thousand, darling." She leaned against the desk to write her check.

"Do you work at the University Hospital, too, Dr. Perelle?" Nicole seemed anxious to use her English.

"Yes. I'm doing some research on . . ." That would get too complicated. "I'm an obstetrician. *Accoucheur.*"

She pumped him for information on his work, where he lived in the States, his family.

"I'd like to pay for this now." Estelle drummed the desk impatiently.

Nicole reached for the check.

"Are you a student?" he asked her.

She nodded. "Music. The flute. I play in a cafe on the weekends."

"Really?" he asked. It would be fun to hear her. "Where?"

She drew him by the arm to the window and began giving him directions. He heard Estelle strike a match behind him and turned to see her light a cigarette. She'd started smoking again since they'd been in Paris, although usually only when they were apart because he complained so much about the smell and the taste. It surprised him to see her lighting up here in this gallery. He turned back to Nicole.

"The Refuge," she said. "Do you know it?"

Estelle had stepped next to them. "I've seen it," she said. "A grimy little joint."

He looked sharply at Estelle, but Nicole seemed to have no idea she was being insulted.

"And if you want an excellent dinner," she continued, "there is—ouch!" She lifted her hand to her lips and looked at Estelle.

Estelle wore a look of horror and remorse. "Oh, I burned you!" She dusted at the back of Nicole's hands. "I'm sorry."

He lifted Nicole's hand and looked at the fresh round burn, then at Estelle.

"It was an accident," she said.

"Let's get it under cold water," he said to Nicole.

Estelle grabbed his arm. "I'm sure she can take care of it herself, can't you, Nicole? We have to get going. Just wrap the painting for me and I'll pick it up next week."

It was well after eight when he reached the condominium. He'd managed to nap for two hours in the sleeping room at Blair, but he was hardly refreshed.

Estelle was waiting for him, wearing a lacy white robe he'd never seen before, her hair a rich auburn against it. "You poor thing," she said, unbuttoning his shirt in the hallway. "What's the chance you won't get called back in tonight?"

"No chance."

"Would you like to soak in the tub a while?"

He shook his head. He'd showered at Blair a few hours ago to try to wake himself up. He looked into her eyes. "We have to talk."

"Not now, Cole," she pleaded. "That can wait. There are clean sheets on the bed. Why don't you crawl in?"

He sighed. The last thing he wanted was a fight. He put his arms around her and buried his face in her hair. "If you'll crawl in with me," he said.

She led him to the bedroom. The sheets were white and crisp, and he could hardly wait to get between them. He let her undress him, let her stroke his body with those cool, familiar fingers.

"You just lie here," she directed him, kissing his hair, the tip of his nose, the weary smile on his lips. "Let me take care of everything."

"Do you remember the good old days, Estelle, when we'd stay in bed for twenty-four hours at a stretch?" Her head was on his chest and her hair felt like satin under his fingers.

"Mmmm." Her voice vibrated against his ribs.

"We'd argue about whose turn it was to go out for sausage sandwiches, and then we'd eat them in bed and get crumbs and green peppers all over the sheets." The memory hurt.

She laughed, deep and throaty. "Ugh. We were disgusting."

"I don't think so," he said, wondering when they'd changed. "We had no problems then." He was talking more to himself than to her.

"We have no problems now, either." Her warning was clear. He let it die. He had no strength for an argument.

He fell into such a deep sleep that he didn't even hear the phone ring.

Estelle woke him. "Darling, I'm sorry," she whispered. "Blair called. Marion somebody is about ready to deliver."

He groaned. The heroin addict. His head was foggy, and he was a little nauseated. He sat up and saw the concern in her eyes. He must look like hell.

"Can't someone cover for you?"

He shook his head. "Kevin will be able to off and on next week. I just have to make it through the next few days."

"I think you age six months every September," she said, helping him find his clothes.

In the bathroom he splashed cold water on his face and avoided looking at his bloodshot eyes in the mirror above the sink. *Marion somebody's had a rotten day, too,* he thought to himself. He'd make her delivery as good for her as he could. He'd even ask her to call him Cole if she liked.

13.

"I'm amazed you made it through this meal without falling asleep." Kit was watching him from across the kitchen table.

He'd dragged dinner out, savoring the anticipation of his first uninterrupted night's sleep in a week. "I can't wait another second for bed," he said now, as he carried his plate to the sink. He felt as if he were sleepwalking.

The phone rang as he started to leave the room, and he froze from force of habit.

"Go," Kit said as she picked it up. "I'm sure Kevin has things under control at Blair."

But it was his father. His father never called him. He took the phone from Kit and frowned into the receiver. "Dad?"

"Cole, your mother's in the hospital. There's . . . uh, a lump in her breast."

Not Mom, he thought. Things like that didn't happen in his family.

"What kind of lump?" He felt Kit and Maris exchange looks across the table.

"Well . . . I think . . . I mean they told her it's cancer.

She's known for a while, I guess, and she had . . . I don't know, some kind of test and didn't tell me. I don't think she told anyone. They're doing the surgery tomorrow morning."

"God." He let his eyelids fall shut for a few seconds. "Are they just planning to excise it?" he asked hopefully.

"She said she's going to sign for them to . . . do a . . . you know, take it all if they need to."

Cole pictured his father nervously doodling on a piece of paper as he talked, a pen gripped in shaky fingers that not so long ago handled the controls of commercial jets. *Hundreds of people depend on me for their lives,* he'd say. He always took that responsibility very seriously.

"Is she at St. Catherine's?" Cole asked.

"Yes."

"I'll come up tonight and see her."

"Good, good." He heard the relief in his father's voice. The vision of his dark bedroom, the waiting bed and feather pillow, moved across his mind and gave him a panicky feeling.

"And, Cole?"

"Yes?"

"Could you call Corinne? I can't talk to her about this."

Why the hell not? he thought. Why did they always have to treat Corinne like a china doll?

"Okay."

He set the receiver down slowly in its cradle. The women were staring at him, waiting for him to say something.

"My mother." His throat constricted. He looked down,

poked at a scrap of paper on the floor with the toe of his shoe.

"I'm sorry, Cole," Kit said. "Is it absolutely necessary for you to go up there tonight? You're exhausted. What good can you do right now?"

"It's malignant, Kit. She's having surgery tomorrow. I have to see her tonight."

"You'd better go, baby," Maris said. "You won't be at peace with yourself unless you do."

He turned back to the phone and called his sister, who put on her usual performance. "Oh my God!" she said. "Oh my God!"

Cut the hysterics, he thought. His patience was ready to crack. "I'm going up there tonight. I can pick you up on the way."

"Cole, you know that's impossible. I hate hospitals. I could never visit her there."

"Don't you think you could put your neuroses on the shelf for one night, for Mom's sake?"

"I can't." She was crying.

"You're so used to saying you can't that you don't even think about it before you answer. What if she doesn't make it through surgery? How will you feel then?"

Kit sucked in her breath as though she'd been wounded. Was he being cruel? He didn't care.

"I can't do it, Cole. I can't go to—"

"Good-bye, Corinne." He hung up and saw that his hand was shaking. He headed for the stairs. He'd need to change, splash some water on his face. He turned back to the women. "Could one of you make me a thermos of coffee, please? Black and very strong."

He let the radio blare to keep himself awake in the car. But then his head started to throb. He drove past the turnoff to Corinne's house and held up his middle finger to the window, feeling a little ashamed of himself.

A sudden image came into his mind. He was seven or so, standing in front of the gas stove in the house in Watchung. He was making pancakes, and he wanted to learn how to flip them in the air the way his mother did. She put her hand over his on the spatula to guide him. He remembered how it felt, her big hand wrapped around his small one, her calm directions in his ear. He pretended to have great difficulty with the task so he could have her hand covering his for as long as possible.

Why was he thinking about that now, for Christ's sake?

Another image. He was seven again. In school, making a Mother's Day card for her. Lacy paper doilies and blue construction paper. He cut designs and pasted them carefully onto the card, trying to make the edges meet perfectly, because things had to be done very neatly for his mother to like them. He thought it looked pretty good, but he wasn't quite sure.

She had a friend over, in the kitchen. He handed it to her quickly, before he had a chance to get too nervous.

"Oh, Cole, this is so nice!" A quick kiss on the cheek while he stood with his hands knotted behind his back. "Thank you, honey."

When he left the room he heard her say to her friend,

"Another little gem to clutter up the front of the refrigerator," and they both laughed.

He'd stayed in his room all that evening, too embarrassed to come down to dinner. For a week, every time he thought about the card, he felt his cheeks burn.

He shook his head to get rid of the memories, but they were rooted to the inside of his forehead. He took a long drink of bitter coffee and wiped at his eyes with the back of the hand that held the thermos.

In the parking lot of St. Catherine's he took the time to study his eyes in the rearview mirror. Even in the dim light he could see that the whites were bloodshot. If she asked, he'd tell her he hadn't slept in a long time. It was the truth, anyway.

His mother was sitting up, her back against the raised white square of the hospital bed. She wore the familiar hospital gown with its faded blue diamond design. His first thought was to tell his father to bring one of her nightgowns and robes from home. She shouldn't look like this, like any other patient.

He pulled a chair close to the bed. "Why didn't you tell anyone?"

She shrugged. "I was hoping it was nothing. Apparently I was wrong." She reached for his hand. Hers was bitter cold. "I've never felt this way before, so helpless and powerless. I'm so used to taking charge, you know." She sighed. "And I've never been so frightened. I can't tell that to your father. He thinks I'm doing fine."

He wished she *could* tell his father. Anyone other than him. He felt burdened by the weight of her fear.

She wanted him to feel the lump in her breast, as though she hoped that when someone who loved her touched it, it would turn out to be no more than a little bump in the skin. She put her right arm behind her head. "It's just below my armpit," she said.

He ignored the queasiness he felt at touching her breast. He felt the round, hard mass, so firmly attached to the skin, and the little hope he'd been clinging to left him.

"It's large," he said, taking his hand away. "You've had it a while." He heard the blame in his voice.

"You get scared, Cole. I never thought I'd react that way. I always thought that if I found a lump I'd go to the doctor right away, but I found it and . . ."

"When? When did you find it?"

"Oh, a month ago. More like two, I guess."

"*Mom.*"

"Don't give me a lecture. That's not what I need. Listen, Cole." She sat forward, gripping his hand tightly. Her nails pressed into his palm. "Your father is handling this very poorly. I don't know what to tell you to do to help him. Just be there for him, okay?"

"He'll be all right."

"And, Cole? If anything . . . goes wrong, if I don't make it through, please—"

"Mom, you're going to be fine." He knew he should let her talk, but he wasn't made of steel as she seemed to think. "Kit wanted to come with me," he said, changing the subject. He'd thanked Kit but told her he wanted to be alone. He needed some time to fall apart.

His mother leaned back. "I guess I won't be having lunch with her for a while. I'll miss that." She looked him squarely in the eye. "I think she loves you."

He nodded. "I love her, too," he said, purposely missing her point. "She's become a good friend."

"Is that all?"

"Of course that's all." He stood up and kissed her cheek, eyeing the door.

"Sometimes I think you're a fool, Cole," she said, as simply as if she were saying the day had been cool for September.

His eyes stung. He thought of telling her to have some respect for his decisions, to realize that he couldn't always take whatever she dished out to him. But what good would it do? And now was certainly not the time.

Kit sat next to him on the ottoman in the library, her arms wrapped around him as though she were trying to hold in his anger. It was black outside the library windows, and there was no sound at all from the ocean, no sound in the room except Kit's breathing and his own. The phone was balanced on his knees. He'd hung up on Corinne again, couldn't stand to hear one more self-serving excuse out of her mouth for why she couldn't visit her mother. For the first time he needed his sister's help, really needed it. He couldn't handle this alone.

His father was useless. He'd left the hospital after his mother's mastectomy, said he needed some air.

"You should be here when she comes out of it, Dad," Cole had said to him.

"You do it, Cole. I'm not feeling too well right now." He didn't look well. So old.

Cole sat at his mother's side in the recovery room for nearly two hours, talking with her in whispers, trying to think of what he would say when she asked for his father. But she never did.

He was shaking beneath Kit's arms, he was so angry. She set her cheek on his shoulder, and he could smell whatever it was she used on her hair. He connected that scent to her. Sometimes a patient would come into his office and he'd catch a whiff of that same scent, and he'd immediately like the woman. It didn't matter who she was.

"You know," Kit said softly. "You have so much patience with the rest of us. We're always turning to you with our little problems and you're always there, ready to listen. But when it comes to your sister, you tune her out."

He put his arm around her waist. "She taxes me," he said. "Do you know what it was like growing up with her? We never went anywhere as a family because Corinne couldn't go. She cost my parents thousands of dollars for doctors and shrinks. If she ever ventured out, to a party or something, she'd call and beg me to pick her up, she couldn't stand to be there another second." His body tensed to remember that time in his life, when Corinne absorbed all his parents' attention. They'd had nothing left over to give to him. "I'm afraid she'll make Wendy and Becky as crazy as she is."

"Does she have friends?"

"You can't have friends when you refuse to leave your house."

"Then she needs you even more than most sisters need their brothers."

"Are you purposely trying to make me feel guilty?"

She shrugged.

"Right now I'm sick of being needed," he said.

She didn't move. Her cheek was still on his shoulder. Her hair smelled so good.

He sighed and began to dial Corinne's number with his left hand, still holding Kit against him with his right.

"I'm sorry," he said when Corinne answered.

She was still sniffling. "I'm afraid I'd cry in front of her."

"So what? I cried in front of her, too." He hadn't really, hadn't even come close to it today. "She knows we're sad. You don't have to hide it. It would mean so much to her to have her daughter with her."

"I'll try, Cole, I really will."

"I'm sorry I lost my temper before, Corinne. I love you." He couldn't remember the last time he'd said those words to her. Maybe when the girls were born. Maybe not even then.

14.

It was dark when she went running in the morning now. She felt like a knife, cutting through chill, black air. Two and a half weeks left until the Somerville Marathon. She'd have to get her speed up, but she was certain she could. She always had something in reserve.

She walked around to the front of the house to look in the garage for Cole's Mustang. Still not there, poor guy. He'd gotten some sleep the night Kevin covered for him, but last night he'd been up and down. The phone woke her three times, and after the third call she heard him moving around his bedroom, talking with Estelle. Then his heavy footsteps on the stairs and the sound of his car starting in the still night, sputtering once before it turned over. She had lain in her bed, wishing she could go in for him, do whatever needed to be done at Blair. He'd changed in the past week. His face was lined and pinched, and his smile, when it was there at all, seemed forced.

She went upstairs, took a shower, and put on her bathrobe. The smell of toast and coffee filled the upstairs hallway. God, she was ravenous. She couldn't stop eating these days. And she never gained an ounce.

She made herself smile at Estelle in the hall. "Cole's had a rough few days, hasn't he?" she said.

"Don't you worry your little pea-brain about Cole," said Estelle. "I'll take care of him. Or do you think you could be doing a better job of it?"

Kit felt the hair on her neck rise. "I'm sorry I mentioned it." She tried to walk past her, but Estelle caught her arm.

"You always have your nose in his business, don't you?" she said. "Maybe you'd better concentrate a little harder on *Sandy.* How long do you think he's going to stick around when you wear Salvation Army specials like this?" Estelle lifted the tie to Kit's seersucker robe and dropped it as though it were infested.

Kit clenched her fists. "Do you want me to hate you, Estelle?"

"Though he's quite a slob himself," she continued as if Kit hadn't spoken. "What's it like to share your lover with other women?" she asked. "Aren't you disgusted when you think of him being in someone else's cunt just hours after he's been in yours?"

"You are such a *bitch.*" Kit turned on her heel and escaped down the stairs, Estelle's throaty laughter behind her.

She found Janni in the kitchen, laying another log on the fire.

"I *hate* that goddamn bitch!" Kit felt her whole body shaking. "You wouldn't believe what she just said to me. How can Cole stand her?"

"*Kit.*" She saw the warning look in Janni's face too late.

Cole stood in the doorway of the pantry, a can of coffee in his hand, his eyes unsmiling.

Kit held up her hands. "Cole, I'm sorry," she said quickly. "That wasn't meant for your ears."

"No, I'm sure it wasn't," he said, walking toward her slowly. She saw the dark circles under his eyes, the lines at the corners of his mouth. He set the can on the counter. "You're always telling me how much you want to be her friend," he said. "How hard you try. Is that just a line you've been handing me?"

"I *have* tried," she said. "But it's useless. She's always putting me down."

"Oh, poor Kit." The sarcasm in his voice made her wince. "Tell her to leave you alone then. Where's your backbone?"

"*You're* the one without the backbone!" she said angrily.

"You *guys*," Janni pleaded. "Don't say things you'll—"

"She lies to you and you swallow every word," Kit said. "She has you wrapped so tightly around her little finger the circulation's been cut off to your brain."

"You'd better just shut up," he warned.

"I'm *sick* of shutting up! We're always protecting you, as though there's some unwritten rule not to let you know what a malicious, conniving, backbiting wench she is."

"Are you jealous of her, Kit? Is that it?" He was mocking her, coming way too close to the truth.

"*No.* It's not just me. Ask anybody." She glanced at Janni who was staring at them, wide-eyed and silent, a log still in her arms. "There's so much tension when she's in the house, I can't stand it," Kit continued. "Are you immune to it? Sometimes I don't want to come home from work because I'm afraid she'll be here."

"Then don't come home from work, if it's so terrible for you," he said. "Estelle's been a part of this group a hell of a lot longer than you have, Kit. If you can't stand being around her, maybe you'd better just move out."

"*Me* move out!" Any second her voice would break. "I've contributed a lot to this household. What has Estelle contributed? Her good looks? She may be beautiful on the outside, Cole, but inside she's ugly to the core."

He shook his head slowly, his eyes hard. "I had no idea what a fucking bitch you can be." He leaned toward her as though he wanted to make sure she heard him. "And you can go straight to hell for all I care." He picked up the coffee can and walked back into the pantry.

He may as well have slapped her. Janni set down the log and walked toward her, one arm outstretched, but Kit shook her head. She needed to get out of the kitchen. Tears burned her eyes as she walked through the living room and up the stairs.

In her bedroom, she sat down on the window seat by the bay window, her arms wrapped around her knees as she stared at the water. A few boats were far out in the ocean. Her run on the beach that morning seemed like days ago.

Maybe you'd better move out.

She couldn't get Cole's words out of her mind. Maybe she *should* leave. The house had served its purpose for her. Her emotional strength was back. She no longer had any need to be coddled. And what good was she doing herself here? Every day she was pummeled by Estelle. And every day she was pulled deeper into this relationship with Cole, a relationship that promised to go nowhere.

There was a knock on her door and she didn't bother to answer. Cole walked in and crossed the room, picking up her dressing table chair and setting it near her. She kept her gaze firmly fastened on the water.

"I've been kidding myself," he said, his voice so flat that she had to look at him. "I keep pretending that she's the old Estelle. She used to be so different. I wish you'd known her years ago, Kit." A little sparkle came into his eyes, but it was gone as quickly as it had come. "Something's not right with her," he said. "I've known for a while but I've tried to ignore it. I didn't realize how hard she's been on you. Why didn't you tell me?"

"I tried to. You didn't want to hear it."

He was quiet. "I knew she could be very . . . well . . . *cutting*. But I didn't think she was capable of being so vicious. Janni told me some of the things she's said to you. I want you to know that I *never* said anything about what you and Sandy do in the privacy of your bedroom."

She looked down at the window seat, played with a thread coming loose from the cushion.

"Do you think she's crazy?" he asked.

"That depends on your definition of crazy. She switches from sweet to sour just like that." She snapped her fingers. "And she's certainly paranoid."

He nodded. "Once during the summer she told me she felt desperate, or something like that."

"She admitted it?"

"Yes, but I didn't encourage her. It bothered me to hear her talk that way."

"She needs help, Cole."

"I know, but she'll never agree to it. Maybe if I gave her an ultimatum. Either she gets into therapy or we split up, though I'm not certain I could hold to my end of the deal."

"It might work. You're the one thing that's important to her." She wondered where her kindness came from. She would just as soon see Estelle flattened by a bus as see her get better.

"Kit, I'm so sorry for the things I said downstairs. You're the least bitchy person I know."

"I'm sorry, too."

"Don't even think of moving out," he said. "I'd hate it if you left." He looked past her through the window, out to the ocean. "This has been a terrible month for me," he said, "not that that's any kind of an excuse for the things I said. But the unit's a baby factory. I'm getting sued. I'll probably lose the funding for the program. My mother has cancer. My father's proved himself to be a Grade-A wimp. And my girlfriend's a sociopath." He looked at her. "And then I hurt my closest friend."

He leaned forward to kiss her cheek, and she fought the urge to take his face in her hands and kiss him back, really kiss him. But it would be the last thing he needed right now. The last thing either of them needed.

15.

He sat on the sofa in Frank Jansen's waiting room, his thigh pressing against Estelle's. She was nervous. He felt an occasional quiver run through her leg. She was reading a magazine, or just pretending to read it; he hadn't seen her turn a page for several minutes.

She'd pleaded with him to come with her and he'd finally agreed. "Just the first time," he said. "Unless he thinks I should continue to come, too." He was willing to do anything Frank Jansen suggested. All his hope was focused on the man behind that big oak door.

He slid his hand into hers now, weaving his warm fingers between her cool ones. She didn't look at him, didn't lift her eyes from the magazine.

Frank called them into his office and motioned them into soft upholstered chairs, set close together. The walls of the room were covered by books and woolly wall hangings that matched the man himself, with his gray mop of hair and full beard. Janni had said he was an overgrown hippie. She told them he knew about the living arrangements at the Chapel House. They wouldn't have to waste time trying to make him understand.

"Tell me why you're here," he asked.

"He made me come," Estelle said.

Frank raised his eyebrows. "Just from looking at you I wouldn't guess you're that easily coerced."

"He told me that if I refused to start therapy he would end our relationship."

"I see. The relationship's important to you, then."

"It's everything to me." Her voice was a whisper. Cole felt cruel.

Frank turned to him. "Why would you make your relationship with Estelle contingent on her being in therapy?"

Cole cleared his throat. "I don't think she's content with herself."

"That's not it," Estelle said. "I'm not the one doing the complaining. *You're* the one who's not content."

Frank looked at Cole, obviously waiting for him to speak.

"I'm the one doing the complaining because she's costing me my friends. She's been . . . verbally abusive to them. She . . ." His mind went blank. "I don't know," he said, feeling foolish.

Estelle smiled, crossing one long leg over the other. "A pretty weak argument for forcing me into therapy, wouldn't you say?"

"Do you two fight much?"

Cole said yes at the same time that Estelle answered no. Frank smiled. "I see," he said.

Cole turned to her. "How can you say that we don't fight?"

"We make love far more than we fight," she said to Frank. "One outweighs the other."

This was going nowhere. "Look." Cole sat forward in his chair. "She nearly got fired because she can't get along with the other women at work. She's so possessive of me that I can't breathe. She's critical of everyone I care about."

"Why are you with her then?"

"I love her."

"You don't make her sound very lovable."

He hesitated, looked at her. "She used to be. She still is, sometimes. When we're together. Alone. She's different then."

Frank turned to Estelle. "Cole's painted a picture of an unhappy, insecure woman, Estelle. Does that fit?"

"*He's* the reason I'm unhappy. He won't live with me. He makes it sound as though I'm the sick one in this relationship. But what do you think of a grown man who's afraid to leave home?"

"Who's in the Chapel House now?" Frank asked.

Cole started to answer but Frank asked Estelle to tell him.

"Janni and Jay. Janni owns the place. You know that, I guess." She went on to describe Jay as unobtrusive, Janni as pushy and interfering. "She hates it when I'm there," she said. "I can feel the icicles when I walk in the door."

"Who else is in the house?"

"Maris Lavender. She's this miserable, funereal black woman who thinks the world owes her an apology for screwing up her life."

"It does," said Cole. He looked at Frank. "Her husband

was killed in a car accident two years ago. Her mother died of leukemia when Maris was fourteen, and a year later her two brothers died in a fire in their house."

"Wow," Frank said.

Estelle looked annoyed. "She probably struck the match."

"*Estelle.*" Cole looked at Frank. *See what I mean?* he said with his eyes.

"And then we have Kit." Estelle turned in her chair to look at Cole, and he was afraid of what she might say. "Kit is out to snare Cole. She's sneaky and subtle. She has this goody-two-shoes demeanor, innocent as a lamb, but what she's really after is getting him into bed with her."

He felt relieved. She thought it was Kit who wanted him. She didn't know she had it backward.

"Assuming Kit is out to get Cole, as you say, do you think she could succeed?"

Estelle shrugged. "He's only human. The flesh is weak." She looked at Cole as if she were examining his weak flesh. "I don't understand why he'd be attracted, really. She's a runner, and she has that look . . . you know, like a mal-nourished greyhound. But Cole is enormously attracted to women. *All* women. That's why he became an obstetrician. To legitimize his obsession."

Cole had to laugh. "You don't really believe that, do you?"

Frank held up a hand to silence him. Estelle was on a roll, and he seemed to want her to continue. "Who else?"

"In the house, you mean? No one. But we haven't talked about Virginia."

"Virginia?"

"Cole's mother. She thinks I'm the devil incarnate. She would do anything to break us up. She had a mastectomy two weeks ago and she clings to Cole as though he's her husband. He's with her nearly all the time that he's not working, and I never get to see him."

"Are you saying that Cole's mother had a mastectomy in an attempt to break you two up?"

Estelle looked suspicious. "Of course not. But she probably would think it had been worth it if it did."

"Estelle, please don't talk that way."

"You want me to tell it all, don't you, Cole? Let out every insane thought in my head?"

He looked at her, not certain what to say.

"Do you think you're insane, Estelle?" Frank asked.

Cole expected her to say no, but she hesitated. "Everybody wonders if they're insane at one time or another," she said, her dark blue eyes serious.

"Yes, many people do," Frank said thoughtfully, tapping his fingers on his chin. He leaned forward in his chair. "Tell me why you nearly got fired," he said.

She recounted the incident enthusiastically, and Cole watched the lines deepen on Frank's forehead as she spoke. He wished he could change the subject or walk out the door. What had he expected? That Frank would have to pull every word out of her? She was exposing so much to him. He hated hearing her sound so transparently crazy. He wouldn't come with her again.

16.

She'd lost sight of Sandy in the crowd of spectators waiting for the race to begin. She was near the middle of the pack. That was best. She wouldn't be left behind and she wouldn't be knocked over. She jumped up and down to keep the blood flowing.

Twenty-six miles in three and a half hours if she wanted to qualify for Boston. Last night, lying with Sandy in their Somerville motel room, she'd been optimistic. But now she felt weighed down. The article in that morning's paper filled her thoughts. *Blair Loses Ground in Fight for Program,* the headline read. In smaller letters beneath it: *Physician Sued.*

Sandy had tried to keep it from her. He knew it was the last thing she needed to see before the race. But she'd grown suspicious at the way he kept that section of the paper to himself, and she finally snuck it away from him.

The article itself said very little. The damage was done in the headline. She called Cole. He'd seen the paper already and he sounded resigned.

"Orrin said the reporters will start calling any minute and I should tell them I have no comment," he said. "It makes me furious. I haven't done a damn thing wrong. It's just the fact that someone sued me, no matter how out of line it is, that can ruin my credibility."

"I know, Cole," she'd said. "Look, 'no comment' sounds like you're guilty. Speak from your heart. What do you have to lose?"

Stupid question, she thought now. He had everything to lose.

The cloth pinned to her shirt read 517. She repeated the numbers over and over in her mind, like a mantra. She looked down at her shoes for what had to be the hundredth time to be certain she'd tied double knots in the laces.

She heard the sound of the gun and suddenly they were moving like one massive animal. She couldn't see the road in front of her or the people cheering along the sidewalk. Just the bodies surrounding her. She studied their fluid, graceful movements until she felt hypnotized by the rhythm.

This was fun. She moved easily, not too fast. Not yet. The air was crisp and cool, clean in her lungs. The trees were beginning to turn, but she let them blur by without taking time to notice their colors. She had to focus on the race, on the way each step felt to her feet and legs. She pushed the Fetal Surgery Program to some back corner of her mind and vowed to keep it there for the rest of the day.

She passed the eight-mile marker at noon. Terrific. Better than she'd hoped for.

She knew there were plenty of hills in the middle stretch. The first loomed in front of her. She heard the breathing of the runners around her as they started the climb. Her legs felt strong. She felt every contraction of the muscles, the way they grabbed and let go. She sailed over the crest and stayed in careful control downhill. No sense giving it your all when you didn't need to. *You were born to run over hills.* She was a little giddy. For about five miles she felt as if she were flying instead of running.

At mile fifteen, though, she came to a narrow hill that curved and dipped, and it took all her concentration to get over and around it. She suddenly felt very tired. Eleven miles left.

Okay, you're tired, she told herself. *Keep moving, one step after the other. What hurts? Nothing much. Really, nothing too much. Calves would like a good stretch, they feel pretty tight. Breathing's good. Very smooth. Weren't you that fat little asthmatic kid?* She was passing people. That amazed her. Of course some passed her too, but that didn't really matter.

She spotted the twenty-mile marker at one-thirty. She wasn't sure if she should trust her watch or not. It was too good. She had a full hour left to run the six miles that would qualify her for Boston. She felt like smiling but couldn't. Everything hurt now. Her eyes burned and teared and a wide band of pain ran across her chest. She had trouble separating one pain from another in her legs and feet. She would spend two miles doing exactly that, she thought. There was a tight pain in her calves, a tighter pain in her hamstrings, threatening to cramp. She wouldn't let herself think about that possibility. The pain in her right hamstring was worse than the pain in her left. Quite a bit worse; it bit into her leg with every step. She'd never be able to make love tonight. *Poor Sandy. No. Don't think about*

Sandy. Back to running. Keep up the pace. The marker for mile twenty-two was just ahead.

The crowd was thick now, roaring in her ears. She kept her eyes straight ahead. For the next mile she'd focus on the sound of her footsteps, the rhythm they made with the footsteps of the other runners. How had it taken her twenty-two miles to notice that pattering sound? Like rain on a tin roof.

At mile twenty-three she began to cry. God, she hurt. The runners in front of her were wavy streaks of color. She must look foolish to the people lining the street. *Don't think about it. You're probably not the only person crying. Get back to the pain. Think about it objectively. Pick it apart.* The right knee, she thought. That was new. And it felt like her feet were bleeding. She didn't look down for fear her shoes had turned red with her blood.

Mile twenty-five. The home stretch. Oh God. There were TV cameras. People on the shoulders of other people. She saw it all through the edges of her vision. She loved the people running near her now. She didn't look at them, didn't know if they were men or women. She thought of how they were sharing something extraordinary. Her right calf was cramping, tight as a fist. She thanked it out loud for waiting until she was nearly done.

The finish line was ahead of her. People she didn't know were jumping up and down and screaming. She ran as fast and as hard as she could across the line and people grabbed her, pulled her to a grassy spot on the side of the road. She let them sit her down. They poured water on her head, made her drink. She must have been holding her calf because someone started rubbing it. And someone else yelled in her ear. "Five-seventeen . . . three hours, sixteen minutes."

She sat across from Sandy in a pancake house the next morning, working her way through a stack of pecan pancakes, high and wide. She hadn't been able to eat a thing the night before.

Sandy had bought a paper from the machine outside, and now he handed it to her across the table. She had no trouble finding the article: *Blair Doctor Speaks out on Lawsuit* was the headline. Her heart thumped against her ribs. It was a short article, and she skimmed it quickly. She smiled as she read Cole's quote out loud to Sandy.

"'There can be no winners in a suit like this. By the time the court makes a decision it will be too late to perform surgery on this baby. The parents will be left with no options, and I'll be left with the knowledge that I could have helped if Blair had had the funds to provide the necessary equipment. It's a situation without blame, and we are all losers.'"

She looked up at Sandy. "A whole lot better than no comment, I'd say."

17.

She lay on her back on the gym mat, five-pound ankle weights attached to her legs. Her stomach was perfectly flat under her blue shorts. She bent her knees, straightened her legs above her, and lowered them with a grimace, gripping the bench behind her with her hands.

The gym had been an unexpected bonus when she moved into the Chapel House. It had once been a second garage, and Jay, Janni, and Cole had gradually equipped it over the years. The room was now complete with weight machines, two ellipticals, a rowing machine, and free weights. There was a mirrored wall with a barre and a stereo system built into the cabinets under the only two windows. The gym seemed out of sync with the aged tranquility of the rest of the house. Nevertheless, it was well used.

She counted slowly to twenty-five, then sat up to ease her breathing. She watched the flakes of snow twirl outside the windows. People were saying it was unusual weather for the first week of November, that it was going to be a cold winter. She hated running in the cold. She could always use the indoor track at the Y, but that would never give her the training she needed. She wanted to break three hours in Boston. She thought she could. In her memory, Somerville hadn't been that hard. Three weeks had passed, and she'd forgotten the pain.

Cole groaned. She turned from the window to watch him. He lay on one of the padded benches, holding the barbell high above his chest. The thick muscles along the backs of his arms trembled. He let the bar down slowly, his face contorted, his chest and arms glistening. There was just a suggestion of extra flesh above the waistband of his black shorts. She liked that—a slight flaw that saved him from perfection.

It was at times like this, when she couldn't get her eyes or mind off him, that she thought again about moving out. Lately, when she made love to Sandy, she found herself imagining he was Cole. That frightened her, struck her as pathetic. She didn't know how she could free herself from that fantasy unless she got away from the Chapel House.

She owned that house on the lagoon in Point Pleasant. It was a good house, airy and clean, with a slip for a boat in the backyard. Her tenants' lease would be up in February. She couldn't think about it. Every time she thought about leaving she got a pain in the center of her chest—a clear warning, she was certain, to put the idea out of her mind.

Cole sat up now and looked at her. "Giving up?" he said.

"It's more fun watching you."

"I'm sure it's a lot easier watching me, too," he said, getting to his feet. He mopped his face with his towel before draping it around his neck. He'd been in good spirits lately. The media coverage of the lawsuit turned out to be a boon for the Fetal Surgery Program, generating far more public support than criticism. And the Carsellis had dropped the suit when a psychiatrist specializing in phobias read about their plight and offered to help Peggy get to Boston. They'd sent Cole a long letter of apology that he'd carried around with him for days, as if he couldn't quite believe it was over.

He sat down next to her on the mat and gave her a little shove with his shoulder. "Get those legs going, woman," he said.

She reached for the buckle on one of the weights. "I'm through for today," she said, pulling at the strap. "I called your mother again this morning. She won't meet me for lunch this week, either." She missed her afternoons with Virginia.

"Don't take it personally. She hasn't seen any of her friends since the surgery. I'm afraid she's never going to pull out of it."

"I thought of forcing myself on her, calling and saying I'm on my way and that I won't take no for an answer. I could bring lunch and she wouldn't have to go out or get dressed or clean the house. She'd have no excuse."

"I'd love you to do that." His old grin was back, lopsided and appealing, and she looked away from him, back outside to the falling snow.

"All right," she said. "I'll go tomorrow."

*

She knocked on the Perelles' door and waited. After a minute she rang the bell. Virginia had said she'd be in. "I don't go anywhere anymore," she'd said.

Kit stomped her feet and hugged the bag of Chinese food closer to her chest. She should have worn gloves and something heavier than her corduroy jacket.

She looked around the expansive front yard, remembering how the trees had formed a canopy over the lawn during the summer. Now the yard was littered with yellow leaves. She could barely see the lawn at all.

Virginia opened the door, and Kit had to force a smile to mask her shock. Before her stood a withered old woman, her skin colorless, her hair dull and uncombed. She wore a droopy beige terrycloth robe, flat where her right breast had been.

"You said not to clean or get dressed up," Virginia said. "I took you at your word."

"Well, I meant it, so that's fine." Kit moved past her, heading for the kitchen. It was hot and dark in the house. She felt as though she were fighting for air.

She pulled out a chair from the kitchen table and settled Virginia into it. She began opening the cupboards in search of plates.

"I'm not too hungry," Virginia said. "I warned you on the phone that I'm not good company these days."

"It doesn't matter. I wanted to see you. I've missed our lunches together."

"I'm not the same woman who used to be your lunch partner."

"It would be hard to go through what you have and

remain the same." She dished out small spoonfuls from each carton onto Virginia's plate, thinking that it looked like food for a child. She scooped twice as much onto her own plate. She was famished, as usual.

She set Virginia's plate in front of her. Virginia picked up the fork in her left hand and began slowly toying with the food.

"You're right-handed, aren't you, Virginia?"

"I can't use my right arm yet," she said. "It's so frustrating. You know what I feel like doing? What I really want to do? I feel like putting my face in this plate and eating off it like a dog. It'd be easier than trying to use my left hand."

"Oh, Virginia." Kit set down her own fork. "I'm so sorry you have to go through this."

"I'm not doing a good job of it either. Really, I thought I was stronger than this. Some days I want to give up. The chemotherapy makes me so sick I wish I were dead. And look what it's done to my hair."

She touched her left hand to her hair and Kit noticed that it wasn't just dull, it was thinning as well. Virginia's white scalp was clearly visible.

"I'm constantly checking my left breast for any changes. I think to myself, well, if I find a lump there I won't tell anyone. I think I'm actually hoping to find one. I'll let it grow and grow until it kills me."

"Please don't let that happen. You would be missed so much."

"Missed by whom?"

"By a lot of people. By Cole, for one, and Phillip. By your friends."

"They don't really care. They called in the beginning. 'Oh, we're sorry, how can we help? Blah blah.' Then they don't call again. Or when they do, they say, 'Cheer up, Ginny! Time to get on with your life.' They don't care about me, about the person that I am now. They want me to be the old Virginia, and she's gone forever." Virginia sat back in her chair. "I look at myself in the mirror and I can't believe what I see. I have to keep reminding myself it's gone for good. I'm not going to wake up tomorrow with my breast back."

"When can you have a prosthesis?"

"I have one," she said dully. "This woman came over from the hospital and brought it with her. I haven't tried it, though."

"I'd like to see it," Kit said. Pushiness seemed to be the right approach.

"Now?"

Kit nodded.

Virginia got to her feet with enormous effort and led Kit to the bedroom. The drapes were still closed, and the air was stale. She went to her dresser, took a plastic bag from the top drawer, and handed it to Kit.

Kit took out the prosthesis. It was made of clear plastic and filled with a jellylike substance.

"It has a wonderfully natural shape." She looked encouragingly at Virginia.

Virginia sighed and pulled a bra out of the drawer. "That needs to go in here."

Kit put the prosthesis in the cup of the bra, and Virginia untied her robe. Kit tried to turn away but she was too late.

There was the purple scar, the flattened chest wall. She wasn't sure what she had expected, but this was worse. She blinked hard, trying to hold back the tears, but they spilled over and rolled down her cheeks before she could stop them.

Virginia looked surprised. She closed the robe over her chest and pulled Kit to her with her good arm. Kit felt the bony frailness of Virginia's body under her own strong arms. She hugged her as tightly as she dared, feeling a part of what Virginia felt: maybe it wasn't worth it.

"I'm sorry, Virginia. It just hit me all at once what this must be like for you." She let go of her and took a tissue from the box on the dresser to wipe her eyes.

Without a word Virginia slipped her robe off. "Help me into this, okay?"

"Is it painful having a bra against it?"

"It's a strange feeling. It feels completely dead, yet overly sensitive at the same time."

She put the robe back on, holding it shut across her chest with her left hand, and looked at her reflection in the mirror. She smiled. "Not too bad," she said.

"No, it looks great!" It really did. She never would have guessed.

Virginia touched her hair and made a face at her reflection. "I can't wash my hair because of my arm. Phillip's done it for me a few times, and Corinne, but it's not enough."

"Let me wash it for you." She was already leading Virginia by the hand back to the kitchen.

"Just one thing, Kit," Virginia said as she leaned over the

sink. "Go gently. I'm afraid one of these times all my hair will go down the drain."

She dried Virginia's hair with a blow dryer, curling the fine strands around her fingers.

"So, how is my son doing?" Virginia asked over the sound of the dryer.

"He's fine. He's in better spirits now that Estelle's in therapy."

Virginia shook her head. "As a psychologist I feel blasphemous saying this, but I don't think therapy can change what's wrong with Estelle. I've never understood Cole's attraction to her. It pains me to think that he's taken in by the way she looks. I thought I raised him better than that."

"You have no reason to be critical of the way you raised Cole. He's a wonderful person."

Virginia smiled. "Are you in love with him, Kit?"

She tensed. "I love him a lot, Virginia, but there's no romance. There. You're dry." She snapped off the dryer and stood back to look at her work. "Pretty," she said. "You look radiant."

She moved to the kitchen table to fold up the cartons of cold Chinese food and to get away from Virginia's far too observant eyes.

18.

She woke to the sound of voices—Estelle's loud and cutting, Cole's a low rumble. She lay as still as possible, trying to make out the words. She caught a few of Estelle's, enough to know that the argument was in French.

She squinted to make out the time on her night table clock. Ten past midnight.

The door to Cole's room slammed shut, and the house shook from the sound. The quick footsteps on the stairs were unmistakably Estelle's. After a minute she heard a car start in the driveway, heard the spray of gravel as it pulled into the street.

Let her go, Cole.

She stared at the patchy moonlight on her ceiling and thought about him alone in his room across the hall, maybe shivering on his balcony as he watched Estelle drive away.

The wood floor was cold under her feet. It took her a few seconds to get her door open—it was stuck as though the house was giving her a second chance to go back to bed and mind her own business.

She slipped across the hall and knocked softly on his door.

"Yes."

She opened the door just enough to see into the dark room. "Do you want someone to talk with?"

"Come in."

He was sitting up against a pile of pillows in his four-poster bed under an old Amish quilt that covered him to his waist. It was strange to be in his room, in the dark, when she was certain he was wearing nothing under that quilt.

She sat down on the empty side of his bed, feet on the mattress, hugging her knees. Even in the darkness she could see the set of his jaw, the unsmiling look she'd seen only once before—the morning he'd called her a 'fucking bitch'.

"We've argued every night this week," he said.

She put her hand on his arm. Estelle's light autumn scent hung in the air around her.

"She actually seems worse since she's been seeing Frank," he said. "I tell myself she probably has to get worse before she'll get better, but she used to at least *try* to control her bitchiness. Now she doesn't seem to care who knows how crazy she is."

He was right. The only change she'd noticed in Estelle was that she no longer waited until Cole's back was turned to aim her barbs at someone. These days Cole himself was often her target.

"What happened tonight?" she asked.

He sighed. "She thinks sex solves everything. She thinks

her body is totally irresistible and when the fighting gets rough, she starts this . . . this come-on. The thing is, it usually works. It's a way of closing my mind to the problems, I guess. Anyhow, I'm sick of it and tonight it had no effect on me. Then she said I must be impotent." He laughed. "It would never occur to her that a man might not want to do it to her if he was physically capable of it."

The rough edge of his words excited her. His arm under her fingers was warm, almost hot.

"I can't be rational about her," he continued. "You know that time you told me I was wrapped around her finger so tightly that I couldn't think straight? You were right. That's why I got angry with you. You were right, and I couldn't stand to have you spell it out for me."

He was finally seeing the light. She felt happy, listening to him.

"She said she'd find someone else for tonight." He waited for her reaction.

"She's only trying to upset you."

"I don't think so. I think she meant it. And she won't have any problem finding someone either. There are plenty of men around here who've wanted her for years." He shuddered. "I can't stand the thought of her making love to someone else."

Kit nodded. "You've been together forever." She lifted her hand from his arm to brush a hair from her eye.

"Don't take your hand away, Kit."

She stared at him, knowing that he was asking for more than her touch on his arm. She could see the color of his eyes even in the dark. He was watching her calmly.

Without stopping to think, she ran her hand slowly across his chest, lacing her fingers in the hair. How long she'd been wanting to do that! She felt the staccato pounding of his heart under her palm. Her own heartbeat was even quicker.

He moved the hem of her robe aside and his hand cupped her calf, squeezing gently. A current of electricity shot through her and she knew that this was it. She couldn't have stopped if a train were about to run her over.

She lowered her hand to his stomach and felt the ridges of tight muscle beneath the soft skin. His hand slid up the inside of her thigh, and she shifted her legs until his fingers were where she wanted them. She clutched the edge of the mattress with one hand and the quilt with the other while he stroked her. She came in an instant.

She leaned forward to kiss him but he held her by the shoulders and laid her back against the quilt. Suddenly he was inside her.

What was happening? It was all too fast.

"Cole . . ."

He didn't seem to hear her. She felt his chin pressing into her shoulder, his movements against her body quick and careless. She stared at the ceiling, not bothering to move with him, and began to cry.

He finished quickly and rolled onto his back, and all she could think about was getting out of his room. She sat up and pulled her robe over her breasts. He hadn't even touched them. They ached from neglect.

"Don't go." He grabbed her arm as she tried to stand.

"I want to leave," she said, her voice breaking.

"Why are you crying?"

"Why do you *think*? I could have been some blow-up doll. You just needed to prove you could do it, didn't you? You needed to get back at Estelle."

He sat up. "I won't take all the blame for this, Kit. *You're* the one who came knocking on *my* door in the middle of the night. You got into *my* bed, and you rubbed my arm. I didn't lay a hand on you. And when I finally did, I don't remember hearing any protest. As a matter of fact, you seemed to enjoy it."

She looked down at the sheet, glad of the darkness so he couldn't see the color in her face. Was he right? Had she been asking for it?

"If I expected anything, it was to be made love to, not to get laid," she said. "I doubt you're usually such a lousy lover."

She braced herself for whatever he might do or say. But he turned and got up, walking slowly to the French doors that led out to his balcony. She lifted the quilt around her shoulders and watched him pull aside the curtain with one finger to look outside. A sliver of moonlight ran down his body. It was minutes before he spoke.

"Do you know how many times I've imagined making love to you?" he said without looking at her. "It was nothing like this. You said once that it would be a mistake for us to do it and I guess you were right. Too many things come into play." He turned toward her. "Maybe it will be out of our systems now. That would make it almost worth it."

Why was it so wrong for them to want each other?

Because she wasn't his type? An embarrassment to his good taste that he occasionally considered making love to her? There was a pocket of hurt in her chest that would never go away.

He was still holding the curtain aside and the thread of moonlight lit the tight line of his jaw and arced over his penis. "Could we please forget this happened, Kit?"

She got up and walked to the door. "There's not much else we can do, is there?"

She avoided him the next day. He called her office a few times but she told them not to put the calls through. She couldn't have put a label on her emotions. She snapped at her secretary for a typographical error, and started crying when a coworker complimented her on a job she'd done.

She didn't see him again until that evening. She was alone in the living room waiting for Sandy when Cole walked in. He had a glass of milk in his hand and he sat on the arm of the blue sofa.

"You didn't take my calls," he said. There was a little line of milk above his upper lip and he licked it off with a flick of his tongue.

"I was busy."

"I wanted to make sure you were all right after last night."

"I thought we were pretending last night didn't . . ." She let her voice trail off as Estelle came in the front door.

"Whew!" Estelle took off her scarf and blue fox jacket and hung them on the coat rack. "It's going to snow any second." She walked to Cole's side and kissed his temple, and he circled her waist with his arm. They had obviously made up sometime during the day.

Kit looked out the window into the dark night, feeling the soup she'd forced down at dinner at the back of her throat.

Sandy arrived around seven. She'd been looking forward to having his company to concentrate on, but his mood was worse than her own.

"Today's been pure shit." He stretched out on her bed. "I got busted."

"Oh, Sandy." She sat down on the window seat. It was hard to feel any sympathy for him.

"Cop stopped me for going ten miles over the limit and he searched my car. Smelled the weed, I guess. I spent a couple of hours locked up."

"They locked you up for marijuana?"

"I had a little coke, too. I don't do the stuff," he said quickly. "I was just transporting it for a friend."

She was too disgusted to speak. What if she'd been with him? She never should have let herself get so involved.

She ended it with Sandy the next day, over lunch in the hospital cafeteria. She was tired of his drug use, she told him, and of his irresponsible lifestyle. He looked hurt and she felt guilty. Her anger wasn't meant for Sandy.

She met with Cole after lunch. There was no way out of it—he had to see the article she'd written for the *Communicator* before it went to press.

He was contrite. "I don't want this to hurt our friendship," he said.

She wished she had the decision to make over again. She liked to think she would walk out of his room the second he touched her. But as she sat in his office, listening to his apology, all she could think about was the warmth of his hands on her skin.

19.

"Dr. Jansen's office." The voice was cold.

"This is Cole Perelle. I'd like to speak with Estelle Lauren, please. She's there for a four o'clock appointment."

He'd been busy at the hospital the past few days and hadn't had much time for Estelle. Tonight they could get back to normal. He'd have her meet him at Pierre's after her appointment and then let her talk him into the condo for the night.

But there was silence on the other end of the phone.

"Hello?" Cole said.

"Mr. Perelle, Ms. Lauren hasn't been to this office since her first appointment."

"I don't understand. You mean she's at some other office?"

"No, I mean she hasn't seen Dr. Jansen since the appointment she had here with you."

He couldn't speak. His mind raced with the lies she'd told him. *Therapy's going fine, darling. I'm so glad you talked me into it.*

He hung up his office phone without saying good-bye.

Maybe there was some explanation he was missing. Maybe she'd found a different therapist somewhere else.

Stop kidding yourself, he thought. *You've been duped.*

No wonder she seemed to be getting worse. She'd been deceiving him week after week. But then he hadn't exactly been honest with her lately either, had he?

He needed to talk with someone. Kit would have left for home by now, but Jay was probably still in his office. He took the elevator up to the fourth floor, his body nearly shaking with anger.

"Are you sick?" Jay asked when Cole walked into his office, and he knew he must look as wretched as he felt. He sat down next to Jay's desk, arms folded across his chest. The sun was setting over the river outside the office window. *His* window would have a view of the sun setting over the goddamn parking lot right about now.

"I just found out Estelle hasn't seen Frank Jansen since the appointment I went to with her."

"She's been lying to you all this time?"

He nodded. "She's crazier than I thought. How can I end it when she's so sick?" He was remembering his father talking about Corinne. "If she were physically ill, we'd do everything we could to help her," his father had said. "It's the same thing."

And they'd done everything they could, and Corinne, to this day, was still nuts. Did he want to spend the rest of his life this way? Why couldn't he end it?

"That was the deal, though, wasn't it?" Jay asked. "She goes to therapy or you split up, right? She knew the rules."

"But she's sick. What if Janni was in a car accident and wound up a paraplegic. Would you break up with her?"

"The analogy is very weak."

"Say she was mentally ill then. I can't see you pulling out on her."

Jay smiled. "What do you want to hear, Cole? Do you want to stay as miserable as you've been this past year? I didn't think you were that much of a masochist. You've given her every opportunity to change, and you've stuck by her through it all."

"I haven't been all that noble." He had to get that out. He was no saint.

Jay looked at him quizzically but said nothing.

"Maybe it would be easier to stay with her," Cole thought out loud. "Give her one more chance."

Jay was quiet for a minute. "It's your life," he said.

He'd been working out in the Chapel House gym for nearly an hour by the time she arrived. She perched on the edge of one of the benches, her legs crossed and everything about her beige and auburn. She looked out of place.

He crossed the room to stand in front of her. "How was therapy?" He hadn't planned on playing that game, but the words were out of his mouth before he could stop them.

"Fine." She smiled at him with her perfect teeth. Where had she been during that hour every week?

"Do you still like Frank?"

"A lot. Jealous?"

"I know you haven't been seeing him, Estelle."

She never lost her smile. "That's ridiculous. I go every week. Sit in that big chair and spill my proverbial guts."

"Stop lying to me."

"I'm not lying to you." How could she look so sincere?

"Look, I *called* there. They said you haven't been back."

"Why were you checking up on me?"

"I wasn't. I wanted to take you to dinner."

"Really? I'd love that." She stood up. "You'll need to take a shower first." She ran her fingertips down the damp hair of his chest.

He grabbed her hand. "Estelle, *stop* it! This is *serious*. I told you we'd split up. Is that what you want?"

She sobered. "Oh please, Cole, no. I love you so much." Her arms were around his neck, her perfumed body held a carefully controlled inch from his sweaty chest.

He pulled her arms away from him. "It's too late for that. I want you to get your things out of my bedroom and leave. Now."

She stared at him, her mouth open.

"Don't leave anything behind for me to bring over to you because I won't. I'll throw it away first."

"Oh, Cole, think what you're doing. *Six years*, Cole. You can't toss them away that easily." There was a catch in her voice that cut into him.

He turned and walked toward the bathroom at the end of the gym. "I'm going to take a shower," he said. "I want you gone by the time I get upstairs."

The following night, he poked at the chicken and rice on his plate while the conversation went on around him. He'd felt sick all day. Twice he thought he would actually vomit. He'd wanted to. He wanted to be cleaned out.

They were eating at the big oak table in the kitchen. Outside it was dark and beginning to snow. He could see the flakes swirling like dust in the light of the terrace. Behind him a fire crackled, the heat burning through his shirt and adding to his irritation.

Janni was talking about the Christmas Open House, worrying about the caterers and the decorations as she did every year. He tried to tune her out, but her voice grated at him.

"I hope the front deck is finished by then," she said. "It'll be an eyesore until they get it painted."

He hated that deck. It was too contemporary, didn't fit the house at all. "An eyesore?" he said. "It's an abomination. This beautiful house and you stick that monstrosity—"

"Cole, sweetie, I think you're exaggerating a bit," Janni said. "And besides, it's *my* house."

Go to hell, he thought.

"How many people usually come?" Kit changed the subject. He watched her scoop a gluttonous second helping of rice onto her plate.

"Last year there were close to three hundred," Maris said.

Cole groaned. He'd forgotten the press of people. In five days he'd be expected to play the genial host, the first time without Estelle on his arm. How would he ever tolerate three hundred people when he could barely tolerate his four old friends?

"What's the matter, sweets?" Janni squeezed his hand. "Are you wishing you didn't have to be here?"

He shrugged, twirling his milk slowly in his glass. "I don't know what I'm wishing," he said gloomily.

"If you want to go to a hotel or something while the preparations are going on . . . I mean if it would help you to have more quiet and privacy while you're, you know, adjusting . . . I'd understand."

"I'd like to move out of my life," he said and then realized how melodramatic that sounded. He smiled at Janni when he saw the serious look in her eyes. "Don't look so worried," he said. "I'm okay."

"I can't believe she left town that quickly," said Maris.

Neither could he. He should have handled it differently. He'd climbed the stairs after his shower the night before hoping she'd still be in his room waiting for one last chance to change his mind. But his room was empty. Every sign of her was gone. The picture of her that he'd kept on his dresser was lying face down on his bed, the glass cracked. He stared down at the dark driveway and thought he could see the reflection of the streetlight on her fender. But his eyes were only seeing what he wanted them to see.

He barely slept. In the middle of the night he changed his sheets to rid the bed of her scent. This morning he'd moved around his office in a fog, confusing one patient with another and thinking of Estelle four floors above him.

At noon he took the elevator up to the Research Department. All eyes were on him as he approached the receptionist. She looked amazed when he asked her to buzz Estelle's office.

"Dr. Perelle, Estelle quit this morning."

His heart beat twice and then seemed to stop.

"Oh yes," he said, as though he'd known all along that had been her plan. He raced downstairs again, anxious to get to the phone in his office.

There was no answer at the condo. He called her brother in Point Pleasant, but he hadn't heard from her in months. He played with the cord of the phone for a long time and then dialed her mother in Connecticut.

"She called this morning because she wanted the account number for an old trust fund," her mother said. "She said she'd be moving to New York and that she'd leave the condominium in the hands of a realtor. She didn't say you two were having problems. I thought you'd be going with her."

"No. We're through."

"Oh. Well, I'm sorry to hear that, Cole," she said. "But I know she could be hard to live with. I know that first-hand."

Everyone else had finished eating, but his plate was still full. It felt as though worms were crawling under his skin. He wanted to clear the table with a sweep of his arm and watch everything go flying. He'd love to see the shock on their faces.

They were beginning to get to him. All of them. Janni with her arrogance, her plans for everyone. Jay who was never bothered by anything. What would it take to get an angry word out of him? Maris and her never-ending neediness. She was sulking across the table from him right at that moment.

And of course, Kit. Every time she looked at him he saw the accusation in her eyes. Or maybe it was his guilt he saw reflected there. She was a constant reminder to him of what he'd done.

"You really don't look too well, Cole," she said now.

He stood up and ran both hands through his hair. "I'm going up to my room," he said.

Silence followed him up the stairs as they waited until he was out of earshot to talk about him. He didn't care.

Only one other person in the world could be feeling this empty. He dialed Estelle's mother again.

"Do you know how I can reach her?" he asked when she picked up.

She laughed at him. "She'll call me when she needs something, Cole, not before. She's probably in a hotel in New York while she's looking for a place to live."

Of course. He tried the two hotels she usually stayed at in the city. She wasn't at either of them.

He sat on the bed, staring at his hands. He wanted to crawl under the covers and go to sleep. But he was far too edgy, as if he'd been drinking coffee all day long.

He jumped when the phone rang and snatched the receiver from its cradle.

"Hello?"

"Cole, this is Stu Davies."

"Hello, Stu." *Estelle, where are you?*

"We've got the contract! Congratulations!"

It took a moment for the words to register, and when they did, he smiled for the first time all day. "That's *fantastic*," he said. "When can we start?"

"It'll be a few months yet. These things take time. But I want you to pick your team and get rolling on the training. Then let's get together with that PR girl so people will know that Blair's about to be put on the map."

20.

She felt like a voyeur. She sat in one of the wing chairs, tucked into the most remote corner of the living room, and watched the party unfold in front of her. She had moved among the guests for a few hours, long enough so that she could withdraw from them now with no pangs of guilt.

She took another swallow of the frothy pink daiquiri Maris had made for her. Her second. Or was it her third? On top of the eggnog and wine. Oh God. Well, it was only once a year.

All these people. They'd have to have the rugs cleaned next week. What a mess. She closed her eyes halfway, letting all the colors fuse together. White, red, silver, and gold. Her own dress was black, cut low in the back and clingy.

She opened her eyes again and spotted Janni in red, moving from group to group, patting arms and overseeing the work of the caterers. Maris looked slinky in silver. She hadn't stopped dancing for the past hour, except to mix drinks. Or maybe it hadn't been Maris who'd made her daiquiri. Kit couldn't remember.

Maris's dance partner tossed her across his back. Maris

might finally have met her match on the dance floor, Kit thought. This guy was good. His name was Sean and he looked like a surfer—long blond hair and a tan that had lasted well into the winter. He couldn't be more than twenty-five, but what did it matter? It was wonderful to see Maris having fun.

She hadn't seen Jay in an hour. Maybe more. Who knew what time it was? But there was Cole. He'd been milling all night, not spending too much time with any one person. News of the breakup had spread quickly and the women from the hospital were out in force. There had to be twenty of them here tonight with designs on him. She could tell by the way they eyed him from across the room and squeezed his arm when they got close enough. On the surface he looked good. Gray suit, dark hair, eyes that were liquefying the women around him. But she knew his smile was frozen in place. It hurt to watch him. She remembered too well how it felt to start over.

It had been a month since that night in his bedroom. They never talked about it. She put it out of her mind as best she could. She imagined that he had forgotten about it, that it took no effort on his part to keep it at bay. He had only one thing on his mind these days and that was Estelle. The breakup had left him dazed, brittle to the touch.

He'd finally spoken to her that morning while she was setting candles on the mantle in the living room. It had been days. She'd felt him pull away from her, from all of them. His eyes had told them to leave him alone as clearly as if he'd spoken the words out loud.

He'd come up behind her as she arranged the candles. "The house looks great," he'd said. "Can I help?"

Nearly everything had been done. An enormous tree decorated with white lights and lace stood in front of the oceanside windows of the living room. There were candles everywhere, holly and pine boughs on the mantel, and far too much mistletoe dangling in the doorways.

"The luminaria still need to be set up around the driveway," she'd said. The paper bags and candles were waiting by the front door.

Cole had looked at them uncertainly.

"Are you sure you want to be here for the party?" she'd asked.

"Where else would I go? Everyone I know will be here." He'd paused. "With one exception."

Now he walked toward her with a smile. "Can I take refuge with you for a few minutes?" He leaned on the arm of her chair.

"Party's getting to you?"

He sighed. "I'm not going to be any good at being single. I don't like all the superficial chatter. 'And what's your sign?'" He batted his eyelashes at her.

She laughed. "Come on. I bet no one's asked you what your sign is. Women are far more direct these days."

"You're right. I've had all types of invitations tonight. The last woman I spoke with asked to see the view from my room."

"What did you tell her?"

"That my room is a mess. She said I could leave the lights off so she wouldn't notice."

"Clever woman."

"I don't know how to respond to that sort of thing. I used to be able to come back with an innuendo of my own, knowing that I'd never be taken seriously with Estelle in the next room. Now I have to tread carefully."

"You really have no interest?"

"None. The thought of trying to get to know someone new is practically repulsive to me. And sex." He rolled his eyes. "I don't think I'll ever do it again. I understand now how you felt about sex when I first met you."

"I can barely remember that feeling. Right now there's little else on my mind." That was the only thing she missed about a relationship with a man these days—the physical side.

"Well," he said, "I spotted Sandy a little while ago."

"Sandy's here?"

"Someplace. I'm sure he'd be willing to oblige."

She shook her head. "That sounds like a bad idea. Besides, I've got my period."

"Really? That's two months in a row, isn't it? Rare for you."

She nodded. She was amazed herself. "This one's nearly over, I think. They're still not normal. Short and light. I guess they've started again because I haven't been running as much."

He was grinning at her. "How much have you had to drink tonight?"

"Why?"

"You're slurring."

"Ugh. Disgusting. Am I really?" Her words sounded perfectly crisp to her own ears.

He looked around the room. "We might have to put a few of these people up for the night if we don't get some coffee brewing. I think you should have the first cup."

"Whatever you say." She handed him the rest of her daiquiri. "If I hold it, I'll keep sipping."

He smiled at her. "Are we back to being friends again?"

"I hope so," she said. "I've missed you."

He leaned down for a hug and they moved apart. "Back to the maddening crowd," he said as he walked toward the heart of the living room, her daiquiri balanced between his fingers.

She should get up and help with the coffee, but the chair was holding her down. And besides, there was Sandy. He was leaning against the wall at the other end of the room, watching her, those big dark marble eyes locked into her own. She let herself stare back at him.

In a minute he was standing at the side of her chair. "You don't seem to be in a partying mood tonight," he said.

"I think I'm partied out."

"How about one more dance?"

"Okay." She stood up and nearly toppled over. "Whoa . . ." She grabbed his arm.

"Tsk, tsk, Kit." He put his arm around her. "Sloppy drunk. You never saw me sloppy stoned, did you?"

She set her cheek against his shoulder and let her head fill with his familiar scent. "I don't know how this happened, Sandy. I was sober one minute and looped the next."

"Let me take you upstairs and put you to bed."

She looked at him for a few seconds. "Okay," she said. "Wait here a minute."

She found Cole and pulled him away from a circle of women. "I'm going upstairs with Sandy." She didn't like the dark look in his eyes. She hooked her fingers in his jacket pocket. "Do you think that's a bad thing to do?"

He put his arm around her. "Take some coffee up with you, okay?" he said. "Just sober up a little before you make any decisions."

"I'm glad we had a chance to do this," Sandy said, after they'd made love. They were lying in her bed. "It'll be the last time. I'm moving."

Sandy leaving the Jersey shore? "Where to?"

"California. Santa Barbara."

"Really? I can't picture you there."

He laughed. "If you can't picture that, try picturing this: I'm getting married."

She sat up. "What?"

"I'm getting married."

"To who?"

"A lady friend."

"You were seeing her while you were seeing me?"

He frowned. "You knew I was seeing other people."

"But how could you have sex with me tonight when you're engaged to someone else?"

"She'd understand."

"Well, I don't." She was suddenly depressingly sober. She envisioned this young woman, innocently planning her wedding in Santa Barbara while her fiancé made love to someone else on the other side of the country.

Although she hadn't thought for a second about Estelle the night she . . .

"I shouldn't have told you," he said.

"Well, now that you have I really would like you to leave."

He gave her a look of disbelief before he got out of bed and pulled on his clothes.

"I didn't think you'd react this way," he said, his hand on the doorknob. "I thought you'd be happy for me."

He closed the door quietly behind him, leaving her feeling sober and a little ashamed.

21.

She let the hospital door fall shut behind her and started running toward the moon. She'd been watching it from her office window for the past hour, watching it lift into a black winter sky, and finally she could stand it no longer. She set her work on the corner of her desk where it would wait for her until morning, changed into her running clothes, dropped her work clothes off with Janni, and escaped.

A few flakes of snow fluttered in the air around her head as her footsteps fell into a steady rhythm on the sidewalk. She turned onto the main road and frowned at the bumper-to-bumper traffic and mounds of dirty snow piled in the gutter. She couldn't run on a street choked with cars on such a beautiful night. No, tonight she'd run home on the beach, next to the water.

She reached the beach by Jenkinson's Pier and ran for a while on the boardwalk, the rides surrounding her like huge, haunting monsters. At the end of the boardwalk she dropped down to the snow-covered sand, then ran out to the water's edge, where the sand was packed and ice-hard. It was eerily quiet. Most of the houses were deserted, boards on their windows, and the splintering sound of the sea was all she heard as the miles fell behind her.

The lights of the Chapel House were in view when she noticed someone on the beach. A huddled figure, sitting near the water.

Who would be out here, sitting alone on the beach on a January night? Some degenerate, probably, warming himself with a bottle of whiskey nestled in a paper bag at his side. Kit slowed her pace, wondering if she should cut back up to the road to avoid an encounter with whoever this might be.

But it was more likely someone like herself, lured to the beach by the moon. She picked up her pace again.

It was a girl. A child? No, a little older than that. Thirteen, fourteen at the most. She was the only patch of color on the beach. Long, pale brown hair, gray pants, and a red sweater. Just a sweater? Kit herself wore a heavy warm-up jacket.

She slowed to a stop and smiled at the girl. "Hi," she said. The sweater was thin, dotted with snowflakes. "Aren't you cold? It's no more than thirty degrees out here."

The girl looked up, her huge eyes shining in the moonlight. Something was wrong with her. Drugs maybe? No, she didn't look the type.

"Are you all right?" Kit asked.

The girl shook her head, and Kit saw that she was holding a blood-stained tissue to her chin. Her left cheek was swollen and bruised.

Kit dropped to her knees. "Someone's hurt you."

The girl looked down at the sand. "Two men," she whispered between chattering teeth. Her lips were blue.

Kit took off her warm-up jacket and wrapped it around the girl's shoulders. "Where? Who?"

The girl shut her eyes.

"Do you live nearby?"

She shook her head.

"Where do you live?"

She hesitated a second before answering. "A few towns over."

"What are you doing out here? Did you know the men who hurt you?"

The girl stared at her sneakers, at the toe where the threads were threatening to pull apart and let in the winter air.

She's frightened by the questions, Kit thought. Trying to fabricate answers in a mind not used to lying. What this kid needed right now was help; the interrogation could wait. "Never mind," she said. "Let me take you to my house. We can get you washed up and call the police from—"

"No, no, no!" The girl shook her head furiously, her hair whipping the air. "They said they'd kill me if I told anyone what happened."

Kit nodded. "I won't let them hurt you." She made the promise as though she knew how to keep it. "Tell me your name."

"Rennie."

"Well, look, Rennie. Let's go to my house and at least get you cleaned up. Let me see your chin."

Rennie held the tissue away from her face, and Kit could

see that the wound was wide, the skin ragged along its edges. It would probably need some stitches. "Keep pressing the tissue against it while we walk," she said. She stood up but Rennie didn't move.

"I don't think I can walk. My chest hurts when I move. Across here." She set her hands on her red sweater, along the bottom of her rib cage.

"Did they hit you there?"

Rennie shook her head. "They threw me against that wall." She pointed toward the house behind them, boarded up for the winter. A long concrete wall ran the length of the patio. Kit winced. This girl was probably lucky to be alive.

Then she noticed the dark stain in the crotch of Rennie's pants.

"Are you bleeding?" she asked.

Rennie looked at her in confusion and pointed to her chin with her free hand.

"No, honey, not there. Tell me, did they rape you?"

The girl began to cry. There was no sound, just rivers of tears flowing down her cheeks. "I can't go home," she said "I *can't*."

"It's all right. We'll get you to the hospital, get you fixed up—"

"No!"

"You have no choice. You're hurt. The hospital will be legally bound to call the police, but you don't have to press charges." She was talking rapidly now, her heart pounding in her chest. What if the girl was hemorrhaging? She had to get her to Blair quickly. "Stay here. Don't move."

She turned and ran toward the Chapel House, glancing behind her to see the girl hunched over her knees again, staring out to sea.

She called the ambulance and then Cole.

"Aren't you on call for the Emergency Room this week?" she asked.

"Uh-huh. Why?"

"I found a girl on the beach who I'm pretty sure has been raped. I called an ambulance to bring her over. Can you meet us in the ER?"

"The ER can handle it without me. Unless she's really messed up."

"I think she may be."

She heard him sigh. It was six-thirty and certainly he wanted to get home, but she didn't have time to sympathize. "Do you know if Janni's still there?" she asked.

"I don't know."

"Could you look out your window and see if her car's there?"

The sigh again. She heard his chair creak as he leaned back to look out the window toward the parking lot.

"Yeah, I see it."

"Call her please, Cole. This kid's going to need a social worker."

If Kit had any doubts about Rennie's story, they disappeared as she watched her being lifted into the ambulance. Lines of pain creased Rennie's face. On the ride to Blair, she squeezed Kit's fingers in her hand each time the ambulance took a turn or hit a dip in the road.

"Don't let them send me home," she begged.

Kit leaned down to give the girl a hug. Rennie nestled in her arms as though a loving touch was so rare that she would take it from a stranger.

22.

He was sidetracked a few times on his way to the E.R. He was certain they could handle this without him. If it were truly an emergency, they would have paged him. God, he hated rape cases. Always felt like the enemy.

He saw her first through the little square window of the treatment room. She sat on the examining table with her back to him, clutching Kit's arm through the warm-up jacket. Janni stood in front of her, talking, writing things on her notepad. The inch or two of the girl's back visible beneath the ties of the hospital gown looked as if she'd been dragged by her heels across a bed of nails.

Janni came out of the room to greet him. She rolled her eyes as she handed him the girl's chart.

"Good luck with this one, sweets," she said. "She's not going to let you near her. She's afraid of her own shadow."

"What's wrong with her back?"

Janni looked through the window of the treatment room. "Scraped raw. So's her front. Plus a cracked rib. And she needed seven stitches in her chin. She's bleeding, too. Don't know what that's all about—that's your department." She paused to take a breath. "There's a couple of swine running loose on the Mantoloking beach. *Mantoloking*. Do you believe it?"

"What do you mean, a couple?"

"There were two of them. Real bastards. I tell you, this kid's a mess. And her family situation leaves something to be desired, too. Said she ran away 'cause her mother's boyfriend was beating her up. I've got to call Protective Services—she'll have to go to the Children's Center for a while, where she'll very likely be eaten alive." Janni made a face. "Poor little kid. She's sweet."

He wasn't really listening. "Did they take evidence yet?"

"Nail scrapings, I think. They're leaving the rest for you. No one wants to hurt her. The doc stitching up her chin stumbled all over himself apologizing to her."

The girl wanted nothing to do with him.

"Hello, Rennie. I'm Dr. Perelle." He held out his hand, but she didn't look up from her lap. He dropped his hand to his side.

Kit moved in front of the girl. "Rennie, Dr. Perelle is a good friend of mine."

Rennie hung her head, the tips of her long, earth-colored hair touching the gown that covered her thighs. Her hands rested limply in her lap, the fingers thin and delicate, the nails chewed short.

"Your chart says you're having some bleeding. Could you be having your period?"

The girl shook her head without looking up. He could see the stitches in her chin, the skin around them raw and bruised.

"Can you tell me when your last period was?"

She shrugged.

He shifted the chart to his left hand. "I know you've had a terrible time, Rennie, and no one here wants to make it any harder for you, but we have to make sure you're all right."

"I'm okay." The childish voice surprised him.

"Do you know what a pelvic examination is?"

"I don't need an examination."

"I explained it to her," said Kit.

"It's very important to find out what's causing the bleeding," he said.

"Please don't." She looked up at him, her blue eyes wide.

Wendy and Becky, he thought. She had his nieces' eyes, ten years from now. He looked at Kit, wondering if she saw the resemblance, but her gaze was on Rennie. She brushed a strand of the girl's hair back over her shoulder.

"It'll all be over in a matter of minutes," she said.

Rennie began to cry, head in hands, shoulders shaking, and he shook his head at Kit. He was not about to hurt this girl with his nieces' eyes.

He called Barb Chrisman in the Maternity Unit and told her there was a rape victim in the ER who could use a woman gynecologist. She examined Rennie while he told the police officer the little he knew. It was hard to concentrate on the questions when he could picture what was happening in the treatment room, step by step. Would they have to take pictures? Probably, with all those scrapes and bruises. And pluck fifteen pubic hairs for forensics. He cringed at the thought. He'd always handed the tweezers over to someone else.

After the police left, he sat in the waiting room watching a rerun of M*A*S*H. Next to him a woman cuddled a feverish-looking toddler, and across the room, a man held a wad of tissues to his son's bloody nose. He focused his attention on the TV. He felt more squeamish out here than he did in the treatment room.

Janni came out of the reception office and sat next to him, her notepad covered with telephone numbers. There was something strange about the way she was looking at him.

"Cole, I did something crazy," she said, her tone confessional. "I talked Protective Services into letting us take her . . . temporarily, I mean, until they find a foster home."

"Are you nuts? What are we going to do with a fourteen-year-old kid?"

"We're going to make her feel welcome and safe, that's what." She took off her glasses and leaned toward him, her bangs grazing the bridge of her nose, and he knew he was in for one of her lectures.

"The county social worker called her mother, who hadn't even notified the police that her daughter was missing. And you know what she said? She said, 'can you keep her somewhere for a while? I'm going on vacation.' Apparently they lived with Rennie's grandmother, who died in June— she was sort of Rennie's protector, I guess—and things have fallen apart since then. Plus, she's got old bruises on her. Stuff from her mother's boyfriend. He's beaten her a few times, and she ran away 'cause he was telling her he'd sneak into her room at night. So tell me, sweets, would you really want to see a girl like that stuck in the Children's Center with all the rowdy kids they've got there?"

"Did you check this idea out with Jay?"

"He'll say yes."

Of course he would. Cole shook his head, thinking that Janni would be delighted if she could fill all ten bedrooms in the Chapel House. "You're one of a kind, Jance," he said.

Rennie's injuries were worse than he'd imagined. Kit came out of the treatment room, glassy-eyed. "They *brutalized* her," she said.

"Why was she bleeding?"

"A tear. Barb had to stitch it. She has a cracked rib. Plus, one of them *sodomized* her."

He winced, happier than ever that he'd turned this one over to Barb.

"I don't think she should be coming home with us," Kit said. "She's afraid of men. She's afraid of *you*."

That bothered him, and he was suddenly glad she would be at the Chapel House. He wanted to win this kid over.

23.

"I've never seen a bedroom this big." Rennie stood at the window that looked out toward the ocean. She had the largest of the spare rooms, at the end of the hall next to Janni and Jay's bedroom. The wallpaper was a bold floral pattern that Kit imagined looked better in this muted, faded state than it had long ago when it was new. But she liked the twin iron beds and huge chest of drawers. She wondered about the history of the room. What self-confident woman in Janni's ancestry had selected this wallpaper?

Rennie moved from window to window, one hand spread flat against her cracked rib. "The only view I ever had at home was of the dumpster in the Safeway parking lot."

Kit sat on the extra bed watching her with a smile, glad now that they hadn't let her go to the Children's Center.

"Do I have to talk to the police tomorrow?" Rennie asked.

"Yes." The police were sending a detective in the morning. "It'll be okay."

"I'm afraid they'll make me go home."

Kit shook her head. "No one is planning on sending you

home." Imagine being fourteen and so afraid to go home that you'd be willing to live with strangers.

Rennie sat down on the bed and stroked the flannel nightgown Kit had set there for her. Her eyes were on the open door. "Is there a key for that door?"

Kit looked at the empty keyhole. "I'm sure there's one somewhere. I'll ask Janni."

"At home I pushed my dresser in front of my door every night, to keep Craig out."

"Your mother's boyfriend?"

Rennie nodded. "He told me he was going to . . . do things to me. I always slept with my clothes on."

"You don't have to do that here. No one in this house would hurt you."

"Can I keep the closet light on?"

"Of course."

Rennie looked at her. "Would Dr. Perelle have done the same things to me that Dr. Chrisman did?"

"You mean examined you and stitched you up?"

"Yes, and . . . everything."

Kit nodded. "Probably exactly the same. He and Dr. Chrisman trained together. He . . ."

They turned at the sound of a knock on the door.

Cole stood in the doorway, holding a blue parka. "Is this your jacket, Rennie?"

"Yes." Rennie looked surprised.

He handed the jacket to Rennie, and Kit smiled her thanks at him. She'd asked him to stop by the house where the attack had happened to see if he could find it. The men had stolen Rennie's knapsack, and the police had taken her clothes for evidence. She was left only with the jeans and sweatshirt Janni'd dug up for her in the hospital's emergency clothing supply. She had nothing of her own.

Rennie bundled the jacket to her chest, hugging it like a teddy bear. She looked up at Kit. "Could you ask him if he found anything else?"

"He's right here, Rennie. You can ask him yourself." She felt sorry for Cole. He was trying hard with her.

"You mean your knapsack?" he asked. "I didn't see it."

Rennie tightened her arms around the jacket. "There was . . . a special thing in it."

"Like what? What would I look for?"

Rennie hesitated. "A plastic box. Just . . . don't open it, please, but bring it to me if you find it."

24.

Cole stayed home with Kit and Rennie the next day, waiting for the detective. Rennie avoided him. She clung to Kit, following her everywhere in the house like a puppy.

He'd spent a half-hour at the boarded-up house just after sunrise, looking for her knapsack. But there was nothing in the yard except melting snow and brittle sea grass.

The detective was a woman, Grace Kelleher. She was dressed in gray slacks and a gray sweater and had silver hair, cut to her chin. A wonderful blend of grandmother and cop.

"I'm glad you're a woman," he said, taking her coat.

"I'm glad I was available."

He led her to the dining room, and the four of them sat at one end of the table. Grace introduced herself and switched on a tape recorder. Rennie glued her eyes to it as if she'd never seen one before.

"Just tell me in your own words what happened," Grace said softly.

It suddenly occurred to him that he shouldn't be there, but Rennie had already begun.

"Well, I was walking down the street by the beach, looking for a place that was, you know, protected a little—like the porch of one of those closed-up houses—where I could spend the night. I was walking past this one house when I saw these two men walking toward me on the sidewalk. I felt nervous 'cause they didn't look like the kind of people who live in a neighborhood like that—like this. They walked right past me. Then all of a sudden one of them grabbed me around the shoulders and I could feel something cold . . . I figured out later it was a knife, against . . ."

"Did you see the knife?" Grace asked.

"Yes. Well. Later I did."

"Go on."

"He said, 'Don't scream or I'll slit your throat.' I don't think I could have screamed, I was so scared." She glanced up at Grace and returned her gaze to the recorder.

"Can you describe the men?"

Rennie hesitated. "It was dark."

"Any information will be helpful. How tall were they?"

"Pretty tall, I think, and more skinny than fat."

"White? Black?"

"White."

"Hair color?"

"I don't know. They both had on, you know, ski caps." Rennie lifted her hands to her head in a halfhearted parody of putting on a ski cap.

"Can you remember their eyes?"

Rennie shook her head. "It was dark and I didn't look at

them long. I tried to, though, 'cause I heard once that if you try to make them see you as a human being then it might make them change their minds. But I couldn't look at them long enough for it to work."

He could imagine her desperately trying to lock eyes with those pigs when she could barely hold the gaze of people who cared about her for more than a second or two.

"What happened after he told you not to scream?"

"The one with the knife dragged me behind that house. He told me to take my jacket off, and I did." Rennie looked at Grace, then at Kit. "Do you think if I'd kept it on they would have just left me alone?"

"I don't think that would have made any difference," said Grace.

"I keep wondering if maybe I might have looked at them when they walked past me or something. And maybe they thought I, you know, wanted them to do it."

Kit was angry. "Rennie, no matter how you looked at them, it's no excuse for what they did. You didn't ask to be raped."

Grace put a hand on Kit's arm. "Please, Kit, let's let Rennie finish her story."

He wished he was sitting next to Kit so he could take her hand under the table. But it was probably better this way; touching her always seemed to be a mistake.

"I took my jacket off," Rennie said, "and then real fast he grabbed the neck of my sweater and like, bent me back over the wall."

For the first time Cole noticed the purple marks on her throat. Wendy's throat. And the way she tilted her head when she asked a question—didn't Becky do that? The muscles in his hands contracted almost painfully. He could kill right then. No problem, no regrets.

He looked at Kit. Her eyes were on him and he wondered what she'd seen in his face.

"The other guy held me back over the wall while the first one, the one in the Army jacket, um . . . did it." She looked directly at Grace. "It hurt," she said in a bewildered voice.

Shit. He looked out the window at the house next door. Salt was eating away at the paint; it was curled and puckered here and there. From the corner of his eye he saw Grace nodding sympathetically.

"Go on, Rennie," she said.

"I don't know what else to say."

Grace waited a few seconds before she spoke. "The exam showed that you were sodomized," she said gently.

Rennie looked at Kit, her eyes questioning. "She means anal sex," Kit said and Rennie looked quickly back at the recorder, blushing to the roots of her hair.

He had no right to be witnessing this. "Would it help if I left, Rennie?" His voice sounded deep and loud to him. She nodded without looking up. "Excuse me," he said to Grace as he rose from his chair.

He picked up his jacket from one of the chairs in the kitchen and walked out the back door. He didn't stop until he reached the far edge of the beach heather. He squinted into the sun. The water was blue-violet, no boats for as far as he could see. Odd for a Saturday with the sea as smooth as glass. He blew on his hands. The icy wind made his eyes tear, but he didn't want to go back inside. It occurred to him how much of his life was spent avoiding anything that could cause him pain. So that was normal, wasn't it? And anyhow, he'd left for Rennie's sake, not his own.

Rennie had looked frightened two days later when he told her the drive to Corinne's would take an hour. He wanted to tell her not to worry. He was harmless. Yet he said nothing. He'd have to show her. Prove it to her. She'd been lied to before.

Now she sat as close to the car door as she could get. Her hand was actually on the handle, which made him nervous. Sixty miles an hour on the parkway and she accidentally pulls back on the handle and then . . . *Don't think about it. And don't tell her to let go of it, either.*

Conversation was strained, at best. She was pretending to be mesmerized by mile after mile of bare trees and snow. She hadn't looked at him since they'd gotten into the car. He tried asking her questions about herself but never got more than a yes or no, whispered against the glass of the window. Poor kid. When he told her he was taking his nieces ice skating, why didn't she come along, she'd looked too scared to object. He loaded her into the car without giving her a chance to say no.

He was smitten by her, by those wide, innocent blue eyes and pudgy little-girl cheeks. Her smile was so rare, so ephemeral that he found himself trying to prolong it. He would stand on his head if he thought it would work.

"How old did you say your nieces are?" She surprised him with the question, her first words spoken without prompting.

"Five," he said. "In kindergarten. Do you like little kids?"

"Yes."

"You don't have any brothers or sisters of your own?"

"No."

"Do you wish you did?"

"Sometimes."

He tried to think of a question she couldn't answer in one or two words. "When was the last time you went skating?"

"I never ice skated before. I roller skated, though."

He had to strain his ears to hear her. "My sister and I used to skate on the lake I'm taking you to practically every weekend during the winter," he said.

She didn't answer. Her breath formed a cloud on the window.

They stopped at Corinne's to pick up Wendy and Becky. The twins were bundled up so snugly they could barely move as he buckled them into the backseat.

"They are *so cute*," Rennie said.

Seeing the three of them together surprised him. Rennie actually looked very little like his nieces. Wendy and Becky had delicate angular features, while Rennie's face was as round as the sun. Their eyes were nothing at all alike. The twins' eyes were greener. How had he ever seen a resemblance?

Rennie was a natural on skates, even with her sore rib. She held Becky's hand while he held Wendy's, and they glided around the lake, laughing more often than not.

Rennie helped him corral the girls when they tried to go off on their own. Watching his nieces, he had to admit that they had no signs of Corinne's craziness, at least not yet. Nothing scared them. If anything, he wished they were a little *more* fearful.

After a while, he pleaded exhaustion so he could sit on a bench and watch the three of them. The girls clung to Rennie, relishing her attention. She was good with them. More comfortable without him there, he thought. Certainly more child than woman. She took to their games as though she'd played them only yesterday. But when Wendy fell, landing with such force that he feared the ice would crack, Rennie wiped the little girl's tears with a tissue. Even made her blow her nose. She kissed her cheek, and then Becky plowed between them to get a kiss of her own. He wondered what it was about Rennie that made you love her from the moment you set eyes on her.

They ate lunch at a tiny lakeside inn, which hadn't changed since he'd eaten there as a child. It still smelled of wet wool and burning wood. They got a table in front of the fireplace, and Cole ordered Reubens for Rennie and himself and peanut butter and jelly for the girls.

"It's hard to believe that was your first time on ice skates, Rennie," he said.

She looked at the flames. "I didn't think I did that good. I wish I could skate backward like you do."

"I'll teach you after lunch. Really, I think you have a natural feel for it."

"Where's my sandwich?" Becky leaned against him.

He put his arm around her. "We just ordered it, Beck. It takes a few minutes for them to make it."

She pouted at him. "Shit," she said.

Shit? Out of the mouth of a five-year-old? She was testing him.

"I don't like that word, Becky," he said.

"Neither does Mommy," Wendy said. "And Becky says it anyway. All the time."

"I do not."

"Okay, enough. Please don't use it anymore this afternoon." He sent Rennie an aren't-kids-something-else smile across the table, and she dropped her gaze to her silverware.

"Last time we were here 'Stell was with us," said Wendy.

"That's right," he said "You have a good memory."

"D'you know 'Stell?" Becky asked Rennie.

Rennie looked to him for the answer.

"Estelle was my girlfriend," he said. "We split up and I haven't figured out how to pass that information on to these two yet."

She nodded.

The waitress set their sandwiches in front of them and the girls immediately lost interest in the conversation.

He had a sudden brainstorm, a way to get Rennie talking. "Do you have any suggestions?" he asked. "I mean on how I can break it to them about Estelle?"

She shook her head and picked at the sauerkraut spilling out of her sandwich.

He took a bite, washed it down with a swallow of Dr. Pepper. "Help me, okay? You're closer to being five than I am. How can I tell them that she'll no longer be a part of my life?"

She bit her lip. "Do they like her?"

"They love her."

"Will they ever get to see her again?"

He shook his head. "Very doubtful."

"Don't tell them that. Tell them she's gone away for a few months or something, and after a while they'll forget about her."

He didn't like the answer, but it was not really good counsel he was after.

"I guess I could do that," he said. "But I'd feel dishonest. Then if they ever figured out that I lied to them, they'd have a hard time trusting me again, don't you think?"

She dropped her gaze, but not before he'd seen the tears in her eyes. What had he said to bring that on? Kit hadn't wanted him to take Rennie with him at all today. Wait until he got home and told her he'd made the kid cry.

"What did I say that upset you?" he asked.

She shook her head, her eyes already dry. "Nothing."

"I wasn't criticizing your answer, Rennie. I was only trying to think it through."

"It's mean to tell a little kid she'll never see someone she loves again," she said.

"Ah." He was relieved. It was nothing he had done. "Maybe you're right. I wonder if there's a way to tell them the truth without being mean."

She was an excellent student. He taught her to skate backward in a couple of minutes. The hard part was not touching her. Not taking her hand or guiding her by the shoulders. He never could keep his hands to himself. Had to be touching somebody all the time. There were probably people in his life who were bothered by it. His male colleagues, no doubt. He'd been careful about touching men until he met Jay. With all those brothers in an Italian household, Jay had never learned it was taboo.

But he didn't touch Rennie. Not until she was getting into the car and he chanced the flat of his hand on her back.

She stiffened. Threw her shoulders back to get rid of him, and he dropped his hand quickly.

Too fast, Perelle.

He scooped Wendy up in his arms and buckled her into the backseat, then did the same with Becky. One day he'd have to stop touching them, too.

25.

Kit wandered around the cafeteria searching for Cole, trying to remember where they'd agreed to meet. Finally she spotted him, waving to her from one of the small tables by the windows. All morning she'd thought about a quiet, private lunch with him. Rennie had been in the Chapel House for only three weeks, but she already owned the rooms and the air that filled them.

She liked Rennie, maybe even loved her. Still, she couldn't shake this irritable feeling that had been dogging her for the past few weeks. Maybe it had more to do with Cole than Rennie. Since Estelle left, he'd thrown himself into his work. She felt more cut off from him now than before.

She'd been thinking again about moving out of the house. It was too late to give her tenants notice that she wanted to move into the Point Pleasant house—she'd let that deadline slip by without a second thought. And what good would it do her to move out of the house when she'd still be working here at Blair, still seeing him each day, still wondering exactly how he was spending his nights? No, if she moved, it would have to be away from the shore, maybe out of New Jersey. But she couldn't leave yet, she told herself, not when Rennie's situation was so uncertain. She was Rennie's main lifeline right now. It wouldn't be fair.

"Do you realize how long it's been since we've had a chance to talk, just the two of us?" she said, setting down her tray.

"I don't have time to think anymore, much less talk."

"How's the fetal surgery training going?"

"Fantastic." He brightened. "Really well. We'll be ready to open the doors March first."

She watched him cut the liver and onions on his plate. His eyelashes were long and straight, his face full of concentration. It had been weeks since she'd let herself study him and she was filled with sadness. She guessed that any attraction he'd felt for her had vanished. After all, he'd had her now, in the flesh, and it had left him with nothing but regret.

He looked over at her tray. "That's all you're eating?" he asked.

She looked down at the tomato soup and corn muffin. "I don't have my usual appetite lately. Haven't been running hard enough, I guess."

"When does the serious training begin?"

"Saturday. Three weeks of speed, then three of hills, three of endurance, and three of putting them all together." And then Boston. Finally.

A nurse dressed in blue scrubs nipped at the waist walked by their table, drawing her hand across Cole's shoulders as she passed. "Hello, Cole," she said, her voice so breathy she sounded winded.

He glanced up. "Hi, Lynn," he said absently.

Kit watched the nurse walk away from them. "Are you ready for someone new?" she asked.

He wrinkled his nose. "No."

"They're ready for you. That nurse and a hundred like her." Women had been calling the house for him since Christmas.

"Lynn is a *doctor*, Kit."

"She is? She looks about twenty-five."

"Twenty-eight, I think."

That depressed her. Where did these women get their role models? How come she'd missed out? She watched Cole take a bite of liver off his fork, and her stomach lurched.

"I have to compliment you on the way you've handled Rennie," she said, trying to get her mind off food.

"I like having her around. I hope it takes them a long time to find a foster placement for her. The whole situation has kept my mind off . . . other things."

She knew he meant Estelle.

"Do you miss her?"

He sighed. "I miss knowing I had someone to talk with and go out with and sleep with. But I don't actually miss Estelle herself, not the way she was at the end, anyway. I think about her, though. I wonder if she'll ever be happy."

Kit thought Estelle's concept of happiness was nothing like Cole's or her own. Pure joy and pure sorrow would never exist for her.

Cole took a swallow of milk and leaned back in his chair. "I wish Rennie wasn't still afraid of me. I feel like an ogre around her. She's such a little waif, and life is so overwhelming for her. If she were my daughter, I'd tuck her away in a closet until she turned twenty-one."

"And when she got out she'd have had no experience coping with anything. You'd have to take care of her for the rest of your life."

"Fine." He smiled.

She picked up a piece of the corn muffin and put it in her mouth. She swallowed it and made a face. "Nothing tastes good to me these days." She pushed her tray away. "I really don't understand why no one ever told me I could be a doctor."

She got up early on Saturday and looked out her window. Good. No snow on the beach. It was January twenty-fourth, twelve weeks before the Boston Marathon. Eight miles to run this morning. She shivered. It must have been the cold that made that task seem monumental.

She dressed painstakingly, wanting everything to be perfect. First the T-shirt, then the sweatshirt, then the sweater. The jacket on top of all that. She smeared Vaseline on her face and pulled her cap low over her ears.

The sand was hard and firm under her feet. Her lungs had gradually adjusted to the cold, but today they were tight. Every breath felt like fire in her chest. She wished she had goggles. Something to protect her eyes. They were watering, and the beach was a blur. *Damn it.* Her nose was running and she had forgotten a tissue. What was wrong with her today?

Maybe the winter would be too much for her after all.

But an indoor track? For the Boston Marathon? She envied those runners with the money to move to a warmer climate while they trained.

She zipped her jacket up to her chin. *Stop being such a baby.*

But something was very wrong. She'd run six miles when she knew she had to stop. She tried to slow down gradually, but a wave of nausea came over her and she dropped to her knees and vomited into the sand. She knelt there for several minutes, shaking and breathless. She couldn't remember the last time she'd gotten sick to her stomach.

She rinsed her mouth with ice-cold salt water and headed home slowly. Was she that out of shape? Pushing too hard too fast? Or maybe it was the flu. She wasn't sure which condition to hope for.

The Chapel House was in sight when she began to retch again. *Oh fine*, she thought, annoyed with herself. *Off to a great start.*

A week later, she felt even worse, barely able to summon the energy to get up in the morning, much less run. That Saturday morning, she stayed in bed, watching her night table clock tick its way to ten-thirty. She was sleeping all the time these days. Janni and Maris thought she must be depressed. *Why aren't you eating?* they'd asked her. *How come you're not training harder?* She laughed their questions off. She had no answers.

She jumped at the sound of a knock on her door and sat

up quickly. She'd hate for anyone to catch her still in bed. But it was only Rennie.

She sat down on the very edge of Kit's bed, her American history book in her lap. "Are you sick?" she asked.

Kit smoothed the blanket over her knees, hoping Rennie wasn't looking for help with her history homework. "I'm just tired and I'm not running well. I'm wondering if I'll ever be able to run a marathon again." She caught herself—she hadn't meant to give words to her fear. "But enough about my problems. What's on your mind?"

Rennie had confided in her the past few weeks. About the times Craig beat her, how his threats of sex kept her in a state of terror. And about her grandmother, but that wound was deep and the words hadn't come easily. She'd told her about the rapists, about their taunting and the pain. She'd told her enough to make Kit sleep fitfully for a week.

"I think Cole thinks it's my fault that I was raped," she said now.

"That's crazy. He doesn't think any such thing."

"That's why I wanted to talk to you. You always know what he's thinking. It's like you and Cole are two people with one mind."

Kit liked the description. "He cares about you a lot."

Rennie looked down at her history book. "Is there something wrong with his eyes?"

"What do you mean?"

"They're so weird. It's like you can see the white through the colored part or something."

Kit laughed. "His eyes are unusual but they're normal eyes. His mother's are like that, too."

It was a few seconds before Rennie spoke again. "I just don't understand why a man would want to be a doctor for women."

So that was it.

"Could you ask him, Kit? Why he's a . . . you know, that kind of doctor, and then tell me his answer?"

"I know his answer, but it won't do you any good coming from me. Why don't I tell him you'd like to talk to him when he gets home today?"

"No."

Kit leaned toward her. She was going to have to get tough on this. It was the only way. "You have to," she said. "You can't continue to live in this house for who knows how long pretending he doesn't exist."

26.

The call from Kit pleased him. He hoped he could finally put an end to the tension between himself and Rennie.

She was waiting for him in the kitchen when he got home.

"I heard you wanted to talk to me." He took off his coat and unwound the scarf from his neck.

She shrugged, looking for all the world as if she couldn't care less. "I guess," she said.

"Well, let me get some milk and we can sit in the library."

She leaned against the counter while he poured his milk, and he felt sorry for her. She was striking a pose of casual indifference, studying the mural of tropical fish on the backsplash, but the frenetic beating of the pulse in her temple gave her away.

"Let's go," he said, guiding her with his hand on her back.

The library was his favorite room for talking. It was quiet, closed in by the walls of books. They sat in the big leather chairs. "Kit didn't give me much information," he lied. "I think she wanted you to tell me yourself."

She stared at the glass of milk he was holding on the arm of his chair. "I don't know what to say," she said finally.

"I know you find me hard to talk to."

She nodded.

"What can I do to change that?"

"Tell me why you're a doctor." She blurted the words out.

"What you'd really like to know is why I'm an obstetrician, right?"

Rennie blushed.

"More people ask me that question than any other, I think."

"They do?" She looked relieved.

"Uh-huh. And there's no simple answer." He moved his milk to the desk and leaned forward. "Have you ever seen a birth, Rennie?"

She shook her head.

"Well, we'll have to arrange that one of these days. The first time I ever felt a new life slip into my hands I knew I wanted that to be a part of my work. I like helping healthy women have healthy babies, and I like figuring out what to do when there are problems. And very soon I'll be operating on babies still inside their mothers. Can you imagine anything more exciting than that?"

She shook her head, the shadow of a smile on her lips.

"And frankly, I prefer women patients to men patients because women are more honest about their feelings. You don't have to guess at what's going on with them."

"Except with me," she said, surprising him with a giggle.

"Well, you *are* a bit of a puzzle, but that's understandable after what you've been through."

"It's made me afraid of everything all of a sudden."

He nodded. "That makes sense."

She looked down at her hands. "Kit said you think it was my own fault I got raped."

He frowned. He was certain Kit had said nothing of the kind. "Why would I think that?"

She shrugged. "I don't know. 'Cause I ran away, I guess. 'Cause maybe you think I asked for it."

He got up and moved to the ottoman right in front of her and she let him take her hands. "It wasn't your fault, Rennie." He looked straight at her, and for the first time she didn't try to dodge his eyes. "Please get that through your head. I know it wasn't your fault. Now you need to accept that for yourself."

27.

Kit sat on the edge of the tub, leaning heavily against the blue tiled wall of her bathroom. The heat was on in the house now that the others were up, but still she shivered. She looked at her watch. Seven o'clock. She'd been sitting there for an hour, fighting the nausea, giving in to it only when she had no choice.

She'd heard Cole answer the phone and leave the house earlier, when it was still dark outside and she was warm in her bed. She'd rolled over to look at the clock and felt the room spin. It was a miracle that she'd made it to the bathroom in time.

How much longer could she pretend everything was all right? She was able to run fairly well at night, but that meant using the sterile indoor track at the Y. She had to be the only person in the world training for a marathon indoors.

She still went out to the beach in the morning. It was part of the ruse. She just walked along the shells now, and it was harder than ever to keep warm. What was wrong with her? She had a new theory every day. Fear of success, poor conditioning, stress at work. Something that could be overcome in a week or two.

She knew Cole had his own theory. He'd met her on the beach the day before. It had been weeks since she'd seen him out there. She felt exposed. He would have seen her sluggish gait, and she wasn't certain her face was clear of her latest crying spell.

He had on his heavy blue jacket and a knit cap pulled over his ears. "Hey," he called when she was close enough to hear him. "You weren't running."

She didn't try to speak.

"You've been crying," he said, very close to her now.

"I don't know what's wrong with me, Cole. I can't run. I feel terrible. When I run hard I throw up."

"Really?"

She nodded.

"And you've been keeping this to yourself, like a little martyr." He took her gloved hand and held it in his pocket as they walked.

"I kept thinking it would get better."

"You haven't had sex with anyone since that time with Sandy at the Christmas party, have you?"

"No." She was annoyed. "And that was at the end of my period."

"Why don't you make an appointment to come in and we'll figure out what's going on."

"I think I'm just nervous."

"Uh-huh." He'd sounded unconvinced and she'd been irritated by his self-confidence and his ability to walk along the beach without the slightest fear of throwing up.

She'd taken his advice and set up an appointment for eleven-thirty this morning. He'd suggested the time so they could have lunch together afterward, but now as she sat dizzily in her bathroom, she doubted she would even be able to watch him eat.

She was still shaky as she sat in the waiting room of Cole's office. The pages of the latest *Newsweek* trembled in her hands.

"You're next, dear," the receptionist told her. "Wait in Dr. Perelle's office. He wanted to talk with you first."

She sank into the leather chair in front of his desk. It felt strange to be there alone, as if she were invading his privacy. She would have felt less intrusive poking around his bedroom at home.

She looked around her as if she'd never seen his office before. The walls were covered with more fat books than a person could read in a lifetime. The shelf by the window held plastic models of body parts and she looked away, repulsed.

Neat piles of paper and charts lined the borders of Cole's desk and a half-full cup of coffee sat in the center of the leather top. The cup had a picture of a tiny doctor on it, standing in the middle of a cornfield. Above the picture it read COLE PERELLE, M.D., and below it, *outstanding in his field*. She'd never known he had a cup like that. She wondered if Estelle had given it to him.

He brought her chart into the room and sat in the other leather chair, frowning at her. "You don't look very well."

"I spent an hour throwing up this morning."

"After running?"

"No. It hit me even before I got out of bed."

He took a pen from the pocket of his white coat and began to write. He was wearing a tie, pleated wool pants. A far cry from his usual jeans or cords. Why was he dressed like that on a regular day at work? She hoped the fetal surgery stuff wasn't going to his head.

"It seems you're getting worse instead of better."

"Not really. I think today was probably as bad as it will get."

He looked at her as if to say, *Who are you trying to kid?* "When was your period due?"

"Never. My periods are never actually due."

"Come on, Kit. You had one in November and another in December." He picked up a small calendar from the desk and handed it to her. "Assuming your cycle was beginning to regulate itself, when would you have been due?"

She counted the days on the calendar with the tip of her finger. "If they were actually getting back to normal, I should have started my period around January seventh."

"Which makes you four or five weeks late."

"If you say so."

"You're really fighting me."

"Sorry," she said.

He set her chart on his desk and stood up. "I want to do a pelvic."

"But, Cole—"

"Humor me, okay? I need to rule out pregnancy before I rack my brain looking for something else. Take the examining room across the hall."

He extended his hand to help her up. She stood and a curtain of darkness dropped over her eyes. "Oh, God," she said, sitting down again.

He leaned over her, his hand on the back of her head. "Put your head down. Kit."

"No, I'm okay. I just stood up too fast."

"Have you eaten anything today?"

She shook her head.

"We'll get you something right after your appointment."

"I don't think I can eat."

"We'll see. Let's try it again." He held out his hand to her. "Slower this time."

Cheryl, the nurse practitioner in Cole's office, took her blood pressure and tried to make small talk, but Kit couldn't concentrate. Cheryl was small and blond, a very young-looking thirty-seven. She was married with two nearly grown kids, and she was going to be on the fetal surgery team. Kit liked her. She knew how much Cole respected her, and at any other time she would have enjoyed talking with her. But not today.

He looked in her throat and her eyes. He listened to her heart and poked at her stomach. It was all perfunctory. She knew what this exam was about, and with every second her shivering intensified.

The speculum felt cold. When he removed it she braced herself for what he would tell her.

"How about a blanket?" was all he said.

"Okay," she said through chattering teeth, and Cheryl took one from the shelf and laid it over her. The weight of it hurt her breasts. She hadn't told him about the pain in her breasts, how they hurt even from the spray in the shower.

His fingers were inside her and with his other hand he pressed on her stomach under the blanket. "You are almost certainly pregnant," he said.

She stared at the mobile of tiny silver sailboats hanging from the ceiling above her head, feeling his eyes on her. "I can't be."

"I don't feel the string of your IUD."

"I checked it last week. It was there." Last week or the week before? Certainly it had been no longer than that.

"Let's do a sonogram," he said to Cheryl. He pulled off his glove and dropped it in the wastebasket.

She took her feet out of the stirrups and sat up, clutching the blanket to her and trying to recapture her dignity. She ignored the dizziness that washed over her. "Cole, I can't be pregnant," she pleaded.

Cheryl handed her a glass of water. "Got to fill your bladder," she said.

"I'll throw up if I drink this."

"Get down as much as you can," said Cole, playing with the ultrasound machine.

She was trapped. She sipped at the water, her throat tightening with every swallow.

Cheryl told her to lie down again so that she could smear some gel on her stomach.

"Look how flat my stomach is," she said.

"You've eaten like a bird for two weeks," Cole said. He

looked at Cheryl, telling her without words to leave them alone. She squeezed Kit's shoulder and left the room.

Cole slid the transducer back and forth over her stomach and studied the images forming on the screen in front of them. Black and white blotches were all she could see.

"Here's the fetus." He pointed to the screen as if he were showing her a hurricane on a weather map. "And there's the IUD."

She frowned at the screen. "I don't see anything," she said stubbornly. Then she noticed the tiny blinking light near the center of the screen and she stared at it in horror. A heart. It had to be. "Cole, the *blinking* . . ."

"Do you want me to turn it off?"

"Oh my God. Yes."

In an instant the gray blotches and the light disappeared. He handed her a tissue and she realized she was crying.

"You're early," he said. "What do you want to do?" His voice was soft, in control. What did he have to worry about? Nothing. This was all in a day's work for him. She felt close to hating him.

She struggled to sit up again and for a horrible moment thought she might throw up on the blanket. The ultimate indignity. "I don't know what I want," she said angrily.

"Let's go to lunch and talk about it." His hands rested in the pockets of his white coat, his face calm.

"I told you I can't eat."

"Kit, come on. I know this is hard but—"

"You can't possibly understand how I'm feeling."

"That's true," he said. "But that's not my fault."

He was right, of course. Innocent by virtue of his gender.

"Give me a prescription for the nausea," she said, hating that she needed anything from him. It wasn't fair that he'd known something about her body that she hadn't known. Or hadn't admitted to herself, in any case.

"There's nothing I can give you."

"What do you mean? My sister always took something when . . ."

He shook his head. "There's nothing currently on the market that's safe enough to prescribe during pregnancy. Not unless you become a whole lot sicker than you are right now."

Bastard. She stared at him.

"Try some saltines," he said. "Drink liquid throughout the day, a few sips at a—"

"How am I supposed to get anything down when I'm so sick I can't even stand to hear you mention food?"

He put his hand on the doorknob. "We can talk about it later. When you've calmed down." He walked out of the room and she jumped at the sound of the door slamming.

The Point Pleasant Library was a converted old brown shingled house on a tree-lined street that reminded her of her grandparents' neighborhood in Seattle. She felt as if she were paying a visit to some old relative, but to her relief, there wasn't a soul she knew inside. A handful of school kids whispered to each other at the tables, and a few old men sat around the nonworking fireplace, chatting and reading.

She picked up a couple of magazines without looking at their covers and carried them to a back corner of the room. She sat in a big, hard wooden chair that faced the side of one of the bookshelves, cut off from everyone's eyes.

She'd never wanted a baby. Not ever. That made her peculiar as a female right from the start. For a year or two she'd played with her Barbie doll, that independent, worldly creature, but she'd cast aside the baby dolls who'd always struck her as limp and perpetually needy.

Once, when the marriage was starting to sag, she'd thought about it. Maybe that was what she and Bill needed—someone to care about other than themselves. It would be easier to have a baby than to split up and start over.

They'd even talked about her having the IUD removed, but she never got around to it. A lot of good it was doing her now. She should have had her tubes tied.

She opened one of the magazines in case someone came near her chair and caught her staring into space. Why was this so hard? From the time she'd first had sex— the night of high school graduation—she'd known that if she ever got pregnant she would have an abortion. Simple. A few minutes in a doctor's office, comfortable in the knowledge that her family would never know and that a girlfriend would be sitting in the outer office, waiting to drive her home.

It would kill her parents. Eight years of pleading with her for a grandchild and she produces one out of wedlock? She smiled at the irony. But her sister would be thrilled. Maybe it would narrow the gulf between them. Paula talked baby teeth and diaper rash, and Kit talked shin splints. They'd never had much in common anyway. Blue-eyed, blond Paula. She'd practically flunked out of school her senior year but no one cared. After all, she'd already been crowned Miss Woodley High School. What else mattered?

And what would Sandy have to say about all this? Better yet, what would his new *wife* have to say? She wished it weren't Sandy's baby. If only it were Cole's. But she'd had a period after she'd been with Cole. She shut her eyes. She didn't like to remember that night.

She could see the corner of the card catalog. She shut the magazine and walked to the bulky wooden case of drawers. An old woman was fingering the cards in the B drawer, and Kit smiled at her as she pulled out the Ps. *I'm pregnant*, she said in her head to the woman. *What do you think about that?* She jotted down the numbers of a few books on pregnancy.

She found only one of them in the stacks. A lot of women in Point Pleasant must have been pregnant. She couldn't imagine when they'd come into the library to get the books. She was the only person of childbearing age there now.

She carried the book back to her chair and began to leaf through it. It was full of glossy, full-page pictures of fetal development. *Just what I need*, she thought, making a face.

She pulled her calendar from her purse and counted the weeks from December fifteenth, the night of the party. Eight weeks and one day. She turned the pages of the book slowly, deliberately, wanting to see and not wanting to. Two weeks, three weeks, four, five . . .

Fetus at eight weeks. She stared in awe, as if she'd never seen a picture of a fetus before. It took up every inch of the page, so that the caption itself had to be on the page next to it. *It's much, much tinier,* she told herself. *Much less significant than it looks.*

The little fingers were stubby, the eyes big and dark. Its skin was lavender mother-of-pearl. On the top of its skull was a shiny area in the shape of a heart. The umbilicus looked wiry and strong. There was no hint of the woman at its other end. No clue as to what she thought of this exquisite little intruder.

She closed the book. She wouldn't check it out. It was just a form of torture.

She could tell by their faces that Janni and Maris knew. They were chopping vegetables at the kitchen counter when she walked in the door.

Janni wiped her hands on a paper towel and grabbed Kit by the wrist. "Sit down," she said, pulling a chair out from the table.

"Cole told you."

"He called hours ago, looking for you. He's worried about you."

They waited for her to say something. She guessed they'd been waiting half the day to hear what was going through her head.

She wouldn't keep them in suspense any longer. "I don't

want a baby." She shuddered at the thought and looked guiltily at their faces. "I feel selfish saying that to you two."

Maris sat across the table from her with her sad gold eyes. "Maybe it's those of us who *want* a baby who are selfish," she said.

"Look, Kit," Janni said, "you can't have a baby you don't want to absolve your guilt over my hysterectomy or Maris's miscarriages, got it? You have to think about yourself, not us. If you have an abortion, we'll go with you and hold your hand, right, Mar?"

Maris nodded.

"I saw the baby's . . . the fetus's heartbeat on the sonogram." Kit shivered. "And then I made the mistake of looking at a picture of an eight-week-old fetus in a book at the library and I'm not sure I can go through with an abortion."

"Eight weeks is nothing," said Janni. "Just a bunch of cells."

"I can't believe that you, of all people, would say that."

"You looked at a picture and suddenly you're caught up in the romance of it all. You need a dose of reality." She poked Kit's stomach. "That little zygote couldn't live outside of you for a fraction of a second."

"I know. That's what bothers me."

"It's fun to imagine what it would look like and what college you'd send it to, but you're not thinking about the twenty-one years of food and care." Janni waved her arms in the air as she spoke.

"You sound as if you *want* me to have an abortion."

"I want you to do what's right for *you*." Janni fell suddenly silent and sat down at the table. "Lord, Kit, you're right," she said. "If I'm honest with myself, then yes, I wish you *would* have an abortion. You've never wanted kids, and it would be hard for me to see you pregnant and with a child. I would be"—she looked apologetic—"so damn jealous."

She was sitting under her afghan on the window seat when Cole came into her room. He hugged her and sat next to her, deliberately on her feet, making them feel snug and warm.

"I've felt like shit all afternoon," he said.

"Me too. I wasn't on my best behavior in your office."

"You had an excuse. I didn't. It was thoughtless of me to do the sonogram. I knew you were pregnant and I wanted you to stop kidding yourself. I should have sent you up to the lab for a test instead to give you more time to get used to the idea."

"I had to face it sooner or later."

"You're not really considering having it, are you?"

"I'm not ruling anything out. Though it seems I won't get much help from my friends if I do decide to have it."

"What do you mean?"

"Obviously you think it's a bad idea, and Janni says she's jealous and wishes I'd have an abortion." She was still shaken by Janni's reaction.

"I'd just hate to see you go through a pregnancy you're unhappy about to have a baby you don't want."

"It does sound stupid, doesn't it? I don't know, Cole. It's incredible to me that there's this little creature in my body.

And it's not like I'm a kid. What excuse do I have for not having it?"

"You don't want children. You've been pretty clear about that. I've never heard you express any ambivalence about it."

"I could have the baby and give it to Janni."

"You're kidding."

The way he said it made her laugh. She didn't want him to know how seriously she'd been considering that plan. "Then I think about Boston. Could I still run?"

"Yes, you could still run, but not in a marathon."

She shut her eyes.

"I want to do Boston more than anything. I haven't wanted something this much for as long as I can remember. But my training schedule's a wreck. *I'm* a wreck. Look at me sitting here like an old lady under an afghan."

"You can have an abortion tomorrow and be training hard by Monday," he said. "It's an option. That's all."

She looked at him. How simple it could be. Why was she making it so hard for herself?

For three days she ate saltines before she got out of bed and ran at night on the track at the Y. She was more introspective than she'd ever been in her life. The others moved around her carefully, allowing her to grapple with her decision in private.

She looked at pregnant women on the street and wondered what they were thinking. Did they feel trapped? Had they considered abortion? How did they make up their minds? But most of them probably had husbands. Their pregnancies had probably been well planned.

A few times she'd strolled past the nursery at Blair. She'd look at the little pink and blue bundles in the plastic cribs and feel a stabbing pain, a longing she'd never known was there. And then one or two of the babies would begin to cry and she'd walk away, the aching gone. She had a career, she reminded herself. She had a passion: running. And she had no husband. There was no room in her life for a child.

If she had this baby, she'd have to put off moving. She couldn't go through this without Cole as her obstetrician. The thought of staying filled her with relief, and she was annoyed with herself. Staying or leaving shouldn't color her decision about the baby.

She was beginning to think she would never be able to decide when the decision was made for her. She dreamt she was walking through a park where everything was lush and green. She was carrying Silver in her arms, like a baby. Silver was wrapped in her afghan, and he looked up at her with his attentive cat eyes. He reached a soft paw up to touch her chin and she hugged him closer.

Then she spotted Paula. Walking happily toward her sister, she covered Silver with the afghan so that Paula would think she was carrying a real baby.

"Oh, let me hold him!" Paula reached out her arms and Kit started to hand the bundle to her, but Silver looked up at her, pleading. He wrapped his paws around her neck and clung to her, burying his furry face against her breast.

She woke up near tears, certain of what she must do for

the first time. She hadn't thought about Silver in years, how she'd handed him over to her sister when he didn't fit into her lifestyle any longer. She'd never been too good at taking care of another living being.

The sky outside her window was beginning to lighten. She put on her robe and walked across the hall to Cole's room. "Cole, are you awake?"

"Not really." He rolled over in a tangle of blankets. The Amish quilt was folded neatly at the foot of his bed. "What's up?"

"I had a dream about my cat Silver. I gave him away and never should have, and I have to have this baby."

He sat up. "Sit." He patted the bed next to him. He took his shirt off the chair next to his bed and put it on. She wondered if he was cold or just afraid of her reaction to his body.

She sat down, facing him. "I've made up my mind."

"A cat is not a baby."

"It's not just the dream. I think I've known from the moment you said I was pregnant."

"What the hell will you do with a baby?" His voice was kinder than his words.

"I don't know. That's my next decision. But I can't abort it."

"I didn't think you were hung up about abortion."

"I'm not. I would still fight to the death for a woman's right to choose, but I can't do it myself. Not right now."

"Are you thinking rationally? What is this about your cat? You're guilty about a cat so you have a baby? Or are you guilty that you can reproduce when the other women in this house can't? Or are you punishing yourself for screwing Sandy again when you knew it was a mis—"

She held up a hand to stop him. "None of the above. And I'm sick of deep self-examination. I want to have this baby."

"What about Boston?"

"*Cole.* Don't *do* this to me. Won't you help me?"

He looked remorseful. "Of course I will."

"Could you hold me, please? Just for a second?"

He pulled her against him. "I don't think I *can* hold you just for a second," he said into her hair. "Ah, Kit. It's going to change your whole life."

Kit sat across from Rennie at McDonald's a few days later, smiling at the light in the girl's eyes as she described her day at school. She was making friends. Two girls had reached out to her. Two young-sounding fourteen-year-olds, like Rennie herself.

Rennie looked good. It wasn't just the new, ready smile and the growing self-confidence. It was more than that. She was taking pains with her appearance, wearing skirts to school, curling the ends of her long light brown hair.

Kit had never heard Rennie string so many words together in such a short space of time as she was doing now. But she wasn't really listening. In a minute she would turn the tables on this kid, ask for some of the same understanding she'd given her for the last month or so.

Rennie stopped talking to take a bite of her hamburger and Kit seized the opportunity.

"I need to tell you something," she said.

Rennie set down the burger. "Do I have to leave the Chapel House?"

"Oh no. Nothing like that." Rennie had that worry hanging over her head day and night. They'd applied to the county to become her permanent foster home, but there was a snag because of the "unusual domestic situation". Rennie knew that at any moment she could be snatched from them. "No, it has to do with me, not you. I wanted you to know that I'm going to have a baby."

Rennie sat back in her chair. "*Why?*"

She hadn't expected that question and she had no answer. *Because I want a baby* was a lie. *Because I had sex with a soon-to-be-married man and it just happened* was the truth but hardly the words she could say to Rennie.

"Some things are hard to explain," she said.

"But you're not married or anything. Who's . . ." Rennie blushed. "I guess it isn't any of my business."

"He's no one you've met." She hadn't figured out yet what role she wanted Sandy to play in this. She wished she could keep him out of her life altogether, but was that fair to him? To her baby? Or would her baby be in for even more heartbreak and confusion if she involved Sandy? As hard as she tried, she couldn't imagine Sandy as a father. He was a child himself.

Rennie looked out the window, her hamburger forgotten. "I don't understand why women ever do it. Have sex, I mean. It hurts so much."

"Rennie, it only hurt you because of the circumstances. When you're older and in love with someone and—"

Rennie shook her head furiously. "I'm never doing it

again." She closed the Styrofoam box around her hamburger, a symbolic gesture. "Kit, would you tell me something? Please be honest."

Kit nodded.

"Did Dr. Chrisman say anything to you about . . . maybe that I'm not normal. You know, not made like other girls or something?"

Kit felt a lump form in her throat. None of them knew the depth of Rennie's suffering, she thought. "You're perfectly normal, Rennie. It hurt because your body wasn't ready. Rape is nothing like making love."

"I'm never going to do it again," Rennie said. "Absolutely never."

Kit smiled and rested her hand on Rennie's. "Tell me that in another ten years," she said.

28.

Traffic was light on the parkway as he drove home from his parents' house. He'd had dinner with them to celebrate his first fetal surgery at Blair, a male with a diaphragmatic hernia. The team had been incredible. He was certain they'd saved the baby's life.

He watched himself on television from the couch in his parents' living room. He looked pretty good, came across sounding more alert than he'd been feeling at the time. He'd just walked out of the OR and couldn't get that euphoric grin off his face.

He only wished Kit had been in town to see the press conference, especially since she'd been responsible for setting it up. But he'd taken her to the airport that morning to catch her flight to Seattle. She'd been nervous. She punched the buttons on his car radio with the change of every song and chewed on the back of her thumb.

"Do I *look* pregnant? Will my parents know as soon as they see me?"

He looked obediently at her stomach, where the denim of her jeans was stretched taut from hip bone to hip bone, and felt a sudden rush. He looked back at the road and locked his fingers around the steering wheel. "They won't know until you tell them," he said.

He kept his physical feelings for her chained down these days. He was getting very good at it. He could almost convince himself that his desire for her had been an aberration. It was only at moments like this, when he was caught off guard, that the feelings came to the surface.

Jay met him now in the Chapel House driveway.

"On your way to Blair?" Cole asked, checking his watch. It was a few minutes before ten.

Jay nodded as he lifted the garage door. "Appendectomy. How's your mom?"

"Good. More like her old self."

Jay paused before getting into his car. "You know, Rennie was a little weird tonight."

"Weird?"

"I can't put my finger on it. Antsy. I was helping her with her algebra and her concentration was nil. She's usually pretty sharp at math."

He felt a flash of panic—something was wrong with Rennie, and Kit was three thousand miles away. But that was idiotic. There were four other adults in this house. Surely they could handle whatever was troubling one fourteen-year-old girl.

He set his ear against Rennie's bedroom door on his way to his own room. He listened for a moment, but all he could hear was the ocean.

It was two in the morning when she cried out his name. He was still awake himself, staring at his ceiling, wondering why he couldn't sleep. He opened her door and the light from the closet lit up her face, wide-eyed and pale.

"Rennie?"

"I'm sick or something."

The room was warm, but Rennie was shaking hard enough to make the old iron bedframe squeak. Cole sat on the edge of the bed and laid the back of his hand on her damp forehead. It was cool. "What's wrong? Are you in pain?"

"No. I don't know what it is. All night I've been kind of nervous and . . ." She swallowed hard and it took her a few seconds to speak again. "My heart's going real fast and it's pounding against my ribs like I'm going to have a heart attack. And I can't catch my breath."

He took her wrist in his hand. Her pulse hammered against his fingertips. He stood up and got a blanket from the closet and laid it over her, thinking that he and Rennie were most likely suffering from the same malaise—a little separation anxiety, with Kit in Seattle. He sat down again. "You know, sometimes," he began carefully, "when a person is upset he has a physical reaction. Maybe his heart races or he hyperventilates—has trouble catching his breath." He tucked the thick stack of blankets around Rennie's shivering shoulders. "I know I feel a little . . . well, like there's an empty spot in the house when Kit's not here. That's probably why I had trouble sleeping tonight." Was that the truth? "Maybe you're upset about it, too."

"I don't understand why she couldn't just call her parents to tell them. Why did she have to go there?"

"It's the kind of thing that's hard to say long distance."

He spotted the phone on Rennie's night table. "Let's call her," he said without thinking. It would be past eleven in Seattle. He'd probably wake her parents.

Kit sounded sleepy when she answered the phone.

"Rennie and I miss you," he said. "I can't sleep, and Rennie's very shaky and her heart's doing the jitterbug, so I thought if we called you we'd feel better."

She was quiet, probably trying to make some sense of his words. "She's having some kind of anxiety attack?" she asked.

"Exactly. Rennie's right here in bed shaking up a storm even though she's under eighty blankets."

"She let you in her *bedroom*?"

"Incredible, huh?"

"I'll say. Put her on."

Rennie tucked the receiver between her ear and the pillow, and Cole walked to the window. The moonlight lay in a narrow sheet of silver on the water.

"Uh-huh," said Rennie. "I just feel like I'm cracking up or something." There was a pause. "But I can't help that my heart's racing." A shorter pause. "Yes." A long, deep breath. Another. And another.

Cole smiled to himself, thinking of Kit calmly working her magic on the other end of the phone. For nearly ten minutes he watched the moonlight playing with the waves, hypnotized. The tension in his own body was melting.

Rennie was peeling off one of the blankets by the time Cole took the phone from her.

"Does she seem better now?" Kit asked.

Rennie had stopped shivering. Her arms were folded across her chest.

"Much," he said. "And how are you doing? How did it go with your parents?"

She sighed. "As well as could be expected. They think I'm the lowest slime that ever crawled the earth, but they didn't disown me."

"Hurry home, okay? I love you."

"I love you too, Cole. Good night."

29

Thank God she no longer lived in Seattle. She lay awake in the bed of her childhood, unable to sleep since hanging up the phone. The familiar streetlight outside her window threw a triangle of white light across the ceiling.

She was a disappointment to her parents. A sudden disappointment, for all her life she'd pleased them. Until the last couple of years. First the divorce, now this.

She hadn't seen them in over a year, and she was stunned at how they'd aged. They moved and spoke with an air of defeat. Had they always been that way? They seemed too old to hurt with her news, and for a moment she thought it would be noble to have an abortion if it meant sparing them pain.

They had stared at her, simply stared, when she told them. After a moment her mother spoke. "I could never love a child who was conceived so . . . haphazardly," she said.

"I'm not asking you to love it. I'm only here to tell you that it exists, and I didn't want to tell you by phone."

"Has the baby's father offered to marry you?" her father asked, his eyes so innocent that it hurt her to look at him.

"I don't want to marry him, Dad."

Her father stared at her again, as if he couldn't decipher the code in which she was speaking. "You're going to make your life and the life of a little child miserable if you have no husband."

"I've had a husband and that made me miserable," she'd said.

Now, the streetlight illuminated her room and she looked at the ragged crack in her ceiling that had been there forever. It still reminded her of a mountain range. She used to pretend there were tiny people who lived on the ceiling and skied down the mountains. Once, she drew little villages around the mountain range with a charcoal pencil, balancing herself on her desk. Her mother had been furious. She made her repaint the whole ceiling. The villages disappeared, but to her relief the mountain range remained.

She could only remember the times her mother had been angry with her. Had there ever been tender moments? She raced through her memory in a kind of panic, but she couldn't think of any. Maybe that was why she felt so little for the baby inside her. You needed to be nurtured before you could nurture someone else.

In the mornings now she felt well—well enough to run smoothly and tirelessly. And her appetite was finally back, like an old friend. The date bread her mother made that morning had disappeared by dinnertime. She felt so well that she was beginning to think about Boston again. It was out of the question, of course, but she wondered if she'd made the decision about the baby on a whim. Maybe Cole had been right. Maybe she should have had the abortion.

She stared at the mountain range and laid her hands on her nearly flat stomach. How could she feel this good and be pregnant? It wouldn't have surprised her if she woke up one morning to discover she'd never been pregnant at all. There was no longer any evidence of it. No need for saltines. No yawning her way through the afternoon. She fed herself well and told people about the baby, but it seemed as though she was giving credence to a delusion. It would be terrible if she had hurt her parents and humiliated herself over some hormonal imbalance.

She sat up and reached for her watch on the dresser. It was three-thirty. She was never going to fall back to sleep. She missed the rhythm of the ocean in her ears. She didn't belong here any longer. This had been no more than a duty call.

The sky above the bay was purple as she climbed the front steps to the Chapel House the following day. In the living room, she held Rennie a long time, longer than the girl might have liked, and she knew very well it was her need and not Rennie's. *I mothered you*, she thought, startled as she remembered talking with her on the phone. *And I did a pretty good job of it, didn't I?*

Kit dialed the phone in the library. She sat back in the chair and let the smell of the leather soothe her. This time she would go through with it. She'd started to call Sandy so many times that she knew the number by heart. She'd memorized her speech as well.

"Hello?" The voice was young, almost girlish. Kit felt an unexpected rush of sympathy for the woman on the other end of the line.

"May I speak with Sandy Cates, please? This is Kit Sheridan."

She sensed the woman's hesitation. "Can I tell him what it's regarding?"

Kit almost laughed. What could she possibly say? "It's personal." Let him work out his own problems with his open-minded, understanding wife.

Sandy's voice was smooth and familiar.

"Sandy, this is Kit Sheridan."

"Kit! How are you?"

"I'm all right, but I need a minute of your time." She drew in a breath. "I need to preface this by saying that I don't want anything from you. I don't want to interfere in your life . . . but I think it's only fair to tell you that I'm pregnant. Nearly four months."

She waited while he chewed on that.

"You're saying that it's mine?"

"Yes."

"I thought you had an IUD."

"I do. It didn't work."

"Hold on a second," he said. She heard a door creak in the background. Heard it click shut. Then he was back on the phone. "Shit, I'm sorry Kit. Here I am trying in vain to make babies in California and you're pregnant in New

Jersey." He laughed. "You're planning on having it, I take it?"

"Yes."

"I would have helped out with an abortion."

"I decided against an abortion. Look, Sandy, I know you have a wife now and you're starting your own family. I don't want to make things difficult for you. I think we just have to figure out what's best for the baby."

"Well, I'll pay child support. That goes without saying. But for right now I think I have to keep this kind of quiet. Kara's upset about not being pregnant herself. She's pretty sensitive all of a sudden and I—"

"It's okay, Sandy." She didn't want to hear about their marital problems.

"Well, could you let me know . . . when it happens? We could talk more about it then?"

"Yes." She was relieved that this phone call was almost over and that he hadn't jumped at the chance to be a father to her child. "I'll call you then."

At first she thought she was dreaming, but then the scream came again, splitting the house from one end to the other. She sat up quickly, her heart pounding in her chest. It had been a long time since she'd heard that scream.

She put on her robe and slippers and walked into the hallway. Maris stood in the middle of the hall in a short nightgown, clutching her pillow to her chest. Cole was already with her, holding her arm with both hands and whispering to her, his lips against her ear. Rennie stood in the doorway of her bedroom in her long flannel night-gown, openmouthed.

Poor Maris. She must feel so exposed. Kit ushered Rennie back to her bed. "Just a nightmare," she said. "There's nothing wrong."

"But she looked so scared."

"She's okay." She kissed Rennie's cheek. "Go to sleep."

Maris was back in her room and Kit decided not to go in. She'd probably had more attention than she wanted, and anyhow, Cole would be with her. She sank back into her own bed, but she couldn't sleep. The ocean made an odd sucking sound, and for the first time she became aware of a feeling unmistakable for anything else: her baby was moving. It was silent and spooky. Some tiny foot or elbow was nudging her, maybe in protest at the rude awakening or to let her know her denial of its existence would no longer be tolerated.

She was supposed to have a husband right now to wake up. Someone to rest a heavy hand on her belly. It was horrible, being alone with this baby. She would have felt only slightly more terror if she thought a burglar was tiptoeing around her room, just out of her sight.

She rolled onto her side, determined to find a position that would stop the movement.

The sun shone like a spotlight on the wall of her room in the morning. She got up to pull down the shades and returned to bed. Sleep was the only solution. She should run instead, but what was the point? The Boston Marathon was one week away and she'd be watching the finishers on TV. *Damn.*

It was Saturday, and she heard morning sounds coming from all corners of the house. The floorboards creaked predictably with each set of footsteps in the hall and on the stairs. Doors squeaked open and banged shut. Voices were subdued by the early hour. She heard Cole and Maris talking in the hallway, and she willed one of them to open her door and ask her what on earth she was doing still in bed.

She pictured them at breakfast. *Where's Kit?* someone would ask. *Must have decided to sleep in,* someone would answer. A third person would suggest they check on her. *It's not like Kit to sleep in on a beautiful Saturday morning.* That would probably be Cole.

But no one came to her room until noon, and by that time she was so consumed by depression she could barely speak. It was Janni who finally knocked on her door. She was wearing black denim jeans and a green sweater that hung to her knees. "Are you going to sleep the day away, Kitty?" she asked.

Kit began to cry and Janni sat on her bed, holding her close. It felt remarkably good to have a woman hold her. Closeness for the sake of closeness. "What's wrong, sweets?"

"I felt the baby move last night."

"That's wonderful!"

Kit shook her head. "It made me feel so lonely. There was no one to tell."

"You're crazy." Janni leaned away from her, her brow furrowed but a smile on her lips. "You live in a house full of people who love you. How can you say there was no one to tell? You should have come to our room and jumped on our bed. We could have celebrated."

I didn't feel like celebrating. She couldn't say that out loud, not to Janni. Cole maybe, but not Jan.

"I've been thinking about this, Kit," Janni said. "If you'd like, I'll be your labor coach. I'll stay with you every minute, and we can pant and push together."

"I'd like that," she said, not wanting to talk about it. She carefully avoided thinking about labor these days. It made her feel trapped and frightened, and she saw no point in worrying about it yet. She took a tissue from the box on her night table and blew her nose.

Janni smiled. "The coaching starts right now. You've got to feed that little critter, especially now that he's going to use up his calories kicking."

"Hers."

"You'd prefer a she?"

Kit sighed. "To tell you the truth, Janni, I don't think I really believed this was a baby at all until last night when it gave me the sign." She got out of bed and picked up her bra and T-shirt from the top of the bureau and began to dress. "I think I'll go for a run before I eat. And Janni?" She touched her friend's shoulder. "Don't tell anyone, please. About the baby moving."

She pulled on her shorts, ignoring the confusion in Janni's face, and slipped out her bedroom door.

Rennie was subdued at dinner that night. Cole watched her pick at her food and swirl the milk around in her glass. Finally she looked across the table at Maris. "I'm sorry you had a nightmare last night," she said.

They all looked at her in surprise. *She sounds like an adult,* he thought. *She sounds like one of us.*

"Thanks," Maris said, buttering a roll. "It's a bitch all right."

He looked at Maris. It was hard to believe that the woman sitting next to him in her slinky jungle-print skirt with her diamond-studded nostril was the same woman who had stood paralyzed in the hallway the night before. She'd reminded him of a deer, frozen in the headlights of a car.

"I've only ever had one nightmare," Rennie said.

"What was it about?" Kit asked.

Rennie shook her head and speared a Brussels sprout with her fork. She did this a lot, teased them with a tidbit or two to make them draw her out.

"Talking about nightmares can make them lose their power," said Janni.

"I think talking about them makes it worse," said Maris. "Life goes on and you have to put the terrible things behind you."

There were times he wanted to hurt Maris enough to make her cry. Times when he wanted to tell her, *Yes, damn it, remember the fire. Remember your brothers' burned bodies. And remember your babies—how old would they be now? How about Chuck's accident, the hours he spent trapped in his car before he died?* Sometimes he wanted to twist her fingers until he saw a tear in those golden eyes. But he never did. He comforted her on her terms—brought her back from the dream to reality, where she could bury her emotions deep inside once again. He wondered if he was really being a friend to her.

Cole turned to Rennie. "I'd like to hear your dream," he said, knowing she was waiting for someone to say those words again.

She looked directly at him, as directly as she could, and then dropped her gaze to the table. "Um . . . well, I dreamt that I came home from school and went to my grandmother's room to see her like I did every day, and I saw that she was asleep. I knew that my mother was out with her boyfriend, so I just walked around my house waiting for Grammy to wake up. I kept walking and all and eating things, just waiting and wondering why she was napping so long. Hours went by, and finally I went to try to wake her up because it was almost time for me to make her dinner. I called her and she wouldn't wake up, and I shook her a little and she was still asleep, and then I saw that her skin looked different . . . and her shoulder where I shook her was cold and kind of stiff . . . and I shook her really hard then and I tried to make her sit up but I couldn't . . . and I tried to make her eyes open with my fingers, and I screamed 'Grammy, wake up!' but she didn't. Because she was dead. I was all alone with her and she was dead and I didn't know what I was supposed to do." She lowered her head, her cheeks crimson.

"What a terrible dream," said Cole.

"I wish it *was* a dream," Rennie said under her breath.

"That's what really happened?" Maris asked.

Rennie nodded, two fat tears starting to fall over her cheeks. "That's why I wanted my knapsack so bad. She was in there."

"You mean you had a picture of her?" Cole asked.

"*No.* I had *her.* In a plastic box. Her *ashes,*" she whispered reverently. "I took them with me when I ran away. My mother didn't care about them. She wouldn't even buy an urn and I didn't have enough money to get one myself. Now I keep wondering where she is? What did they do with her?"

Cole looked at the others, four openmouthed faces. What would those bastards have done with an old lady's ashes?

The snow had long ago melted from the yard but the house was still boarded up and Cole began his methodical search, starting at the corner near the patio, kicking through the sand. It was fine and pure and offered nothing more than a few clam shells. But when he reached the beach heather, he spotted something blue jutting out of the ground. He dug at it and unearthed a blue knapsack, empty except for a yellow sweatshirt and a plastic box filled with ashes.

She loved running in the rain. There was no escaping it, so it made no sense to try. She let it soak through her T-shirt and plaster her hair to her scalp. The sand was as dense as concrete beneath her feet and she sent wet clumps of it behind her with every step.

Cole had been right. At four months, better than four months really, Boston would have been a mistake. She felt wonderful and strong, but to put a baby through twenty-six miles of jostling would be cruel. Even on these four-mile runs home from work, she imagined that something would pull loose or that her baby's little head might take one too many knocks against the wall of her uterus. Cole said that was nonsense, but still she worried.

The house rose up in front of her like part of the rain-soaked landscape, its features blending into the gray evening sky so that it was hard to tell where the sky ended and the house began. It reminded her of the photograph that hung above the mantel in the living room.

Jay met her at the sliding glass doors of the kitchen, water dripping down his raincoat. His hair clung to his head and he looked tired. His face was full of lines.

"Have you heard anything from Cole?" he asked.

"No. Why?"

"I thought he'd be home by now." Jay rubbed his hands together, slowly, as if he were trying to flatten a piece of clay between his palms. "He left the hospital around two, and he wasn't in very good shape. He lost a patient today."

An obstetrician losing a patient? "A mother patient or a baby patient?" she asked calmly, as if the answer didn't matter.

"Abortion." Jay took off his raincoat and laid it over the back of a kitchen chair. "It was bad. He had this patient, forty-one or forty-two, I think, with severe cardiac disease. Really obese. Nice woman. Nice husband. Anyway, she gets pregnant after twelve years of a childless marriage. First pregnancy." Jay's Brooklyn accent was almost too thick to follow when he spoke fast. "There's no way she could have had this baby. Her cardiologist said she couldn't survive the pregnancy. Her husband wanted her to have the abortion. Cole recommended it too, of course. She was only ten weeks. She knew she had to abort, but that didn't stop her from being really upset about it. Crying on the way into the treatment room and all. I'm sure Cole felt like shit. Then in the middle of the procedure her heart stops."

"Oh, God." She pictured the scene in her mind: the glaring lights, the woman draped and asleep—or maybe she'd only had a local? Maybe she knew exactly what was happening the whole time. She could see Cole, his eyes above the mask full of terror. Or panic. Or maybe he'd stay perfectly calm through something like that. She really didn't know.

"Cole did everything he could," Jay continued. "He did everything right. No way was it his fault. But you feel like it at times like that, like, damn, maybe I could have done something else. They worked on her twenty minutes but . . ." He turned his palms up in a gesture of defeat. "I saw Cole afterward and he was really shaken up. Cheryl too. She blew lunch in the scrub sink. Cole spent some time with the husband, and then he said he needed to get out of there and left."

She wondered where he was. Driving in the rain? What was he thinking? Did he blame himself?

They were still in the kitchen when he came home. He walked through the room without a word and threw his raincoat on the table, knocking over a vase. Kit rescued it before it fell to the floor and grabbed a paper towel to mop the water from the oak tabletop. Either he didn't notice it or he didn't care. He walked into the library and slammed the door behind him.

If he still wanted to be alone, he wouldn't have come home, Kit thought. She walked toward the library.

"You've got guts, girl," said Jay.

He was sitting in the chair closest to the window, and the cool April rainstorm cast a gray tint to his face. He stared out at the darkening beach.

She closed the library door behind her and stood in front of it, ready to make an escape. "I'm sorry," she said.

"Lousy weather."

She hurt for him. "Jay said there was nothing you could have done."

He made a noise in his throat as if he were choking on a laugh, and a sick-looking smile came to his lips. "Nice of him," he said.

"You don't agree?" She walked toward him and sat on the ottoman. She was shivering. She still had on her wet shorts and T-shirt.

He spoke without looking at her, and she saw the reflection of the rain in his eyes. "I knew there were risks. I thought I'd taken every precaution. I *did*. It just wasn't enough."

She shrugged. "These things happen."

"Tell that to her husband."

They were both quiet for a moment.

"Maybe I should have let her try to carry that pregnancy and not pushed so hard for the abortion," he said.

"Could she have lived?"

"I don't see how. And she was taking drugs for her heart that would have damaged the fetus. But she was happy about being pregnant. At least she could have tried."

"That's ridiculous. You know you're not responsible for her death, and you're scraping the bottom of the barrel for ways to blame yourself."

"*Don't* counsel me." His eyes hit her like bolts of lightning. "The last thing I need right now is a goddamned counselor."

She stood up, ready to retreat, but he caught her hand.

"Don't go," he said. I'm sorry."

She sat down again, thinking that maybe she'd better just listen. She watched his face as he spoke, studied the sharp, strong features that couldn't save him from looking vulnerable. She wished she could hold him, comfort him. But for months now they'd been cautious in their touching.

He was still holding her hand, though, and he stroked the back of it with his thumb. His eyes had softened. "Her husband fell apart," he said. "She was all he had and they really doted on each other. Did Jay tell you she was one of my first patients?"

She shook her head.

"She had such complete trust in me. *Shit*. I keep remembering her face when they wheeled her into the room." He shuddered. "She was crying and I thought, *she's not ready for this*. But she squeezed my hand and said, 'Do what you have to do, Cole.' *She* was comforting *me*."

"It was as if she knew."

"Exactly. It was just like she knew."

"Where did you go, Cole?" she asked. "Today, when you left Blair?"

"The inlet."

The muscles in her chest contracted but she kept her face calm. "Why?" she asked. "Did you have a sudden urge to watch the boats go out to sea or was it the condo?"

He smiled. "I can't say. I just drove straight there. I walked out on the jetty for about ten minutes, and I could feel the condo behind me saying, come on in, Cole, it's been a while. And when I looked up I half expected to see Estelle on her balcony."

"You were hoping."

"Yeah, I guess I was hoping. I don't know why. She was never much good at comforting. Anyway, I went in and talked to the guy at the desk. It's sold. I thought maybe she'd just rent it out, but she sold it. So . . ." He shrugged, let out a sigh. "Then I went back to my car and sat there watching the boats and the fishermen and feeling sorry for myself."

"Oh, babe." She wrapped her arms around his calves and laid her cheek on his knee. It felt good to be this close to him.

He set his hand on the back of her head. "This has implications for you. Kit." His voice sounded different, and she lifted her head to look at him. He wound a strand of her damp hair around his finger. "I did a lot of thinking this afternoon and I decided that I don't want to be your doctor any longer."

"*Cole.* You *have* to be." She felt panicky.

"If anything happened to you, I could never forgive myself."

"Nothing's going to happen. Cole, I've been counting on you. Please."

"You shouldn't trust me as much as you do. I'm not infallible. And I don't think straight when my emotions are involved."

"You did Janni's hysterectomy without any problem."

He groaned. "That was *torture* for me. She was so excited, finally thinking she was pregnant after all those years, and I told her not only wasn't she pregnant but I was going to take away any chance she'd ever have of getting pregnant. You know she didn't talk to me for two weeks after the hysterectomy? It's wonderful, taking care of a patient who won't talk to you."

"I wouldn't do that."

"I'm asking a favor, Kit. Let me refer you."

She felt hot tears forming in her eyes and put her head on his knees again so he wouldn't see. "How would you feel if you referred me to someone else and *they* made some terrible mistake while they were taking care of me?"

He was quiet and she hoped she'd hit a nerve.

"I'd rather die at your hands than at anyone else's."

He laughed. "That's a pretty inane statement." He sat back in the chair, sighing again. "Let me think it over," he said. "What happened today is too fresh in my mind."

32.

Her cheeks were turning pink in the May sunshine. It was just one more change in her body. She'd never burned before, or tanned for that matter. But now, as she ran the last block to the pier, she felt her cheeks beginning to sting.

She stood on the end of the pier and squinted out at the expansive blue circle of water in front of her. This part of the bay was bordered by large, sturdy-looking houses. She imagined that living in one of them would be the next best thing to living on the ocean.

The *Sweetwater* was somewhere on the bay today on her first outing of the year. They'd worked on her over the weekend, scraping and painting. She'd been impressed by how hard Rennie had worked on the boat. As hard as any of them.

Kit wished the county would put aside its concerns and approve the Chapel House as Rennie's permanent foster home. It was obvious they had no place else to put her. Why not let her stay with people who wanted her, with people who, to be honest, would grieve if she were taken from them?

She sat down on the bench and stretched her legs out along the seat, wondering if for once they might tan. They were still tight and strong-looking.

She was working hard to convince Cole that she didn't have a fragile bone in her body. The tougher, the healthier she seemed, the less he'd regret his decision to keep treating her. She'd twisted his arm on that one, but she'd had no choice. The terror she felt at going through it all without him had shaken her. She began to wonder if she'd continued the pregnancy just to guarantee his closeness to her.

She lifted the leg of her shorts and smiled at the pink and white line the sun was making on her thigh. Setting her hand on her stomach, she shut her eyes. It was taking her longer to catch her breath today. Every day she was a little more winded than the day before. Cole had told her to slow her pace a little, to listen to her body. But she had to keep running so she could get back into training right after the baby was born.

She wished the next four months could be compacted into one week. Feeling quick and slender again was only part of it. She wanted to hold her baby in her arms. That was a surprise. The feeling had crept up on her out of nowhere. Sometimes her arms ached to have her baby in them. She liked the way strangers stared at her in the grocery store, and she couldn't resist thumbing through the magazines in the checkout line, hunting for articles on pregnancy and babies. She shopped for maternity clothes with Janni and Maris. At work she felt on display, and she didn't mind a bit. She was providing grist for the rumor mill: she was definitely pregnant and she was definitely not married. The others were probably getting pumped for the facts, though they never spoke to her about it.

The bench shook from footsteps on the pier. She turned her head and squinted at the man walking toward her. Khaki pants and a brown plaid shirt. Dark hair, nice build.

"Hi, Kit," he said.

It took her a moment to recognize him. "Orrin?" She sat up straight, immediately on guard. "Don't tell me there's another lawsuit."

He laughed and took off his sunglasses. "Nothing like that. I stopped by your house because I wanted to see you. One of your housemates told me I'd find you out here."

"What did you need to see me about?"

"I don't *need* to see you about anything." He smiled. "I was wondering if we could have dinner together sometime soon."

She stared at him, at those gray eyes rimmed by dark lashes and his smooth, black hair. Couldn't he tell she was pregnant? For the first time in weeks she wished she weren't.

"Orrin, I'm five months pregnant." No use dragging it out.

He glanced at her stomach, then back to her face. "I didn't realize you were seeing someone."

"I'm not."

"Oh. Well then, the dinner invitation still stands."

She cringed at the polite tone. "Thanks, Orrin, but I don't think either of us would feel too comfortable."

"It doesn't have to be anything serious. I like you. I enjoyed working with you. Let's have dinner as friends."

They made plans for Saturday night, dinner and the symphony in Philadelphia, and she watched him walk back up the pier, smiling to herself. This was amazing. Too bad the timing was off. What could she possibly wear that would camouflage the bulging center of her body? Her baby gave a kick in protest and she stroked her belly. "You come first," she whispered. "Don't you worry."

Orrin arrived at the exact stroke of five. "I'd love a tour of this place," he said as he walked into the living room. "What a view." He stood at the back window. The ocean was performing perfectly tonight, the waves a deep glassy blue with just a sliver of white water reaching for the beach.

He wore a gray suit and blue-striped shirt. He looked terrific. *Too* terrific, every hair in place. She found herself wondering if he'd had his nails professionally manicured. She felt sloppy by comparison. Her blue maternity dress was nondescript. No matter what she wore these days, she felt like a beach ball with stick arms and legs protruding at odd angles.

"I'll show you around," she said.

Orrin had something nice to say about everything. The living room had character; the cherry wood dining room furniture was elegant. He studied the tile mural of tropical fish in the kitchen, mesmerized by the color and detail.

She thought twice about taking him upstairs. She would usually show a guest her room with its ocean view and maybe the den. But she couldn't get through the second story that easily these days. They'd transformed the room next to hers into a nursery and it drew her in. It was hard to walk past it without stepping inside, imagining what it would be like in a few months. She could see herself in the one-armed nursing rocker, coaxing her baby to sleep while she watched the rise and fall of the waves. She doubted very much that Orrin would be interested.

But he was. Or at least he pretended to be.

"My birthday was last week," she explained, "and as a surprise Rennie and Maris painted and the others bought me the furniture." The white crib was from Janni and Jay, the rocker from Cole. It already smelled like a baby in here, and she took a deep breath.

"You're all set," he said. He touched the rainbow mobile. "Cute."

This had to be boring for him, but she wasn't ready to leave the room yet. "This is from Maris." She held out the gold charm she was wearing around her neck. "It's called an Ashanti medallion, and African women wear them to ensure the beauty of their babies."

He held the charm on the tips of his fingers. "It'll be a lucky baby, with these built-in aunts and uncles," he said. "Your life is very settled, isn't it?"

"You mean by the pregnancy?"

"No. By this house. By your friends. You have everything you need."

She frowned at him, wondering if he was right. What was wrong with her that she felt no sense of contentment?

*

They had a table by the window at the Liberty Inn. Outside, a thunderstorm sent spikes of rain into the sidewalk.

"Does it feel awkward, being out with a pregnant woman?" She felt awkward enough for both of them.

"I've done it before," he said. "When my wife was pregnant."

"Are you divorced?" She realized she didn't know a thing about him.

"Widowed."

"Oh. I'm sorry." She hadn't expected that. "How long has it been?"

He leaned back, and it seemed to take all his powers of concentration to remember. "Almost four years."

"You must have a child then."

"No. Bruni was pregnant when she died."

She took a bite of salad. Was that why he was interested in her? Some unresolved thing about his wife?

"Does my pregnancy have anything to do with your wanting to go out with me?"

He looked surprised and then laughed out loud. "Relax. Nothing like that. And you don't look a thing like her, either. She was Swedish. Very blond."

"Oh."

"I haven't been in a hurry to start another relationship. I want to move slowly. So I wasn't terribly upset when you said you were pregnant."

"Drat. And here I was hoping you had some perverse craving for pregnant women." She laughed, but he barely smiled. God, this was uncomfortable. "How did she die? Or does it bother you to talk about it?"

"Cancer," he said, setting his fork on the empty salad plate. "And yes, it really does. Bother me, I mean."

"I'm sorry. I didn't mean to pry."

"You weren't." He smiled at her. "You know, I only make it to Blair a few times a month, but they send the *Communicator* to my home and I have to say that since you've been working on it it's improved one hundred percent. I used to feel embarrassed for the editor when I read it, it was so cutesy. Now it's readable and it gets the facts across without insulting the reader's intelligence."

"Thank you. That was exactly my goal, so it's nice to hear I've succeeded, at least with one reader."

"How long have you been divorced?" he asked.

"Nearly two years."

Orrin tapped his wineglass with his finger, and she wondered again about his smooth, square nails.

"Someone told me you ran in the Boston Marathon," he said.

"Next year, I hope. I'll have to requalify in another marathon first." She pressed her hands together in her lap. Her palms were as wet as the rain coating the window.

The waiter brought their entrees, and she was relieved to have the food to attend to. This was intolerable. How would they ever rise above this superficial plane? It was hard to imagine ever telling him a secret, a treasured thought. He was too polite, too squeaky clean. She took a bite of salmon dripping with hollandaise, and thought with some dismay that she'd rather be at home with the others, eating tuna fish casserole.

33

Cole was edgy. He sat on the living room floor, in the middle of the Persian carpet, playing Hearts with Rennie and Maris. He was barely able to focus on the game. Every minute or so he needed to shift position. He was getting too old to sit on the floor. Outside, the rain spilled through the darkness.

The others were jumpy, too. Maris was on her second glass of wine, and Rennie cringed each time lightning pierced the sky outside the window. Janni sat in the over-stuffed chair, a book upside down on her thigh, and her eyes on Jay, who was trying to get a second wind out of the dying fire.

It wasn't the storm that had them tense, Cole thought. It was what he was coming to think of as the Kit's-not-home syndrome. It was midnight. They should be on their way to bed, but here they sat, dragging out their activities in the unacknowledged ritual of waiting for Kit to come home.

They all started at an ear-splitting crack of thunder. With this rain it could be another couple of hours, he thought.

The phone rang, and he set down his cards and walked toward the library.

"Please don't be the hospital," Janni said.

It was Kit. There was laughter in her voice. "Cole? We got out of the symphony and Orrin's car wouldn't start. So we've taken a room in a little bed and breakfast place and we're trying to dry off. I'm going to have to stay here tonight. There's no way to get home."

"No, of course not. I was worried about you two driving in this storm anyway." His mind was racing.

"You should see this room, Cole. There's a fireplace and it's very homey. So don't worry about me. I'm not sure what time I'll get home tomorrow, though."

"You don't need to hurry. Just be good, okay?" He grimaced. Why did he say that?

"Do I have to? I mean, is there any reason, physically speaking, why I have to be good?"

Damn it. She wanted to sleep with Orrin. He forced a laugh. "No, of course there isn't. Enjoy yourself."

The rain wouldn't let him sleep. It sounded like waves breaking on his balcony. He tried to block out the picture taking shape in his mind—Kit and Orrin alone in a room with a fireplace and just one bed. Well, it would be good for her. She wasn't feeling that great about herself lately. A little body image problem. This was probably just what she needed.

Was he jealous? He rejected the word, told himself it didn't fit the situation. They were friends, very good friends, nothing more. He just missed knowing that she was right across the hall.

She came home the next afternoon, still wearing the blue dress she'd left in the night before. He thought she looked secretive. She was craving bouillabaisse, she said. She wanted to make it for dinner. She invited him to go to the fish market with her, and he jumped at the chance. He wanted some time alone with her.

He climbed into the passenger side of her car. She'd changed into a white jersey, sleeves pushed up above her elbows, a blue silk scarf tied at her throat. She'd pinned her hair up in back and it fell around her face in soft, honey-colored wisps. He studied her profile, the nearly perfect nose with its five or six pale freckles, the truly perfect lips. What had those lips done last night?

He looked back at the road. "How was the symphony?"

"Wonderful. Philadelphia's not that far. We should go more often."

He wondered who she meant by "we". He felt so far away from her, so separate. He wanted to bridge the gap between them but had no idea how to go about it.

She parked the car in front of the pier, where shirtless men scrubbed the deck of a fishing boat. She switched off the ignition and turned to look at him.

"There's an unasked question hanging in the air of this car," she said.

"There is?"

She nodded. "And the answer is: I slept in the bed, he slept on the couch."

He smiled, the muscles in his face giving way before he could stop them. "Oh," he said. She had done it for him—cut through the distance.

She squeezed his hand. "Let's buy some fish."

He watched her in the crowded fish market, using skills she must have learned in Seattle—rapping clams together, sniffing scallops, lifting the gills of whole fish to peer inside. He stood apart from her, lighthearted, drinking in the rich smell of the sea. Occasionally she held up a crab leg or a handful of mussels and looked over at him for his opinion. And each time he nodded. He wanted to prolong her shopping so he could continue to stand there, leaning against the rough wooden wall, feeling good.

She paid for the seafood and handed him the heavy paper bag, but he blocked her path when she headed for the door.

"Let's not go yet," he said.

She looked surprised. "Why not?"

"I like it here."

She laughed. "Come on, our fish will rot." She pushed past him through the door, blue silk catching the breeze, but he took his time. He wanted to stay there for the rest of the day, with Kit, in a cold little shop filled with fish and crushed ice.

34.

The sun was a thin gold thread on the horizon when she spotted Cole. She wasn't surprised to see him. He'd been meeting her for a couple of weeks now, since she'd started seeing Orrin. Yet she ran tensely those few minutes before she caught sight of him, dreading the possibility that he'd slept in.

He walked toward her with his hands in the pockets of his green warm-up jacket. "Good *morning*," he called.

"I'm winded." She slowed to a walk. "I feel as though I ate lead before I ran today."

He put his arm around her, his fingers warm against the bare skin of her arm. "I wish you'd pay better attention to what your body's trying to tell you and slow down a bit."

She hated him to talk that way. It made her feel guilty.

They were nearing the house and they walked silently for a few minutes. The sand looked like it contained a billion tiny lights, and somehow the scent of flowers had found its way to the beach and mingled with the salt from the ocean. She wished that every morning could begin like this one.

"Cole?" She hooked her thumb through the belt loop of his jeans.

"Hmm?"

"Will you be my baby's godfather?"

His arm tightened around her shoulders. "I thought you didn't believe in God."

"I don't think I do, but I'd like you to have a special connection to my baby and that's the only way I know to institutionalize it."

"I would be honored. And I really see no conflict between atheism and god parenting."

"You don't?"

"The godparent's supposed to make certain that the child is raised in the faith of the deceased biological parent, right? Since you have no faith that would be quite simple."

She laughed. "Actually, I'd just like you to lavish presents on her and give her piggyback rides and let her call you Uncle Coley."

"Pretty sure it's a girl, huh?"

"I hope so." She felt her eyes begin to burn. "Will you help me with her, Cole? She's not going to have much of a father."

He pulled open the sliding glass door to the kitchen. "It's a promise," he said, his face as serious as she'd ever seen it.

"I'm out of my element," she said to Orrin as they smiled their way through the throng at the Devlin Foundation dinner. She had the feeling everyone else in the hall had spent the day on their yacht.

"You look like you fit right in." Orrin led her by the elbow to the head table, where Cole was already seated. He looked relieved to see them. He was probably as nervous as she was. They would both be expected to perform tonight. He stood up and pulled out a chair for her, a few seats from his own.

"It's better politics if we spread out a bit," he whispered.

She knew he was right, but she would have preferred sitting next to him, nestled safely between him and Orrin.

The hall was peculiar. Dozens of round tables were set with white tablecloths and glittering silver and crystal. Yet the room itself with its woody scent and exposed rafters reminded her of a boathouse.

George Calloway, the red-nosed and jowly president of the Devlin Foundation, pumped her hand and took his seat next to her. His wife was already sitting next to Cole, talking in his ear and gripping the sleeve of his oatmeal-colored suit in her hand as she spoke. He looked mouth-watering in that suit. It made his eyes more startling.

Winn Meyer, her white hair knotted at the back of her head, sat next to Orrin, scooping him into conversation with the skill of the PR professional that she was. How did she do that so effortlessly? The Devlin Foundation had a real find in her. Some people were born knowing how to handle other people, Kit thought. And here she sat, smiling at George Calloway's veiny nose and feeling obscenely pregnant.

Cole had told her she looked good pregnant. "You have this tight, muscled body, and your belly just looks like one more muscle," he said.

She loved the description, but right now she wondered if he saw her as a liability. How did he explain her pregnancy to people like these? Maybe they would think that Orrin was her baby's father. That would probably be worth hoping for. Let them think she was married to Orrin but had kept her own name. She looked down at her ringless fingers and dropped her hands into her lap.

Ridiculous to worry about it, she thought. Who cares what they think? She looked around the table. There was one empty chair left, between Cole and Winn Meyer's husband. She was certain Cole had told them he'd be coming alone. The empty chair gaped at them.

"Will this be your first?" George Calloway leaned toward her.

"Yes." She smiled.

"When . . . ?"

"September twentieth."

"My oldest son was born in September. He's a professional golfer now. Travels all over the country."

"How many children do you have?" she asked politely.

"Four." He reached into the pocket of his suit jacket and she expected him to pull out photographs, but instead he produced a crumpled handkerchief and blew his nose. "Julie's at Princeton, Roger's the golfer, Patty's teaching in Collingswood . . ." He looked up suddenly, his attention caught by a woman standing behind the vacant chair. "Ah! Here she is." He stood up. "This is Cynthia Britten, without whom the foundation would fold up like an umbrella. She's our accountant."

The men stood and Kit stared. She was exquisite. Her

hair was as dark and shiny as Orrin's, her skin a rich bronze. Her dress was made of some feather-light fabric that fell in layers low on her breasts. It was exactly the color of Cole's eyes. The way she moved and her throaty voice when she apologized for being late reminded her of Estelle. But her beauty was different—innocent and unpolished, as if she hadn't yet learned its power.

Cole spoke to her as she settled into her seat, and they laughed like old friends. Kit smoothed her green silk dress over her stomach and shifted in her seat. She'd scoured every maternity shop between the shore and Princeton for this dress. She'd have done just as well at the local Kmart.

Cynthia caught her eye and smiled at her, and Kit smiled back, captured. She longed to reach across the table and stroke her fingers over the exposed part of Cynthia's breasts. If she felt that kind of pull, what on earth must Cole be feeling?

They made their way through salads and stuffed flounder. Kit listened politely to the Calloways' detailed descriptions of their children's exploits, wishing Orrin could rescue her somehow. But he was chatting on and on with Winn Meyer and her husband as if he was having the time of his life.

With half her attention she watched Cole and Cynthia. At times they didn't seem to notice the others around them. Every once in a while Cole smiled at Kit across the table with a look that said: How could I be this lucky?

Applause broke out table by table as George Calloway made his way to the podium. He held up his hands to quiet them. Kit's heartbeat quickened and she barely heard a word he said. Something about all of them knowing why they were there and the foundation's great pride in being a part of a program that was so exciting. Then he introduced her.

She walked up to the front of the hall and had her cheek bussed by his damp, rubbery lips. She settled in behind the podium and looked out at the expectant faces in the audience. She wasn't up to this tonight. It would have been better to let Cole do all the speaking, but she hadn't been given that choice. She only hoped that her carefully memorized speech sounded more spontaneous than it felt.

"Blair Medical Center has always been an exciting place to work," she said, her voice echoing. This *had* to be a boathouse. "When you talk to the employees, you get a sense that they like their jobs, regardless of the level at which they're working. They have a commitment to their work and to the patients, and they know they're part of something very, very important. But in recent months, since the Devlin Foundation provided financial backing for the Fetal Surgery Program, I've noticed a change in the level of excitement. It's higher than ever before. You can feel it in the air—the sense of pride of everyone there in knowing that lives are being saved and changed in a way they had never imagined possible in their lifetimes."

She paused for breath and glanced at Cole. The rest of what she had to say would put them all to sleep. They'd told her she had to talk about Blair itself. Its history. Its other programs. Leave the fetal surgery stuff to Cole even though she was the one who'd been making the speaking engagements all along.

She wrapped it up quickly, trying to ignore the polite

staring into space of the audience, and turned the podium over to Cole.

The applause shook the crystal on the tables and for a moment she feared they would all stand. He'd hate that. He would say something humble about how he didn't deserve that kind of deification. Yet as she watched him take the podium, smiling patiently while they applauded, she had to admit he had charisma. Was it that suit or had he had it all the time? He jumped right in, speaking to them as though he were sitting over a cup of coffee in their living room.

"Last week, a couple came to me after a doctor diagnosed their unborn child with a deadly kidney disease. I was able to tell them there was a very good chance the life of their baby could be saved, and that it could be a very full and normal life as well. A year ago I would have had to tell them it was hopeless and watch them walk from my office knowing that they would have to see through to the finish a pregnancy that would result in certain death for their baby. I can't begin to tell you the gratitude I feel—and the parents I'm treating feel—toward the Devlin Foundation, which has made this possible."

He was twisting the truth, exaggerating the Foundation's impact as though the Foundation itself were responsible for the surgical techniques. And really, he should have reversed the order of the example he'd used. He should have said that a year ago he would have had to tell the parents that there was no hope, but now he was able to offer their baby a chance.

But it didn't matter. The audience listened intently, all

eyes and ears. Cynthia smiled, stroking her water glass with long, polished fingernails.

Cole spoke for about twenty minutes and left the podium to more applause. He sat down again, and it was Cynthia, not Kit, who got his first smile of relief.

People were beginning to rise. Many of them were approaching Cole, patting his shoulder and shaking his hand. A few were headed in her direction.

"Time to mingle," she said to Orrin.

It had to be an hour later that Cole finally worked his way toward her. "You were great," he grinned.

"You, too. You had them spellbound."

"I think Cynthia and I are getting out of here."

She waited, hoping he would suggest that she and Orrin join them but he obviously wasn't thinking in that direction at all.

"She seems really nice," she said. There were strange, tingling pains in her chest.

George Calloway broke between them. "A complete success," he said, his breath fuming in her direction. It was hard to get any air in her lungs at all. She couldn't take much more of this.

She excused herself from the two of them and found Orrin waiting for her by the front door.

"Ready?" He reached for the door, as if he knew she wanted to make the quickest exit possible.

She nodded and pushed past him, filling her lungs with the fresh night air.

*

"Your blood pressure's one-twenty over eighty." Cole frowned into her chart the next morning.

"That doesn't sound all that high," Kit said from her perch on the examining table.

"It's not, except that it's unusual for you and it merits watching. You've put on a little more weight than I'd like to see, too, which might mean that you're eating too much or it might be an early sign of PIH—pregnancy-induced hypertension."

"Toxemia."

"Right. It's not that uncommon in older . . ."—he smiled, touched her arm—"in women over thirty expecting their first baby."

"So what do I have to do?"

"Rest. Lots of protein. Lie down most of the time when you're at home. Forget running."

"I *have* to run."

"No running. You can walk on the beach, but not far and not fast."

She knew toxemia could be dangerous, but she felt fine. She wanted to tell him that if she stopped running, that's when she'd get sick, but the look on his face told her not to. "Okay," she said. "I'll be good."

35.

The crowd at the band shell expanded so rapidly that he wondered if he'd ever be able to find Cynthia. But then he caught sight of her, walking toward him with a smile and a wave. Her gauzy white dress deepened her tan, and she carried a dark red sweater over one arm, a basket over the other.

"I was afraid we'd miss each other in this mob," she said, helping him hunt for a spot on the grass where they could spread his blanket.

"I wouldn't have left here until I found you."

They had to put the blanket close to the lake, quite a distance from the band shell, but he was pleased. He wanted the music to provide the background for the evening, nothing more.

Cynthia pulled a bowl of red grapes from her basket. She reached in again and produced a bottle of white wine and a plastic bag packed with wedges of cheese. He uncorked the wine while she arranged the cheese on a little china plate. She handed him a plastic wineglass, along with a pink cloth napkin.

He watched her busyness with a smile. Her bare arms were perfectly shaped, her fingernails the color of roses.

It might have been a mistake, meeting her at the band shell. He'd come here often with Estelle, though certainly not to hear Debussy. Estelle loathed Debussy. *Too sweet*, she said. But the music seemed a perfect fit for Cynthia. She was a gentle presence next to him. Soft, almost shy, although he imagined a steel core inside of her that had gotten her where she was professionally.

She wanted to hear about fetal surgery, the technical details.

She followed him easily, said she was a frustrated nurse trapped in an accountant's body. Her brown eyes rarely left his face as he spoke, unless he touched her or reached for her hand. Then she'd turn her head away from him. He had the feeling she'd been wounded once or twice.

In the middle of *La Mer*, she slipped a grape between her lips and leaned back on her arms. "I don't understand your living arrangements, Cole. They sound . . . odd."

"It's simple. When I was in medical school I lived with Jay DeSantis, who is now a surgeon at Blair. Then his girlfriend Janni moved in with us. Then Janni inherited the Chapel House and we all moved in there. Janni and Jay hired an architect to make some changes on the house and when her—the architect's—husband died, she moved in with us. Then about a year and a half ago, Kit moved to New Jersey from Seattle, and she was a friend of Janni's so she moved in. Then we took Rennie in as a foster kid." He loved recounting that tale. And he loved the stunned look on Cynthia's face.

"My God. Do you know how bizarre that sounds?"

He shrugged innocently. "Does it?"

"You live on a commune. Do you grow your own vegetables?"

He laughed, hoping she didn't mean to be as cynical as she sounded.

"Orrin doesn't live there?"

"No."

"Aren't he and Kit . . . I assumed he was the father of Kit's baby."

"No. That was someone she's no longer seeing."

"Oh." She looked pained. "It would be terrible to have a baby without the father around."

"Well, she's hardly lonely. Besides, Kit's pretty tough."

Cynthia looked thoughtful. "What will happen when you want to settle down?"

"There's always room for one more."

"You mean you'd *stay* there? In that house with a million other people?"

He sighed. He'd hoped she'd understand. "It would be very hard to leave."

She shook her head. "There's something unhealthy about it. Six adults living together. Professional adults. If you were all students or people just getting your feet on the ground, I could see it. Maybe."

"Five."

"What?"

"There are only five adults."

"However many. It just isn't done."

"We'll have a baby there too in the not too distant future." He was baiting her shamelessly.

"When is Kit due?"

"September. If she makes it that long. She's having a few problems, and I'm not happy with some of her test results."

"You sound like you're her doctor."

"I am."

She leaned back, and he could only read the look on her face as horror.

"You live with her, you work with her, you're her obstetrician . . . Don't you think that's a peculiar arrangement?"

"It's not a problem," he said. He was growing uncomfortable with her questions. He poured himself another glass of wine and leaned back on his elbows. "If you're done criticizing me, maybe we can listen to the music."

She looked stricken. "Cole, I'm sorry. Here I am with somebody that I really like for the first time in a long while, and I'm destroying it before it's begun. It's a bad habit."

She seemed human again, and he risked it now, taking her hand. "We all have our vices," he said.

36.

Kit leaned over the side of the boat and ran her fingers through the cool water of the bay. She'd spent the morning on the *Sweetwater* with Maris, Jay, and Rennie, teaching Rennie to ski. Rennie was good; she lasted four minutes on her first try and looked great out on the water, with her hair flying behind her and her body in the early golden stage of a tan. It was fun watching her confidence grow. But Kit would be glad to get back to solid ground. Every time they bounced across the wake of another boat, she worried that the jostling might be too much for her baby.

Jay turned the *Sweetwater* toward shore, and Kit spotted two figures on the distant pier. Probably Cole and Cynthia, back from the church breakfast. Cynthia's idea, of course. Cole had looked embarrassed when he told Kit about it. He had to be hooked to put up with that sort of thing.

She knew he was intrigued by Cynthia. He'd told her so. He told her everything, much as he had with Estelle. She knew the details of their dates, what Cynthia said, what he said in return. And she knew they were not yet lovers. Cynthia was holding him off.

Each time he came home, she was afraid he'd tell her

they'd crossed that line. She didn't want to hear it. She didn't want to think of him making love to Cynthia, imagining how it would compare to the quick, uncaring way he'd made love to her the night he fought with Estelle.

The figures on the pier came more clearly into view. They were both men, and they had a boat, sleeker and more powerful than the *Sweetwater*. One of them was getting ready to board.

"Who's that?" Maris asked.

Jay shook his head. "I don't know." Only a few other people shared their pier and none of them had their boat in the water yet this season.

Rennie looked toward the pier and caught her breath. She jumped to her feet, nearly knocking herself off balance, and grabbed the wheel out of Jay's hands. She turned it sharply to the left.

Jay caught her arm. "Rennie, what the hell are you doing?"

"It's them!" she screamed. She broke free of his hand and scrambled to the side of the boat. She had one foot in the water before Kit and Maris caught her. She fought like a caged animal, and Kit held her at arm's length, frightened of taking a blow to her stomach.

"Rennie, calm down," Jay said. "We're back out in the bay. You're safe."

"They're the ones who raped you?" Kit felt some of Rennie's terror.

Rennie went limp in Kit's arms. "Why are they *here*?" she cried. "I thought they'd gone away."

"I'll drop you off a few blocks down, Rennie." Jay turned the boat south.

The *Sweetwater* pulled alongside a pier behind a white shingled house. Kit followed Rennie's eyes back to their own pier. The men were still there, one of them in the boat.

"They can see me get off here," Rennie said.

"I'll go with you." Kit climbed onto the pier.

Jay turned off the engine. "We'd all better get out here," he said. "We'll call the police from the house."

37.

He woke up thirsty in the middle of the night, thirsty enough to get out of bed for a glass of water. Probably that corned beef hash at the church breakfast. It had been an awkward morning, meeting Cynthia's friends, though they were obviously primed to meet him. "We've heard so much about you," they said, and "Cynthia seems so happy lately," and "How did you ever inspire her to apply to nursing school? We've been trying for years."

Cynthia told him that some of her friends were zealous anti-abortionists who might try to put him on the spot. He felt rigid, watching his Ps and Qs. He was surprised that he cared what her friends thought of him. And he was surprised when Cynthia told him that she herself had protested the opening of an abortion clinic earlier that year. He had created an image in his mind of who she was and what she was like, and she was chipping away at it bit by bit.

He opened his bedroom door and nearly tripped over Rennie. She was asleep on the floor, curled up under her blanket, one arm circling her pillow. He stepped back in his room to put on his pants and a T-shirt and went back into the hall. He knelt next to her and shook her gently by the shoulder.

"Rennie," he whispered. "Wake up."

Her eyelids flew open, and he saw the crimson in her cheeks at being caught.

"Were you afraid in your bedroom?" She'd been jittery and preoccupied since that morning, when she'd spotted those bastards on the pier.

"I can't sleep in there, Cole."

"Come on," he said, helping her up. "You can't sleep out here on the floor, either."

The shades in her bedroom were tightly drawn, the closet door wide open, filling the room with a yellow light. She'd been sleeping in the dark the past few weeks, and it saddened him to see the light on again, to see how this had set her back.

He pulled back her covers. "Get in."

She climbed into the bed obediently and lay back, looking him squarely in the eye. At least she was no longer afraid of *him*. He sat on the edge of her bed.

"The house is full of noises tonight," she said.

He nodded. "You can lock your door."

"But then I'd feel even farther away from everyone."

He smiled. "Quite a dilemma."

Her eyes clouded over. "I keep thinking about Grammy," she said. "I'm glad she didn't live to see me raped. She couldn't have taken it. It would have killed her." She surprised herself with a giggle and clapped her hand over her mouth. "That's not funny," she said.

"I bet your grandmother would have laughed at that herself."

"She was so sick. At the end she couldn't talk at all. Sometimes she didn't even know who I was."

He was aware of Grammy watching them from inside the plastic box on Rennie's bureau. "Let's get her an urn," he said.

She brightened. "Can we?"

"Tomorrow." He stood up and switched off the light. "Good night."

"Cole?"

"Yes?"

"Are you in love with Cynthia?"

"No. Why do you ask?"

"Just wondering," she said.

He closed the door, but not before he saw her smile in the light from the closet.

He told the others he'd be getting home late that night. Very late. He even considered packing his clothes for the next day and slipping his toothbrush into his pants pocket, but he decided he'd better not push his luck.

She lived in a boxy little house a block from the river. Estelle would never have lived in a house like that, with its tiny rooms and packrat furniture. The living room was a collage of colors and textures—every chair, every pillow in a different print. It was a soothing blend, though he never would have thought to put all that stuff together himself.

"Have a seat," she said. "I'll get some wine. Or would you prefer coffee?"

"Wine." He sank into the sofa, the fattest and softest he'd ever seen. He took off his tie and undid the top buttons of his shirt.

She came into the room carrying the wine and two glasses and set them on the coffee table on top of a lace doily. Every surface in the room was covered by some kind of fabric. Even the arms of the chairs and the sofa had lacy things hanging over them.

"That was the best king crab I've ever had," she said, pouring the wine.

"You hardly touched it."

"That doesn't mean it wasn't wonderful. In certain situations, my appetite just disappears." She smiled and looked away.

He took the glass she handed him. "You mean when you're nervous?"

"Not nervous. When I'm excited." She blushed. "I don't mean *excited*. Just *anticipatory*."

"What's wrong with being *excited*?" He said it the same way she had. "I am." An understatement. He couldn't forget the way she'd looked at him across the table at dinner, the way she'd licked the butter off the strands of crabmeat, teasing him from the safety of her chair in a public restaurant.

"It's heathen. Only the lower species give in to that primitive sort of feeling." She laughed, embarrassed. She nearly knocked over the wine bottle as she set it on the coffee table. "I don't know why I said that," she added.

She really *was* nervous. He set his glass down and stood up. She was right next to him and she didn't try to move away, not even when he put his hands on her waist. He kissed her, and her arms slid around his neck. The second kiss was her doing, longer and deeper, and suddenly he was the one who was nervous. It had been so long. She wasn't Estelle. Her body was a stranger's against him. What would she like? What would she *need*? He'd relished the routine of making love to Estelle. He'd never grown bored with it—her scent, the shape of her body, the pre-dictability of her orgasms. How did you start all over?

"Can we go to your bedroom?" he said into her hair. He pictured a bed with plump blankets and dozens of lacy pillows stacked high.

She started to pull away from him. "No."

He wanted to ask her why not, but stopped himself. He moved to the sofa, and she let him lower her into the downy cushions. He pulled off his shoes and lay next to her, kissing her and working at the buttons of her blouse, his heart pounding.

Damn. He thought miserably about birth control. He should have asked her what she was using. Something, surely. She wasn't stupid.

When was the last time he'd kissed a woman for so long with all his clothes on? He stood up and switched off the lamp and began to pull his shirt from his pants.

"Cole," she said. "Maybe we'd better not."

The moonlight was soft on her face and breasts, still snug in her bra. He took off his shirt and sat on the sofa next to her, holding her hand. "You look so beautiful right now," he said. She really did. Beautiful and worried. "Are you using something?"

"Diaphragm."

"Is it in?"

She hesitated. "Yes."

He felt a little guilty, making her admit she was ready for this, that she'd expected it.

He ran his fingers down her throat and over her breast and slipped his fingertips under the waistband of her skirt. He heard her draw in her breath. "Are you sure you don't want to?" He stretched out next to her again and felt her hands on his back. He unhooked her bra and found her nipple with his mouth. Her breasts were as smooth as ivory against her tan. Her body began to move rhythmically next to him, and he held her hips tightly against him.

She pushed him gently from her so she could slip out of her blouse and bra. He helped her, and there was no hint of protest now. He knelt on the floor in front of her, slipping his hands beneath the fabric of her skirt, running his palms over the hot skin of her thighs. He pushed her skirt up to her waist and was kissing the inside of her thigh when she caught his chin in the palm of her hand.

"Please don't do that, Cole."

He looked up in surprise. "No?"

"I don't like it."

"Maybe you've never had it done well."

"The thought makes me sick. I hate oral sex."

He leaned back on his heels with a sigh, his erection fading. "Wow," he said.

She pulled her blouse from the arm of the sofa and laid it over her breasts. "There's a lot more to making love than going down on each other," she said.

"Of course. Sorry. You just surprised me. I really like it."

"And I really hate it."

"Is there any room for compromise?"

"None." Her mouth was set.

"Why are you so adamant?"

"By the time you're twenty-nine you know what you like and what you don't."

"But let's say that you and I were together for a long time. Let's say we really cared about each other. Would you still be unwilling to compromise if you knew it meant a lot to me?" Why the hell was he making an issue out of this?

"I could lie to you so you'd stay." There was the slightest quiver to her lower lip, and he leaned forward to erase it with a kiss.

"It's not important," he said. "Sorry I pushed."

They made love on the sofa. She came quickly and it was just as well because he came only seconds later. Even with the wine. It had been a long time.

They lay in each other's arms afterward, a sad tension between them. He stroked her hair and touched her face with his fingertips. "I don't usually come that quickly," he apologized.

"It's all right. I got mine."

"Yes, I noticed."

She began to cry. "I'm sorry." She wiped at her tears with her fingers. "I care for you more than I have for any-one in a long time."

He didn't feel like comforting her. He was thinking about getting out of this house, driving home with the car windows wide open. "That's nothing to cry about," he said.

"I'm afraid now that I'll never see you again."

"Men haven't treated you very well, have they?"

"Not very."

"Of course I want to see you again." He was certain that he did, that he wasn't lying. He had fantasies of permanence with this woman that he wasn't ready to let go of. But he wanted her to be different next time, not crying, not so emotional. Not so uptight. He sat up, wondering if it would be bad etiquette to leave so soon. "I should get back," he said. He stood and groped on the floor for his pants.

"Couldn't you stay tonight?"

He shook his head, although that had certainly been his plan. "I should be there in the morning—I don't want Rennie to think I stayed out all night." A good, moral argument he was certain would appeal to her. "Plus I need an early start tomorrow; I have a few patients due." *You're a real creep, Perelle*, he thought to himself. "I'll call you in the morning?"

She had curled herself into a corner of the sofa. "Please do."

He leaned down to kiss her good night. "I'll let myself out." He turned to find the door, wondering what he had gotten himself into with Cynthia.

38.

Paddy cake, paddy cake, baker man, Bake me a cake as fast as you can, Roll it and knead it and mark it with B, And put it in the oven for Baby and me.

Was that the way it went? Kit rocked in the darkness of the nursery, stroking her baby through her robe.

So Cole was making love to Cynthia tonight.

She pulled her chair closer to the dormered window so she could see the stars. The sky was alive with them. Had it only been a year since she'd sat on the beach with him listening to him describe the constellations? It was as though she'd known him all her life.

He'd been sure of himself tonight, excited as a little kid before a party.

"Aren't you glad she's made you wait?" she asked, feigning excitement for him. She was always faking. It would be the story of her life if she stayed in Mantoloking: Cole with a bright and beautiful woman, Kit in the background, encouraging him, pretending to be happy for him. Not sure enough of what she wanted to go after it herself. She was certain he had no idea of her deception. He knew her so well. He knew the parts of her she never let anyone see. Yet between them hung this major lie.

Earlier tonight she'd pulled out her portable typewriter and updated her resume. Tomorrow she'd have copies made and she'd send them to the medical centers with large PR departments. Nothing on the west coast, and nothing where the winters would be too cold for running. She'd enclose a simple cover letter, noncommittal, a little careless. An expression of her ambivalence.

A stupid time to think of moving, perhaps, but moving would be less stressful than lying awake at night thinking of Cole with Cynthia. She could handle this pregnancy without him. She would have to.

She spotted him through the sliding glass doors of the kitchen the next morning as she tied her shoes. He was sitting on the arm of one of John Chapel's heavy beach chairs, his feet on the seat and his elbows on his knees. A long blade of beach heather dangled from his fingers. She hadn't expected to see him at all this morning. She'd thought he would stay over at Cynthia's.

He stood up with a grin when she walked into the yard. "You look awfully cute," he said.

She smoothed her gray sweatshirt over her belly. "I can't imagine getting bigger than this. My stretch marks have stretch marks."

"You've got a long way to go yet." He put his hand on her back as they walked toward the line of shells left by the high tide.

"When did you get home?" she asked.

"About one."

"That early?"

"It wasn't the greatest night of my life."

She hated herself for taking pleasure in those words. "What went wrong?"

"Nothing actually went wrong. But the earth didn't move, you know what I mean?"

She slipped her arm around his waist. "Cole, you're thirty-five years old. Don't you know by now that it takes time to get the earth moving? You have to work at it."

"I need to know now if it's possible. Otherwise I want to end it before she gets hooked on me."

"Is she moving in that direction?"

"Rapidly. At the risk of sounding egotistical."

"I can't blame her for that. You're probably the prettiest thing she's seen in a long time."

"Talk about pretty. God, she's gorgeous."

"Yes. She is."

"And so bright. But the bottom line is, we don't get along very well. We haven't seriously talked politics but I'm sure we're miles apart. She thinks my lifestyle is unhealthy and maybe a little immoral. And she hates oral sex."

She bit her lip to keep from smiling. "Some women feel that's just too intimate to do the first time they're with a lover," she said, proud of her generosity toward Cynthia.

He shook his head. "She said she'd never do it."

"Did you talk to her about it? Try to find out what the problem is? Maybe she has false teeth."

He laughed. "She won't even allow herself to be the *doee*."

"Oh. The woman's nuts." She said it before she could stop herself.

Cole smiled. "She's not a glowing example of stability, and it worries me to get involved with another crazy lady."

"Well, is it worth taking the chance? Do you like her?"

"Yes, I do. At least I think I do. I like her head—her intellect. And I admire her ambition. But I don't know. Something's not clicking."

He sounded worn out, and she felt evil for wishing him anything other than good fortune with Cynthia. "Why not enjoy it one day at a time?"

"That's easy for you to say. You're not interested in settling down."

It was odd to hear him say that. It wasn't lack of interest so much as sheer terror. It would be like one long, never-ending asthma attack.

"You're trying to fit ten years of intimacy into a few weeks," she said.

He looked at the horizon, squinting, as though the pale morning sunlight hurt his eyes. "I wish I knew where Estelle was."

So, he was still thinking about Estelle.

"You know what I hope?" she asked. "I hope Cynthia can make you not give a damn where Estelle is. I really do." She knew as she said it that she meant every word.

39.

Cole sat next to her on the sofa in the den. "One-thirty over eighty," he said as he took the cuff off her arm. "Do you know what those numbers mean?"

"No more walks on the beach?" she asked. That would be the final blow. Week by week he'd been reining her in, following her around the house with the blood pressure cuff.

"You're not even going to walk from the living room to the kitchen. You're staying upstairs. Your bed or this sofa. I'm talking bed rest."

Bed rest. She stood up. "I just don't feel sick."

"Trust me, you're sick. You're not even thirty-one weeks. You're spilling protein. And look at your ankles."

She didn't need to. She knew they were ballooning above her shoes.

She sat down again, defeated. "I'll go crazy, Cole. I can't spend the rest of this pregnancy lying flat on my back."

"I don't want you to lie flat on your back. Your left side is preferable."

"God, you're vicious."

"And you're stubborn."

"You're treating this so lightly, as though it's a simple thing for me to suddenly stop living."

"Don't be so dramatic. Look." He leaned forward. "This is serious. I wouldn't be at all adverse to you going into the hospital right now. We're looking at an early delivery unless we get this under control."

Rennie took up a collection to buy her a few magazines and Kit spent the day reading in the den. It was an underused room. That seemed like a terrible waste to her now as she looked around her. It was a good room with an enormous blue and rust serape rug on the floor and a white Victorian mantel over the fireplace. It was next to Cole's room and shared his view of the bay. The only TV in the house was in here. That said something about all of them, she mused, that they were strangers to the only room with a TV.

By early evening the small of her back was beginning to ache from lying in one spot for so long. Her housemates brought dinner upstairs and spread out in the den to eat. "We don't want you to have to eat alone," Janni said.

"We can eat with you every night," said Rennie. "And I can buy you more magazines every week."

Kit groaned. *Every week*. She could see her future mapped out in front of her. They'd come upstairs to have dinner with her each night and then they'd get up and leave. They'd go out to the beach and run, swim, play volleyball. And she would stay here, glued to the couch. *Nine more weeks*.

There was a dull pain creeping across her temple. She knew it. Bed rest was going to make her sick.

Two weeks later, Janni sat cross-legged on the end of Kit's bed. She had on her traveling clothes—faded jeans and a T-shirt that read *I wanted a NEW JERSEY but all I could afford was this T-shirt* across her chest. She looked all of thirteen. "You're sure you don't mind if I go?" she asked.

Kit picked up the pillow cover she was stitching and poked the fat needle into the backing for the thousandth time that morning. "Of course I don't mind. I'd feel terrible if you missed San Francisco to stay here and play nurse to me." She'd give up her nine pairs of running shoes if Janni would skip the conference and stay home.

"I don't know how you stand it, sweets. I think about you constantly. It must be awful to be stuck in one spot all day."

"I know every square inch of this ceiling intimately," Kit said, pointing to the ceiling with her needle. Two weeks in bed and she was ready to scream. One wrong move from anyone and it would come out. Shock the hell out of them. They thought she was doing all right. She pulled a piece of blue yarn out of her needle and replaced it with a long strand of brown. "Janni," she said slowly, "what if I need a c-section?" She was getting scared. Things weren't going the way she'd hoped.

"You need a section, you have a section." Janni shrugged.

She poked the needle back into the flower design. She couldn't tell Janni what a section would do to her. More time in bed, more time until she was running again. To

Janni, it would be worth going through a dozen surgeries if the end result were a baby.

"I want to be there even if it's a section," Janni said.

"I'm counting on it. When I picture it, I've got you next to me, holding my hand."

Janni grinned and jumped a little on the bed. "I can't wait!" she said. "It's so exciting!" They were jovial around her, as though she were lying here for their entertainment. Only Cole ever mentioned that she wasn't improving.

She woke in the middle of the night, her right foot curved in on itself with a pain so intense she gasped. She reached around her belly to grab her foot, trying to pull back on the toes. They were locked in place. She pushed her foot against the footboard of her bed, frightened now. She had to walk on it. She jumped out of bed and switched on the light. The room seemed hazy, as if she were looking at it through plastic wrap. She wiped at her eyes but nothing changed.

"Cole!" She pressed her foot into the floor. Her breathing was choppy, her chest tight. "*Cole.*" There were parts of the room she couldn't see. Blind spots that moved with her wherever she turned her head. She looked down at her foot and didn't recognize it. Was it her blurred vision that made it look so enormous?

He came into the room zipping his jeans. "Lie down," he said taking her arm.

"I have a cramp in my foot." She was crying.

"I'll rub it. Lie down." He eased her onto her side and

took her foot in his lap. He began working the cramp out, inch by inch, and she felt the muscles unwind.

"There's something wrong with my eyes," she said. "And my head's going to explode."

He got up without a word and returned with the blood pressure cuff. He put the stethoscope in place and listened without looking at her.

"I'm taking you to Blair," he said, gently pulling the cuff from her arm. "Do you have some things packed?"

She shook her head guiltily. She'd forgotten his request to be ready for something like this.

"Someone can bring things over for you. Come as you are." He tugged the hem of the baggy extra-large T-shirt she was wearing. "Don't bother getting dressed. You'd just have to get undressed once we got there."

They put her in a labor room by herself and turned the lights down low. They strapped thick folds of towels to the rails of her bed. It was as if they were creating the softest atmosphere they could for her. But it was only an illusion.

They drew her blood, stabbing her arm a few times before they found the vein. It had disappeared. Like Cole. He was around somewhere, obviously responsible for all that was happening to her, but she hadn't seen him in hours.

They inserted a catheter in her bladder, linking her to the plastic bag on the side of the bed. They checked her reflexes, frowning at the way her body twitched and jerked, out of her control. An IV line ran into her arm, into the one willing vein they could find. A monitor was strapped around her belly, hooked up to a machine that let her hear her baby's heartbeat. It was a wonderful sound, but she couldn't relax, afraid that at any moment it might stop.

Cole walked in around six. He sat in the chair at the side of her bed, annoyingly calm. "Well." He smiled. "Let's see what we can do for you here."

"Where have you *been*?" she asked, hoping she didn't sound as upset as she felt.

"I checked on a couple of other patients, ordered some tests for you. Had a cup of coffee to wake myself up."

"It's been *hours*, though, I thought you'd gone home. Just left me here." *Don't cry*, she told herself. *You're a grown woman.*

He frowned and leaned toward her. "Kit, we got here at five. It's now a few minutes after six."

One hour? "I'm sorry," she said. "I guess I lost track of the time. If you have to leave, will you please tell me?"

"Of course." He stood up. "You'll be on much stricter bed rest here. I don't want you up for anything. The goal is to keep your baby inside you for as long as we can without endangering your health, and the good news is that he or she seems to be doing well. So for now we have to wait and see."

There was nothing to look at in this room. No window. Empty white walls cloaked in shadow. She had a right to be confused about the time. There was no way to measure it. She thought of her watch on her dresser at the house and longed for her room, probably sun-soaked by now, and for the never-ending hum of the ocean. What if she never saw the house again?

"Come on, now," the older nurse with the glasses told her when she noticed her tears. "You're making a big fuss over nothing."

"I think the monitor sounds different than it did before." The heartbeat was very faint. "Is my baby all right?"

The nurse didn't even glance at the monitor. "Your mind can play tricks on you," she said. "Everything's just fine."

She was positive it sounded different. There'd been nothing to concentrate on but that sound ever since she'd been in the room. She wanted to ask the nurse to look at the screen and its little green lines, but she said nothing. She couldn't afford to have them annoyed with her.

She was certain they already were. She asked too many questions, she was too fearful, she pushed the call button too much. Their smiles were practiced and patronizing. When they walked out of her room, she thought she could hear them in the hall whispering about her. Complaining. *A couple of spots in front of her eyes and she thinks we should drop everything and hold her hand.*

There was no phone in the labor room. She wanted to call Cole's office to find out when he'd be in to see her. It had been so long.

The nurse with the glasses came in again to check the blood pressure cuff that was now permanently attached to her arm.

"Do you think Dr. Perelle will be in soon?" Kit asked timidly.

"You're not his only patient, you know."

She felt a flash of anger, but it was overshadowed by her fear. "I'm sorry," she said. "I'm not too good at this."

"At what?"

"At being a patient. I'm not used to it."

The nurse laughed. "You're doing fine, dear. But it doesn't help to worry about things. Only makes it worse."

Cole made it very clear that she was not his only patient. He came in just before noon, still dressed in his scrubs from the morning's c-section. There was a sickening blotch of blood on the blue pants. It was a complicated surgery, he said, trying to account for his long absence. Now his office was backed up, the waiting room overflowing.

And was everything okay with her? Good, fine. He'd see her later.

At noon she had a new nurse. Alison Peters. Young enough to make her feel too old to be having a baby. Bright and quick. She touched everything. The buttons on the monitor. The band around her belly. Inspected everything with intelligent eyes. Kit watched her silently through hazy vision. She would not speak, would not alienate this one.

Alison finished her work and sat on the edge of Kit's bed. She smiled and squeezed her arm. "Must be scary," she said, "locked in here with a bunch of machines."

Kit started to cry and Alison took her hand.

"Do you understand everything that's going on?" she asked.

"Is the baby all right? I thought the monitor sounded different."

"The sound changes as your baby moves around,"

Alison said. "It's harder for the ultrasound to pick up the heartbeat if your baby moves out of its range. That doesn't mean the heart's not still strong and healthy."

"Oh," Kit said. That made perfect sense. "Do you think the baby could survive if I had it now?"

"The Intensive Care Nursery has a lot of experience with premature babies. There's a very good chance that your baby could do quite well." Alison handed her a tissue. "Would you like a back rub while we talk?"

"I'd love that," she said. She could keep this woman with her, right next to her. "But don't you have other patients you need to get to?"

"No." Alison began to untie the back of Kit's gown. "You're my only patient. I'm afraid you're stuck with me."

Cole came in at three. He looked tired. "Rennie's in the hall," he said. "She's on her way home from summer school and asked if she could stop in to see you. Is that okay?"

"Absolutely!" It would be wonderful to see anyone from home.

"I'll tell her to keep it short," Cole said, opening her door.

Rennie stood at the end of the bed, biting her lip.

"It's sweet of you to stop in, Rennie," Kit said.

"What's the matter with your face?" Rennie asked.

She touched her cheek. "I didn't know there was anything wrong with it." She looked at Cole.

"Her face is just a little swollen," he said to Rennie.

She had to find a mirror. She'd had no idea.

"Are you going to have the baby now?"

"I don't know." She looked at Cole again. He shrugged.

"If you don't have the baby today, can you come home?" Rennie turned to Cole. "Could she?"

"I think we'd better keep her here for a while, Rennie," he said.

She waited until the door had completely closed behind Rennie before she spoke. "I'd like the mirror out of my purse, please."

He looked at her for a moment as if deciding how to answer. "There's a mirror inside the top of your tray table," he said, rolling it closer to her.

She hesitated, her hand on the top.

"You don't look that bad," he said.

She opened the top and caught her breath. Her cheeks looked as if she'd had all her teeth pulled at once. And her *eyes*. The lids were puffy white sausages that hid her lashes. "I had no idea I looked like this," she said, closing the top.

He sat down on the chair next to her bed. "Let's talk," he said.

"I don't want any more visitors." No one should see her like this. Her coworkers from the PR office were planning on coming down that afternoon. "I don't want to see anyone," she said.

"Don't worry. The nurses know not to let anyone in. I thought a minute or two with Rennie wouldn't hurt, but I guess I was wrong."

"No, that was okay." She gently touched her fingertips to

her eyelids. They were ready to burst. She gritted her teeth together to keep from crying.

"Your pressure's gone up a little higher," Cole said. "I'm putting you on magnesium sulfate to ward off . . . any problems. If things don't improve, you'll have to deliver."

"Now? You said yourself it's too early."

"There comes a point when you . . . when *I* have to decide if your baby would be better off in the Intensive Care Nursery than inside of you."

For the first time it hit her. Her baby was in real trouble. "Cole?"

"Yes?"

"If I'd been more obedient about taking it easy, would I be lying here right now?"

"I don't think it would have made any difference. And there's no point to thinking that way, anyhow, so no guilt trips. Okay?"

"I can tell you your baby's sex, if you'd like to know." He was watching the ultrasound image on the screen.

"Oh, yes."

"You have a daughter."

"What?" She needed to hear him say it again.

"A daughter. A girl-child. My goddaughter, remember her?"

She looked at the image on the screen. "Alison," she said.

He looked surprised. "Alison?"

"I just like it."

"Alison as in Alison Peters?" He hadn't lost that stunned look.

"She's been wonderful." The one human touch in a room full of plastic and machines.

"A little impulsive, don't you think? You know someone for a couple of hours and name your baby after her?"

"It's a good name, Cole." It was perfect. Alison was as real to her as if she were already lying in her arms.

40.

He could tell by Cheryl's face that his problems had gotten worse overnight. She handed him the computer sheet with the latest lab results and sat down in the chair by his desk, putting her feet up on the other chair. He felt her blue eyes on him as she waited for him to react.

He studied the sheet for a long time, as if he could change the numbers by concentrating. "Well," he said, "I guess inducing labor would be just short of infanticide."

Cheryl looked calmer than he felt. "If her pressure goes any higher, you'll have to choose between that and matricide."

She was only half joking, maybe not joking at all. He hated these decisions about any patient. That it was Kit terrified him. His judgment was clouding over.

"The nurses are getting nervous, Cole. They're afraid she's going to seize."

She was thinking he'd waited too long to start the mag sulfate. He wondered about that himself.

"Cheryl"—he leaned across his desk toward her—"I don't want to deliver her until I have no other choice."

"I don't understand what you're waiting for."

This was what he usually loved best about Cheryl—the way she'd stand up to him, make him think. But right now it irritated him.

"You seem to be thinking only of Kit," he said.

"And you're thinking only of the baby."

Was it his imagination or was Cheryl giving him dirty looks in his office examining room? He hoped his patients couldn't pick up the tension between them. The nurses on the unit were grumbling about him. That he knew for certain. Cheryl was keeping it no secret. Maybe they were right. Maybe he was overcompensating for his tie to Kit. He wished he could extricate himself from the whole mess. He could stand off in a corner and with complete objectivity say, *this is what should be done.*

"My head is killing me."

He lowered the railing and sat on the edge of Kit's bed. "I'll get you something for it," he said.

"How am I doing otherwise?"

He shook his head. "Not so good. I've decided to induce you." He'd made up his mind at lunch. He'd done all he could for that baby. She was on her own now.

Kit looked at the ceiling. Her eyelids were so swollen that he couldn't have guessed the color of her eyes.

"I'm worried that Alison won't make it." She looked at him and he guessed she was hoping for reassurance.

"She's doing surprisingly well inside you," he said. "That's why I'm hesitant to induce. But since you're—"

"What if I said no? What would happen?"

"Convulsions are a strong possibility." He didn't mention stroke or coma. See if convulsions would be enough for her.

She sighed. "Oh, shit."

"And your baby will run into problems getting enough oxygen."

She played with the wire to her call button. "My baby's not even born and I'm already a lousy mother."

"Don't do that to yourself."

She pulled a tissue from the box at her side and blew her nose. "So what happens now?"

"We'll add some Pitocin to your IV to bring on your labor." He should warn her that it might not work. "Your cervix isn't very favorable for induction so you may not be able to deliver vaginally even with the Pitocin."

She frowned. "A section?"

"It may be our only option."

Her contractions didn't start for nearly an hour, but when they did they were just what he had hoped for—hard and fast.

She was miserable. He felt sorry for her. She told him she felt trapped. He sat on her bed and smoothed the damp curls off her forehead. Every part of her body was hooked up to something. She *was* trapped.

"The pain is worse than I expected," she said.

He nodded. "The anesthesiologist is on his way." They would both be more comfortable when she had some pain relief.

"I'm sorry I'm such a shitty patient."

He smiled. "You're not."

"Yes, I am. I'm a shitty patient and a shitty mother and a shi—" She gasped with the sudden grip of a contraction.

He watched the monitor. "Breathe through it, Kit," he said. "Don't hold your breath."

She went limp as the contraction ended, tears rolling down the sides of her face and into her hair. "I'm not ready for this, Cole," she said.

She was right, in more ways than one. Her cervix wasn't performing, still thick and closed. He'd be amazed if this worked. "Listen"—he leaned closer to her ear—"I have to get back to the office. I'll stop in between patients."

She grabbed his sleeve. Her eyes asked him how he could leave her.

He looked at his watch. "It's three o'clock," he said. "My last patient's at four-thirty, and then I'll be all yours." He squeezed her hand. "I'm just down the hall."

He couldn't concentrate on his patients, shouldn't even charge them for their visits. He saw Kit between appointments. There was little change, except that each time he saw her she looked at him with more fear in her eyes, more awareness that the induction wasn't working.

He found Jay in the lounge. He poured his tenth cup of coffee of the day and sat next to him at the table. Jay watched him expectantly.

"Here's the picture," Cole said into his coffee cup. "She's been having good contractions for a couple of hours, but her pressure's still up and her cervix isn't doing a thing."

"If it were some other patient, what would you do?" Jay was whispering. There were other people in the lounge.

Cole took a swallow of coffee. It tasted like iodine. "It's not some other patient," he said.

Jay rested his hand on Cole's shoulder. "Are you all right?"

Cole shut his eyes and felt his head spin. "I'm playing with fire here unless I do a section."

"So section her."

Was it that simple? He looked up at Jay. "Would you assist?" They rarely operated together anymore, but right now he wanted Jay with him.

"I was hoping you'd ask."

There was chaos in the hallway by the labor rooms. One of the nurses grabbed his arm. "She's seizing."

It was like a scene from a horror movie. Kit's arms and legs thrashed in spastic rhythm; saliva ran from the corner of her mouth.

"Start the Valium," he said hoarsely.

Alison Peters was working with the IV tubing. "Already have," she said without so much as a glance in his direction. An older nurse he didn't know leaned over Kit, watching her body rock convulsively on the bed.

He should have started the mag sulfate sooner. Not that it would have been any guarantee.

"Give her a bolus of mag sulfate," he said.

"Yes, Doctor," said Alison.

He watched helplessly, gripping the metal arm rail of

her bed. He tried not to think about what the seizure might be doing to her. To the baby.

Kit's violent movements subsided and he felt his own body go limp. His knees were about to give out, but he had no time to waste. The gurney appeared, and he and Alison lifted Kit onto it and raced down the hall to the OR.

It was the quickest section he could ever remember doing. Even with Jay assisting—Jay who only performed c-sections these days when Cole asked him to—it was smooth sailing. They were perfectly matched today—Cole with the greater knowledge of the procedure. Jay with the calmer approach. They balanced each other. When they were finished and the pale, limp baby girl had been rushed off to the Intensive Care Nursery, it was all he could do to keep from telling Jay he loved him. It was the closest he'd ever come to getting those words out.

The house did not look welcoming as he pulled into the garage. The windows were dark, except for those in the living room, and no one had turned on the front lights. He felt his way across the gravel driveway in the darkness.

Janni, Maris, and Rennie were in the living room, but the house felt empty. Jay was still at Blair, and Kit was lying asleep in the recovery room of the Maternity Unit, unreachable. She didn't exist for him tonight.

He wanted to be surrounded by friends. Friends who wanted nothing of him other than his quiet company. Friends who would massage the knots out of his shoulders. He was too tired, too empty to offer anything in return.

But as he stood near the front door, looking into the expectant faces of his three housemates, he knew that he would not find what he wanted here. There was too much tension in this room.

"You're back," he said to Janni. She was wearing a San Francisco T-shirt.

"I missed the whole damn thing, didn't I?" she said. "I called the hospital and Jay said there wasn't much point to my coming over, that Kit's out of it. How's the baby?"

"Not good." He looked around the room. He felt disoriented. "I need milk," he said.

"Well, get your milk and join us," said Janni. There was a curt snap to her voice. He pretended not to hear it, as if ignoring it would make it go away. He needed Janni's warm side tonight.

"I don't know." He buried his hands in his pockets. "I'm exhausted. I might just go to bed."

"But we want to hear about the *baby*," Rennie whined.

And I don't want to talk about it.

"Come on, Cole, stay with us a while," Maris pleaded.

"Okay," he said, against his better judgment. "For a few minutes."

He went to the kitchen and returned with a glass of milk.

"The baby's not going to die or anything, is she?" Rennie asked as he sat next to Maris on the couch.

He shrugged. "I don't know. She could. She has severe respiratory distress."

"That's crazy," Rennie said. "Babies don't die."

He felt as if she were blaming him.

"Poor Kit," said Janni. "It must have been horrible for her."

He nodded and leaned back. He couldn't sit up on his own any longer. "Yes, it was," he said. "For me, too. I made a decision that I'm never going to do this again. I won't have a friend as my patient." He'd felt enormous relief when he'd come to that conclusion. As soon as Kit was back on her feet, he'd refer her to someone else.

"Where does that leave me?" Janni asked.

"There are plenty of good gynecologists around, Jance."

"I have no say in the matter?"

"Janni." He sat forward and frowned at her. "Have a little compassion, okay? I don't think I use my best judgment when I'm making decisions about a friend's welfare."

Janni was quiet, but only for a moment. "Cynthia called this afternoon," she said.

He groaned. *Cynthia.* "Did you explain to her that I didn't intentionally stand her up last night?"

Maris squeezed his arm. "She knows that, baby."

"You could have called her," Janni said.

"It was just about the last thing on my mind."

"I think she's figured that out. She's catching on that when it comes to Kit she'll always have to take a back seat."

He felt his face redden. "That's not true. My mind's on Kit right now, but . . ."

"But *what?*" asked Janni. "How can you expect to have a normal relationship with another woman if you come home and tell Kit everything that went on with her? That was the problem with Estelle too, wasn't it?"

He felt backed into a corner. "Why are you being such a bitch?" he asked.

"Really, Cole, it's so unfair to Kit." Janni plowed ahead. "She's never going to get something going with Orrin or any other man as long as you keep her as your confidante. When are you going to admit to yourself that you care more about Kit than anyone else in the world?"

Cole set his milk on the coffee table and stood up. "I don't get why you're doing this to me," he said.

"Why didn't you *call* me?" The tears started down Janni's cheeks, and he looked away. He didn't want to feel any sympathy for her. "I promised Kit I'd be there for her and you cut me out."

"Janni, if you're angry with me, why don't you just *say* it instead of throwing all this other shit my way?" He didn't wait for her answer. He turned and headed for the stairs, for the haven of his room.

It was a long time before he fell asleep. He couldn't get Janni's words out of his mind. She was right. He used Kit. He'd go out with Cynthia, have a good time, come home, and use Kit as his therapist. And she did the same with him. He'd made her dependent on him.

Tomorrow he'd start fresh with Cynthia. He'd tell her everything that came into his head. He hadn't given her a chance to get close, really.

And he would cut back on the time he spent with Kit. This would be the perfect time to do it. She was out of the house. She was no longer pregnant. It would just be one change among many for her.

The phone woke him from a sleep that left him more tired than refreshed. Someone in another part of the house answered it, and he lay still waiting. The clock on his night table read quarter to six. A bad sign. *Let it be the baby and not Kit.*

"Cole!" It was Janni, calling him from downstairs. She must not have slept well either. Good.

He picked up the receiver. "This is Cole Perelle." The rasp of his voice surprised him.

"Dr. Perelle, this is Valerie in the nursery. I wanted to let you know that the Sheridan baby died about an hour ago."

He shut his eyes. "Does her mother know yet?"

"I don't think so."

"I'll be right there."

They'd moved her to a private room on the Maternity Unit. It was small and sterile and smelled antiseptic.

She was inhumanly pale, her lips white and papery. She smiled weakly at him. "Hi," she said.

He sat on the edge of her bed and took her right hand, the one that wasn't attached to the IV. "Hi." He leaned over and kissed her warm cheek.

"Is today Friday?"

"No. It's Saturday. About seven-fifteen in the morning."

"I lost a day somehow."

"Yesterday was a hard one for you." He touched her hair,

smoothed it away from her face with his fingers. It was the only color in the room.

"Did Janni get back yet?"

"Yes, last night. She was upset about not having been here for you."

"Tell her not to worry about it. How's Rennie?"

"Okay. She misses you, but she's doing all right."

She smiled a little and turned her eyes away from him.

He had to tell her now. He opened his mouth but she stopped him.

"Jay helped yesterday, didn't he, or did I dream that?"

"Yes, he assisted," he said.

She looked at the ceiling and blinked hard. "The longer I keep you talking about other things the longer I can pretend Alison's all right." She looked at him then, waiting for him to speak.

He tightened his grip on her hand. "She died this morning, Kit."

"No! Shh, *please!*" She pulled her hand away from his to cover her ear.

"I'm sorry."

He waited while she cried, her face as colorless as the sheets.

"I didn't even get to see her," she said.

"You can. As soon as you feel up to it we can bring her over for you to see."

"Today?" There was childlike hope in her voice.

"I think tomorrow would be better." He wasn't being fair. She was probably ready right now. He was the one who wouldn't be able to handle it today.

"Don't let them do an autopsy until I get to see her."

"They won't. You have to sign for an autopsy."

"But what if they do it by mistake?"

"They won't, sweetheart." He touched her cheek and his fingertips came away wet.

"But what if she really wasn't dead and they thought she was and they put her in the refrigerator and she—"

"Kit." He leaned down and took her in his arms. "She died, honey. Alison's dead. Her lungs weren't ready."

"I shouldn't have run." She sobbed against his neck. "She'd still be safe inside me."

"That has nothing to do with it."

"But if only I—"

"Shh." He rocked her gently as if she were a child, not wanting her to say another word. "It'll be all right."

Cynthia sat across from him at dinner, in a soft, appealing gray pantsuit, her eyes never leaving his face as he told her about the past two days. She reached across the table to take his hand and murmured words of sympathy, and he began to feel manipulative. It was like flicking a switch, the way he could get her to care about him.

After dinner they went back to her house and made love. She lay smiling in his arms afterward, and he softly scratched her back, but his mind was on Kit. He hadn't spoken to her since that morning when he'd told her about the baby. He'd called the unit a few times to check on her condition, but he deliberately avoided calling her. Janni said she'd spend the afternoon with her. That was better.

She should have a woman with her right now. He'd only be a reminder of yesterday's nightmare.

They were eating pizza at the kitchen table when he got home.

"Please join us," Janni said.

"I'm not a masochist."

"Give us a chance to make up to you for last night," said Maris.

Rennie's face was turned up to him, anxious little lines etched around her wide blue eyes.

"Sit down, Cole." Jay pulled out the chair next to him, and Cole lowered himself into it, inside an invisible suit of armor.

They obviously had a plan. They went around the table in order, competing with each other in the eloquence of their apology. They were sorry for not giving him more support, they said. He felt hard and annoyed. He listened without comment. Janni spoke last and there was an almost hysterical quality to her voice as she begged him to forgive her. He thought of telling her that the wedge she'd pounded between them would take a long time to dislodge, but she wasn't worth the strength it would take to get the words out.

When she was finished, Cole let them stew for a minute in silence. "Are you all through?" he asked finally.

They nodded.

"Good night, then."

He rose and walked toward the stairs, pleased by the

vibrations of disappointment he left behind him. In the morning he would be kind. But for tonight, there was no other way.

41.

Was it Sunday? Kit wasn't certain, although otherwise she was painfully lucid. She knew *where* she was. She was in that closet-sized room at the end of the hall in the Maternity Unit. It was as far from the nursery and the cries of the babies as they could get her. And she was thinking clearly enough to know she was lonely. Janni'd spent much of Saturday with her and she'd been wonderful, letting her recount the same dim memories of the past few days over and over. Kit couldn't stop talking and Janni encouraged her. Helped her separate one piece of pain from another. Janni knew what helped and what didn't.

But when Janni left, she was alone. She thought for certain Cole would come in to see her, but he didn't. Her sister called, begging Kit to let her come, but the last thing she wanted was to have Paula in Mantoloking. It would be more of a responsibility than a relief.

Jay stopped by Saturday evening to check her incision. He kissed the top of her head and told her he loved her. They'd all be happy to get her home, he said.

And Orrin sent flowers. *I was very sorry to hear about*

your loss, he'd written on the card, as if she were no more than a client.

She cried most of Saturday night, imagining Alison in the morgue. She pictured her in a little wooden box, walnut-colored and highly polished. Sometime near morning she realized that Alison was more likely in a suffocating plastic bag than a box and she cried harder. She couldn't get the image out of her mind.

It was ten in the morning by the time Cole came into her room. She felt as though she'd been holding her breath all night and could finally let it out.

"You're doing very well," he said, her chart in his hand.

"Can I see her today?"

He nodded. "Are you up to it now?"

"Yes." She tried to sit up but a dagger of pain pierced her side.

"Well"—he looked hesitant—"if you really feel up to it we can bring her over. Or you can wait until this afternoon."

Now. She wanted to see Alison now. She didn't let her face show pain as he cranked up the head of her bed.

Her nurse appeared at the door to her room. "Shall I get the baby?" she asked. She looked as though she would rather walk across hot coals.

Cole stood up. "I'll go," he said. At the door he turned back to face her. "She'll feel very cold, Kit."

She made herself nod. She thought of dead adults she'd seen at funerals, ethereal and untouchable, and her heart jiggled its beat. She didn't want to be afraid of her own baby.

It seemed like a long time before he returned, wheeling one of the little plastic cribs from the nursery. Inside was a pink bundle. Her hands shook uncontrollably as he came closer, and she locked them together in her lap.

Cole lifted the bundle out of the crib as carefully as if he were handling a live baby and set it on Kit's thighs. She felt the cold through the blankets. He pushed the one chair in the room against the far wall and sat on its edge.

She was glad Alison was completely covered by the blanket. She needed to go slowly. With a trembling hand, she reached forward and gently tugged the blanket away from the baby's face. She caught her breath. Alison's features were perfect, carved in pale wax.

"My God, she's beautiful." Her hand was steadier now, and she ran her fingers over the miniature nose, the ear like a delicate seashell.

"So much hair." She smiled, smoothing the pale copper fluff, so soft she could barely feel it, under her fingertips. "This was the color of my hair when I was a baby."

Cole didn't answer, as though he knew her words weren't meant for him.

She pulled the blanket away slowly, taking in every part of her baby and seeing with an overwhelming sadness that she was perfect. Down to the tiniest toe and speck of a nail.

She looked at Cole. "There's nothing wrong with her," she said, as if asking him how he could possibly think this was a dead baby he'd placed in front of her.

"It's inside," he said.

"I want to hold her."

He stood up. "With or without the blanket?"

"Without." The bare skin of her arms tingled.

Cole set the baby in her arms, the tiny head resting in the crook of Kit's elbow. It felt perfect. Even with the cold and the shivery weakness that ran through her. Skin against skin. Her breasts ached. If Cole weren't here, would she try to fit her nipple into Alison's mouth? Yes, she thought, a little alarmed, she probably would. She'd heard about that—mothers who went a little crazy when their babies died.

"Alison." She said it without thinking. "I'm sorry . . . I never knew this would happen." She was vaguely aware of Cole rising, turning to look out the window of her room. "I wish I had it to do all over again," she whispered. "I'd do it right this time." She watched one of her tears land on Alison's cheek and roll over her lips and across her chin, as if the baby had cried it herself. "My baby." Kit hugged the little body to her, afraid she would never be able to let go.

Cole turned and walked toward her.

"One last look," she pleaded, setting Alison back on her thighs. She traced her face with her fingers, trying to commit every line of it to memory. "She's really pretty, Cole, isn't she?"

He nodded.

"I wish I'd seen her eyes."

"They're blue. I think they'll probably stay . . . I mean, they would have stayed blue."

"Like Paula's." She thought of her sister's clear blue eyes. "She looks a little like Paula, I think."

"Ready?" He was probably getting impatient with her. She nodded, and he lifted Alison out of her lap and placed her back in the crib. He picked up the blanket and set it in a crumpled mound on top of her.

"Could you smooth it, Cole?"

"Hmm?"

"The blanket." She blushed. "I . . . it's just that I'd feel better if you'd smooth it out a little."

He picked up the blanket, folded it in half and set it neatly over the baby. "Okay?" He smiled at her and she nodded. "I'll be back in a minute," he said.

He walked out the door and she had to stop herself from calling him back.

Orrin visited on Monday. He looked impeccable as always in a navy blue suit, sitting a few feet from her bed, staring at her. She knew she looked terrible. Her hair hung limp and unwashed around her face. She wished she could hide from his eyes.

As good as Orrin could be with words, he was at a loss for them now. She wished he would talk. Fill up the silence with his usual rhetoric.

"Would you like to see a picture of Alison?" She felt shy, asking him. She'd been showing it to everyone who came in her room, this paper-thin substitute for a baby. It was all she had.

He nodded.

She pulled the Polaroid snapshot from the drawer of the

hospital night table and handed it to him. "The nursery took it before she died."

He barely glanced at it before handing it back to her. "It's hard to see what she looked like," he said.

Kit wanted to point out what he'd missed—the tufts of hair and button nose, the tiny fingers clutching the yellow wire attached to her chest—but she said nothing.

Orrin shifted in the chair. "I have to go out of town for a few days so I won't be able to visit for a while."

"Oh. Where are you going?"

"New York. There are some depositions I have to take up there. I'll be gone about a week I think."

"Will you call me when you get back?" She was suddenly afraid of losing touch with him. With anyone.

"Of course," he said, standing, ready to make his exit.

"Thank you for coming. And thanks for the flowers."

"Sure." He was practically backing away from her. "I'll see you in a week or so," he said, turning quickly toward the door.

When she got back to the Chapel House, she would have to check the dictionary to see if she were a leper or a lepress.

There was no doubt about it. Cole was pulling away from her.

At noon on Wednesday Jay announced he was driving her home. "Cole's really swamped today," he said when he saw the surprise in her face. "He said he'd see you at the house tonight."

Her bed in the house was an invitation. Someone had

made it up with flowery pink sheets. Somehow she found the energy to change out of her pants and cotton top into the baggy man's T-shirt she'd worn while she'd been pregnant and she climbed into her bed, tucking Alison's picture under her pillow. She felt pleasantly pressed into the mattress. She would never get out of this bed. Cole would tell her she had to get up and walk around. He'd been after her about it since Sunday. But what was the point? This was the place to be.

Except for the heat. Jay brought the fan into her room before he went back to Blair, and it blew hot, damp salt air across the bed.

She slept all afternoon. Cole woke her at six. "Dinner's ready." He stood next to her bed. He was wearing his oatmeal-colored suit and looked newly tanned.

Maybe he would be different now that she was home. She tried to sit up, but her body was too heavy to move. "I couldn't get up if I wanted to," she said.

"You need to keep moving, Kit. And you need to eat. Now come on."

"Just for tonight," she begged. "Tomorrow I'll get up, but for tonight I just want to lie here."

He frowned at her. "Okay. I'll ask someone to bring your dinner up." He looked at his watch. "I have to go. I'm supposed to pick Cynthia up at six-thirty."

So that was why he was dressed up. She grabbed his wrist, the bronzed wrist of a stranger. "Wait," she said. "I'm so out of touch. You haven't told me how things are going with her. I'm not so full of my own problems that I can't listen." It was a desperate ploy to keep him with her.

She didn't care how things were going with Cynthia. She didn't want to hear about Cynthia at all.

"Things are better," he said. "We've seen each other a lot this week."

She pictured the two of them, sunbathing on the Chapel House beach while she lay crying in her airless hospital room.

"That's good," she said. She had the feeling she was keeping him. He stood first on one foot, then the other. "Well, have fun tonight."

A quick smile. "I will. Bye." He left without touching her.

Thursday morning he didn't even come in her room. He stood in the doorway, badgering her to eat, before he left for Blair.

When did this start? She pressed her fingers to her temples. He'd been very kind the morning he brought Alison to her room. Kind, yes, but a little distant. Even that Saturday, he'd come to tell her about Alison's death, and then he didn't come back. He'd hugged her, though. Her body ached to remember it—his arms around her, the scent of his neck and hair. But maybe he'd felt he had to. She'd been crying, talking fantasy nonsense about Alison. She'd left him little choice but to comfort her. It embarrassed her to remember it.

No, she could trace the change right back to the day of Alison's birth. She'd been so demanding, as if she were his only patient. Whiny and childish. What a drain she'd been on him. He probably lived for those moments when he could get away from her complaining and her fear. By the end of that day she must have been no more than a repulsive mass of body parts to him.

Could she ever erase the image he had of her now? Not this way. Not lying here, glued to her bed with sweat.

She moved slowly through a shower. It took her forever to wash her hair. She planned to get dressed and go downstairs. Maybe eat something. But she began to cry again for no reason, and her bed with its hot, rumpled pink sheets drew her in again.

She slept until one o'clock when Rennie knocked on the door.

"Cole said it would be okay for you to sit out on the beach with me," she said, stepping into the room. She had on a white eyelet beach jacket Kit had never seen before. Her tan had deepened to a rich golden brown.

"Oh. Thanks for asking, honey, but I'd rather stay here."

Rennie made no movement toward the door.

"Is there something else, Rennie?"

The girl stared down at her bare feet. "I wish you'd get better soon. Things are different."

"Different how?" She didn't have the strength for this.

"Nobody gets along as well. I get afraid sometimes things won't ever be the same again."

"I get afraid of that too, Ren," she said, knowing that was not what Rennie needed to hear. "I'll be all right in a few days. I'm just very, very tired."

"Can I bring you something to eat? Some cookies or something?"

She smiled. "I'm not hungry."

Rennie stared at the floor again. "Cole said if you didn't eat you'd have to go back to the hospital."

A current of alarm shot through her. Would he do that? Did he want to get her as far away from him as he could?

"Okay, honey. Bring me some toast, please." She'd flush it down the toilet, but she wouldn't let him put her back in the hospital.

Cole looked genuinely concerned that night as he sat on her bed.

"Maris said all you had today was some toast."

And I didn't even have that. "Maybe I'll get my appetite back tomorrow," she said.

"You need to eat, and more than just toast. And you're hardly drinking anything. And you need to get moving, Kit. When you wouldn't exercise in the hospital I thought maybe you just needed to get home with us."

She looked at his hands instead of his eyes and said nothing. She felt ugly.

"Kit"—he looked uncomfortable—"I thought I might ask Frank Jansen to come see you."

"I don't need a shrink," she said.

"It's normal to be depressed after you've lost a baby but I'm concerned that your depression's taking a toll on your health."

He was talking to her gently, doctor to patient. *He'll be glad to get out of here*, she thought. Glad to get to Cynthia. She pictured Cynthia's sleek dark hair and slender body. Was she going down on him now?

"All right, I'll drink and eat and get up," she snapped.

"Okay?" She rolled onto her side and shut her eyes, relieved to escape his scrutiny.

She woke to the sound of a baby crying. She stared at the ceiling, lacy with moonlight, trying to get her bearings. It was her own room, not the hospital. It was very early Friday morning and somewhere—down the hall, maybe in the nursery—a baby was crying.

She lay still, willing the sound to come again, but the murmur of the sea was all she could hear.

She sat up, a thin veneer of perspiration coating her body. *I'm going crazy*, she thought. She got out of bed, startled by the weakness in her legs, and walked slowly to the door. She had to stop there to catch her breath.

She opened the door and stepped into the hallway, feeling a pang of sadness when she saw Cole's door in front of her. How confidently she'd knocked on that door in the past, knowing she was welcome on the other side. It was the last door in the house she would knock on now.

She moved slowly, breathlessly down the hall until she reached the nursery. She turned the knob. *Please, God, let there be a baby inside*. She held her breath as she opened the door. There was no need to turn on the light to see that the nursery was empty. The moon washed any mystery from the room with its stark light. She could see the shine of the blue plastic mattress in the bottom of the crib.

She was relieved to get back to her bed. The mattress was molded to the shape of her body now.

Was she going out of her mind? She had to do something, take some action. She would talk to Cole. She had little left to lose. She'd tell him that she needed him. *No.* Too demanding. Should she tell him she knew he was disgusted with her? Then he'd try to defend himself. She'd never needed to think through her words to him before.

She was tense the second she opened her eyes in the morning. She didn't remember falling asleep, just rehearsing in her mind what she would say to Cole. He would stop in her room before he left for work and she would tell him, "Cole, I miss you." She would try not to cry, but thinking those words to herself put a lump in her throat.

He knocked on her door at eight-fifteen. "How are you doing?" he asked from the doorway.

Please come in. Her heart was pounding. "Better," she said. "Do you have a little time to talk?" She said it so coolly, so casually that he would never guess the trepidation behind the words.

He looked at his watch. "I wish I did, but I have a slew of patients starting at nine," he said. "I'm sorry. I'll call you later."

"No, it's not that important. I just haven't really talked with you in a while." She steeled herself. "How about after work?"

He shook his head. "Cynthia and I are going to an early movie and then out to dinner. But, listen," he added suddenly, "I can cancel with her . . ."

"No, don't do that." She smiled. "It's nothing."

For the first time she became aware of the house functioning without her. From her window seat, she watched

Rennie and one of her girlfriends on the beach, stretched out on blankets. Even at this distance she could see that Rennie's hair was streaked blond from the sun. She could hear indecipherable snips of their conversation as the hot salt air blew through her window. At noon, she watched Maris dive into the water and swim back and forth beyond the breaking waves. Kit felt dead to them now. Everyone was doing fine without her.

Janni yelled at her. The new tack. Long hours of gentle talk about Alison and patient encouragement to get out of her room hadn't worked.

"Look, Kit, you're *rotting* in here," she said in a voice that was painfully loud. "I want you to come downstairs. I don't care if you're miserable as hell down there, you need to get out of this . . . this tomb."

Yes, a tomb. Her room seemed to fit that description now, holding her in, shrinking in size with each day.

"Please leave me alone," she said.

"And you need a shower," Janni added with brutal frankness. She came over to the window seat and grabbed her hand. "Come on, sweets. You and I are taking a shower together. You'll feel much better, you'll see."

"Not so fast!" She nearly fell. God, she was weak. It would be easier to go with Janni than to fight her.

She let Janni wash her hair and soap her body while she leaned against the shower wall, eyes closed. It took all her effort just to stand there and breathe at the same time.

Maris changed her sheets while she was in the shower. Someday she would have the strength to thank them for this, but not now. She headed in the direction of the bed.

"Oh no you don't." Janni grabbed her arm. "You're coming outside. On the beach."

"No, Janni, please." She began to cry.

"Kit, Rennie misses you. She needs you." Another new tack. "Come on, sweets."

She sat on her bed. "Let me stay here, Janni. Please."

There was some pleasure in seeing Janni give in.

She felt undeniably better now that she was clean and lying between fresh sheets. Maris had propped her pillows up for her, and she leaned back against them with a sigh. It had been a rough hour.

Alison's picture. She leaped up and threw the pillows to the floor. Nothing beneath them but the pure white cotton sheet. What if Maris had put it in the laundry? Her heart raced as she pulled open the drawer of her night table. There it was, resting on the tissue box. She clutched it to her chest, breathing hard. She could hear the wheeze when she exhaled like the string section of an orchestra.

She turned away from Cole when he came to her room the next morning. Her head throbbed and she didn't want him to see the red in her eyes. He turned her face toward him with two fingers on her chin.

"You look dehydrated."

She shrugged.

"What do you want to drink? Water? Juice? Iced tea?"

"It doesn't matter."

"I think we need to lock your bedroom door the next time you go to the bathroom so you can't get back in here."

"Then I won't go to the bathroom."

He sat down on her bed with a sigh. "You know, I don't know how to help you."

"I'm not asking you to help me."

"I thought you were doing better yesterday. You seemed in better spirits when I saw you in the morning and Janni said you ate more."

She had eaten nothing. Everything had gone in the toilet.

"But you've got to get out of this bed, Kit. I don't expect you to be cheerful, but you should at least get dressed and eat your meals at the table with the rest of us. You haven't been downstairs since you came home."

Downstairs. She'd forgotten this house had a downstairs. It had been nearly three weeks since she'd seen it. She pictured the airy comfort of the kitchen, imagined walking out to the beach, the white sand hot under her bare feet.

She picked at a flaw in her sheet. She had nothing to say to him.

He looked at his watch and stood up. "I've got a baby to deliver." He caught himself and made a face. "I'm sorry. That was tactless." She felt his eyes on her. "What can I do, Kit?"

She slid down into the bed and pulled the sheet over her face. She didn't even hear him leave the room.

It wasn't until that afternoon that she remembered what day it was. Saturday. Exactly one week since Alison's death. She still remembered everything about her, every eyelash, the swirly pattern of her hair on the top of her head, the bow-shape of her mouth. By now she would have been a week old. Everyone in the house would be fighting to hold her, maybe joking about how her crying kept them awake at night. But she never would have let her cry for long. She would have sat up with her in the rocker or brought her into bed with her to nurse.

She was plummeting. As low as she'd been all week, she was falling even lower. By the time Virginia Perelle appeared at her door, she'd been crying for over an hour.

"Can I come . . . Kit, dear, you poor thing." Virginia walked briskly across the room and sat on the chair at the side of the bed. "Janni told me you've been crying for days. It must hurt terribly to lose a baby."

"It's not just the baby, it's your goddamned son!" She bit her tongue, too late.

But Virginia looked unflustered. "What's my . . . goddamned son . . . done?"

"He's forgotten I exist, except as a baby machine. An inferior one at that."

"Oh, Kit, he cares so much for you. I can't believe for an instant that . . ."

Kit shook her head. "He's avoiding me. I'm not imagining it." She told her about his brief visits to her room from the safety of the doorway, how he only seemed concerned with her physical well-being.

"You need to talk with him," Virginia said.

"I'm afraid to."

"When you see him tonight just say, 'I need to talk to you.' It's simple."

"And he'll look at his watch and say, 'Oops, sorry, Kit, gotta run.'"

"'Cole, I really need some of your time and I need it now. Tonight.'" Virginia was pretending to be Kit.

Kit decided to play along with her. "Okay," she said. "What is it?"

"I've been feeling as if you've changed toward me since I had the baby."

"I haven't changed."

"Yes, Cole, you have."

"All right!" Kit sat up straight, her eyes flashing. "I'll tell you. You *disgust* me. You're a whiny bitch. You look like hell, all washed out like that. You look twice your age. I can't get it out of my mind that I cut you open, that I had my hands in your guts. And your baby *died*. You never really, completely wanted her and you balked at taking good care of yourself. So I feel like a failure because I delivered a defective baby and it's your goddamned fault. There's this . . . this aura of death around you. I can smell it when I come in your room. How the hell can you expect me to still care about you?" Kit's voice broke and she fell back against the pillows, tears running down her cheeks.

"Oh, Kit," Virginia said softly. "Your last sentence sums it up, doesn't it? How can you expect him to care about you when you're thinking about yourself that way? They were *your* words, dear, not Cole's."

She knew by Cole's face that he'd spoken with his mother. He stood at the foot of her bed, leaning against the wooden footboard.

"How do I begin?" he said.

"She had no right to tell you anything."

"I've been dense, Kit. I never would have figured this out on my own. I'm sorry."

What had Virginia told him? She felt her cheeks burning, but he didn't seem to notice. He was lost inside his head, struggling to get something across to her without words. He used to be able to do that so easily, but it wasn't working now. He sat on her bed near the footboard, looking down at his hands.

"The night Alison was born," he said, "I had a conversation with Janni. I don't want to go into it all . . . some day I'll tell you, but not now."

She couldn't imagine where this was leading, but she felt sorry for him. It was as if she was seeing his face for the first time in days, and it was full of misery.

"She was critical of our relationship," he said.

"Yours and mine?"

He nodded. "You know, that we're too dependent on each other, that I hold you back from having a healthy relationship with Orrin or whoever, and vice versa." He waited for her reaction.

"She's right," she said. She was drowning in her dependence on him.

"Yeah, I thought so too. So I've stopped telling you everything and I've tried confiding more in Cynthia." He smiled. "That's been a challenge. But it's worked, I think. I feel closer to her. I thought this would be a good time to do it. I figured that you'd be so involved with yourself and getting better that you wouldn't miss me telling you all my troubles."

"But how do you think I've felt this week having you ignore me?"

"I thought I was doing the right thing. Increasing my attention to Cynthia, decreasing my attention to you. Like a mathematical equation. I forgot there were people involved."

"Maybe it *is* the right thing to do, I don't know. But you can't leave me out of the decision. I didn't know what was going on, Cole. I misinterpreted things. I've been acting crazy. At times this week I think I actually *was* crazy. One night I thought I heard a baby crying and I . . ." She stopped herself. It had been so long since she'd told him anything. She wasn't certain he'd care.

"You what?"

"I went looking for it," she said softly.

"Oh, Kit." He moved up next to her, wrapped his arm around her shoulders. He was quiet for a moment, and when he spoke again there was hurt in his voice. "How could you think you disgust me?" he asked.

She blushed. *Damn Virginia.* She shrugged and leaned her head against his shoulder, then lifted it quickly. He pulled it back against him with his hand.

"I don't want to cling to you," she said.

"You never have. No harder than I've clung to you, anyhow. I missed you this week. I felt like an addict with withdrawal symptoms."

She nearly laughed. "Bring me up to date, then."

He stood up. "Why don't you get dressed and we'll have

dinner with the others," he said. "Then we can lock ourselves away somewhere to talk."

She was glad that he left her alone to get dressed because the whole process was a struggle. Her muscles shook as she buttoned her shirt and her breathing reminded her of the time in high school when she'd had pneumonia. But she didn't pay her body much attention. It felt too wonderful to be in real clothes again to worry about anything as mundane as asthma. And dinner at the big dining room table sounded close to nirvana, if she could just make it down the stairs. She was so hungry.

She smiled at herself in the mirror on her closet door as she pulled a comb through her hair. *You are a simple person,* she thought, *to be able to go from empty to full in the space of an hour.*

42

She was sitting on one of the beach chairs, a stack of stationery resting on its broad arm.

"Hi," he said, walking toward her through the beach heather. He felt sand slip into his shoes.

She smiled up at him, the sun catching the gold and red in her hair. Her cheeks were pink and the dark hollow look was beginning to fade from her face. She looked pretty again.

"Catching up on letters?"

"They're not too easy to write."

He nodded. "I need to talk to you." He'd been thinking about this all afternoon, how he would tell her. He still wasn't quite sure.

"Have a seat." She gestured toward a vacant chair.

He looked out at the beach where Rennie and her girl-friends were sprawled on blankets. "Do you mind if we go in the house?"

A look of concern came over her face, and he said nothing to erase it. She got to her feet slowly. Still weak from not eating, he thought. He'd been stunned when she told him she'd been flushing her food down the toilet.

In the library, he pulled the two ottomans close together, and she sat on one while he shut the door.

"You look very serious and I'm getting very nervous," she said.

He sat down on the other ottoman. "I'm the one who needs to be nervous. I don't quite know how to tell you this."

"What's wrong?"

"I called Sandy this morning, like you asked me to, to tell him about Alison. He said he was just about to call you. His wife's been having trouble conceiving so he had a sperm count done last week and they told him his sperm were too few and far between for him to impregnate anyone."

She frowned. "How could his sperm count drop off that quickly?"

"It didn't," he said. "You're not following me. I asked him if he knew his blood type. He said it's AB. Blood type doesn't usually prove anything but I had Alison's autopsy report on my desk so I figured I might as well check. Kit, Alison's blood type was O. So is yours. It's impossible for her father to be AB."

There was a crease between her eyebrows as though it was a strain to follow him. "But . . . Sandy was the only possibility."

"Not if that period you had in December wasn't actually a period. I remember you saying it was light." He sat back and watched her face as his words sank in.

"Oh my God." She covered her mouth with her hand. "I'm O."

She couldn't speak. He could guess at the things racing through her mind, since they'd been in his own hours earlier. They should have been partners in this whole thing from start to finish. Instead she'd gone through it alone. He cursed that night; he'd never forgive himself for it.

"You didn't even get to mourn," she said.

"Mourning's the last thing on my mind. I can't even adjust to the idea that I . . . fathered a child." The word *father* wrenched his heart.

They sat in silence for several minutes, their knees touching. "Kit." He looked out the window. He wasn't certain how she would take this. "I can't keep this to myself."

She nodded. "Of course not. You had a child. How can you pretend something like that didn't happen?"

He smiled at her. "I was hoping you'd understand. All day I've been feeling sentimental and thinking how ridiculous that is. But who knows if I'll ever have another child. I don't think it's a secret I can carry around with me for the rest of my life."

"Who do you want to know?"

He sighed, folded his hands on his knee. "Jay already knows. I had to talk to someone. Sorry."

"What did he say?"

"After 'holy shit'? He was sad, I think. Sad that we didn't know from the start. And a little amazed that I would do something like that when I was still with Estelle."

"Does anyone else know?"

"No, but I want to tell Janni and Maris."

Kit nodded. "We have to keep it from Rennie, though," she said. "She'd never understand."

He nodded. "Absolutely." He would keep it from Rennie at all costs.

It was warm out on the bay, and oddly quiet, the only sound the hum of the *Sweetwater*'s motor as Jay steered her toward the setting sun. The houses along the water's edge looked as though they'd been painted there, still and peaceful. It was quiet inside the boat as well. *They're mulling over the news,* Cole thought. He stretched out on the seat at the back of the boat, watching them. Janni and Maris sat next to each other on the *Sweetwater*'s left side. He'd told them about the baby only an hour ago and surely there could be nothing else on their minds. Janni caught his eye now and winked. She was making it easy for him. She'd cried when he told her. He'd seen the curiosity burning in her eyes, all the questions she was longing to ask. He knew it was hard for her to refrain from probing deeper. That she didn't pry the slightest bit touched him.

And Maris had surprised him with her look of delight. "I've never understood why we don't all make love to each other whenever we feel the need," she said. "Sure would keep me happy." Then she'd put her arms around him and kissed him. "Come on, Cole. Give me an aquamarine-eyed black baby." She'd diffused a lot of his guilt right then, joking about it.

Kit sat on the right side of the boat. She'd wrapped a white sweater around her shoulders and she sat up straight, letting the breeze whip her hair around her face. Rennie sat next to her, looking miserable. They'd all be talking about the baby right now if it weren't for her. She hadn't wanted to come with them, but Kit insisted. "Please, Ren, I want everybody with me tonight."

It had been Kit's idea, the evening boat ride. They doused themselves with insect repellent and walked the two blocks to the pier in silence, Rennie lagging behind.

What was wrong with Rennie? He watched her now. She stared at the deck of the boat, the tips of her blond-streaked hair grazing her thighs.

"Do you have a lot of homework tonight, Ren?" he asked, trying to get her talking.

She didn't answer. From where he sat, her eyes looked glassy, her nose swollen.

"Cole asked if you have much homework," said Kit.

Rennie looked up at Kit. "Was Cole your baby's father?"

He sat back against the plastic cushion and felt the vibrations of the engine up his spine. How could she know? "Why do you ask that?" he said.

"Was he?" Rennie repeated to Kit.

Kit gave him a resigned look over Rennie's shoulder. "Yes," she said, "he was."

Rennie clapped her hand to her mouth, and for a moment he thought she was going to get sick. Apparently Kit did too. She turned Rennie's shoulders to face the water. "Over the side, Rennie," she said.

But Rennie twisted free of her. She lifted her feet onto the seat and hugged her knees, her eyes glued to the horizon. Jay cut the engine and the *Sweetwater* started to drift.

"How did you know?" Cole asked. He looked at Janni and Maris for the answer but they shook their heads.

"I heard you talking on the phone."

His mother. He tried to remember exactly what he'd said to her, what his end of the conversation would have sounded like to a just-turned fifteen-year-old girl, around whom he acted as if he'd taken a lifetime vow of celibacy.

"I was talking to my mother, Rennie. And you must have heard me tell her that I didn't realize the baby was mine until after she was born." He hoped that would somehow make him more innocent in Rennie's eyes.

"How could you *do* that to Kit?"

"It was a mutual decision," Kit said quickly. "Cole's not to blame."

"No one's to blame." Janni moved closer to him and rested her hand on his knee. "It's just a fact, plain and simple. It happened. Kit and Cole made a baby together. You're getting tangled up in right and wrong."

"But Kit got so sick. She almost *died* because of . . . him."

So, he was suddenly reduced to a *him.*

"It's not Cole's fault that Kit got sick," said Jay.

Rennie turned to Cole again. "If you'd known it was your baby, would you have married her?"

She was offering him a chance to redeem himself, but the thought of marriage had never entered his head. He looked at Kit and saw with relief that she was smiling at him. "It's impossible to say what we would have done," he said.

"You should still marry her if you had sex with her," Rennie said solemnly.

Maris laughed. "Yeah, Cole, make an honest woman out of her."

Rennie scowled. "Jay, can we go back?" she asked abruptly.

Jay nodded. "Sounds good to me."

The motor started up again, and the *Sweetwater* cut back across the bay, toward Mantoloking and the Chapel House. No one spoke, and he wondered how he could ever erase the look of betrayal in Rennie's eyes. He'd presented himself to her as a good man. Now she knew the truth.

43.

She reached the hotel in Atlanta around five. For a moment she was afraid to get out of the taxi. Her head was light; she was not certain her legs would hold her. She didn't want to pass out on the sidewalk of a strange city, alone.

You're not the fainting type, she told herself as she paid the driver and got out of the cab.

She'd only brought an overnight case with her. Her suitcase was too heavy and bulky for her to manage. Physically, she shouldn't be here at all—Cole would give her hell if he knew. But he *didn't* know. No one did. They thought she was having a restful visit with an old friend in Pennsylvania, a person she'd fabricated in a few minutes' time.

She'd received the call from the University Hospital in Atlanta two days ago. She'd almost forgotten that she'd sent out those resumes. The hospital had a PR position open, the man told her, and Kit sounded custom-made for the job. Could she come down on such short notice?

Of course, she'd said, not allowing herself to think it through. She was not allowing herself to think at all. She should have asked him if she could put the interview off a week. She wasn't strong enough for this quite yet.

She knew that now, as she leaned against the hotel's registration desk trying to catch her breath so she could ask for her room. She'd order a little something to eat from room service, she thought, then get in bed and stay there until morning.

The interview went smoothly the next day. She met with the PR director first, then with her six potential coworkers. She liked them. She liked the soft twang in their voices and felt their warmth. She was wearing a disguise, though, the facade of a woman who was glib and good humored, who was yearning for a new professional challenge. No one would guess that just four weeks ago she'd delivered and lost a baby. Her interviewers were such gentle people that for a moment she considered telling them. She caught herself, frightened by the near lapse in judgment that would have cost her this job, because surely she would have cried. Surely she would look like a woman about to fall apart.

The director called her at her hotel that night. They wanted her, he said. He outlined the offer: more money than she was making at Blair and better benefits.

"I'll need to give at least four weeks' notice," Kit said.

"You can have six," he answered. She could hear the smile in his voice. They were pleased to have found her.

She accepted the offer and got off the phone feeling numb. This would be fine, she told herself. She'd live alone for a change. She'd make new friends—she was good at that. She would make a new start on her life. Again.

She had little strength left to hunt for an apartment, but she had no choice. She didn't want to make a second trip down here. The first apartment she looked at was stark and glassy and overlooked a shopping mall. Her furniture would look ridiculous in it, but it didn't matter. This would be temporary, she thought, until she could find a house.

She stared out the living room window while the landlord rattled on about the cleaning deposit, garbage pickup, the laundry room. The huge square shopping mall stretched out below her. It covered a full block, maybe two, and lines of cars snaked around it. She could hear an occasional car horn and the squeal of brakes.

"Do you have any questions?" the landlord asked.

She thought of the sunrise over the ocean, the cymbal crash of the waves, and turned to face him.

"Let me write you a check," she said.

44.

In the summer, the Seaside Heights boardwalk was a world all its own. Kit was drawn to it and repelled by it at the same time. The shadowy beach and black ocean were eerie and mysterious in stark contrast to the activity on the boardwalk. The lights were garish, the calls of the kids working the concessions grating. They had promised Rennie a night at Seaside to celebrate the last day of summer school. She brought her two girlfriends with her. Laurie and Chris were turning Rennie into a giggly teenager. It was good to see her laughing and happy.

It had been a week since her interview in Atlanta, and Kit had told no one about her plans. It relieved her now to watch Rennie, to see how well she was doing. She didn't need Kit. She would be fine without her.

Rennie had been cold to Cole for a couple of weeks after she learned about the baby, but now she was talking to him again, acting as if she'd never been angry with him in the first place. Probably it wasn't anger she'd been feeling as much as confusion, Kit thought. Rennie hadn't been sure how to act toward him, so she'd chosen not to act at all.

They separated from the girls by the frozen custard

stand in the middle of the boardwalk. "We'll meet back here at ten," said Janni.

The girls groaned.

"Okay. Ten-thirty."

The adults headed south, the girls north. Cole looked back at them over his shoulder.

"You worried?" Kit asked him.

He looked embarrassed. "A little."

"She can take care of herself." She knew he was down tonight. His surgery that afternoon on a hydrocephalic fetus had been a disaster. That was the word he used, and she hadn't pressed him for details. It was obvious he didn't want to talk about it.

"You are neurotic, Perelle," Janni said. "What is the worst possible thing that could happen to Rennie? Tonight, I mean."

He smiled. "Well, I was a teenager myself on this board-walk once upon a time, cruising around, looking for girls—like those three—to pick up. My friends and I would see who'd be first to get a girl under the boardwalk."

"Rennie's unlikely to go under the boardwalk with any-one, no matter how he sweet-talks her," said Kit.

They were nearing the rides at the south end of the boardwalk and rock music blared from the concessions surrounding them on all sides. It was an incredible cacophony, and they had to yell to hear each other. People were packed together, eating thin-crusted pizza and frozen custard.

"God, I'd forgotten how tacky this place is," said Cole.

Jay nodded. "It's great, isn't it?"

"Jay and Maris and I used to come here a few nights a week during the summer," Janni said to Kit. "But Cole almost never came with us because Estelle was afraid her hair would frizz in the night air."

Cole managed a laugh at that.

"It still smells exactly the same now as it did when I was a kid." Maris took in a long breath. "Wood and onions and cigars and salt spray."

They were at the Flume, a massive conglomeration of fiberglass slides filled with rushing water.

"Let's ride it!" Kit said, suddenly excited. "Come on." She tugged at Maris's arm.

"Oh no," said Maris. "I long ago outgrew the desire for these torture chambers."

"Uh, I'm going to pass too, Kit," Janni said as a car of screaming girls plunged from a remarkable height into a pool of water. "I'd lose my dinner."

She felt the disappointment show in her face. She wanted to do this. She wanted to scream and laugh without having to think through every response before she made it.

"Come on, Kit." Jay took her hand and grabbed Cole by the arm. "We men with nerves of steel will go with you."

She sat sandwiched between them in the hollowed-out log. Cole put his arms around her and her breasts rested on his hands. It was wonderfully unavoidable. She leaned into his chest and pulled Jay snugly against her.

She screamed the second they took off. She gave her lungs free rein, and it felt as though they'd had bad air trapped inside them for weeks. She felt Cole's laughter in her ear more than she heard it. At every turn, cool water poured over them like a baptism, and when they finally got off she felt completely rejuvenated.

The five of them stopped to buy pizza and birch beer and stood in a huddle, swooning over the tastes. She felt so close to them. How was she going to leave?

They began slowly walking north and soon the beach was next to them again, as black and obscure as the ocean behind it.

"Do kids actually do it under the boardwalk?" she asked.

"Oh yes," said Janni.

"Come on, Kit." Cole took her arm. "You need a tour of the Underwood Motel."

He steered her toward the ramp that led to the beach. They took off their sandals when they reached the sand and made an abrupt about-face to walk under the boardwalk. It was dark and eerie. Thousands of footsteps thundered above them, and the wood muffled the music from the concessions.

"Did you really have your way with girlfriends down here?" Kit peered into the darkness and saw a few couples here and there.

"Numerous times, although I like to think it was their way as well as mine. I had a system. First we'd eat some pizza. Then we'd play pinball for about fifteen minutes— that was before the video games took over—and if it was a new girlfriend I'd try to win her something. I had a friend from Watchung who worked the wheel at one of the concessions so it wasn't hard to win a big teddy bear or something."

"You were a devil."

He peeled a big splinter from one of the boards and leaned against a pole, playing with the sliver of wood. "Then I'd bring her down here and take off my shirt to put under her head so she didn't get sand in her hair and then whatever happened, happened."

"And all we had in Seattle were the backseats of cars," she said.

He looked good in the patchy light that lit his eyes and hair, and she thought of kissing him. It haunted her that they had created a child together without kissing. Just one kiss now. One retroactive kiss before she left.

"Well." He dropped the splinter of wood and reached for her hand. "We'd better get going or we'll never catch up to the others. We'd have a hard time convincing them of our innocence."

They walked on the beach just outside the boardwalk. She pressed her palm into his.

"You're feeling sexier these days, aren't you," he said. It was a statement, not a question.

"What do you mean?" She was surprised.

"You seem more like your old self this week. More confident. I guess getting back with Orrin helped. You look good, and you're back in your non-maternity jeans . . ."

"One size larger than I used to wear."

". . . and there's something of the provocateur in you."

"There is? Are you provoked?" Brave, Kit. It was easy to be brave when you had one foot out the door.

She could feel his shrug more than see it. "A little. I figure it's Orrin you're directing it at and I'm just picking up the residuals."

He had it so wrong. She felt nothing for Orrin, though he'd certainly been good to her since his return from New York. He apologized for his coolness to her in the hospital. It brought back memories of when his wife was sick, he said. She understood that and felt warmed that he shared it with her. He was lighter with her than he'd been previously, more open, telling her that he wanted to make love to her. She wasn't supposed to have sex for another couple of weeks, she told him. She was relieved to have two more weeks of celibacy to help her in the transition from mother to lover.

But despite the deeper topics, there was still an emptiness in their relating that she couldn't break through. Or perhaps she'd stopped trying. That was just as well. It would make leaving easier.

They'd reached the amusement rides at the north end of the boardwalk and turned toward the stairs. She held him back.

"Cole?"

He looked at her, eyebrows raised, waiting.

"I'm moving to Atlanta."

"*What?*"

"I've accepted a position at the University Hospital there. I have an apartment. I leave in a month."

"When did you . . ."

"I went to Atlanta when I said I was in Pennsylvania."

He looked at her sharply, then looked away, out to the

beach. He stared so long at one spot that she followed his eyes to see what was holding his attention, but there was nothing there.

"I guess our friendship wasn't what I thought it was if you'd keep something like this from me." He was hurt. She heard it in his voice. She felt tears well up in her own eyes.

"I was afraid you'd try to change my mind if I told you."

"I still will," he said. "Please don't go, Kit."

"I have to."

"Why?"

She couldn't tell him her reasons. He was too much a part of them.

"The winters are warmer there," she said, wishing immediately she could take back the words. They were cruelly simplistic, an insult to their closeness.

He stared at her, the look on his face bruised and angry. "Fine," he said, climbing the ramp to the boardwalk. "I hope you're never cold again."

45.

She and Orrin were first to arrive at the restaurant. They sat on a sofa in the bar, waiting for Cole and Cynthia. Kit played with her strawberry daiquiri, licking the pink crystals off the straw while Orrin sipped his gin and tonic. He was talking about another case he had at Blair, but she wasn't listening. She was remembering her appointment that afternoon with Barb Chrisman. It had relieved her to see a woman gynecologist again. The second she walked into Barb's office, she'd felt a bond.

She told her she wanted her tubes tied, but Barb shook her head. "Let me give you a diaphragm for now, Kit," she said. "You should wait a couple of months before you have the tubal. I'll give you the name of someone in Atlanta."

Kit didn't protest. She wished she were more certain of her feelings. Another pregnancy was unthinkable. Yet there was that raw ache deep in her belly each time she thought of Alison.

"There they are," she said now as Cole and Cynthia appeared in the doorway. She was struck again by how well-matched they were in their handsomeness, both tan, both in blue. She suddenly saw herself sometime in the future, sitting in her living room in Atlanta, opening the wedding invitation. Opening the birth announcement. She put the thought out of her mind and reached up to take the hand Cynthia offered.

Cynthia pulled a chair close to the sofa and sat down.

"I wanted to tell you how sad I felt about your baby," she said in a near-whisper.

Kit squeezed her hand. "Thank you."

"I can't imagine what it's like to carry a baby all that time only to lose it."

She's good at this, Kit thought. There were a few seconds of silence and she took a deep breath. "I'm sure it wasn't easy for you either, finding out about Cole and the baby."

Cynthia smiled. "Oh well. It happened before I met him." She brushed a strand of her long, dark hair behind her ear. "How are you feeling?"

"Better. I actually ran yesterday. Not far, but it felt great."

"You were in such good shape before, it shouldn't take you long."

The men were leaning against the wall near the bar. They looked bored. "I think they're waiting for us." Kit nodded in their direction.

They had a table in the middle of the dining room next to the dance floor. She was starving. She talked them into ordering three different appetizers.

She worked on an artichoke heart while Cole fed Cynthia plump sautéed mushrooms from his fork. It was odd to watch him with a woman other than Estelle. Their relationship was obviously different. He was in much greater control.

She was pleased at how little tension there was between herself and Cole tonight. He seemed to be pretending she'd said nothing to him last night about leaving. That was fine with her. She would handle it the same way.

"This is a little better than last night's dinner, wouldn't you say, Kit?" he asked her now.

She laughed. "We ate junk food at the boardwalk last night," she explained. "We took Rennie and her friends to celebrate the end of summer school." She added that quickly, not wanting Orrin and Cynthia to think it had been just the two of them, alone.

"I've never understood why Rennie's in a foster home instead of a reform school," said Cynthia.

"She doesn't need to be reformed," said Cole.

"But you said that she ran away from home. Shouldn't a child who runs away be disciplined in some way other than sending her to live in a house on the beach?"

Cole looked exasperated. "She spent her life being neglected by her mother and getting beaten up by her mother's boyfriend. What else was she supposed to do?"

"Sometimes running away is the healthiest thing a kid can do," said Kit.

"I suppose. I just can't imagine families like that. And it amazes me that they'd put her in the Chapel House instead of with a normal family."

"I think she's lucky," said Orrin. "She has five foster parents all to herself."

Good for you, Orrin, Kit thought. "The county's not happy about having her at the Chapel House either, Cynthia.

They're trying to find a so-called normal family to place her with."

"Hopefully they won't," said Cole. There was an edge to his voice that Kit couldn't read.

"Did you have another rough day?" she asked him.

He looked surprised. "Not really. A nasty abortion I wished I could have passed on. But it worked out all right."

Cynthia made a face. "*All* abortions are nasty," she said. "I wish you didn't do them. I lie to my friends when they ask me if you do."

"And I wish you didn't lie," Cole said quietly.

Orrin leaned back as his prime rib dinner was set in front of him. "What if the fetus were so damaged that it'd be born with severe handicaps or a terminal condition?" he asked Cynthia.

Cynthia shook her head. "There's no reason I can think of that would justify taking the life of a baby." She turned to Cole. "What was the reason for the abortion today?"

"She had four kids already and she didn't think she could give a fifth child all the attention he'd need."

"She should have thought about that before she got pregnant. Anyone who's dumb enough to get pregnant when she doesn't want . . ." Cynthia's cheeks reddened. She looked at Kit, immediately contrite. "I'm sorry."

Kit laughed, more amused than angry. "You'd better watch out, Cynthia," she said. "Birth control isn't foolproof, and I know for a fact that the gun you're playing with is loaded."

"*Kit.*" Cole looked at her in disbelief, but she knew he

was fighting a smile. "Let's move on to some other topic, okay?"

They turned to their food, filling the silence with the sound of forks clinking against china.

She danced with Cole near the end of the evening, thinking that dancing was a wonderful invention. She could hold him close to her for an extended period of time and no one would guess at the pleasure it gave her.

"Orrin's a nice guy," he said, "but I don't think he's good enough for you. Maybe you'll find someone better in Atlanta."

"Maybe." She wasn't certain she was pleased that he acknowledged her leaving in such an offhanded way.

"I won't stand in your way, Kit, if this is what you want."

"Thank you." She was ashamed of herself that she preferred his wounded reaction last night to this one.

"Do you see the problem with Cynthia?" he asked. "She's so conservative. She was in the Girl Scouts until she was twenty. That's pathological, don't you think?"

"There *is* a very sheltered quality about her. But she's a warm person. She said some nice things to me about the baby."

"Yeah, she's nice all right. But there are these basic differences between us that seem practically insurmountable."

"She's just different from the people you're used to. I think you expect her to change her values for you when you wouldn't dream of changing yours for her."

"Oh no? My sex life is suddenly limited to the missionary position. If that's not surrendering to her values, I don't know what is."

"Poor Cole," she laughed. "Maybe I should take her aside and give her a pep talk."

"Why don't you just take *me* aside and . . . I'm sorry. I was about to say something completely inappropriate."

She felt herself blush and he hugged her with a laugh.

"I never knew you were so easily embarrassed," he said.

"I'm not," she said, her voice teasing. "That's not the blush of embarrassment. It's the blush of unresolved desire."

"Oh really? I wonder if Orrin knows what he's in for." He hesitated and slowed his dancing to a near standstill. "Or is it really me you'd like it from?"

She looked up at him, at a face more serious than she'd anticipated. His eyes were looking inside her. She struggled to think of a witty comeback but nothing came to her. She put her head against his neck.

"Let's change the subject," she said, telling him all she needed to.

He let go of her hand and wrapped both his arms around her and they finished the dance in silence.

Sex with Orrin was lackluster. She lay in his arms afterward, empty and unsatisfied. She had to admit she'd been pretty mechanical. Two weeks were up, it was time, he was more than willing. His prettiness wasn't lost on her, but she felt nothing for him.

He was quickly asleep, and she got out of bed and stood at his window, staring into the dark woods. She ran her fingertips across the scar on her stomach. Cole was with Cynthia tonight. In another few weeks she could stop torturing herself with those images. She would no longer know his whereabouts every night.

And she'd no longer see his smile at breakfast or feel his arm around her on the beach. She swallowed hard to keep the tears back. She wished she'd never met him. She had too much and not enough of him at the same time.

46.

He closed the door to Cynthia's house quietly behind him and crunched across the gravel driveway to his car. He'd expected to stay the night but he didn't want to argue any longer and he doubted they'd be able to talk civilly to each other until they'd had some time apart. His headlights picked up the Jersey pines across the street as he pulled onto the deserted road.

What was he going to do about Cynthia? They'd never agree on sex. And sex was not the real problem—it was just where their differences were most blatantly apparent. He'd been pretty ugly tonight, comparing her to Estelle, disparaging her as a lover. He'd even threatened to end it with her, knowing that would hurt her far more than it would him. He'd been cruel. When would he learn to think before he spoke?

He'd been in a bad mood to begin with, ever since seeing that baby in the elevator. He'd started to tell her about it, then changed his mind. She wouldn't have understood.

He spotted a pay phone at an isolated gas station and

pulled over, feeling in his pocket for a quarter. Cynthia's phone rang ten times before she answered.

He ran his hand through his hair. "I wanted to apologize for the things I said."

She was still crying. She cried like Estelle, with no loss of her beauty to the tears. She didn't answer him.

"I don't know how we can ever resolve the problems between us, but I know getting ugly about it doesn't help and I'm really very sorry."

"Cole, I *love* you, but I can't be everything you want me to be."

"I know. It's okay. I'll call you tomorrow, all right?"

"Cole? It would help me so much if you'd tell me you love me."

She was asking him to lie.

"I can't say that."

"Because it's hard for you to say or because you don't?"

"I don't love you now, but that doesn't mean I couldn't at some point." He was kidding himself as well as her.

In the Chapel House, he knocked on Kit's door and opened it when there was no answer. A splash of moonlight lit up the white crocheted bedspread. He walked glumly to the bay window. He wished he could talk with her. She would scold him and then say something to make him feel better. He looked at his watch. One o'clock. She was probably staying over at Orrin's. Damn. He was beginning to need her more than she needed him. It was a little too late for that.

She'd looked so pretty tonight in that black jersey dress cut high on her shoulders. Very sexy, too sexy for Orrin.

How could she leave? He could never do it, leave the Chapel House, leave *her*. He admired her for it, for knowing what was best for her. Certainly he had done her no good, and the house could only hold memories of this last unhappy year for her. She was wise to get away. He loved her too much to try to block her path.

He walked back to her bed and sat down, close to the night table. He switched on the lamp and squinted against the light as he pulled out the drawer. Alison's picture was where he thought it would be, on top of the box of tissues, next to the little bowl of smoothed glass Kit had collected from the beach. He took it out and held it under the light.

My own daughter. A tragic little thing. She should never have been conceived.

He looked up, startled by the sound of Kit stepping into the room. He hadn't heard her car. He was caught red-handed, snooping and intrusive. But she smiled at him.

"I look at her picture at least ten times a night," she said, making everything all right. She sat next to him and draped her arm around his shoulders. "It's getting a little frayed around the edges." She gently touched the border. It was all that was left of his child, this much-handled photograph.

"Her hair would have been just like yours," he said.

"Do you think so?"

He nodded.

They were quiet for a moment, staring at Alison's picture as if they'd never seen it before.

"I think I'm having a delayed reaction to losing her," he said. "It took me so long to realize she was mine. I had to adjust to that before I could adjust to the fact that she died."

"I know, babe. You were gypped."

"Something happened today."

"What?"

"It's going to sound silly."

"Come on."

He sighed. "Well, I was in the elevator and this guy got on. He was carrying a baby, six months old or so. He was holding her like this." He pulled one of Kit's pillows out from under the spread and set it upright in his arms. "Her ear was right against his lips." He laughed, feeling ridiculous. "It drove me crazy. I couldn't take my eyes off them. She was this little black baby with a pink bow in her hair. Every once in a while he'd kiss her ear. I kept thinking about how wonderful it would feel to kiss my daughter's ear."

"Oh, Cole." She knelt next to him on the bed, her arms around him, and to his horror he began to cry. He clung to her, remembering how he'd followed the father and his baby off the elevator and into the gift shop, how he'd bought a roll of mints he didn't want just so he could watch them longer.

"You need a friend to sleep with." Kit took the picture from his hand and set it on the night table. Then she stretched out on top of the bedspread, still in that black jersey dress, and pulled him down next to her. He nestled his head against her breasts, feeling content for the first time all day.

She smoothed his hair. "I'll make you a copy of Alison's picture before I leave," she said.

47

Her bedroom door was open and he could hear her packing, bureau drawers sliding shut, hangers clacking on the wooden rod in her closet. He changed out of his work clothes into his shorts, listening, trying to remember what the house had been like before she arrived. He tried to picture her room before she'd put her heavy dark furniture in it. He remembered the emptiness of that room, how his footsteps used to echo when he stepped inside.

He walked across the hall and stood in her doorway. She was kneeling in front of her bureau, shifting piles of sweaters from the bottom drawer into a box at her side. There were boxes everywhere, neatly stacked, *bedroom* written across the sides. Her closet door was open. There were just a few things hanging up inside and a couple of pairs of shoes on the floor, clothes she'd need for her last two days at Blair.

She looked up at him. "A lot of work," she said. She'd pinned her hair up off her neck and her forehead was damp.

He needed some time with her. They hadn't talked, not really. Just bits and pieces about her plans for her apartment. She seemed to want to leave with no more than a wave good-bye. Surely they had more to say to each other than that.

He didn't want to let her go without telling her how much her friendship meant to him.

He didn't want to let her go.

"Would you like to go out later tonight?" he asked. "Just for ice cream or something?"

She sat back on her heels and sighed. "I won't have time, Cole. I have so much I have to—"

He held up his hand to stop her. "It's all right," he said. He didn't want to watch her struggle to make up excuses. He turned and walked back to his room feeling the emptiness growing behind him.

On paper the surgery was simple: partially remove the fetus from its mother's uterus, make the necessary corrections to the neural tube—or rather, attempt to make the corrections—and sew the fetus back in. It was the fact that his would be the first medical team ever to attempt it on a human patient that kept him from sleeping the night before and had him in his office by six in the morning going over every step in his mind, every possible thing that might go wrong.

By the time he arrived in the operating room, the amphitheater above him was packed, and he could tell he was not the only tense member of the team. They spoke to each other in hushed tones as if they were in church. He liked every one of them. They were skilled and dedicated, with a collective sense of humor that had carried him through some rough hours in this OR. They'd absorbed everything he'd taught them and then studied on their own, some of them traveling to other parts of the country to learn all they could and bring the knowledge back to him.

He looked at them now. Eight men and women dressed identically in blue and hovering at various distances from the woman on the table. They were absolutely rigid today. Maybe he'd made a mistake asking Aguillerio to join them. They all knew the California neurosurgeon's reputation as a perfectionist. But politically, Cole had had no other choice. Aguillerio had perfected the technique on primates. If Cole had attempted this procedure without him and failed, he would have left himself wide open to criticism for not inviting Aguillerio along for the ride.

He knew within minutes that worrying had been a waste of time. The team functioned like clockwork. They were calm and methodical in spite of their anxiety. He'd have to remember to compliment them later. He couldn't fault any of them. He smiled beneath the mask, thinking of himself as a choreographer with his dancers smooth and precise in every step.

Aguillerio was a pleasant surprise himself. He was a tiny man and he held back, offering no more than an occasional suggestion or comment, as if he knew he could intimidate too easily and that intimidation could only hurt the performance.

Near the end of the surgery Cole saw the smile in the little man's eyes and his own thoughts were confirmed: almost without a doubt they had turned the life of this baby around. It wasn't over yet. They'd have to wait months before they knew for sure. Yet he left the operating room almost dizzy with a sense of victory and a craving in the back of his throat for champagne.

48.

Kit climbed out of the tub and dried herself slowly with the towel. She smoothed lotion over her body, digging her thumbs into the tight muscles of her thighs, relishing the pain. She ran her fingers through her hair and slipped on her new robe, a gift from Paula. *Short and satiny*, Paula had written. *Life goes on.* She looked at herself in the mirror. The robe was a deep charcoal gray. The perfect color for her.

Okay, she thought. *Mind's clear, let's try it again.* She picked up the press release she'd been working on all afternoon, ever since the surgery, and leaned against the bathroom wall to read it once more. She wrinkled her nose. Still not right. She'd hoped that a long soak in the tub and a little self-indulgence would give her a fresh outlook. This was the last press release she'd write at Blair. It had to be good. The best. She'd have Cole take a look at it.

She found him in the gym. He was straddling the bench of one of the weight machines, straining to lower the bar behind his head. Janni was on the elliptical in the corner, a towel draped around her neck as she pumped her legs up and down.

"You don't look like you're dressed for a workout," Janni said.

"No time to work out," Kit said as she sat down on a mat across from Cole. "I need your advice," she said to him.

He let the bar down slowly and wiped his hands on the towel lying across the bench. "Is the press release done yet?"

She smiled at the excitement in his voice. She'd never seen him quite so high before. "That's what I need your advice on."

"The most critical thing about that press release is to spell Aguillerio's name correctly. Two 'l's, one 'r'. The man's ego is tied up in that procedure."

"And yours isn't?" How odd this was, bantering with him as though tomorrow wasn't her last day at work, her last day in the Chapel House.

He smiled. "Let's hear it."

She cleared her throat and began to read. "In the first case of its kind, specialists at Blair Medical Center may have saved a child from the crippling disease spina bifida by operating on the fetus ex utero—outside the mother's womb. Under the direction of Blair's Chief of Maternal and Fetal Medicine, Dr. Cole Perelle, the Fetal Surgery Team used bone particles suspended in an agar medium to close neural tube fissures in a twenty-week-old fetus." She looked up. "Now here's where my problem begins . . . What are you smiling at?" He looked as though he hadn't heard a word she'd read.

"Sorry," he said, trying to make his face serious. "You just look amazing in that robe."

She felt her nipples press against the soft fabric. Out of the corner of her eye she saw Janni slow down on the elliptical, and she knew without looking that Janni wore a grin.

Cole turned to Janni. "Would you get out of here, please?" he asked.

"You bet!" Janni all but leaped off the machine. She grabbed her towel from one of the benches and tossed it around her shoulders. "And I'll lock the door on my way out." She hit the light switch as she left, leaving them in the filtered light from the windows.

Kit looked down at the paper in her hands, impossible to read in the dim light. She raised her gaze to Cole's.

He leaned toward her. "I want to make love to you," he said.

"We can't."

"Why not?"

"Please, I just don't want to."

"The hell you don't."

"This release, Cole. I have to—"

"I'll help you with it tonight," he said.

Just this once, she thought. It would be all right as long as she could keep herself from wanting anything more than that. At this point she had little to lose.

He followed her with his eyes as she walked toward him. She straddled the bench facing him and he ran one hand up her arm. "I hope you don't mind a little sweat," he said.

She lowered her head to taste the salty dampness of his chest. He lifted her chin and kissed her, teasing her with closed lips. She licked at his mouth and he pulled away with a smile.

"You're impatient," he said, running his finger across her lips. "Let's take it slow this time. Make up for the last time."

"Do you know we've never kissed before?" she said, thinking she shouldn't speak at the same moment the words came out of her mouth.

"Oh, we must have. When we . . . ?"

He didn't remember.

"No," she said. "We didn't."

"*Kitty.*" He hugged her to him and she fought tears, glad of the darkness. They kissed again, his tongue gently probing. She was afraid of this, going too slowly. It was harder to stay in control. Her body trembled.

Her diaphragm. Damn.

She jerked her head away. "Cole . . ."

"The diaphragm." He laughed into her neck. "Shit."

"I'll get it."

"No." He held her arms. "Let me go. I'm afraid you won't come back. Where is it?" He stood up, cupped her cheek in his palm.

"It's packed. The box on my bathroom counter."

He took her hand and pressed it between his own. "Listen," he pleaded. "Don't go anywhere. Don't think of anything. I'll be right back."

She obeyed him, afraid not to. If they didn't make love now, she would go out of her mind. She wouldn't let herself think of what it might mean. Would it make it harder or easier to drive away from the Chapel House on Saturday?

He was back in seconds, out of breath and smiling. She reached for the diaphragm and the tube of jelly but he held it away from her.

"I want to do it," he said.

"I don't want to feel like you're my doctor."

"You won't." He took her hand and led her to one of the blue mats on the floor. She watched him fill the diaphragm with jelly and set it next to them on the mat. "Later," he said.

He left the robe on her, reaching inside it with his hands and his mouth, unhurried, taking time to tell her the things he liked best about her body.

"You know my body as well as I do," she said. "Better in some ways."

"I feel as though I've never seen it before." He raised himself up on his knees and opened her robe, and she shut her eyes, strangely unshy. She felt his eyes on her, then his hands, softly stroking her skin. Her body was a million nerve endings all reaching up to him, begging him to touch her harder, longer.

He lifted her hips, leaned over her until her scar was against his mouth, and kissed it softly, then moved his lips lower. He held her thighs apart with his hands and made her come with his mouth, his fingers, his mouth again until she felt deliciously drained. He knew her so well. It was as if they'd been lovers all their lives.

She reached for him, letting her hand brush against his penis, and he leaned toward her as if he hoped the touch had been more than accidental. She guided him onto his back and he tugged off her robe. It was suddenly in the way. He kissed her, his mouth feverish, and she caught her breath in surprise as he slipped the diaphragm inside her.

She lowered herself between his legs, struck by the stony hardness of his thighs under her hands. Harder than her own. She felt the tension mounting in his body. He'd considered himself deprived for so long. He treated everything she did, every kiss, the touch of her fingers, the feel of her mouth on him, as a gift, and now she wanted to go slowly to let him savor the pleasure.

She teased him with her tongue and teeth until he finally held her head down on him with both his hands. She unwound his fingers from her hair and lifted her head to look at him.

"I want you to remember this for a long time," she said. "You'll thank me later for making it last."

"Sweet torture," he murmured.

She finally relented and took as much of him in her mouth as she could. She wished she could see his face at the same time. She imagined the smile was gone. His face would be lined with concentration, a look of pain that had nothing to do with pain at all.

He tugged at her shoulders, and she stretched over his body for a kiss, this one slow and delicate, and then he was inside her.

He held her hips tightly against him, but her concentration was ebbing away. She was distracted by fear. She felt her body gripping his. So full of him now. In a moment she would lose him. She heard the ocean roaring in her ears like city traffic. A couple of gulls fought over something outside the window. She heard Janni call the others to dinner. It seemed like hours since they'd begun, and it was about to end. She'd known it all along, hadn't she? That it would end? That all this could leave her was more vulnerable than before?

He came with a catch of his breath and a series of shudders, and she pulled off him so quickly that he opened his eyes in surprise.

"No," he said. "Stay."

"We'd better go to dinner." She kissed him lightly. She wanted to get away from him before he said anything else.

He put his arms around her to keep her from getting up. "Dinner will wait. We need to talk."

"We don't have time. We're taking Rennie skating after dinner, remember?" *And I'm moving out of your life tomorrow.* She pulled free of him and groped on the floor for her robe.

He sat up too, grabbing her shoulder to turn her toward him. "You're acting as though I suddenly have the plague."

"There's nothing to talk about. It was just this once, Cole. I don't want any more of you than that."

"I love you."

"Shh." She put her finger to his lips and stood up. "I need to shower." She walked toward the door on legs that threatened to buckle beneath her. "I'll see you at dinner."

It was hard to be polite to Orrin when she suddenly resented his entire existence. He was telling her how he wanted to keep in touch, how he didn't mind a long-distance relationship. She hung on to his arm as they skated around the rink, cursing the skates, her ankles, and the slick floor. She was no good at this. Her concentration was off. She couldn't think about anything other than that afternoon in the gym. Her mind tormented her with the image of Cole stretched out beneath her. He'd been soaked, his hair damp against his forehead, his skin glistening. She could still smell him in her hair. Surely Orrin could tell.

Dinner had been an ordeal. It was obvious that Janni had told the others. The disappointment in their faces was clear as they picked up the tension between her and Cole. Cole was upset with her, snapping at her a few times across the table. But he apologized later and asked her if they could go out for breakfast in the morning, just the two of them. She'd agreed. Now as she watched him with Cynthia, holding her hand, skating smoothly in time with the music, she wished she'd risked talking with him in the gym. She was afraid, though, of what he might say. Sappy promises he'd regret later, the next time he saw a woman who looked like she stepped off the cover of *Vogue*.

"Penny for your thoughts," Orrin said, taking her hand.

"I was thinking how amazing it is that I can run as well as I do but I can barely skate at all. My calves are killing me." She took her hand out of his. "I think I'll take a restroom break."

The ladies' room was spacious but not very clean. Kit avoided looking at the dirt-spattered sink as she washed her hands. She was combing her hair with her fingers when Rennie walked in. Their eyes met in the mirror for a second before Rennie looked away.

Kit leaned back against the sink and folded her arms across her chest. "I have a feeling there's a lot you want to say to me," she said.

Rennie picked up the filthy bar of soap and began washing her hands. "I just don't understand how you and Cole could do what you did and then come here with Orrin and Cynthia," she said.

What explanation could she offer? Should she label it a mistake—their second?

But Rennie didn't wait for an explanation. "I thought it meant you two were finally serious. That you'd *stay*. Everybody thought that. Janni and Maris were talking about celebrating and everything. But now here we are at this stupid skating rink and you're with stupid Orrin and Cole's with stupid Cynthia . . ." Rennie shook her head. "I *hate* Cynthia. I know it's not fair, but I *do*. She talks to me like I'm a child, in that high voice. She just pretends to be interested in me so Cole will like her. Why doesn't he see through her?"

"Rennie . . ." She wasn't sure what to say. "Some things are too complicated to explain."

Rennie started to cry. "I don't want you to go. I want you and Cole to be together."

Kit hugged her. "I know," she said. "I know that's what you want."

Orrin was waiting for her at the side of the rink. She skated over to him and boosted herself onto the wall.

"Aren't we going to skate?" he asked.

"I'm sorry," she said. "I can't seem to get into it."

A young woman skated by, her eyes on Orrin instead of the herd of children in front of her, and she tripped and went flying. The kids helped her up and she smiled sheepishly, skating away with a limp in her stride.

Kit laughed. "You have an admirer," she said. From this angle, Orrin's thick eyelashes looked as though they brushed his cheeks when he blinked.

"I wish she weren't the only one."

"I'm sure you have many."

"In this skating rink I mean."

Did he have to pick tonight for that kind of talk? She was in no mood for it.

She took a deep breath. "Orrin, Cole and I made love this afternoon." It was a relief to say it out loud. If it meant the end of her relationship with Orrin, fine.

But he laughed. It was the last reaction she'd expected. "Well, I'm not surprised."

"You're not?" She spotted Cole skating toward them and cringed at his timing. He looked as though his stomach hurt.

"I have a problem," he said, speaking to Kit. "Rennie told me you two had a little chat in the restroom about . . . this afternoon." He chose his words carefully, his eyes on Orrin. "I guess you didn't realize that Cynthia was in there. Now she won't come out."

Cynthia was there? She played back the conversation with Rennie in her mind and shut her eyes. Poor Cynthia. "Oh, Cole, I'm sorry."

He started to untie the laces of her right skate. "Will you go get her, Kit?"

"*Me?* I'm the last person she wants to see."

"Please. I can't go in there."

"What can I say?"

"That I want to talk to her." He pulled off the skate and began to untie the other, one hand holding her ankle in a way that was completely unnecessary to the task of loosening the laces.

He lifted her off the wall, keeping his hands around her waist for a few seconds after she was on solid ground. She shut her eyes, knowing the message in them was too raw for the moment, in a public skating rink with Orrin standing next to them. When she looked up, he was smiling at her. He could read her whether her eyes were open or closed.

"And I want to talk with you, too," he said. "Later."

She possessed power she didn't want. Cynthia sat on a brown metal folding chair, the only chair in the restroom, and looked up at her with red eyes.

"Cole asked me to tell you that he wants to see you," Kit said.

"And you do everything Cole asks you to do. Meet his every need, I'm sure." Cynthia began to say. "I'm sorry," she said. "I don't mean to sound bitchy."

Kit knelt at her side. "You couldn't sound bitchy if you tried. I feel terrible, Cynthia. I know Cole does, too. We didn't mean to hurt you or Orrin."

Cynthia looked at Kit, riveting her eyes. "Will you finally let go of him when you're in Atlanta? You bled him dry when you lost the baby and you're still hanging on to him."

Kit stood up. "He hangs on to me, too," she said, turning to leave the room. She had no more to say. Any words she had left were for Cole, not Cynthia.

When she opened her eyes, the room was bathed in silver light from the moon and Cole was sitting on her bed, his back against the footboard, his legs stretched out next to hers.

"What time is it?" she asked sleepily.

"Quarter after one," he answered without checking his watch.

"What are you doing?"

"Watching you. Watching the moonlight on your face while you sleep. Do you mind?" He squeezed her foot through the sheet.

She smiled at him. "It's a little spooky, being watched while I'm sleeping."

"Were you dreaming?"

She struggled to clear her head. "I don't remember."

"I was."

She sat up. "But you're awake."

"I dreamt that you woke up and I told you I wanted to marry you and you said yes."

She stared at him. He pulled something from his shirt pocket and handed it to her.

"This is for you," he said.

It was a ring, very old. A pool of diamonds set in silver filigree. She looked up at him.

"It was my grandmother's. I drove to my parents' house

to get it after I left Cynthia last night. After I *split* with Cynthia."

She felt a chill. "Cole . . ."

"Please, Kit. Put it on."

She slipped it on the ring finger of her left hand. It caught the moonlight at a thousand angles. "I'm scared," she said, covering the ring with her other hand, as if she were afraid she might lose it. It was the tiniest bit too large.

"I promise not to suffocate you."

She leaned forward to kiss him. "I love you."

"I've been waiting the whole goddamn day to hear those words from you," he said.

She called the movers in the morning, the phone resting on the bed between Cole and herself. *Don't bother coming,* she told them. *I'm not going anywhere.*

Then she called the PR director of the University Hospital in Atlanta. She couldn't take the job, she said. Something personal had come up, something she hadn't predicted. The conversation was polite on both sides, full of platitudes, and she was relieved to hang up the phone.

Cole wrapped his arms around her and she snuggled against him, thoroughly content. Some other woman must have planned that move to Atlanta, she thought. Some woman who thought she could survive outside the circle of Cole's arms.

49.

The twentieth of September was a Sunday and she woke early with a headache. Cole was asleep next to her, his body curved around hers, his hand flat on her stomach above her scar. She got out of bed and swallowed two aspirin in the bathroom. Then she sat on the window seat, pulling the afghan around her shoulders. It was a sparkling morning. The sun glittered off the water and a crisp breeze blew against her from the open window. But the beauty of the day was offensive.

Today had been her due date. If everything had gone as it should have, she'd be delivering Alison right about now. A different Alison than the baby she saw in her hospital room. This baby would be seven pounds, maybe more, with a healthy set of lungs and a cry that would shake the rafters.

"Going for a run?"

She started at the sound of his voice. "Headache," she said without turning around. She didn't want him to know what had her upset this morning. It would only add to his problems. He was already too harried at work, stretched too thin. Besides, she thought entirely too much about

Alison, what might have been. Why did she have to hang on to the grief when she had so many good things going for her? She'd been promoted to Assistant Director of the PR department at Blair—her reward for staying. And in a few months she was getting married to the only man she could imagine marrying.

They'd picked the first of January for the wedding. It was the best way she could think of to start the new year. Cole would have been happy if they'd gotten married the night he asked her, but she needed time to put the events of this past year behind her. She wanted the year of her marriage to be unencumbered by memories of the past.

Cole got out of bed now and sat behind her on the window seat, wrapping the afghan around them both.

"I was wondering if you'd be all right today," he said. "And you're not, are you?"

He knew. She shook her head and leaned back against him. His chest was warm against the bare skin of her back.

"You weren't going to tell me." He spoke softly against her ear, but she knew he was scolding her.

"It's about time I let go of it."

"It hasn't been that long."

They were silent for a moment before he spoke again. "Please don't keep things from me, Kit. I would have misinterpreted your sadness this morning if I hadn't known. Can we make it a pact? No secrets?"

She nodded. She was relieved. She'd been afraid of losing that part of their relationship, that openness. She rested her head against his shoulder, wishing that he didn't have to work today. They could sit here under the afghan and watch the day run its course on the ocean.

"Another dinner without Dr. Perelle." Jay was the last to take his seat at the kitchen table the following night. "You can tell the month of the year by counting how many times Cole misses supper."

"Well, one thing I've learned from living in this house is that I don't ever want to be a doctor," Rennie said.

Jay looked crushed. "How can you say that? Look at the glamorous lives Cole and I lead, sewing episiotomies and taking out gallbladders."

Rennie wrinkled her nose. "Don't you ever get tired of them calling you all the time?"

"You get used to it. It's the price you pay for being able to live in luxury and eat like a king." He held up a forkful of baked beans as the phone rang. He smiled at Rennie. "It's probably 'them' calling me right now, don't you think?"

He walked to the counter and picked up the receiver. "Hello?" He held up a hand to silence the others, a frown on his face. "Cheryl, slow down, I can't understand you."

Something in the tone of his voice made everyone turn to look at him. He grasped the edge of the counter and held tight, his knuckles white. "What kind of accident?"

Kit felt her pulse quicken in her throat. Jay glanced at her, then looked away.

"What was he . . . Cheryl, come on, head wounds bleed that way, you know that . . . oh, God."

He looked directly at her, and she knew it was Cole. She

stood up, scraping the tops of her thighs on the table and knocking over her water.

"How long has he been out? Yes, I'll be right there. You calm down, okay?"

He hung up the phone and turned to her. "Cole was in an accident. He was riding in an ambulance with a patient and it was hit by a truck. The driver and an attendant were killed, and Cole has some kind of head injury."

She struggled to keep her head clear, her voice calm. "How bad . . . ?"

Jay shook his head. "He's unconscious. Cheryl really doesn't know much, just that he looked bad when he came in because of the blood and . . ."

Jay seemed rooted to the floor. She grabbed his arm. "Let's go," she said.

For the first five minutes of the drive to Point Pleasant she and Jay said nothing to each other. She played the words *dear God, let him be all right* over and over in her mind. It was evidence of her helplessness, praying to a God she had little faith in.

When they turned off the ocean road, Jay took her hand and held it on his thigh. "This is bizarre," he said. "I can see my own life passing before my eyes."

"Do you think he's okay?" she asked. Jay was a doctor, for heaven's sake. He should be able to tell her *something*.

But he didn't seem to hear her. "When I look back at my own life, it's full of Cole. I've seen him practically every day for the last twelve and a half . . . thirteen years, except when he was in France. It's like I'm married to him." He laughed. She held his hand tighter, afraid of the calm in his voice, the faraway look in his eyes.

"When I look at the future," he said, "Cole's still there. He's got to be." He let go of her hand to turn the steering wheel. They were going over the canal bridge now. She felt sick when she looked down at the water. "He knows what his friendship means to me, don't you think. Kit?"

"Of course he does," she said, thinking how odd it was that she'd been given the role of comforter here. She'd gotten into the car fully expecting to fall apart and let Jay piece her back together again. But it was better this way. Better right now to think about Jay than Cole.

She'd expected to see a horde of physicians hovering over him but except for Cheryl and another nurse, Cole was alone in the treatment room of the ER. He was flat on his back, a cervical collar on his neck and a wide, blood-soaked bandage wrapped around his head.

Cheryl smiled at them, a damp washcloth in her hand. "He's conscious," she said. Kit saw his eyelashes flutter.

"Thank God," said Jay. He walked across the room and leaned over to hug him, his lips brushing Cole's cheek.

That's from me too, Cole, she thought. She couldn't move.

"I'm all right," Cole said softly, his lips barely moving.

Her hand was still frozen on the doorknob. He didn't look all right. His face was scratched raw in most places and the skin that was still intact was purple.

Jay turned to her. "Come over here, Kit."

She walked toward them slowly.

"I can tell by your face that I look pretty bad," Cole

whispered. "Just a concussion." He lifted an arm to point to his head and winced.

"And a few broken ribs," Cheryl added. There was another bandage wrapped around the lower part of his rib cage, and EKG leads ran from his chest to a machine next to the gurney.

Kit leaned over to kiss his forehead, below the bloody gauze. "I love you," she said.

"Mm. I'm afraid I'm going to be very sick."

Cheryl produced a plastic basin from the counter behind his gurney and Cole swallowed hard.

"How am I going to do this, Cheryl?" he asked. "I can't move."

Cheryl looked at Jay. "We have to roll him," she said. "The cracked ribs are on this side, so roll him toward you."

"I'll talk to Dr. Gold about a nasogastric tube," the other nurse said, heading for the door.

Kit watched helplessly while they turned him in one gentle movement, like rolling a log. Cheryl folded the washcloth and held it on the back of his neck.

Cole moaned.

"Hang on, Cole." Cheryl held his head in her palm and slipped the basin under his cheek just in time. He vomited violently, his whole body shaking. Then he vomited again.

Kit felt the room spin. She glanced at the sink, wondering if she was going to get sick herself.

Jay took her by the shoulder and pointed her in the direction of the door. "Go call the others," he said. "Cheryl and I will stay with him."

She called the house and then sat in a chair outside the

room. She watched doctors and nurses go in and out, ignoring her. She heard him vomit a few more times before they got the tube down him. It had to feel like you were suffocating, having that thing stuck down your throat. She dug in her purse for a piece of gum, something to get the stale taste out of her mouth. She was useless. Too cowardly even to hold his head while he threw up. What would she have done if Alison had gotten sick in the middle of the night?

It seemed like a long time before Cheryl came out. She pulled a chair out of one of the other treatment rooms and sat next to Kit. "It's bad," she said, "but it could have been a lot worse. He has no memory of the accident at all. He doesn't remember his patient or even that he was in an ambulance. He doesn't know anyone was killed."

"No one told him?"

"Dr. Gold said it's better to let things proceed naturally. We answer his questions as he asks them instead of offering a lot of information. I told him his patient's name but it meant nothing to him. She's new."

"I don't understand why he was in an ambulance."

"Neither does he. I pieced it together, though. His patient was in the ER at Shore Memorial and he wanted her transferred over here. She was in premature labor and terrified. She asked him to ride with her. You know Cole, he couldn't say no."

No, Kit thought, he wouldn't.

"I'm so glad you were here," she said to Cheryl. She hated to think of him waking to a bunch of cold, professional faces. Cheryl would have been almost like family.

"I was just about to leave for the night and the ER receptionist called and said, 'I thought you might like to know that we've got Dr. Perelle down here.' It was awful when they first brought him in. And the two who were killed. One guy's head was attached to his shoulders by a thread of skin. I saw the two of them first and then I saw Cole and I thought for sure he was dying." Cheryl looked away from her, toward the reception desk, and Kit saw the tears in her eyes. "I know I really upset Jay on the phone—I should have checked out Cole's condition a little further before I called."

"I'm glad you called right away."

"Dr. Gold's going to admit him to a private room. They'll have to wake him up every hour or so. You can stay with him if you like."

She wanted to stay. She couldn't change his bandages or hold the basin while he threw up. Spending the night at the hospital seemed the least she could do for him.

He spoke and moved in slow motion, as if he were afraid he would break. He was bothered by his sketchy memory of what had happened, and he felt just well enough to be grumpy.

"I wish I could remember," he said. "I never go in ambulances with patients. I feel like I'm cracking up."

She ran her hand up his arm. It was perfect, without a scratch. "That's to be expected after a bad conk on the head."

"Tell me about this morning. I want to see what I remember."

She searched her own memory. "We slept in my room and we got up too late to go for a run because of our activities during the night. You remember them, don't you?"

He smiled weakly. "Afraid not. Don't take it personally. I'm sure it was wonderful."

She felt a little sad. "What's the last thing you do remember?" she asked.

He squinted as he thought. "Did all of us go out for ice cream sundaes last night?"

"That was the night before. Do you remember that?"

"Yes," he said, and a look of amusement crossed his face. "I have a selective memory, I guess."

She slept most of the morning on a sofa in his office. He was groggy when she went to see him in the afternoon. They'd taken the collar off his neck and they were letting him sleep for three hours at a time.

He held her hand loosely. "I've never hurt so much in my life," he said. "Everything aches. My head feels like it has a hatchet in it."

"I know, babe."

He suddenly brightened. "My patient came to see me and I remembered her."

"Really?"

"Yes. She's new in town, so I hadn't been seeing her long. I still don't understand how it all happened, though. She said I rode with her because she was scared." He looked at her. "Did you know I was such a nice guy?"

She smiled. "Oh, yeah."

"She said she felt guilty about the accident."

"Poor thing."

"I told her not to, that I'll be all right. I just feel bad about her baby."

She could see the light dawning in his eyes and knew she was on shaky ground.

"What about the driver?" he asked. "The ambulance driver. Was he hurt at all?"

How should she do this? "Yes, he was. There was a driver and two attendants."

"Are they here at Blair?'

She tightened her grip on his hand. "One attendant is here and he's doing very well. The driver and the other attendant—a woman—were badly hurt and they died on the way in."

Cole turned his face toward her, his eyes huge in their blackened sockets. "Jesus, no. Why didn't you tell me?'

"Dr. Gold said it would be better to tell you when you asked."

"Oh my God. It's my fault. I could have driven her in."

"Cole, no way was it your—"

"Two people are dead. And the *baby*. Shit." He let go of her hand. "I've been lying here complaining about my little aches and pains, and three people are dead. How could you let me do this?"

She leaned back in her chair, not saying anything. Nothing she said could make any difference.

50.

There was a percussion section in his head, and the room moved in and out of focus. Someone in white blurred past him and he struggled to bring her into clear view.

She walked toward him with the thermometer in her hand. A very pretty nurse he'd never seen before. "Well, you're finally awake," she said, slipping the thermometer under his tongue. "I've been trying to perk you up for about ten minutes now, and I was getting a little worried."

Her voice was an ice pick in his ears. He shut his eyes and tried to drift off again.

"Oh, no you don't, Dr. Perelle." She removed the thermometer. "Come on, eyelids up. Just for another minute."

She stood near the end of his bed, her head tilted to one side. "Even with those black eyes you're every bit as pretty as they say."

"Who's they?" he asked. "My parents?"

"Oh, I'm sure you know who they are," she said with a wink. "Sweet dreams, Doctor."

He was asleep before she'd left the room.

*

He was dreaming that he was being caressed by some faceless woman, her hands cool and heavy on his chest. She was massaging him, cool fingers on his stomach now, below the bandage. Then lower, under the sheet, grazing his erection. He opened his eyes, his breathing heavy. He wasn't dreaming. Someone was stroking him. He tried to get his bearings in the darkness.

Estelle? He touched the back of her neck as she leaned over him, her lips on his chest. It was not Estelle's neck. Someone with short hair.

Damn. The nurse.

He had to stop her, but he would die if she stopped. Just die.

"What are you doing?" he said hoarsely. His tongue felt like a boulder in his mouth. "Please stop." He grabbed her hand.

"I don't think you really want me to," she whispered. "You're holding my hand right where you want it."

She was right. He pulled her hand away from him and saw that it had not been her hands stroking him but a warm, damp washcloth. Yet certainly this had been no innocent bath.

She sat up straight. There was victory in her eyes. "You didn't seem to like my other methods for waking you so I thought a bath might be nice."

"I didn't appreciate it."

"You certainly seemed to." She smiled. "And let's see what it did for your BP."

She strapped the cuff on him and he turned away from

her, recoiling from the touch of her fingers on his arm. He wished his breathing would settle down.

"Wow," she said with a little giggle. "I'll have to adjust these numbers or they'll wonder what happened at ten o'clock to raise your pressure."

"Please leave." He slipped his hands under the covers so she wouldn't see that they were shaking.

"Come on, Doctor. You can't tell me you didn't enjoy that." She looked smug.

He was afraid of her. "Get out," he said.

"Okay, love. See you later." It felt like a threat.

He wouldn't let himself sleep. The thought of her touching him while he slept sickened him.

He thought of calling Kit, but he didn't want to wake her or worry her. He wished he could tell her what just happened. It was ironic. Three weeks ago the words would have slipped out easily, but now he felt cut off from her by their closeness. This would upset her too much. He would have to keep it from her.

He lay still with the growing urge to urinate. How could he call her in for the urinal now? His face grew hot with anger. He pressed the buzzer.

"Yes, Doctor?" she said from his doorway.

"I want a change in nurses."

She looked stricken. "Why?"

"You know why. Get me another nurse."

"I don't understand. And we're horribly short-staffed."

The picture of innocence. Maybe he had dreamt it after

all. But he remembered those blond curls against his hand, tickling his chest.

"Look, what you did was wrong. I can call your supervisor. I've been here a long time. I have credibility. You're new; you don't. Get me another nurse."

He watched her trying to choose her reaction. Finally she gave in.

"All right. I don't know what you're talking about, but if you feel that strongly I'll see what I can do."

"And I want her right away, understand? If I don't have a new nurse in five minutes, I'll be on the phone to your supervisor." Whoever the hell that was.

"Yes, sir!" She saluted him and walked out the door.

He felt drained. Within a few minutes the familiar face of Sue Astor was at his door. She was a tall, big-boned woman who nearly filled the doorway, and he was overjoyed to see her. He was suddenly connected to the safety of the outside world.

"Hi, Cole," she said. "Dana and I swapped assignments. She said you needed something?"

"The urinal." He didn't bother to mask the relief in his voice.

Sue frowned at him. "Dr. Gold said you could have bathroom privileges after eight tonight. Didn't Dana tell you?"

"No. She didn't."

"You poor guy," she said. "It's no fun being tied to a bedpan. Think you can get up?"

She helped him to the bathroom and then settled him back in bed. "God, what beautiful roses," she said, pointing to a vase on his nightstand.

Roses? He looked at his night table and saw the dozen blood-red roses in a white vase. He tried to think. The shelf that ran the length of the wall opposite his bed was covered with flowers from patients and colleagues. There was a big bouquet from his parents. But he'd never noticed the roses before.

"I must have been asleep when they brought them in," he said, adjusting himself carefully in the bed. "Who are they from?"

Sue handed him the little beige envelope. He pulled out the card and caught his breath. The card smelled like soap and roses and earth and he knew who the flowers were from without reading the signature.

He cupped the card in his palm. "Thanks, Sue," he said, dismissing her.

He switched on the bedside light and studied the card, his heart pounding.

Darling,
I heard about the accident, and that you are all right.
That means everything to me.
E.

He stared at the familiar handwriting for a long time before he opened the drawer to his night table and slipped the card into his wallet.

He knew this was the second thing he would keep from Kit tonight.

*

He could see the ocean from the wicker sofa in the living room. A flock of gawky-looking pelicans flew along the beach, just on the other side of the beach heather. They made him smile. He was grateful to be home, to be alive.

He heard the school bus squeal to a stop in front of the house and the crunch of gravel as Rennie walked across the driveway.

"You're home!" she said, her eyes bright and warm. She was a beautiful kid. "Does your head still hurt? Kit said you were in a lot of pain."

He touched the bandage. "It's a little better today. It's at its best when I sit still."

Rennie settled herself next to him on the sofa. He put his arm around her and she didn't budge. She still had little-girl hair that rested like gossamer on his hand. "You tell me everything you need and I'll get it for you," she said. "You don't have to move."

Jay came home earlier than usual and shooed Rennie from the room. "I need to talk to Cole," he said, and his serious look was enough to make Rennie leave without an argument.

Jay's thirty-sixth birthday was in a few weeks. He looked at least that old today, except for that incredible mop of black hair. He sat down in one of the wicker chairs and frowned at Cole.

"I don't know what to make of this," he said. "Cheryl came to see me today, pretty upset. She said there's a rumor on the grapevine that your nurse last night gave you more than the usual TLC."

"You're kidding." How many ears had it gone through to get all the way back to Cheryl, from the tenth floor to the Maternity Unit? "What did she say? How much more than the usual TLC?"

"The works."

"Well, then, she's lying. Exaggerating at least." He recounted the events of the night before and Jay frowned.

"This is bad news, Cole. She's telling tales that put you in jeopardy as well as herself, you know."

"I didn't think she'd be stupid enough to talk about it."

"She was stupid enough to try something in the first place. You'd better either get her to clam up or take it to administration. I'll talk to her tomorrow, if you like."

"She's on evenings. I'll call her tonight. What really bothers me is that other people at Blair think something happened and will feel as though they have something over Kit."

"Kit doesn't know?"

He shook his head.

"How come? You two closing down on each other?"

"I didn't want to upset her."

"*Cole.*" The word was a reprimand.

"I'll tell her."

51.

She held Cole's hand tightly at the funeral. The driver and attendant had been friends, apparently from old Point Pleasant families, and the funeral was a joint affair. Their bodies lay in open caskets in the side aisle of the chapel and her eyes were drawn to them, imagining Cole in their place. She'd never be able to tolerate more than one loss every few years. Alison was enough for now. Everyone else in her life had better hang on.

How strange this must be for Cole, to be at a funeral he felt no part of. There wasn't a familiar face in the crowded church. The first few pews were full of people in black, hunched over and white-faced. Cole sat stoically next to her, the clean white bandage on his head and the ghostly green and yellow bruises on his face making it clear to any observer who he was and why he was there. But no one could see the pain inside him. She worried that he still blamed himself for the accident or for his patient's baby—or for letting that bitch act out her fantasies on him in the hospital.

It scared her that he hadn't planned to tell her. They'd

made that pact to be open with each other and he'd broken it already.

Cole pushed her toward the line of people filing past the caskets. She knew this was what he was waiting for. He was hoping he'd remember them when he saw their faces. The air in the church thickened, and she kept her eyes on the door instead of the bodies. She remembered Cheryl's description of the driver, how he'd been nearly beheaded. She didn't want to see how they'd made him presentable for an open casket.

"So young," Cole whispered to her.

She shut her eyes and leaned against his shoulder.

"They're strangers," he said. "It's as if I never laid eyes on them before."

He was quiet when they got home. Closed in on himself. He wanted to go to bed although it was not yet dinnertime. He swallowed a couple of pills, and she followed him up the stairs at the snail's pace he set. He was still stiff and fragile. And so withdrawn. He ignored her. She would have guessed he was angry with her if she hadn't seen the tightness in the muscles of his face and known his head was hurting. He sat on the edge of her bed and stared out the window at the sea while she pulled down the covers.

"Get in, babe," she said, wishing he would speak to her.

He undressed and moved woodenly onto his back, his eyes squeezed shut and his teeth clenched. He stretched out slowly, sighing like an old man. She lay down next to him and watched his face.

"Is there anything I can get you?" she asked.

He pressed his fingers to the space between his eyes, as if waiting for the pain to pass before he answered. "No," he said. "I'm sorry I'm grouchy. I'll be okay when the medication takes hold."

"You're not grouchy. You're just depressed."

He looked up at the ceiling. "I'm wondering how to face Dana. Not to mention Cheryl and anyone else who might have heard the rumors."

"You're an innocent victim, Cole. As surely as if you were a woman accosted on the street."

He made a face. "It feels like shit. I can understand why Rennie thought we'd blame her after she was raped. Except I'm a grown man. It's humiliating."

"You were as incapable as an infant to prevent it."

He looked into her eyes. "Thank you," he said.

"For what?"

"For saying that. For understanding so well. For going to look at dead strangers with me. And for coming to bed with me at five-thirty in the afternoon so I don't have to be depressed alone."

"You're welcome."

He ran his finger across her cheek. "I'd like to make love to you," he said, "but I'm limited by my disabilities."

"I accommodate the handicapped," she said.

He took her head in both his hands and kissed her and there was no doubt in her mind that they'd find some way to make love.

She woke up alone in the morning. Cole had obviously decided to go in to work. She hoped he'd only work the morning. He wouldn't make it through a day of examining patients, not the way every little movement made him wince.

She pulled on her shorts and running shoes and picked up the wastebasket to take downstairs to empty. A small beige envelope lying among the white tissues caught her eye. It was addressed to Cole, in fluid, European-looking handwriting. She remembered that writing.

She took the envelope from the basket. It couldn't be from Estelle. He would have told her. She slipped the card out of the envelope and read it slowly.

Darling,
I heard about the accident, and that you are all right.
That means everything to me.
E.

She remembered Cole the night before, making love to her, laughing with her. She remembered the feel of his warm body next to her the whole night through. Surely they were okay. And he'd thrown the card away, parted with it next to a bunch of soiled tissues.

But why hadn't he told her?

52.

She sat on the corner of his desk, her legs crossed at the knee, one shoe dangling. It was remarkable how she could look as comfortable in a suit as she did in her running shorts and T-shirt. He'd always loved this suit on her. He was thinking of slipping the jacket off her shoulders, unzipping her skirt. It didn't matter what she wore these days, he wanted to take it off her. But he restrained himself. She was shifting her position on the desk, getting ready to talk business.

She handed him a pile of letters. "There are three requests from talk shows in this stack," she said with a smile. "Select carefully."

"How am I supposed to choose?"

"Visibility and audience. I don't know why Davies is adamant about you picking just one."

"I'm glad he is. This makes me nervous."

"You should pick the most serious audience, so it doesn't seem exploitative. You know what would be great? If you could have a patient do it with you."

"Maybe," he said, thinking of who might be willing. He

wasn't at all averse to sharing the spotlight—or the butterflies.

Her face was suddenly serious. "Will you have some time to talk tonight?" she said. "About a topic we've been avoiding?"

"What's that?" He was certain she meant Estelle. He'd thought of Estelle only twice in the last few months—when he received her card in the hospital and before that on the drive back from Watchung with the ring. In his mind that ring had always belonged to Estelle. And she'd known it was waiting for her. Once she'd asked him if she could have the diamonds reset in gold so it would match the rest of her jewelry. He'd laughed, thinking she was joking. Looking back, he wasn't so sure.

But the moment Kit slipped the ring on her finger, he knew that was where it belonged. He watched it now as she unpinned the hospital ID from her lapel. "I want to sign the consent form to have my tubes tied."

"Oh." He was relieved. "You're sure you want to?"

She picked up his coffee cup and rolled it between her palms. "Yes." Her voice pleaded with him to understand. "I just couldn't go through it again, Cole."

"I'd never ask you to."

"But I'm afraid you want children."

He shrugged. "Estelle didn't want kids and I got used to the idea of never having any. As a matter of fact, I should have a vasectomy rather than you—"

"No." She looked upset. "What if we split up and you met someone who wanted children?"

"We're not going to split up." He didn't like her to talk that way.

"What if I died?"

He took her hand, had to pry it away from the mug. "My desire for a child just isn't that strong." He wondered as he spoke if he was telling the truth.

"If I wanted children, you'd go along with having some, wouldn't you?"

He thought carefully. Yes, of course he would. Babies that looked like Alison. Little girls like Wendy and Becky. His to tuck in at night and read stories to when he came home from work.

But how to answer her? She was trying to trap him. Make him admit he wanted a child so she could torment herself with guilt over not wanting to be a mother. It was one of her favorite pastimes.

He stood up, put his hands on her shoulders. "Listen, I'll answer your question honestly. But first you have to tell me if you're firm in your decision."

"Completely."

"Even if I said I was desperate for a child, you would still have a tubal?"

"Yes, but I'd feel terrible about it."

He smiled at the warning in her voice. *Please don't make me feel terrible.* She was so easy to read. Sometimes it amazed him that she had the political savvy she needed to do her job.

"The important thing to me is that I'm with you. I could enjoy being a father, but it's not something that I *need*."

She stood up and leaned against him, and he circled her with his arms.

"This is the world's softest, sexiest suit," he said.

"You're changing the subject."

"I thought we were through with that subject."

She set her head on his shoulder. "Maybe we could make Wendy and Becky more a part of our lives," she said. "They could spend weekends with us sometimes. It would give Corinne some time for herself."

He was touched. "I'd like that."

After she left he picked up his file on the patient in labor. He opened it but didn't read a word inside. He was remembering the day the twins were born. He'd only been with Estelle a few months then. She wouldn't go to the hospital with him to see Corinne. Didn't want to see *babies*. The word alone made her blanch. "How can women do that to their bodies?" she'd said. He'd thought then that he could change her thinking. He would have to. Back then he couldn't imagine his life without children. He remembered holding those babies, one in each arm. He loved the way they'd looked up at him even then as though he were someone special.

If only he'd held Alison. If only Alison had lived. *Damn it.*

He closed the file and stood up, felt in his pocket for his car keys. *You are going to spend the rest of your life delivering babies without ever holding one of your own.* He switched off his office light, and the darkness overwhelmed him. He hurried through the dark waiting room and breathed a sigh of relief when he reached the bright corridor of the Maternity Unit. He pushed open the double doors and stepped into the fresh air.

Then he smiled, catching on. Kit was not so easy to read after all. This had been her plan, the reason she'd pushed him. She wanted it to really sink in so he'd do his grieving now and not hold it against her later.

So he would have no children. No orthodontia bills, no bickering in the backseat of the car. No interruptions in the middle of the night. Except when Kit wanted to make love and couldn't wait until morning to have him.

He sat on top of the big desk in the library and motioned Rennie into one of the leather chairs. He'd been looking forward to this moment all day. He'd asked Janni to let him be the one to tell her. Rennie knew something was up. She wore an expectant look on her face.

"The paperwork's completed, Rennie," he said. "You're staying here."

Her expression didn't change. "Staying here? In the Chapel House?"

He nodded.

"I won't have to go to some other foster family?"

"No." He could almost see the cloud that had been hovering over her head disappear. But then she surprised him.

"What makes you think I want to stay here?"

"*What*?"

"I'm *joking*." She grinned.

"Oh." He smiled. "Well, I'm glad this is finally settled. I

couldn't stand the thought of you moving out, living with people you don't know or don't feel safe with."

"I wasn't going to. I was going to kill myself first." She said it so matter-of-factly that he laughed.

"You're joking again?"

"No. I hadn't figured out how to do it yet, but I wasn't going to go to another foster home, or worse than that, back to my mother and Craig."

He felt his smile go flat. She was serious. "*Rennie.*"

"It's okay now," she said quickly. "I get to stay here and that's really all I wanted."

He leaned toward her. "If you ever, ever, feel that way again, you tell me. Understand?" He heard his voice rising. They could probably hear him in the living room. "How do you think we'd feel if you killed yourself, huh?"

She stood up. "Don't yell at me!"

He looked at her in surprise.

"All my life I've been yelled at for things I didn't do until I'm so confused I can't figure out whether I actually did something wrong or not. But I know I didn't do anything so terrible right now for you to be yelling at me."

She was standing up to him. He resisted a smile. "You're right," he said. "I'm sorry."

"Can I still stay here?"

"Of course."

She left the room and he sat on the desk for a few minutes longer, looking out at the dark beach, smiling to himself.

*

The cafeteria was nearly deserted and he looked at the clock. Six-thirty. He'd been staring at the grilled cheese sandwich on his plate for fifteen minutes. He couldn't eat it. Hadn't been able to get a thing down all day and probably wouldn't be able to sleep tonight, either. He'd never known this about himself, that he would fall victim to stage fright. He could perform the most delicate surgery with a steady hand, but he was terrified of facing Claudia Marks tomorrow. It was hard to believe. Tomorrow Claudia Marks herself would be interviewing him for her nationally televised talk show. He wondered now if he'd be able to utter a single coherent word.

"There you are."

He turned to see Cheryl walking toward him. "Why are you still here?" he asked.

"I'm leaving in a minute. But I thought you'd want to know that the hydrocephalic baby you operated on back in August was delivered by c-section this afternoon."

The Garry baby. He remembered that surgery, the only one he'd performed at Blair that was a clear-cut failure. He set his napkin on top of the sandwich. "Alive?"

She nodded.

He'd had nightmares about this baby. Its head must be swollen to the size of a melon by now. "Have you seen him?" he asked.

She nodded again. "Pretty sad," she said. "He won't last long."

He left his grilled cheese untouched and walked over to the Intensive Care Nursery.

"Hi, Doc. You here to see the Garry baby?"

He didn't recognize the nurse who greeted him, but she apparently knew who he was.

"If I may," he said. He imagined the entire ICN team would be surrounding the baby. He probably wouldn't be able to get near him. But after he'd scrubbed and gowned, the nurse led him to one of the small isolation rooms where the baby was the sole occupant. No one was working on him, not a soul. They knew better than to try to save this baby.

His head seemed to fill one end of his little plastic Isolate. Cole had never seen anything like it.

"Damn it," he said quietly, shutting his eyes.

"You all right, Doc?"

"Yes. It's a shock, that's all." He moved closer, determined to study this infant in the most clinical sense possible. He told himself he would feel nothing, not horror or revulsion, pity or guilt. Nothing.

Blue veins mapped the pale surface of the baby's scalp. The facial features were off-center, dwarfed by a head larger than an adult's. Cole swallowed hard. What had gone wrong with that surgery? This baby should be wailing in his mother's arms right now.

He wouldn't let Kit handle the PR on this. She mustn't see this baby—it would tear her apart. He wanted her away from babies altogether for a while.

But Kit had other ideas. She met him at the front door of the Chapel House. "Dr. Davies called me," she said. "He wants me to have a press release ready to go in the morning. He said a lot of people are waiting for something like this to happen to use as ammunition against fetal surgery."

Cole shook his head. "No. Uh-uh. I don't want you on this. Call someone else in the PR department to do it for you."

She looked at him in surprise. "You don't think I can handle the PR?"

"No, it's not that." She was by the far the best in the department. "I just think it's too soon for you to have to deal with a dying baby. It would be too painful for you."

She hesitated a moment before giving in. "All right," she said finally.

He was relieved. He was never sure anymore where her pain left off and his began.

53.

All of her energy these last few weeks had gone into the plans for Cole's interview today with Claudia Marks. Running was the only other activity she hadn't allowed to suffer. It had actually been a relief to turn the Garry case over to Terri, one of her PR colleagues. She wouldn't have time to handle a situation like that today.

The television crew arrived in Cole's office at ten o'clock. She stood in the doorway watching them, fascinated. There were at least twenty people, each with his or her own sense of purpose. She was glad that everyone seemed to know exactly what he was doing. Her part of this job was nearly over. The arrangements, the diplomacy, the soothing of jittery nerves were behind her.

"You just relax," she'd told Blair's director that Monday. "You can sit back and watch Blair's reputation grow as one of the most exciting and innovative medical centers in the country. On national TV."

All she had to do today was take Claudia Marks to lunch and make sure everyone was in the right place at the right time. It was Cole who was carrying the nerve-wrenching responsibility now.

She found him in her office, pacing.

"They kicked me out of my office," he said.

"I know. They told me."

"I should have worn a suit." He was wearing navy blue pants and a light blue shirt, open at the neck. They had told him to wear whatever he usually wore in his office. Taken from that perspective, he was a little overdressed.

"You look fine. You have that casual, it's-all-in-a-day's-work look about you."

"Who's handling the PR on the Garry baby?"

"Terri. Don't think about that now, Cole. It'll be fine."

Claudia Marks was taller, more imposing in real life. They met in Kit's office at eleven, and Claudia wanted a tour of the hospital before they went to lunch. Kit watched her with admiration as they traveled from unit to unit. Claudia had an eye for a story, and she riveted her attention on people and situations she could twist into something marketable. She spent so long watching the triage nurse in the ER evaluating the victims of an accident that it was past noon when they reached the restaurant.

"Dr. Perelle was in an accident himself a few weeks ago," Kit said after the waiter had taken their orders. She cringed at the gleam in Claudia's eyes.

"Kit, that's exactly the kind of information I'm missing on this story. We know a great deal about Dr. Perelle as a physician and a researcher, but very little about the man himself. Was he badly hurt?"

She'd meant it to be small talk, not fuel for her program. "He was hospitalized for a few days with a concussion."

She made it sound unimportant, but Claudia was very hungry, for more than lunch.

"Were other people hurt? Whose fault was it?"

"He was riding in an ambulance with a patient, and some people were killed. You'd need to get the rest of the information from him, though I doubt very much that he'd want to talk about it."

"He doesn't need to talk about it," Claudia said. "We can toss it into our narrative." She lit a cigarette. "I can't tell you how refreshing it is to be able to feature someone who's a bright light in a scientific field and young and attractive at the same time. Not to mention eligible. The combination is hard to find and unbeatable in the ratings. He's a local hero now, but just wait until the rest of the country gets a look at him. We're planning plenty of close-ups, so those eyes of his can work their magic on the viewers."

"I think he'd rather have the focus be on his work."

"Oh, of course." Claudia waved her cigarette in the air. "We won't make an issue out of anything other than his professional endeavors. But the average viewer will be receiving a subliminal message through strategically placed tidbits about Cole Perelle as a person. It works every time. Is he gay?"

Kit laughed. "I beg your pardon?"

"Why is a good-looking man still unattached at the age of thirty-five?"

"He *is* attached."

"Really?" A new spark in Claudia's eye now. "To a female?"

"Oh, yes."

Claudia leaned forward. "Tell me more."

"I can't, Claudia," she said, as the waiter set a seafood salad in front of her. "I think any information about his personal life had better come from him."

Five minutes into the interview, she knew he was starting to relax. She leaned against the door and tried to block out the camera crew from her vision to imagine how the interview would actually look on television. It was warm in the room and the lights bathed everything in a hot white glow. She wondered how Cole could stand them right in his eyes.

Claudia sat in one of the maroon leather chairs at the side of his desk, while he sat behind it. He was telling her why he'd become interested in fetal surgery. He was good at this. Why he got so nervous beforehand she didn't know. He was smiling, his eyes sparkling in the lights, and the words he used were packed with emotion. Claudia looked ecstatic. He was turning out to be even more of a winner than she had anticipated.

"And now,"—Claudia Marks smiled into the camera—"we are very pleased to have with us a former patient of Dr. Perelle's and her parents." She turned to face the couple sitting on her left. The woman held a robust-looking baby in her arms. "This is little Megan Kelley," Claudia murmured reverently. "Fran, tell us how you felt when you first learned there was a problem with the baby you were carrying?"

Claudia did a nice job of getting the Kelleys and Cole to describe the successful surgery Cole had performed on

Megan's blocked kidney. Kit could see with relief that the interview was drawing to a close. But suddenly Claudia's questioning took a new direction. Her voice became that of an investigative reporter, calculated, probing.

"But fetal surgery is not always successful is it, Cole?" she asked.

Kit came to attention. What was she up to?

"There's a baby some are describing as a 'monster baby' right here—today—at Blair Medical Center," Claudia continued. "That baby is the result of fetal surgery you performed."

Monster baby? Who was describing the Garry baby in those words? She watched Cole struggle with his anger.

"The surgery wasn't able to improve the condition of the fetus," Cole interrupted her, "but it did nothing to worsen it," he said. "The baby would have been born with this problem whether I—"

"Is the baby going to die as a result of the surgery?"

Kit watched in disbelief. *Manipulative bitch.*

"No," Cole said, with more control than Kit expected. "The baby will *not* die as a result of the surgery; the baby will die as a result of hydrocephalus."

Claudia looked at the camera. "So, as you can see, there is no guarantee of a happy outcome with fetal surgery."

The camera stopped rolling, and Kit saw Cole lean toward Claudia, hissing something at her under his breath. She would let him take care of Claudia. She had her own work to do. When this interview aired there would be reporters breaking down the hospital doors.

She left Cole's office without speaking to him, before

he'd have a chance to change her mind. She called Terri in the PR office.

"I'm taking the Garry assignment back," she said. "It's going to get very hot."

"It's all yours," said Terri. "Have you seen that baby?"

"I'm going over there now."

"Well," Terri said, "steel yourself."

She hung up the phone and walked to the nursery, wishing the route were longer. It had been months since she'd been in this hallway. She avoided it—it was too hard to tune out the crying. But she didn't really hear it today. She had a task to do. She'd take a quick peek at this baby to see what all the fuss was about and to ready herself for the questions from the media. Then she'd prepare a press release. She'd beat Claudia Marks to the draw.

She scrubbed at the sink outside the nursery and let a red-headed nurse wrap her into one of the yellow gowns. She made idle chatter with the nurse, pretending this was all in a day's work.

"He's in the isolation room," the nurse said, "on the warming table. He's not doing too well today."

The first thing she noticed was his face. It was a perfect face, as perfect as Alison's. His eyes were open, and she thought he watched her as she slipped her finger into one tiny hand. His head was huge, no doubt about it, but God, what a face. His pale lips quivered with each raw-sounding breath. Kit bit her lip. It hurt him just to breathe.

"Do you want to hold him?"

She turned around to see the red-headed nurse behind her.

"May I?" Could such a delicate little thing be held?

"You'd better sit down." The nurse pointed to a chair by the door. She carefully lifted the baby from the warming table and rested him in Kit's arms. "His head is super-heavy," she said. "You have to give it lots of support."

He was so warm. She smiled down at that wonderful little face, the eyes most definitely looking back into her own. "How long does he have?" she asked.

"He won't make it through the night." The nurse looked over Kit's head toward the door. "Hi, Dr. Perelle."

Kit turned to see him standing in the doorway, arms folded across his chest.

He sat down in the only other chair in the room. "Claudia Marks pulled a fast one there, didn't she?" he asked.

"The nurse said he's going to die tonight."

Cole sighed. "I wish you hadn't come over here to the nursery."

"I had to. And I'm fine." The baby wrinkled his nose for a second and squirmed in her lap. Her left arm shook from the weight of his head. "I've taken this assignment back from Terri, and what I need from you is a written explan-ation of the surgery in layman's terms, including what went wrong with this little guy. I also want a simple description of hydrocephalus and some illustrations of the fetus and how the shunt's inserted, et cetera. Do you have something like that?"

He smiled. "Yes."

"Can I have it by five?" It was four now.

"I'd better get busy." He stood up to go.

"And Cole?"

"Yes?"

She looked down at the fragile life in her arms. "I'm going to cancel my tubal," she said.

54.

They had taken a bottle of champagne to bed with them and now he had quite a buzz. He lay with his head on Kit's lap while she sat propped up against the pillows, stroking his hair.

The Claudia Marks show had aired a few hours earlier, with the incriminating last five minutes of the interview cut. Claudia had sent a telegram of apology to him. What choice did she have? Kit had saturated the media with the facts about the Garry baby. She'd left no room for rumor or accusation.

"I think we spilled." Cole felt the damp spot on the top sheet.

"This was worth an extra load of laundry." She reached for a pad and pen from the night table and began to write. "We have to add champagne to the list for the reception."

He was grateful for her organized mind.

"I wish I could meet your family before the wedding," he said.

"They're going to love you. As long as they never know you were the father of my baby, that is. I'm sure they'll view you as this wonderful stable guy who's rescuing their daughter from her depraved lifestyle."

She was quiet a moment, and he knew she was thinking about his father, who had reacted to the announcement of their engagement with a silence so cold it drained the color from Kit's face. Ever since Phillip had learned of her pregnancy, he'd distanced himself from her. "She never seemed like that type of girl," he'd said.

"I wish I could redeem myself in your father's eyes," she said now.

"He'll come around, Kit. He thought the sun rose and set on Estelle. She had a real knack for turning Perelle men into gullible fools."

He hoped he was right, that his father wouldn't boycott the wedding. It would be here at the house, in the living room, overlooking the water. He couldn't imagine it anywhere else. They'd invited just their families and a few close friends. And Rennie, of course. He'd been thinking a lot about Rennie lately. He looked up at Kit. "Is it possible to adopt a teenager?"

"Of course. It's just rarely done because no one *wants* to adopt a teenager."

"I do." He surprised himself with the words.

She set the pad back on the night table. "I've thought about it too, Cole. But I don't think they'd let us as long as we're living in this . . . arrangement. Look at how hard it was just to get approved as a foster home."

"So we'd have to leave the Chapel House." He said it simply, curious to see how the words felt on his tongue. Not too bad. The terror he'd always felt at that thought wasn't there. His reactions must be deadened by the alcohol.

"Do you think you could move out?" Kit asked.

"If I had you and Rennie . . . I think I could." He thought of Jay and shut his eyes. He'd lived a third of his life with him. "If we didn't move too far." He smiled.

"We'd better save this conversation for sometime when we're sober and—"

The screams from the room next door silenced her. Cole felt his body tense, but he made no move to get up. Maris would be all right. It was already quiet, although he knew she would be trembling and glassy-eyed, making that groaning sound deep in her throat, that sound that substituted for tears.

Kit stopped stroking his hair and leaned down to kiss him. "Do you want to go to her? It must be days since you've rescued anyone."

He laughed at how sweetly she'd insulted him. She was laughing too, noiselessly. He could feel it in the fleshy part of her stomach under his cheek. The part she hated and he loved. His baby had been in there.

He sat up and was about to say yes when he got a good look at her in the light from the window. Warm gray eyes that demanded nothing of him. He belonged in this room, with her. "I'll stay here," he said.

She shook her head. "I know you want to go."

He sighed. "She's so used to having me there. I've got you, Janni and Jay are together, and she has no—"

"I know. It's okay. Go." She gave him a little shove.

She was in one of her independent moods. He still wasn't used to it. He'd had to explain every move he made to Estelle.

55

Rennie chewed her nails as Kit drove her to the police station. Her rapists—alleged rapists—had been apprehended the night before after raping another girl in Point Pleasant, and Rennie had nervously agreed to identify them in a line-up.

Cole had been upset when Kit told him about the call from the police. She'd caught up with him in his office yesterday afternoon. He was eating lunch at his desk, munching an apple and drinking milk straight from the carton. Claudia Marks had made a big deal out of his milk drinking—his wholesome image—on her program. That show had been a hit. Kit spent most of the day on the phone with the major networks. Suddenly everyone wanted to do a feature on fetal surgery.

"She finally seems to be getting over it, and now to dredge it up again . . ." said Cole. "I don't even feel like telling her after that talk about suicide."

She'd persuaded him that it was only fair to tell her, to leave the decision to prosecute up to Rennie herself. Now as she watched Rennie biting her nails to the quick, she was not so sure.

"Shannon doesn't want to prosecute." Grace Kelleher, the detective who'd spoken to Rennie back in January, sat across the desk from them. "She has that right, just as you do."

"She won't even try to identify them?" Rennie asked.

Grace shook her head, her short gray hair grazing her chin.

Kit wanted to take Rennie's hand, do something to comfort her. Rennie had spoken in the car of having someone to share this with. Now she was going to have to do it alone.

The other girl was afraid, Grace explained. Did Rennie remember how frightened she'd been at first?

Rennie nodded.

Well, that's how this girl was feeling now.

Rennie shut her eyes for a moment, and Kit felt her own heart pounding. She thought of telling Grace to forget it, just let her take Rennie home. Cole had been right to worry about putting her through this, making her live it all over again.

"So what does that mean?" Rennie asked, looking straight at the detective.

"It means the men—if you identify them—will be tried on the basis of the crime they committed against you. And only you."

"But that's not fair. It's only half of what they've done."

Grace looked thoughtful. "Would you like to talk with Shannon, Rennie?"

Kit leaned forward. "No, I don't think that's a very good

idea." Grace obviously didn't have Rennie's best interests at heart.

Grace continued as if Kit hadn't spoken. "Perhaps if she heard how strongly you feel . . . perhaps if she felt she wasn't going through this alone . . . ?"

Rennie shook her head quickly. She turned to Kit. "I can't. It would be like watching myself suffer."

"It was just a thought," Grace said.

"What happened to her?" Rennie's hands tightened on the arms of her chair: "I mean . . . was it just like what happened to me? Don't tell me the details, please. Just . . . in general."

Grace nodded. "It was their . . . um, their style, that led us to suspect it was the same men. It was very similar. They threatened Shannon with a knife, same as you. Some of her injuries were worse than yours, some of yours were worse than hers."

"I feel so sorry for her," Rennie said. "Maybe it would help her to meet me."

Kit covered one of Rennie's hands with her own. "Honey, I really don't think—"

"Kit, you don't *know*," Rennie said. "You don't understand. Maybe I can *help* her." She turned to Grace. "I'll do it," she said. "I'll talk to her."

Grace led them to the conference room where Shannon Lewis was waiting and pulled Kit aside. "You can stay, but let Rennie do the talking," she said. "She'll be fine."

There were twelve chairs around the long conference table, but Shannon wasn't sitting. She leaned against the window sill, her eyes, one of them blackened and bruised, riveted on Rennie. Kit wanted to step between them to protect Rennie from that glare. Shannon looked about as vulnerable as a tiger. It was hard to believe she was only fourteen. Eighteen would be more like it. She wore black jeans that were so tight she'd probably had to lie down to zip them. Her breasts were full under a purple sweatshirt that hung off her bare left shoulder. Her eyebrows were plucked to a skinny thread above dark lashes, chunky with mascara.

"Hi," Rennie said.

"Do you have a match?" Shannon pulled a cigarette from a pack of Kools.

Kit and Rennie shook their heads as they sat down at one end of the table.

"I've gotta find a match," Shannon said. She left them alone in the room for a minute.

"Rennie, you don't have to do this."

Rennie didn't answer her.

Shannon came back, carrying an ashtray and a book of matches, her cigarette aglow. She sat at the opposite end of the table and inhaled deeply, eyes closed.

"I promised Detective Kelleher that I'd talk to you," she said, opening her eyes behind a shield of smoke. "But it's not going to do any good. My mind's made up." Her hand trembled as she tapped her cigarette into the ashtray.

She was not as tough as she looked, Kit thought. Rennie seemed to notice it too, for she suddenly found her voice.

"Don't you want to see them punished?" she asked.

"Don't you want to keep them from doing it to anyone else?"

Shannon laughed. "You don't know much about life, do you . . . what's your name? Ronnie?"

"Rennie," Kit said.

Shannon looked at Kit. "Are you her spokesman or something? Let her speak for herself." She leaned forward on the table. "*We're* the ones who'll be on trial. They'll ask how many guys we did it with before and . . . how many guys *have* you done it with?"

"I've never done it with anyone."

"Oh." Shannon looked out the window. "You might be naive enough to pull this off. You can get sympathy, little golden girl. I've never gotten any, and I don't expect to get it now."

"You have *my* sympathy," Rennie said.

Rennie was right, Kit thought. She couldn't understand. There was a bond between these two that transcended their looks and their lifestyles.

Shannon looked at Rennie. "How did it happen to you?" she asked quietly.

"At night," Rennie answered. "Last January, on the beach."

"Did they . . . cut you?"

Rennie shook her head.

Shannon stood and pulled her sweatshirt up to reveal a long bandage across her third or fourth rib. "They didn't actually stab me, just sliced a little." She chuckled mirthlessly, then sat down again and stared at the table. "Oh fuck," she said, stubbing out her cigarette. Her eyes were glistening.

"I'm sorry," Rennie said.

Shannon looked up. "Did they do it to you . . ."—she stumbled over the words—"you know . . . both ways?"

Rennie nodded.

Shannon shook her head. "That was a first for me, let me tell you." She was half laughing, half crying.

"It was terrible, right?" Rennie said. "Doesn't it make you want to make them suffer the way you did?"

"Look, Rennie, I was *hitchhiking*. I wasn't building sand-castles, or whatever you were doing, on the beach. The judge is going to say I asked for it, led them on or something. Maybe I *did*. I get confused about what happened."

Rennie leaned forward. "Did you ask for that?" She pointed to where Shannon's sweatshirt covered the bandage. "And your black eye? Did you ask them to do it to you from . . . in both ways?" She sounded pleased to have the euphemism.

Shannon began to cry in earnest now, and Rennie looked at Kit for the first time, as though she was frightened by her own power. She had probably never made another person cry in her entire life. Kit nodded her encouragement and Rennie looked back at Shannon.

"They took pictures of you at the hospital, right?" she asked. "Pictures of your injuries?"

Shannon nodded.

"The judge will see the pictures and know that nobody in her right mind would ask to be hurt like that."

"My own mother thinks I made the whole thing up."

"Well, I don't. What happened to you is too close to what happened to me. If I testify by myself against them, it wouldn't seem like they're so bad. But together you and I can get them locked up forever."

Kit smiled to herself. Rennie was dynamite.

Shannon lit another cigarette. "I want to forget it. I don't want to have to go over it again and again."

"You won't be alone." Rennie turned to Kit. "Do you have a piece of paper?"

Kit felt in her purse for a scrap of paper and came up with only a chewing gum wrapper. Rennie opened it and wrote the Chapel House phone number neatly across the middle.

"Here." She walked around the table and gave the wrapper to Shannon.

Shannon looked at Rennie. "Didn't Detective Kelleher say you're a foster kid?"

Rennie nodded.

"But you're so . . . you're just not like someone who's from a foster home. Most foster kids are so fucked up."

Rennie blushed. "Call me, okay? When you're scared, or any time. I know how you feel. I really truly do."

"You feel all right?" Kit put her arm around Rennie as they waited behind the one-way mirror.

"I'm fine."

Grace stood behind them. "You don't need to rush, Rennie. There will be two sets of six men. Take all the time you need."

Rennie nodded and Kit tightened her hand on her shoulder.

"Kit, I can hardly breathe, you're so close."

Kit backed away a little. "Sorry."

The first group of men walked in. Kit searched the unfamiliar faces. All of them were wearing ski caps and looked like they'd been scraped out of the gutter. Where had the police ever dug up such ratty-looking human beings? And which were the rapists? What would it be like to have those dirty, rough hands touching her? She shuddered.

Rennie shook her head. "None of them." She turned to Kit. "Maybe the guys who did it to Shannon weren't the same ones after all."

The second group moved onto the platform, and Rennie began to tremble under Kit's arm. She looked into her lap.

"Rennie?" Grace said.

"The two on the left," Rennie said without looking up.

Kit looked at the two ordinary faces. They could be men she passed any day on the street, only uglier, something hideous in their features. She felt a well of hatred forming inside her chest. It was good Cole wasn't with them—he'd be through the mirror and on them in a second.

"Rennie, I have to ask you to look at them again," Grace said. "You barely glanced at them, and we have to be very certain that you're identifying the right men."

She looked up, right into the eyes of the ugly bastard on the far left. "Are you sure they can't see me?"

"Absolutely positive," said Grace.

"The one on the very left was the one with the knife. He

held me over the concrete wall and gave me all those scratches on my back. The one next to him—"

"Honey," Kit interrupted. "I don't think you need to go into all the detail."

Rennie looked at her. "I'm all *right*, Kit," she said. She looked back at the men. "The one next to him was the one who did the sodomy thing."

Grace spoke into the microphone, instructing the men to leave the room. Then she turned to Rennie. "You did an excellent job, Rennie," she said. "I admire your composure. You've done a lot of growing up in the past year, haven't you?"

"I guess."

"And I owe you one," Grace continued. "I don't know how you did it."

"Did what?"

Grace smiled. "Shannon's agreed to prosecute."

56.

He leaned across the Monopoly board to set two hundred dollars in paper currency at Kit's side. Then he sat back and continued doing what he'd been doing for the last half-hour—watching Rennie.

Sometime in the last few days she'd moved the part in her hair to the side and curled the ends so they fell softly on her shoulders. She had to be one of the prettiest girls at Point Pleasant High School. And she'd grown cocky. He loved to see it in her.

The trial was scheduled for the second week in January. He and Kit would cut short their honeymoon in St. Thomas to be with her. And then, if she were willing, they'd start the adoption process.

What would it feel like to introduce her as his daughter?

She took a card from the pile and screwed up her nose. "Jail again." She picked up the little tin shoe and moved it to the corner of the board. How long would it be before she had no interest in playing board games with them?

He reached for the dice as the phone rang. Janni stood to answer it, and they were quiet, waiting to see who it was for. Cole was certain he knew. He had a baby due any minute. And three more tomorrow. But then he'd have the weekend in Miami with Kit, just the two of them. They both needed the time away.

She was already nervous about the qualifying marathon. He looked across the circle at her. She was sitting Indian-style, bouncing her knees on the floor. He smiled to himself. She could not sit still.

Janni raised the phone to her ear. "Chapel House," she said. Then she looked at Cole, her eyes wide, and his hand froze above the board. "Hi, Estelle," Janni said. "Yes, he's here."

His heart skipped a beat. He felt Kit watching him from across the board as he got to his feet, his gut suddenly roiling. He ran his hand over Kit's head as he passed her, not daring to look into her eyes.

He took the phone from Janni, lifting it to his ear. "Estelle?" He turned his back to the others but stayed in the doorway. Better to stay there than to go into the library, as if he had something to hide.

"Cole! How are you? It's so good to hear your voice."

She sounded animated. He ached a little. "It's good to hear yours, too," he said quietly. "Where are you?"

"In Point Pleasant, at my brother's house. He and Marilyn finally got married so I came for the wedding. Did you know?"

"No." He had intentionally lost touch with her family.

"Well, they did. I've taken a few days off work to house sit while they go on their honeymoon."

"Where are you working?"

"I have a spectacular job, Cole. As a matter of fact,

everything in my life is spectacular. I'm working at a huge medical center in Hartford and—"

"Kessler?"

"You've heard of it?"

"Yes, of course." He was impressed.

"They're paying me a third more than I was making at Blair, and the variety of research is astounding."

She was so full of life. He'd forgotten the vitality that had once attracted him. "How long have you been there?" he asked.

"About six months. I started in May, which was also my third month in therapy. You were right, Cole. I needed it. I don't know how you tolerated me that last year."

He'd done the right thing then, by ending it with her, casting her out on her own. He'd always wondered.

"So how are *you*?" she asked. "Recovered from the accident, I hope?"

"I'm fine. How did you know about it?"

"A little blurb in the paper. I called the hospital and they said you were okay. I also heard the Fetal Surgery Program was funded."

"Yes, it's going very well."

For a moment, neither of them spoke. "I'm dying to see you, Cole," she said finally. "Can we have lunch tomorrow?"

The thought of seeing her electrified him. "Yes, if I can get away." He fidgeted with the doorknob. "But I need to tell you that Kit and I are together now. We're getting married in January." He tensed, waiting for her reaction.

There was a brief silence on Estelle's end of the line. "I

could have guessed that," she said finally. "I'm happy for you, Cole, if that's what you want. I really am."

He couldn't have asked for a better response. "I'll meet you at noon tomorrow, or as close as I can make it."

"Pierre's?"

"Fine," he said, thinking of all the quiet lunches they'd shared there, twining their hands together across a table in a dark corner. "I'll see you then."

He hung up and walked on eggs across the living room to take his place again in front of the Monopoly board. No one said a word, and he wished he were not sitting directly across from Kit. He didn't want to meet her eyes. He felt as if he'd betrayed her.

The silence made him uneasy.

"You're meeting her for lunch tomorrow?" Kit asked.

"Yes." He paused. "Are you upset?"

She shrugged. "I knew all along that you'd need to see her again. I just don't want you to fall in love with her again."

He was certain no one else had picked up the telltale catch in her voice. "You don't need to worry," he said. "We'll talk later, all right?"

She nodded as the phone rang again. He rose to answer it himself, knowing that this time it had to be Blair. He couldn't be lucky twice in a row.

57

It was one in the morning when she finally went to bed, alone. For a dismal moment she imagined that the phone call from Blair had been Estelle calling back to persuade Cole to meet her now. Tonight. She forced the thought out of her mind, angry with herself for her insecurity.

But he'd been so damn pleased when she called. He could barely control his excitement. He'd never been able to resist her before. How would he do it now? She could picture Estelle meeting him at Pierre's, perfumed and dressed in something sexy. He'd have to be superhuman to say no to her.

She woke with the alarm to find him sleeping next to her, his arm across her stomach and his lips against her shoulder. She stroked his hair and watched him sleep a few minutes longer before she pulled on her shorts and running shoes and headed outside to the beach.

He was just leaving the house when she returned. "I'll call you after lunch," he said, hugging her to him.

"If you get the time," she said generously, feigning calm.

She took the day off. It wasn't like her, but she'd never

be able to concentrate on work today. She moved from room to room in the house, staring out the windows, disgusted with herself for her lethargy and her fear.

Janni called her from Blair around noon. "You know how much he loves you," she said.

"Yes."

"Even if he sees Estelle at lunch and finds himself drooling in his vichyssoise, don't you think he's wise enough to recognize the feeling as lust, not love."

"I'd like it if he didn't even feel lust," Kit said.

"Well, forget that. Lust is Cole's most pervasive emotion."

Kit smiled to herself. "I know."

"Why don't you meet me for lunch?"

Kit looked at her watch. Ten past twelve. If Cole and Estelle met on time, they were being seated now, appraising each other. "No, thanks. I'd rather sit around the house and feel dismal."

He'd said he would call after lunch, or had she misunderstood? He should have been back in his office by two. Two-thirty at the latest. It was after three now. She thought of calling him, but he was probably swamped. Otherwise he would have called himself, right?

She turned on a soap opera in the den and stretched out on the sofa with a box of cookies.

She couldn't get the card Estelle had sent him out of her mind. *Darling*, Estelle had called him. Kit had never called him 'darling'. It would take some level of sophistication she didn't possess to use that word—she doubted she could force it off her tongue. Would he want her to? Would it make a difference?

When the phone rang at three-thirty she raced to her room to answer it.

"Hello?" she said breathlessly, with no pretense at indifference.

"Kit, this is Estelle."

It would take all her strength to be civil. "Hello, Estelle, how are you?"

"I'm very well, thank you. Very, very well."

She waited for her to continue, but Estelle was playing coy.

"Did you meet Cole for lunch?" Kit couldn't stand the silence.

"Yes. Yes, and that's why I'm calling. I thought this call might be a little easier for me to make than for him."

"I don't understand." She would refuse to understand.

"No, I guess I'm not making myself clear." Estelle hesitated for a moment, as if she were trying to select the right words. "Let me start by saying that I'm a very different person from the woman you knew a year ago. I know this is late in coming, but I'd like to apologize for the way I behaved toward you back then. I wasn't a happy person and I took a lot of it out on you."

"That's in the past," Kit said without warmth.

"I don't wish you any ill, Kit. That's why what I have to say is difficult. Cole and I . . . well, we realized we've never stopped loving each other. We go back a long time. We talked about it at lunch, and there was no doubt in either of our minds that we want to give it another try."

Okay, she told herself, *you knew this could happen. Stay calm.*

"Kit, are you there?"

"Why didn't Cole call to tell me this?"

"He thought it would be better to tell you tonight in person rather than over the phone. I wanted to clear the path for him a little, make it easier for him. And I also wanted to let you know that I understand how important your friendship is to him. I told him I wouldn't stand in the way of you two seeing each other, or running together if that's what you'd like. It's all right, as long as it's me he comes home to at night."

Her wrist hurt from gripping the phone. "Estelle, I'd prefer to hear this from Cole." She hung up the receiver before the words had finished leaving her lips. She sat down on the bed and stared blindly at the wall.

She and Cole had found a house on the bay just the weekend before. It was gray, like the Chapel House, and had a solid, symmetric beauty to it. One of its previous owners had glassed in the entire back wall so that the living room, dining room, and master bedroom all had a view of the water. They planned to move in in February. She wondered now if they would ever live in that house. She wondered if they would ever live together anywhere at all.

58.

With any luck, he'd have an hour to himself. It was already four o'clock. He hadn't had a chance to catch his breath from the moment he'd left Pierre's. One thing after another, complete with emergency surgery that left him weak-kneed. Too much in one day.

Estelle had looked good. Never better. She must have dressed with him in mind that morning, remembering that green was his favorite color. That dress was a knock-out. Eyes turned when they walked into Pierre's. He'd forgotten the commotion she could cause merely by look-ing the way she did. And as always, she seemed coolly oblivious to the stares.

Jacques had been surprised to see them. "Dr. Perelle, Miss Lauren!" he'd exclaimed with a little bow. "It's been too long." Jacques remembered which table they'd always requested and seated them ahead of waiting customers. Estelle settled in across from him, smiling, with no hint of the nervousness he felt.

"You look wonderful," he said.

"So do you."

He'd thought all morning about how much he should

tell her. About Kit's baby? Certainly not that Alison had been his child. He could picture her reaction to *that* piece of news. Should he tell her about Cynthia? No, he couldn't tell her any of it. He realized with a jolt that he'd always censored his communication with her. He didn't even want to tell her about Rennie, as though sharing her with Estellé would tarnish her in some way. He didn't trust her to respect the things he cherished.

She told him about her therapy. In the beginning they'd put her on medication, she said, though not for long. She wasn't taking anything now.

Psychotropic drugs. How could he not have known she'd been that seriously ill? A big help he'd been to her back then.

"I progressed very rapidly," she said. "The shrink was amazed." She smiled and looked at him. "Losing you really opened my eyes."

He didn't want to talk about the breakup. "Have you made any friends up there?" he asked.

She nodded. "I joined a health spa and I've made some friends through that."

"A health spa? With exercise classes and all?"

"Uh-huh."

"That's fantastic." He grinned at her, trying to picture Estelle in tennis shoes. "How about men?"

She was quiet while Jacques poured her wine. Cole held his hand over his glass. He couldn't afford a light head with all he had to do that afternoon.

"No one special yet," she said when Jacques walked away. "I've been seeing a couple of men but"—she shrugged—

"no chemistry." She took a sip of her wine. "How's your mother?"

"She's fine. I'd say she's fully recovered, both physically and emotionally."

"Corinne and the girls?"

He was surprised by her warmth. She had definitely changed. He put his doubts aside and told her about Rennie and the possibility of adopting her. He told her the details of the accident and found himself loving the look of concern that came into her face. He stopped short of telling her that he and Kit had found that house on the bay. It would be cruel to tell her they were moving out when she'd begged him for years to do exactly that and he'd refused.

Their lunches were served and they began to eat in a comfortable silence. After a few minutes, she set down her fork and looked up at him. "Cole," she said. "I miss you."

"There are things I miss about you, too," he said carefully, suddenly afraid of the intensity in her eyes.

"Don't be angry with me for saying this, but I still love you. I think about you so often. I'm afraid I'll never meet anyone like you."

"Why would I be angry with you for loving me?" he said. "You'll find someone, Estelle. It takes a little time, but you will."

"Do you still love me?"

He put down his own fork and reached across the table to take her hand. "I don't love you the way I once did, but I still care about you," he said. "I was very pleased that you called, but—"

"Don't say 'but'," she said quickly, gripping his hand

with both of hers. "Cole, *please*. Let's try it again. I'm different now. You can tell, can't you? It can work this time."

He was stunned. "Estelle—"

"We can live in Mantoloking if you like." She was speaking French now, her ultimate weapon of seduction. "I don't care where I live as long as we're together. My priorities have changed. *I've* changed. I wasn't responsible for my actions back then. I was *sick*. Don't punish me for something I had no control over."

"It's not a matter of punishment," he said in English. "It's—"

"It would be so different now."

"Estelle, I'm in love with Kit."

For an instant he caught a glimpse of the old Estelle hiding behind the new facade. Narrowed eyes, a twisted smile. But she caught herself quickly.

"I know you are," she said. "But can you really tell me it's as good with her as it was with me? In our good years, I mean?"

"How can I answer that honestly without hurting you?"

Her eyes filled with venom, and he withdrew his fingers from hers quickly, repelled.

"You fell right into the trap she set for you. Can you actually sit there and tell me that Kit can give you everything I can?" Her voice was rising and people glanced at her from other tables.

"Estelle," he said quietly. "Lower your voice."

"I will *not*! And talk to me in French, damn it."

"You're still sick," he said in French, not to please her as much as to prevent the other diners from understanding their conversation. "Maybe sicker than you were before. Are you still in therapy?"

She threw her head back with a laugh, embarrassingly loud. "I never *was* in therapy. You think that's the answer to everything, baring your soul to some stranger. Forget it! I'll never do it."

The woman at the next table let out an irate "Shh!"

"If you don't lower your voice, I'm going to leave." He watched her face change again. Now she looked weak and desperate.

"I'm sorry," she said. "Don't go. All right, I understand. For whatever reason you want to stay with Kit. I have to accept that. But please, I'm only here for a few days. Couldn't you spend some time with me?"

He knew what she wanted, and it had little to do with time. "Absolutely not," he said.

"You said you still care about me. The Kensington Hotel is right next door, remember? Remember all those after-lunch rendezvous?"

"I'm leaving." He pushed his nearly full plate away from him and stood up.

"Cole, I'll kill myself. I swear to God I will."

He leaned forward, his face inches from hers. "You need help, Estelle. But I can't be the one to give it to you anymore."

59.

"How could you have believed her?" He sat on the window seat watching Kit pace the floor, her face still puffy from crying.

"She was very convincing. And I think I'd prepared myself to hear it."

"Is that how little you think of me?" He spoke gently. She'd been through a lot that afternoon, and he didn't need to make it worse.

"It's how little I think of myself."

"There must be something radically wrong with our relationship if you think I could pick up with Estelle again."

"There's something radically wrong with *me*. Don't you see? I've let it happen. I can't live without you, damn it!" She kicked the basket she used for wastepaper across the room, and he had to smile.

"Come here, baby." He reached out to her.

"No. I don't want you to comfort me."

"What do you want?"

"I want to know that I could live without you."

"You could."

"But not happily." She stopped her pacing to look at him, and he stood up and put his arms around her.

"What's the crime?" he asked. "You need me, I need you. I like it, frankly." He wished he knew the magic words that would end this conversation. He wanted to make love, not talk. He stroked her hair. "Why didn't you call me after she spoke to you? I could have cleared the whole thing up and we'd be laughing about it right now."

"I was afraid to talk to you. I felt as though I didn't know you."

"You *don't* know me if you think I can be seduced so easily."

It was a few seconds before she spoke again. "Cole, I saw the card she sent you while you were in the hospital."

"You did? How?" He couldn't remember what he'd done with that card.

"It was in the wastepaper basket when I emptied it."

"Why didn't you tell me you found it?"

"Why didn't you tell me you received it?"

"*Touché,*" he said. "I didn't think it was worth worrying you about."

"I really did put it out of my mind. Things seemed so good between us. But when *this* happened, I thought of the card and how you hadn't told me about it. I figured you must have other secrets, too."

He shook his head, thinking that he would have drawn the same conclusions—or worse—had he been in her place. "No other secrets," he said.

She leaned her head against his shoulder and sighed. "Just hold me for a couple of minutes."

He held her against him, feeling the tension leave her body bit by bit. She felt so good, her hair soft against his cheek. He felt his erection growing between them and heard her muffled laugh against his neck.

"How can you think of sex at a time like this?" she asked.

He felt appropriately guilty. "All afternoon I was thinking about us going to Miami tomorrow, and how tense you're going to be, and how you're probably not going to be in the mood while we're there . . . so I thought tonight might be my—excuse me, I mean *our*—last chance for a few days."

"You dog." She kissed him, a long, satiny kiss that cleared his mind of the afternoon. She began to unbutton his shirt.

He led her to the bed and lay down next to her, slipping his hands under her sweater to unfasten her bra. Her breasts were warm.

"I can't wait, Cole," she said. "I'm in better condition now than I was before Somerville. When we're finished do you think we could pack?"

"Shh." He kissed her. She seemed to have forgotten they were making love.

"Sorry. I'm just excited about tomorrow."

"Forget about tomorrow, at least for the next hour or so." He unzipped her jeans and she helped him slide them off. "I'd better make sure these legs are ready to run twenty-six miles," he said. He leaned down to kiss the top of her thigh and heard her moan softly. She'd already forgotten tomorrow. He would make her forget today as well.

60.

Kit had their new matching suitcases packed and waiting by the sliding glass doors of the kitchen.

She couldn't relax. What a day of torture. She'd been keyed up from the second she opened her eyes that morning, and then to have to make two presentations and sit through a bunch of meetings . . . She could have screamed. The entire day she'd thought about one thing: running. What if she were kidding herself about her condition? What if she didn't make the time she needed for Boston and had to miss it again?

"Here he is." Maris looked through the sliding glass doors. Cole's old white Mustang was pulling into the driveway. "I'll be glad when he gets you out of here. You're too antsy."

The phone rang as he walked in the door and Kit looked at him in alarm. He held up a hand. "Don't worry," he said, "Kevin's covering. I'm free until Monday."

Maris answered the phone, then held it out to Cole. "Blair for Cole Perelle," she said apologetically. "Sorry."

Damn Blair, she thought. Why couldn't they leave him alone for once?

"This is Cole Perelle," he said. He frowned at the floor, then ran a hand through his hair. "Oh, no." He looked at Kit, but she had no idea what was behind the worry in his eyes. "What are her vital signs?" He listened a moment. "No, I'd rather not," he said. "She has family. I'll try to get in touch with them." He hung up the phone and turned to her. "Estelle swallowed a bottle of sleeping pills. She's in a coma."

Kit sat down at the kitchen table. She could see outside to the terrace where Cole had stacked the lumber he'd bought the day before. He was going to build beach chairs like John Chapel's to set in their new backyard on the bay. He was anxious to get them built, he'd told her. Anxious to see a part of himself in that house.

Why a coma, damn it? Why couldn't she have done the job right?

"Do they expect her to make it?" Maris asked.

Cole leafed through the phone book. "They're not saying." He picked up the receiver and dialed. Kit listened as he spoke with Marc, Estelle's younger brother. It was obvious from Cole's end of the conversation that Marc had no idea Estelle was even in town. He hadn't seen her since before she'd left New Jersey. Then Cole began arguing with him. Wouldn't Marc go to Blair to be with her, and what did he mean, he really didn't care if she lived or died? Cole hung up the phone and began dialing again, this time Estelle's mother. The conversation was even shorter than the one with Marc.

"Unreal," he said, hanging up the phone. "What a cold bunch of people."

She comes by it naturally, Kit thought.

"Her mother said, 'Well, if she wakes up, then I'll come down, but I don't see the point in coming all the way to New Jersey if she's unconscious.' Her *mother*. Can you believe it?"

"She didn't even endear herself to her own family," said Maris.

Every muscle in her body was tight, waiting for what was coming next. She knew him too well. The way he was looking at her, the apology in his eyes before he spoke. She felt her own eyes fill with tears before he'd uttered the first word.

Please don't do this to me, Cole.

"I have to stay here," he said.

"No you don't."

"What if she comes out of it and there's no one there? Not a soul who cares about her?"

"You can't stay out of guilt."

"It's not guilt. She tried to *kill* herself. If she wakes up alone, she'll . . . I don't want her to regret that she didn't succeed."

"But this is my *marathon*. I want you with me."

"If it were one of my nieces or Maris or Jay or anyone, I'd do the same thing."

She knew that was true. She stood up. "You're not going with me then?" She forced the words past the knot in her throat.

"I'll take you to the airport."

She shook her head. "I'll drive myself." She stood up and squeezed his shoulder. It was the most she could manage just then to let him know she understood. Or at least a part of her did. She walked toward the stairs. "Your suitcase is the one on the left," she said without turning around.

61.

Saturday was the longest day of his life. Strange, spending the entire day at Blair without working. He sat next to Estelle's bed in the Intensive Care Unit, reading. First the newspaper. Then the stack of professional articles that had been mounting on his desk for the past few months. It was hard to concentrate, though, with her lying in front of him.

He wouldn't have recognized her. If he'd been walking through the ICU and noticed her, he might have thought she looked a trifle like Estelle, enough to make him think of her, but no more. It was the pallor and the tubes. The bruises around her mouth where they'd intubated her. She was tied to the respirator and the sound of it nauseated him.

He watched the clock the entire day. If she came out of it before noon, he would spend a few hours with her and then fly to Miami. When noon came and went he changed his plans to catching a night plane—that was if she woke up before six or so. He even called the airport. The last plane was at ten-thirty.

By five he knew there was no chance of making it to Miami that night. He went to his office and sat in the welcome darkness, away from the bright lights and machinery, and wondered if Kit was as lonely for him as he was for her. He hadn't thought this through too well. It wasn't fair to her, yet no matter how long and hard he'd considered the options, he would have made this choice. It would have been harder for Kit if he'd been with her, worrying about Estelle the whole time.

He'd call her later, when he was feeling better. The last thing he wanted to do was fall apart on the phone.

After dinner he went back to Estelle's cubicle in the ICU. Nothing had changed. It could go on forever this way, he thought, the only change being that her body would gradually wither. She'd be a haunting presence in the hospital. He'd always know she was up here. If it went on too long, he'd pull the plug on her respirator.

He was thinking nonsense. It did something to your mind, sitting in one spot all day watching a person trying to die. A person he'd loved. Or had he? Suddenly he wasn't sure if it had ever been love that tied him to her. He couldn't remember. How had he felt in those first few years? Had it been love or just the excitement of having a woman like Estelle? He didn't know anymore. Whatever it was he felt for Kit made every other emotion seem hollow.

She didn't sound pleased to hear from him, and he struggled to keep conversation rolling, his voice even. "Have you met other runners there?" he asked, after he'd asked her about the flight, the hotel room and what she'd eaten for dinner—cereal and water.

"The hotel's crawling with them," she said.

"I wish I was there with you." He said it quickly.

"You could have been."

He was silent.

"I'm sorry," she said. "I wish you were here, too."

He still couldn't speak. He held the phone away to take in a deep breath.

"Cole?"

"I love you."

"Are you crying?" she asked.

"It's been a long day."

"How's Estelle?"

"No change. All day I've been hoping she'd come out of it and then I could fly down there and . . ."

"But it didn't work out," she said softly.

"No."

"It's all right, babe. I'm really fine. I can concentrate better by myself."

"You're very sweet," he said.

"I know."

He hung up with a smile. His first all day.

62.

She had no intention of enjoying Miami. If Cole had been with her, it would have been different. But aside from a couple of easy runs, she stayed in her room. The woman from room service probably thought she was a recluse. She felt a twinge of loneliness just once, when she went down to the lobby to buy the evening paper and saw the gathering of people. Obviously runners. They looked scrubbed and fresh and fired up for tomorrow. For a moment she was tempted to join them. It was where she belonged. But she turned back to the elevator and rode to the ninth floor of the hotel alone.

She would have felt worse if he hadn't called, but now he was planted firmly in her mind, and that she didn't need. She'd have to get the cobwebs out by tomorrow at eleven.

She fell asleep so easily that she was surprised to find the sun streaming in her room when she opened her eyes. The night had been far less painful than she'd expected.

She ate half a piece of toast and drank a few glasses of water in the hotel restaurant. She tipped the waitress well for all the trips with the water pitcher. Then she put on her running clothes and went out front to wait for a taxi. She had to share one with two other runners.

She would have thought they were in town for a party instead of a race.

"Where you from?" the man asked her. He was incredibly skinny, and she wondered what the muscles of his legs looked like under his warm-up pants.

"New Jersey."

"Whew!" said the woman. "How d'ya ever train in that kind of weather? I visited some friends of mine there once at Christmas time and just about froze my tail off."

"What a loss that woulda been," said the man, giving the woman's tail a little squeeze.

Kit didn't bother to ask them where *they* were from, and after a while they gave up trying to make conversation with her and babbled to each other.

She felt flat and it worried her. She pinned her number on the front of her T-shirt and planted herself in the middle of the throng. *If I don't make it, Perelle, it's your fault.* She shook her head at how stupid that sounded.

It wasn't until the tenth mile that she realized that running emotionlessly might not be so bad. She passed marker ten in seventy smooth minutes. She hadn't even concentrated that hard on her pace. She worried that she was running too fast, that she'd tire too early to keep it up. But she felt fine. Maybe she actually *could* break three hours.

At mile eighteen, though, she started to falter. Everything hurt. Everything was wrong. She couldn't filter anything out. The sunlight was blinding and splinters of pain stabbed her eyes. But hadn't she been running into the sun for the last hour? This was ridiculous. Her shorts felt like they belonged to someone else. The waistband was too loose, and she spent precious minutes trying to decide whether or not to hitch them up. She chose not to, and then imagined they were slipping bit by bit as she ran.

And the *bystanders*. The cheering mob was thickening by the minute and she couldn't keep her eyes off them. Five men in the length of one city block reminded her of Cole. She even looked back at one of them, thinking that maybe he'd made it after all. But then he would be at the finish line, not along the course.

Unless he'd flown in just seconds earlier and this was as close as he could . . .

Poor Cole. She was certain he was not here at all. He was back in New Jersey, doing what he thought was the right thing. It was simply the way he was. He'd always do what he thought was right no matter what it cost him. As long as she was with him, there would always be someone else. If not Estelle, then his mother or Rennie or a patient. Always someone he thought needed him a little more than she did at that moment.

And he'd probably be right.

The woman she'd been keeping pace with suddenly sprang ahead, and Kit's attention snapped back to the race. She had no idea what mile she was running or how she was doing with the time. She was only running now because it was a habit developed over the last couple of hours.

A good habit, though. She finished in two hours and fifty-eight minutes and sprawled on the grass at the side of the road, alone and smiling.

63.

The cottage was one of dozens that dotted the sand between the ocean and the street. But it was the only one inhabited in the middle of December.

"This is like a honeymoon," she said, moving closer to the fire Cole had built in the stone fireplace. The tiny living room glowed warmly from the blaze.

"A premarital honeymoon." He sat on the dumpy sofa, sipping his cocoa and watching her.

"I've almost adjusted to the quiet," she said. It was odd to be without the others. Only Rennie had trouble understanding that they needed some time away alone *now*. That it couldn't wait until after the wedding.

"I like having you all to myself." He put his feet on the hassock. "This has been a wonderful uncomplicated day."

She leaned forward to stir the fire and made a face at the pain in her legs.

"Stiff?"

"I hurt even more than I did last time."

"You ran harder."

"Wait till you see me in Boston."

"I hope to." He stood up and walked into the little

kitchen for more cocoa. "Oh wow," she heard him say. "The sky is full of stars. You want to bundle up and go out to the beach?"

She smiled to herself and stood up. He was already holding her jacket and mittens out to her. He pulled her ski cap down over her ears and picked up a couple of blankets from the table.

The beach was right outside their front door. Janni had made an excellent choice. She'd handed Kit the keys to the cottage when she met her plane from Miami. "This is your early Christmas present," she'd said. "Three days for you and Cole, away from the house. I figure you both need it after this weekend."

The air was cool but not cold, and it smelled of the smoke from their fire. They spread one of the blankets on the hard sand and pulled the second over them as they stretched out under the glittering sky.

"I see Orion," she said, pointing to the three stars of Orion's sash.

"Very good!" He sounded impressed. "Now find the scorpion."

She smiled in the darkness. "You can't fool me. They're never in the sky at the same time." How long ago had they had that conversation? It was so fresh in her mind. "Orion's the victor this time around."

They were quiet for a few minutes and the familiar churning of the ocean was all she could hear. Summer or winter, the sea sounded the same.

Cole broke the silence with a sigh. "Sometimes I wish she'd died," he said.

"Why?" she asked quietly.

"So I'd be free of her." He rolled onto his side to look at her. "I'm responsible for her now, you understand that, don't you? I mean . . . her family's worthless."

"I understand that you'll do whatever you have to do to be at peace with yourself," she said.

"I want to be certain she gets the right kind of care. And I'll want to visit her sometimes, if they think that will help."

She felt him searching her face for some objection that wasn't there. "It's all right," she said. "I don't need to hold on to you that tightly."

He rolled onto his back again and put his arm under her head. She looked up at the stars and thought of the house on the bay, waiting to be filled with love and tradition. In a few weeks they would set their furniture inside it, hang curtains at the windows, and make it theirs. They would watch these same stars from their own solid wooden beach chairs.

Their names would be carved beneath the seats.

Epilogue

TWENTY-FIVE YEARS LATER

From her van, Kit spotted Maris standing in front of the arrivals terminal and she broke into a smile. Maris had put on some weight since Kit last saw her and she now wore her hair in a short coppery pixie style, but the cinnamon skin, the long artsy earrings, the African print skirt, and the regal way she held her body—all of it was pure Maris.

Kit drove carefully through the clot of vehicles until she reached the curb. She nearly jumped out of the van, waving and calling Maris's name as she ran toward her, and Maris's face lit up when she saw her.

"I love your hair!" Kit said, pulling her into a hug.

"I can't believe I'm finally here." Maris drew away and held Kit at arm's length. "Damn, girl, you look good!"

"*Hey!*"

They turned to see a cop pounding his hand on the side of the van. "You can't stay here!" he shouted. "Take your mutual admiration society on the road!"

Kit held up her hands in surrender. "We're on our way," she assured him. She lifted the handle of one of Maris's enormous black suitcases and began rolling it toward the van.

It took both of them to hoist each of the two suitcases into the rear of the van, and Maris wedged her carry-on between them. "I know it looks like a lot," she said, "but a month is a long time. Plus I needed to bring my tools of the trade."

"No problem." Kit nearly had to shout over the cacophony of car horns. "We've got plenty of room."

Once inside the van, Kit navigated carefully into the line of cars jostling for space in front of the terminal and in a few minutes they'd reached the entrance to the parkway, heading down the shore.

"So," Kit said, settling in for the drive, "I was trying to think how long it's been since I've seen you. Nine years?"

"I haven't been to Mantoloking in more than twenty," Maris said, "but when did you and Cole and the kids come out to visit? '03? '04?"

Kit nodded. "'04, I think, so ten years ago. Hannah would have been twelve and Aidan and Thomas were ten." She reached over to touch Maris's shoulder. "It's been *way* too long," she said.

"Don't I know it! We've been so busy at the firm, and my first impulse when Janni called was to say 'no', even though I really wanted to say 'yes', but Sean said if I was waiting for a slow time to get back to Mantoloking, I'd be waiting forever."

"You guys are that busy?"

"We are," Maris said. "It's a double-edged sword, of course. Great money, and we love what we're doing, but we don't have a minute to catch our breath." She tilted her head at Kit. "What are you smiling at?"

Kit sped up to pass a car, then glanced at her old friend. "I was just remembering the first night I met Sean," she said. "It was the annual Christmas party in the Chapel House. Do you remember? You and Sean were dancing and I thought he was some hot young surfer dude you'd picked up on the beach. I had no idea he was an architect friend of yours and I *certainly* never thought you'd end up married to him."

Maris laughed. "He *still* looks like a hot surfer dude," she said, "just not so young anymore. His hair's still long, but it's mostly gray now."

"Wait till you see Jay and Cole," Kit said. "Completely gray, though I have to say that they wear it well."

"They both look good in those Christmas card pictures," Maris said, then she laughed. "Interesting how Jay and Cole have gone gray but you, Janni, and I haven't."

"Yeah, it's a miracle." Kit smiled. "Janni actually doesn't color hers. She's only now getting a few silver strands in her hair."

"She still looks like a kid, at least in pictures."

"She does. I think she weighs what she did in high school. I blame my extra twenty pounds on pregnancy because I have to blame them on something."

"Oh, well." Maris shrugged. "Twenty pounds. Thirty. Forty." She patted her thigh through her skirt. "Gray hair. Wrinkles. Sagging boobs. None of it really matters in the long run, does it?"

Kit nodded. "I think we worried about all the wrong things when we were younger."

"We were babies back then."

Kit pulled back into the right lane and turned on the cruise control. She took her foot off the gas and felt her body relax. "I remember back when I moved into the Chapel House," she said. "I was just starting that Public Relations job at Blair and I was what . . . thirty? Thirty-one? And I thought about how hard it was going to be to change careers at that advanced age." She laughed. "I've changed two more times since then."

"I love stumbling across your articles, Kit," Maris said. "I can hear your voice when I read them and it makes me miss you. I read the piece you wrote for the *Huffington Post* a couple of months ago—the one about adopting teen-agers? It was excellent."

"Rennie was a huge help with that one," Kit said. It had been a challenge to pin Rennie down long enough to pick her brain, but her input had made the article that much richer. Kit had been able to tell both sides of the story.

"Rennie will be at the house today, right?" Maris asked.

"I hope so." Kit didn't bother correcting her use of the word "house". They all did it. "She and her husband and kids were already there when I left, but while I was waiting for you, Cole texted me to say that Rennie got called to Blair for a delivery."

Maris slowly shook her head, a smile on her face. "It's still hard for me to imagine Rennie as an *adult*, much less a doctor," she said.

"She's amazing. You should hear conversations between

her and Cole. Cole's got the experience, but she keeps up with every advance in the field. You'd think she invented obstetrics."

"Uh oh." Maris laughed. "Does that create some tension?"

"It can get a little heated sometimes, but honestly, I think Cole gets a kick out of it. He's extremely proud of her. She's taken over the bulk of his practice and he's mostly doing fetal surgery these days."

"Just . . . mind-blowing," Maris said. "Whoever could have guessed that's how things would turn out?"

"I know. It's wild."

"What do you think would have become of Rennie if you'd never stumbled across her on the beach?"

"Oh, Maris, I can't even go there." It wasn't the first time that thought had crossed Kit's mind, and it was impossible to imagine. "All the 'what ifs'," she said. "What if I'd never met Janni at that conference nearly thirty years ago? It was such a fluke." She shuddered at the thought of an alternate life she might have lived. "I think we all got lucky," she said.

"I remember when you first moved into the Chapel House," Maris said. "You'd had it with men. You never wanted to get married again. You didn't want to be tied down. You *certainly* didn't want to have kids. All you wanted to do was run."

Kit laughed. "I remember that woman," she said. "She was running away from everything."

"I'm glad you stopped running from Cole." Maris's voice was gentle.

Kit glanced at her again. "He seemed like a dangerous person to give in to back then," she said.

"I know," Maris agreed. "You always had the specter of Estelle to compete with."

They fell quiet and Kit guessed they were both thinking about the same thing.

Maris finally broke the silence. "I think you were amazing back then, Kit," she said. "The way you dealt with that whole situation."

"Thank you." She bit her lip, remembering. "I only wish it could have turned out differently. It was so hard on Cole."

"He didn't blame himself, did he?"

"A little, I think. But to be honest, it's the one thing we've never really talked about. He said she took up too much of our energy when she was alive and he wasn't going to keep giving her that power."

"He tried so hard to help her," Maris said. "And you were so understanding."

Kit shrugged. "I just kept reminding myself that he'd chosen to be with me," she said. "I knew it was me he loved."

"*Everyone* knew it was you he loved," Maris said. "Everyone, including Estelle. We knew it way before you did."

Kit smiled. "Lucky I figured it out before it was too late," she said.

They were quiet as she drove through Point Pleasant and over the canal bridge, and Kit tried to see the shore through Maris's eyes. She'd been away so long. When they turned onto the ocean road, Maris rolled down her window. "Ah, the Atlantic!" she said as the warm salt air filled the van. "I swear, the Pacific has never smelled quite right to me."

"Oh, I think San Francisco has other charms to make up for it," Kit said.

"It doesn't look too bad here," Maris mused as they drove past Bay Head homes that had already been repaired.

"Well, nearly two years have passed since Hurricane Sandy," Kit said. "I can show you a video of how it looked through here after the storm. Completely flooded."

"Did your house have much damage?"

Kit tightened her hands on the steering wheel at the memory. "All the Mantoloking houses were damaged," she said, "but we were lucky, especially considering we're right on the bay. A house a block away from us was completely destroyed. We had flooding and needed a lot of reconstruction work done to the downstairs and it was a mess, but it could have been so much worse." She looked at Maris. "Did you know the storm cut a new inlet right through Mantoloking, from the bay to the ocean?"

"I saw pictures of that on the news," Maris said. "I couldn't believe it, seeing little Mantoloking on CNN. It's not still like that, is it?"

"No, they've done a remarkable job of rebuilding the coast in that area."

Maris leaned close to the windshield, squinting at the road ahead. "Where *are* we?" she asked. "I can't get my bearings."

Kit understood how she felt. "This is Mantoloking," she said.

"You're kidding!"

The landscape had changed shape dramatically in the last two years as homeowners tried to rebuild their lives. The houses were newly elevated on pilings, or covered in Tyvek sheeting, or in some cases, simply gone. Construction trucks were everywhere. But Maris hadn't seen the worst of it yet. That was about to come. And she seemed to know it.

"My heart is pounding," she said.

They drove in silence for a short distance and then Kit made a left turn onto a wide sandy lot bordered by the scrubby trees and shrubs so common along the coast. She parked next to Aidan's station wagon, right behind a slightly off-kilter Port-a-Potty tucked into the trees.

"Why are we stopping here?" Maris asked.

"Oh, Mar." Kit bit her lip at the confusion in Maris's voice. "This is it." She pointed to the barren lot. "This was the Chapel House."

Maris stared at the flat expanse of sand in front of them, a look of disbelief in her eyes. Then she did what they had all done: She cried.

"I didn't expect to feel this way," she said once she'd pulled herself together and they had gotten out of the van. "I mean, I *knew* it was destroyed . . . I know that's why I'm here . . . but this is just so . . ." She shook her head. "It's so in your *face*. How can it be totally erased? All the life that was in that house!" Her voice cracked. "All the memories."

"We've still got them," Kit said. "Nothing can take them

away." She tugged Maris's arm. "Come on," she said. "Are you ready to see everyone?"

Maris looked blankly at the empty lot. "Everyone?" she asked. "Where are they?"

Kit nodded toward the ocean. "Just over the dune on the beach."

The sun was sinking low in the sky behind them as they skirted the rows of newly planted beach grass on the dune, and Kit could hear the squeals of Rennie's kids above the rhythmic sound of the waves. A blue striped beach umbrella came into view, along with Janni and Jay's white beach canopy. Half a dozen folding beach chairs were scattered on the sand. John Chapel's old wooden chairs were somewhere out to sea.

Cole was waist deep in the water, jumping the waves with Janni and Jay's three-year-old granddaughter Brigit on his shoulders, and in the distance, Kit saw her own daughter and twin sons straddling their surfboards, waiting for a decent wave.

Maris stopped walking. "Who *are* all these people?" she asked with a laugh. "Is that Hannah out there on the surfboard?"

"Right. With Aidan and Thomas."

"*That's* Aidan and Thomas?" Maris looked incredulous. "Oh my God, Kit. They've turned into men!"

Kit laughed. "I know. I swear, it happened overnight." She pointed to a man sitting on a surfboard several yards north of the others. "And the guy over there is Hannah's fiancé, Jordan. Then those four girls sunbathing are Aidan and Thomas's girlfriends, and Elizabeth, Janni and Jay's daughter and . . . I'm honestly not sure who the fourth one is." She laughed. "Kids multiply around here. That guy body surfing out there is Janni and Jay's son, Derek."

"He and Elizabeth are brother and sister, right?" Maris asked. "I mean, biological?"

"Right. They were four and five when Jan and Jay adopted them and total hellions." Kit shuddered at the memory. "But they're sweethearts now, especially now that Derek's a father."

Maris put her hands on her hips. "I'm totally over-whelmed," she said. "All these people who didn't even *exist* last time I was here. Unreal." She nodded toward the boy and girl playing in the sand at the water's edge. "Are those two Rennie's?" she asked. "I recognize them from her Facebook page."

"Yes, and their dad is—"

"Maris!" Janni appeared from around the corner of the white canopy. She raced toward them across the sand, her ponytail bouncing in the air. "You're here!" Janni stood on her tiptoes to wrap her arms around Maris. "You're such a wonderful friend to do this!"

"I'm so sorry about the house, Jan," Maris said, as they pulled apart.

Janni held up a hand to put an end to the sympathy. "Thanks, sweetie, but we're looking forward now, not back," she said, though the words still sounded like they took some effort. Kit didn't think Janni would ever get over losing the house that had been in her family for generations.

"Hey, you're here!" Jay called as he walked toward them from beneath the canopy. He hugged Maris, then held her by the shoulders and studied her face. "Wow, look at you!" he said. "You look fantastic."

She reached up and tousled his wild gray hair. "I *love* this," she said. "I'd kill for this thick head of hair."

Cole had spotted them and was walking through the surf toward the beach. He lifted Brigit from his shoulders and set her down in the sand next to Rennie's son and daughter, then headed toward them. Maris didn't wait for him. She kicked off her sandals and ran toward him across the damp sand. Kit watched her with a smile. She knew Maris had always loved him. Did she still? Did she see the same thing Kit saw when she looked at him? How his white hair only brought out the blue-green of his eyes? How his smile still produced those sexy dimples in his cheeks?

Cole held his arms out wide, grinning as he waited for a hug. "I'm wet!" he warned Maris.

"I don't care!" she said, and they came together in an embrace that lasted long enough to put a lump in Kit's throat. She wished Maris still lived close by. She wished they could all be together in the house again, this time with their kids and grandkids.

She wished she could have the impossible.

"So, are you really allowed to have a fire on the beach these days?" Maris asked a couple of hours later, as sparks rose into the dusky air above them. They sat on the folding beach chairs in a half circle around the fire Cole had built close to the dune, just the five of them now, toasting marshmallows on long skewers. "Or are we breaking the law?" Maris added.

"What exactly is there left to burn down?" Jay asked, his voice somber.

Janni poked him with her elbow. "We're looking forward, remember?"

He held his toasted marshmallow out to her in apology, and she plucked it from the skewer and popped it in her mouth.

An hour earlier, they'd eaten sandwiches and salad with the kids. Rennie had arrived just in time for dessert and she'd looked beautiful and tired as she hugged Maris and gathered up her exhausted children and sunburned husband. Then everyone else disappeared as if by magic, murmuring "boardwalk" or "movies" or words Kit didn't catch. She was certain her own sons and daughter knew that tonight, the Chapel House beach belonged to this coterie of old friends.

Maris looked over her shoulder, and Kit knew what she was seeing: the milky, wide-open evening sky where the house had stood for over a hundred years.

Jay followed her gaze. "We know if we rebuild, the sea could take it the day after it's finished, Maris," he said. "We might hesitate if it had only been a summer house. A getaway. But this was Janni's home. Her *family* home. We have to do it."

"I don't blame you," Maris said. "Not a bit."

"That's why we wanted *you* to work with us, Mar," Janni said. "You'll understand better than any other architect what the house meant to us." She threaded another marshmallow on the end of her skewer. "Are you still game?" she asked.

"Absolutely," Maris said. "I've spent the last couple of weeks studying the new restrictions and floodplain requirements, but frankly, I think we should go above and beyond all of them. Make this a house that's ready for whatever comes down the pike in the future." She looked at Janni. "We can make it look at least somewhat like the Chapel House, Jan, but the bones will be a lot stronger. If you've got the guts to rebuild, I'm ready and willing to design it for you."

"Oh, I've got the guts," Janni said. "I want it for our children," she said. "For *all* our children, including your stepchildren if you can ever get them out here. The Perelle kids practically grew up in the Chapel House."

Kit nodded. It was the truth. Although they lived no more than three blocks away in a beautiful house on the bay, Hannah and Aidan and Thomas had been drawn to the Chapel House and its beach since they were babies.

Maris stood up, brushing sand from the hem of her skirt. Hands on her hips, she looked toward the lot. "The biggest obvious difference will be that the house has to be elevated," she said. "By a lot. And I'll tell you something. You're going to have one hell of a view with that new elevation. But we need to think about . . . Well, come with me." She waved at Janni to follow her. "Before it gets too dark, you and Jay should show me where you were hoping to have the garage. I want to start thinking about this."

Janni handed her skewer to Kit and she and Jay got to their feet. Kit nibbled the toasted marshmallow as she watched them climb the dune to the site of their future home. She turned to look at Cole.

"It's scary," she said. Ever since the storm, they'd had long talks with Janni and Jay about rebuilding. It had felt like an absolute necessity in the beginning, but now, with Maris here and plans moving forward, the reality of building a house so close to the treacherous sea was sinking in.

Cole stabbed his empty skewer into the sand near the fire. "Come closer." He tugged at her chair.

She moved her chair snugly against his and he took her hand.

"If the storm had taken our house," he said, "we would have rebuilt. You know we would have."

She nodded. "I know. And I know they've thought it through. But I'm still worried about them."

They were quiet for a moment. Kit looked toward the dune, thinking about her friends walking through the sand as they tried to imagine a house that would not disappear in a heartbeat.

"Maris has changed," Cole said.

"In a good way."

"A very good way. She seems . . . so much more sure of herself."

"I think she's really happy."

"Nothing like she was when we were all living together," he said.

"No."

Cole took the empty skewer from her and stuck it in the sand next to his. "It's got to feel strange to come back to the house she used to live in only to find an empty lot and a dozen or so kids in her place," he said.

Kit rested her head on his shoulder. "Did you notice

how quiet all the kids were while we were eating?" she asked. "I think they feel just as sad as we do. Hannah and the boys have such great memories of the house. All the birthday parties and the sleepovers and just hanging out with Elizabeth and Derek and their friends on the beach." She smiled. "I'm pretty sure two of our kids lost their virginity in that house."

"Oh, I think it was all three of them, actually."

She drew her head away to look at him. "What do you know that I don't know?" she asked.

He shrugged with a smile, and Kit knew she'd get no more out of him. Most likely he was already kicking himself for breaking a confidence.

"Life goes on," he said, gently pressing her head back to his shoulder. "Our grandkids will have their parties and sleepovers and lose their virginity in the new house. Their memories will be just as meaningful as ours. And when we're old, we can sit on the porch in our wheelchairs with our rheumy eyes and tell them, 'We had awesome parties in the old days and we'd play games in the living room, and there were these great big old wooden chairs on the beach that we could tip back to look at the stars', and our grandkids will listen politely for a few minutes before they roll their eyes and carry their surfboards out to the beach to get away from the doddering old folks who keep talking about some old house that means nothing to them."

"Wow." She laughed. "That's depressing. But probably accurate." She looked at their hands where they were locked together on the arm of Cole's chair. The fire bounced sparks of light off the diamonds in her ring. "I have an absolute favorite memory of the house," she said.

"What's that, babe?" he asked.

"The night I woke up to find you sitting on my bed with your grandmother's ring."

"Mm." He ran his thumb over the back of her hand. "That's a good one, but I think my favorite memory is the first time we made love. Remember? In the gym?"

"That wasn't actually the first time," Kit pointed out.

"It was the first time worth remembering," he said.

"True." She turned her hand to lace her fingers with his. "So," she said, "my favorite memory is romantic and yours is sex."

He laughed. "Whatever."

"I'm just glad both of them happened." She lifted her head from his shoulder as a sudden peal of laughter came from the dune above them. "I like the sound of that," she said.

"Let's go listen in on the plans," Cole suggested.

They walked hand in hand up the dune to find the others standing in the middle of the sandy lot. It was growing dark, but not too dark to see Janni's smile. "This will be the kitchen," she said to them. "And we're going to make it a whole lot bigger than the old one." She put her arm around Kit's shoulders, and in a moment all five of them stood in a huddle, arms around each other, breathing in the evening air.

"I was thinking," Maris said after a moment. "It would be cool to frame some of the really old photographs of the

Chapel House and hang them somewhere in the new house."

"Except," Jay said slowly, "we lost them all. All the old albums are gone."

"Oh," Maris said. "Oh, damn. I'm sorry."

"We should have scanned them," Janni said. "It never occurred to us."

"Cole and I have some pictures of the house on our computers," Kit said. "They're recent, though."

"We'll make them work," Maris said.

For a while no one spoke, and Kit wondered if they were thinking the same thing she was: photographs could tell only half the story. They could never capture the ancient woody, salty scent of the house, or the familiar creak of the stairs, or the way the angle of the early morning sun made you squint when you walked onto the porch. Pictures could never capture the lives that had unfolded in those old rooms. The tender words, the impassioned fights, the late night conversations, the early morning lovemaking. They could never capture what she felt right here, right now, standing with her friends in the place they would all start over.

The love, she thought.

But they needed no pictures for that.

OUT NOW

PRETENDING TO DANCE
Diane Chamberlain

When the pretending ends, the lying begins . . .

It's the summer of 1990 and fourteen-year-old Molly
Arnette lives with her extended family on one hundred
acres in the Blue Ridge Mountains. The summer seems
idyllic at first. The mountains are Molly's playground and
she's well loved by her father, a therapist famous for books
he's written about a method called "Pretend Therapy"; her
adoptive mother, who has raised Molly as her own; and
Amalia, her birth mother who also lives on the family land.
The adults in Molly's life have created a safe and secure
world for her to grow up in. But Molly's security begins to
crumble as she becomes aware of a plan taking shape in
her extended family – a plan she can't stop and that threat-
ens to turn her idyllic summer into a nightmare.

Pretending to Dance by Diane Chamberlain, the bestsell-
ing author of *The Silent Sister*, is a fascinating and deftly
woven novel that reveals the devastating power of secrets.

OUT NOW

THE ESCAPE ARTIST

Diane Chamberlain

Tell the truth and you lose your child.

When Susanna Miller loses custody of her eleven-month-old son, Tyler, she goes on the run instead of turning her little boy over to her ex-husband and his new wife. She dyes her hair, changes her name and escapes from Boulder, Colorado, leaving behind everyone she knows, including Linc Sebastian, the man who has been her best friend since childhood and who knows her better than anyone.

Susanna lands in Annapolis, Maryland, lonely, frightened, and always looking over her shoulder for someone who might recognize her. Just as she's beginning to feel safe in her new surroundings, she stumbles across information that could save the lives of many people . . . if she's willing to take it to the police. But going to the authorities means revealing her identity, admitting her guilt and, worst of all, losing her son.

OUT NOW

FIRE AND RAIN
Diane Chamberlain

Should you ever trust a stranger?

Valle Rosa, a small, drought-weary town in Southern California, is under destruction from deadly wildfires. Into the midst of this crisis rolls a handsome stranger calling himself Jeff Cabrio, who claims he can cure the town's troubles by making it rain.

But Cabrio's entrance into the community brings more than just potential rain, and it's not long before the residents' interests turn from the weather to their mysterious neighbour. For tragedy-afflicted sculptress MiaTanner, Cabrio unearths old wounds and new loves. For struggling journalist Carmen Perez, Cabrio brings the possibility of revitalizing her career through uncovering the truth about him. And ex-major-league player Chris Garrett is offered the chance to come to terms with the demise of his career as a professional baseball pitcher. As their lives become irrevocably entwined, it's not long before each is forced to face the ghosts of the past.